THE IDES
of APRIL

THE IDES
of APRIL

A Flavia Albia Mystery

Lindsey Davis

MINOTAUR BOOKS
NEW YORK

THE IDES OF APRIL. Copyright © 2013 by Lindsey Davis. All rights reserved. Printed in the United States of America. For information, address St. Martin's Press, 175 Fifth Avenue, New York, N.Y. 10010.

www.minotaurbooks.com

Designed by Steven Seighman

The Library of Congress has cataloged the hardcover edition as follows:

Davis, Lindsey.
    The Ides of April : a Flavia Albia mystery / Lindsey Davis. — First U.S. Edition.
        p. cm.
    ISBN 978-1-250-02369-8 (hardcover)
    ISBN 978-1-250-02370-4 (e-book)
    1. Private investigators—Rome—Fiction. 2. Murder—Investigation—Fiction. 3. Rome—Fiction. I. Title.
    PR6054.A8925I34 2013
    823'.914—dc23

2013011921

ISBN 978-1-250-04855-4 (trade paperback)

Minotaur books may be purchased for educational, business, or promotional use. For information on bulk purchases, please contact Macmillan Corporate and Premium Sales Department at 1-800-221-7945, extension 5442, or write specialmarkets@macmillan.com.

First published in Great Britain in 2013 by Hodder & Stoughton

First Minotaur Books Paperback Edition: June 2014

D 10 9 8 7 6 5 4 3 2

THE IDES
of APRIL

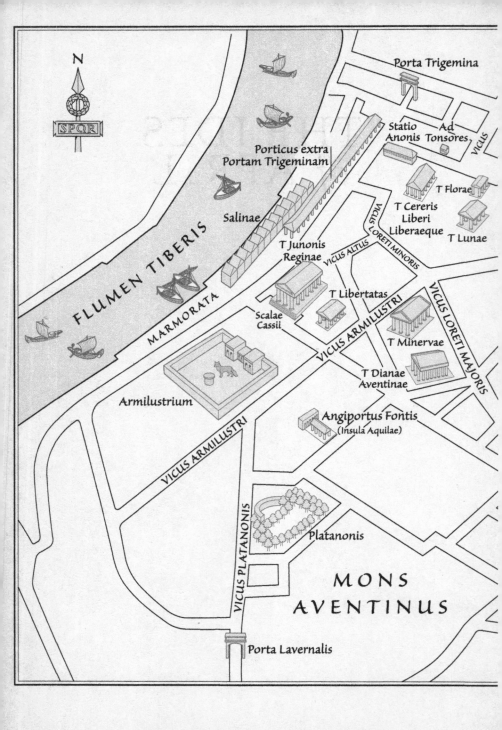

N
SPQR

Porta Trigemina

Porticus extra
Portam Trigeminam

Statio
Anonis

Ad
Tonsores

VICUS

T Florae

T Cereris
Liberi
Liberaeque

T Lunae

FLUMEN TIBERIS

Salinae

T Junonis
Reginae

VICUS ALTUS

VICUS LORETI MINORIS

VICUS LORETI MAJORIS

MARMORATA

T Libertatas

VICUS ARMILLUSTRI

T Minervae

Scalae
Cassii

T Dianae
Aventinae

Armilustrium

Angiportus Fontis
(Insula Aquilae)

VICUS ARMILLUSTRI

VICUS PLATANONIS

Platanonis

MONS
AVENTINUS

Porta Lavernalis

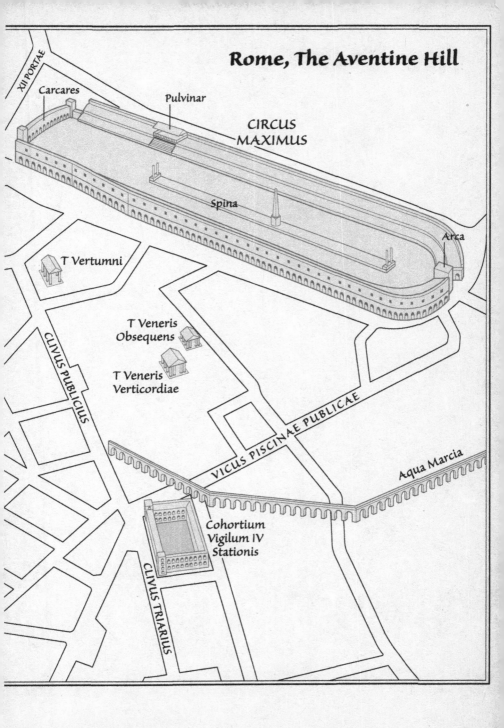

Rome, The Aventine Hill

XII PORTAE

Carcares

Pulvinar

CIRCUS MAXIMUS

Spina

Arca

T Vertumni

T Veneris Obsequens

T Veneris Verticordiae

CLIVUS PUBLICIUS

VICUS PISCINAE PUBLICAE

Aqua Marcia

Cohortium Vigilum IV Stationis

CLIVUS TRIARIUS

THE CAST

NEIGHBOURS AND FAMILY

Flavia Albia	ready for anything, expecting nothing good
Marcus Didius Falco & Helena Justina	her mother and father, typical parents
Julia and Favonia	her younger sisters, normal girls
Postumus	their little brother, a very strange boy
Ferret	looking for trouble
Junillus	a cousin, deaf but far from dumb
The late Lentullus	a good man who died young
Rodan	a bad gladiator who won't die
Prisca	a bathhouse proprietor
Serena	her small strong masseuse
Chloe and Zoe	big strong gladiating girls
The Mythembal family	local cover for Albia
Robigo	an urban fox
Titus Morellus	a vigiles investigator, useless but useful
Cassius Scaurus	his superior, an inferior tribune
Felix	Falco's driver, a decoy
Kicker	his mule, a good mover
Piddle, Diddle and Willikins	three hens involved in law evasion

THE DEAD AND THEIR MOURNERS

Lucius Bassus	deceased aged three, a tragedy
Salvidia	deceased, the client who never pays
Metellus Nepos	a misguided client, who does pay
Celendina	an elderly victim who said too much
Kylo	her son, who remembers nothing
Lupus	deceased, aged 15, another tragedy
Lupus' father and brothers	who saw nothing fishy
Julius Viator	aged 23, fit, boring and deceased
Cassiana Clara	his forlorn widow, hiding something
Laia Gratiana	in the Ceres cult, a woman with a past
Venusia	her maid, saying nothing
Marcia Balbilla	a rival cult initiate, a woman of surprises
Ino	her maid, deceased, a touching memory
A funeral director	doing well out of all this

OTHER INTERESTED PARTIES

The Goddess Ceres	bringer of plenty (of trouble)
Andronicus	an archivist, a curiously attractive prospect
Tiberius	an undercover agent, with questions to answer
Manlius Faustus	a plebeian aedile, an unknown quantity

ROME, the Aventine Hill:
March–April AD 89

I

Lucius Bassus was three years old when his mother took her eyes off him and he ran out of the house to play. They lived on the Clivus Publicius, a steep road on the Aventine Hill, where he was knocked down by a builder's cart. The cart, which escaped its driver's control as it sped down the slope, was owned by Metellus and Nepos, an outfit that worked from a yard on the hill. Nobody talked about Nepos; at first I thought he might be an invention for some tax fiddle.

This business was no more shady than most in Imperial Rome. It carried out refurbishments for bar owners who wanted to move up from blatantly sleazy to a pretence of hygiene. The custom was that the Metellus crew would tender for a full deep-clean and fancy renovation, promising to complete in eight weeks max. In practice, every project took two years and they skimped on the fittings. They would re-grout the marble counters, put in a new doorstep, provide a misspelt signboard and charge the earth for it. By then their clients, unable to operate in the permanent dustcloud, had lost their custom and were going under. It amazed me that other bar owners saw what happened yet still used the firm, but they did. Over the years Metellus and Nepos had done very nicely out of Roman rotgut-sellers innocently trusting them. But killing a child, in the close-knit Aventine community where we had *some* standards, just might be commercially stupid.

Lucius died at once from his injuries. He never stood a chance.

He expired on the kerb. Inevitably, at that very moment his distraught mother came out of the house. It helped fuel local outrage.

The ramshackle cart had been overloaded. The draught oxen were both past their best. Their driver was blind drunk, no question. He denied that on principle, the principle being that Salvidia, the vinegary widow who had inherited the shopfitting business from the husband she had driven to his grave, would not pay his wages if he told the truth. There were witnesses, a large group of whom gathered in the Clivus and took an interest, but they all disappeared when a busybody produced a note tablet and started collecting names.

Once the funeral with its pathetic tiny coffin had been held, well-meaning neighbours started to suggest that the family were entitled to payment for their terrible loss. Everyone agreed they should immediately hire an informer to look into the legal aspects. If being hit on the head by a falling flower tub could be worth cash to the victim, what price a child's life under civil law? Someone (it was rumoured to be the note tablet busybody I mentioned) even wrote up on a wall a plea for concerned citizens who had been present at the accident to come forward. It must have appeared before the first of April, because I saw it that day, the Kalends. The poster sounded official. While not actually offering payment, it implied possible advantage. As a professional, I read it with interest. I found it subtly done.

By then, I had become involved. Any investigator who was favoured by Fortune would be taken on by the heartbroken mother to negotiate compensation. This was a public-spirited task, where a reputable person could maintain a clear conscience: you look into the facts, you put those facts to the guilty party succinctly, you say, "I am a top informer, this is meat and drink to me; a toddler is dead and a jury will be weeping into their togas, but nobody wants this to go to court, do we?" The guilty cough up, and you cream off your percentage.

Not me. Fortune never favoured me and the problem with being a woman was that sometimes I could only obtain business that all the male informers had sniffed and refused. This was one of those months. *I* was hired by Salvidia. The owner of Metellus and Nepos wanted me to help her beat off the mother's claim. Typical.

From what I have already said about this construction group, you will guess my employment was on a "no win, no fee" basis. Indeed, I was starting to feel its basis might amount to "win, but even then the bastards never pay up"—like so much of my work, unfortunately. After a week, I was ready to abandon the miserable project, but I had already put in quite a few hours and, besides, I never like to be defeated. The poster asking for witnesses suggested someone else felt the same way.

The wall graffiti included an address where people could make statements, so as my enquiries were stuck, I went along to see if any had done so. My line would be that as I was assisting a party in the dispute, I had the right to ask. As a female I had no rights at all in matters of law, but why let that stop me? Either way, I was hoping to plea-bargain. Anything to have this finished fast, so I could drop the case.

The address was the Temple of Ceres. It was close to my home and office, though on a far grander street than the blind alley I lived in. Anywhere would be finer than that. Fountain Court holds no attractions for the founders of fine religious buildings.

Arranging assignations at temples is common in Rome. For strangers it is neutral ground. For instance, married men find the steps of temples convenient for picking up prostitutes. The grander the temple, the lousier its hangers-on. Inured to the seamy side of our city, the public pass by without noticing. Suggesting a meet at a temple was, I presumed, simply for convenience. Thinking little of it, I went along on spec.

Only when I asked for the contact on the wall notice did I learn he was a big prawn in a purple-edged toga who belonged to an ancient order of magistrates. The Temple of Ceres was their headquarters and archive depository.

I reconsidered. Then I went home and made alterations to my

5

appearance. I was visiting the office of men of great consequence in Rome: men of wealth and power. I did not suppose "Manlius Faustus" had chalked up graffiti on the Clivus Publicius in person, but some minion certainly did it in his name. That minion must have felt confident Faustus would enjoy throwing his weight about. By definition this magistrate was one of those menaces who drive traders wild checking market weights. I had been trained by my father to avoid such types, though in fact those over-promoted snoots don't tangle with me. I have contacts, but no one that important.

Still, it always pays to respect the opposition. So I changed into a full-length tunic in a neutral shade, not white, not quite unbleached linen, but neat, tidy and unthreatening. It did have an embroidered neckline that suggested money, which in turn hints at a woman with influential men behind her, one who should not be too quickly or too rudely dismissed.

My earrings were plain gold rosettes. I added a row of bangles, to give me confidence. Hair pinned up. Three dabs of a discreet perfume. A large stole: the demure, respectable widow look. I really am a widow, so that part was right.

Mother had taught me how to pose as a meek matron. It was ridiculous and hypocritical, but the act now came as second nature and I could manage it without laughing.

So, feeling convinced that I was as good as them and could handle these bastards, I set off for my first encounter with the plebeian aediles.

II

The Temple of Ceres was so local to me that I normally ignored it. It sat on the northern slope of the Aventine, a short walk halfway uphill from the starting-gates end of the Circus Maximus. A chunky edifice, it was designed in the remote past and looked more Greek than Roman in an archaic way; the heavy grey columns surrounding it had thick bases and curious capitols that, if you care to know such stuff, were neither Ionic nor Doric. I believe the word is "transitional." I don't suppose the distinction bothered many people; most probably never looked up high enough to notice. But I had spent my childhood a thousand miles from Rome, in a backwoods town that had been laid waste in a revolt and still lacked interesting architecture; when an effort has been made to build something unusual, I pay polite attention.

The truth is, after I was brought to Rome by the family who adopted me, I had to learn fast about the people and the place; as a result I often know more about the myths and monuments than most of the city's natives. I was about fifteen then, and curious about the world. Education was made available. While being taught to read and write, I devoured facts. Sometimes now it helped in my work. More often, it just made me marvel at the weird history and attitudes of these Romans, who believed themselves masters of the civilised world.

At least they had a history. They knew their origins, which was more than I could say.

The temple was home to a Triad: three gods, bunking up together, all holy and cosy amid the incense and deposited must cakes. In addition to Ceres the Earth Mother, a well-built dame bearing sheaves of corn who was one of the twelve grand Olympian deities, it also housed Liber and Libera, two lesser gods that I bet you've never heard of, Ceres' children, I think. This triple cult was rooted in fertility rites—well may you groan!

Needless to say, an organised body of religious-minded women fussed about the temple. No serious shrine can fail to have such busybodies importantly organising themselves into a sniffy coven; it's one way local matrons can get out of the house once a week. My grandmother loved it—a bunch of upper-crust women dabbling in neighbourhood benevolence, heads down over gossip, then having wine together afterwards without their husbands daring to disapprove. My senatorial grandmama was a wonderful woman, only surpassed by her plebeian counterpart, whose domestic rule was legendary all over the Aventine. If I mentioned *her* at the stall where she used to buy roots for her broth cauldron, the greengrocer still mimed running for the hills.

A temple cult can be a good argument against letting women control things. Although Ceres was bringer of plenty, especially favouring commoners, I found that her devotees included a scrawny bird who had been spoiled from birth and thought herself *very* superior. Forget liberality. The public slaves who swept the steps and acted as security directed me to her because I was a woman, for which I would not thank them. Possibly they could see I was a different type entirely and they were hoping for a laugh.

Sisterhood did not feature at our meeting.

The supercilious sanctum queen was called Laia Gratiana. The public slave had told me that; she would not introduce herself, in case I dirtied her name by using it. She was fair and I am dark; that was only the start of the distance between us. I told myself she was older than me, though in fact she may not have been. She behaved like a domineering old matriarch with five generations of cowed family who all feared she might alter her will if they as much as sneezed. Her garments were rich cloth, elegantly draped with many folds, though in a revolting puce colour that some sly dyer must have been delighted to offload on an idiot. When she swept up, intent on facing me down, I felt my hackles rise by instinct. I saw she felt the same—in my view, with much less reason.

"What do you want?"

"I am looking for Manlius Faustus."

"He won't see you."

"Suppose I ask him that myself. I am responding to a public notice he put up."

When I stood my ground, it unsettled her. Grudgingly, she deigned to mention that the aediles worked from an office in a side street alongside the temple. I guess she only told me because I could have found out easily from anyone.

We parted on poor terms. If I had known then that Gratiana and I were to have history, I would have felt even more sour.

My two romantic little sisters believed that being so carefully dressed up as I was that afternoon guaranteed that you would meet the love of your life. Not today, apparently. My first encounter was certainly dire; while I sized up a nondescript building that must be the aediles' headquarters, a male menace barged out into the street and crashed into me. He snorted with irritation. It was his fault, absolutely. He was too busy hunching up to make himself look like a nobody, an effect he achieved without trying. The shifty blaggard was all hemp tunics and chin stubble. Absolutely not my type. Sorry, hopeful sisters!

"Oh, don't bother to apologise!—Is this the aediles' office?" He refused to answer, skulking off head down. Rubbing my bruised arm, I sent a soldier's gesture after him, though I fear it was wasted.

As I tripped inside the building, I replaced a scowl with my bright-eyed charming face, to impress any occupants. There was no one in sight.

Small rooms led off a dark little entrance hall. Beyond it was a meagre courtyard with a miniature fountain in the form of a shell. It produced a trickle of water that glugged in pathetic hiccups, then leaked into a trail of green slime down the outside of the collection bowl. Mosquitoes clustered hopefully.

I stood still for a moment, listening. I didn't knock or clear my throat. My father was a private informer too, and according to some (him, for example), he was the best in Rome. I was trained to take my chance, to open doors, to look around.

You always dream of finding an unattended diary that reveals an eye-watering love affair—not that I ever had. Everyone was too careful now. Under our latest emperor, when people committed adultery—as they did like rabbits, because he was a despot and they needed cheering up—they did not write down details. Domitian saw it as his sacred role to punish scandalous behaviour. His agents were always looking for evidence.

Repression had spread to the aediles. Encouraged by our austere and humourless ruler, the market monitors were extra conscientious these days. They were cracking down on docket-diddling, fraudulent weights and pavement-encroachment, though their most lucrative target was prostitution. Here in their lair, I saw massive armoured chests, where all the fines from miserable bar girls could be stored. Bar girls were fair game for the purity police. Traditionally, whenever a waitress served a customer a drink, he could order a bunk upstairs as a chaser. That's if he wanted to catch the crabs or risk having to slip an officer a backhander if the authorities paid that bar a surprise visit, looking for unregistered whores—and inevitably finding them.

Bribes, I presumed, would go straight into the aediles' belt pouches. Could Manlius Faustus be paid off with a bribe, I wondered? How much of his income came from sweeteners?

The building smelled of dust. It was a place of unused reference scrolls and faded wall maps. Old wooden benches inhabited uncomfortable interview rooms in which members of the public, hauled in for questioning, could be made to feel guilty about the kind of rule infringement everyone expects to get away with. One thing startled me: a cage containing leg irons, though currently no prisoners.

Someone had turned up behind me.

"I see you are admiring our facilities!" I spun around. The charmer, who was neat and suave, purred appreciation of my physical appearance. He pretended to assume I had come for a guided tour. "His eminence has already cleared out the captives today, so I can't show you any, I'm afraid."

Some days the sun just comes out and lightens your world. We understood one another immediately. That magic spark.

I gazed at him, a pleasant experience. He was roughly my age, not a real redhead but he had gingery-brown eyes, hair, eyebrows, beard and moustache, even the fine hairs on the backs of his hands and his arms—the complete matching set. Background?—hard to say, though his accent was cultured. If he worked in a public office he was almost certainly a freedman, probably first-generation. I don't despise ex-slaves. I could be one myself; I shall never even know.

"The used gruel bowl looks recent." I nudged it with my toe. The toe had been pedicured; my sandal was new. I often wore shoes more suitable for a lame old lady, laced from front to ankle, in case I had to do a route march; on this visit I had treated myself to more feminine footwear. The soles would make a mark if I kicked someone, but the uppers consisted of just two thin gold straps on a toe-post. If this clerk was anything of a foot fetishist, my high instep would set his pulse racing. "I'm glad I am not compelled to steal the keys and set someone free behind your back."

"You sound as if you would really do it!" he murmured admiringly.

"That's me."

The tips of his ears had a little turn forward that gave him character, which I could tell involved personality, humour and intelligence. His slim build suggested a plain life; like me, he had probably known struggle. What I liked most was that he looked as if the sun came out for him too, when he found me in their anteroom. I fell for it happily.

"Andronicus," he introduced himself. "I work here as an archivist."

"Hundreds of records of market fines?"

"That would be tedious!" Andronicus said, although I myself had been neutral. Scrupulously kept public records can be a windfall in my line of work. I never despise bureaucracy. "The plebeian aediles receive decrees from the Senate, which they must deposit for safe-keeping next door in the Temple of Ceres. All those records become my responsibility." He was exaggerating his own importance, though I did not blame him. "I tend them devotedly, even though no one ever asks to consult anything."

"But of course if you ever did misfile a scroll or let a mouse nibble one, that would be the only occasion ever that some pompous piece in purple would requisition it."

"You know the world!" Andronicus' grin was rueful and charming; he was very aware of that. "Life has its high spots. Sometimes, the aediles hold a meeting, all four of them—we have two plebeians and two patricians, as I am sure you know. To save them getting ink on themselves, I then have the privilege of being their minutes secretary. I bet you guess that means compiling action notes that none of the spoiled boys will carry out."

I knew he was playing me, or he thought he was. Even though I was enjoying the moment, I never forgot that men were sneaky. "Do you always flirt with visitors?" I asked him.

"Only the attractive ones." He was respectably dressed; his tunic was clean, not even splattered with ink—yet he managed to give the impression his thoughts were dirty. I liked him enough to share them, though I didn't show it.

"Ah don't expect me to fall for blather, Andronicus. I spend a lot of my time explaining to inane women that plain male treachery is the reason their husbands have vanished. Even though my clients' husbands are always supposed to be the loveliest of men, none of whom would harm flies, nevertheless, my enquiries tend to show they have uncharacteristically run away with a bar girl. A piece with an ankle-chain, invariably. And by then, five months pregnant."

"Ooh," the archivist crooned. "Are you part of the emperor's morality campaign? Do you take these absconders to court?"

"No, I track down loose husbands for abandoned wives who can't afford to go to law. My clients have to settle for battering the bastards with heavy iron frying pans."

"I get the impression you hold the men down while it happens?"

Andronicus was smiling broadly. Why spoil his party? I smiled back. "That's my de luxe service . . . You mentioned your superior," I hinted broadly, dragging us back to the point of my visit. "I think it's him I need to see. Is the notable who calls himself Manlius Faustus available? Or are you going to spin me the old line—'sorry, you just missed him'?"

He gave me a wry gleam. "Faustus is, genuinely, out. I hardly dare say this, but he did leave the building just before you came."

"Not that lout who nearly knocked me over on the step?"

I thought something flickered in the archivist's gaze but he answered calmly, "Oh that would have been our runner." He paused, then added, "Tiberius. Did you speak to him?"

"No." Why would I? "He was a grim bastard. And what's Faustus like?"

"Couldn't possibly comment. He is much too aware that I owe him this job."

"Not on good terms?" I guessed.

"Let's say, if you think our runner is dour, you will not like Faustus."

Andronicus seemed keen to move on the conversation. He asked what brought me, so I explained about the accident in the Clivus

Publicius and that notice calling for witnesses with Faustus' name on it.

"Sounds like him," Andronicus commented. "He's quite a meddler."

"Well, I suppose it is his job . . . Have any witnesses shown up in response?"

"Only you."

I smiled with the complicity we had developed between us so nicely. "I wouldn't have come if I hadn't been stuck . . . Are you going to mention me to Faustus?"

"Why? You haven't told me anything." Andronicus gave me his own conspiratorial grin. I did like dealing with this man. He came so much cheaper than the clerks I usually had to badger or bribe.

"I want to ask a cheeky favour. If anyone does bring in a story, could you possibly let me know?"

"Love to." Showing how keen he was, Andronicus then asked, "So where do I contact you?"

I always considered this carefully. People can find my office; I could not work otherwise. But there was a difference between clients who were too preoccupied with whatever trouble they were already in to cause any other trouble, and chancers who might have tricky personal motives in coming after me.

Andronicus worked for a magistrate. That guaranteed he was reliable, surely? I told him where I lived.

Anyway, I had Rodan. "It's a climb and not easy to find. But my doorman brings up visitors. Rodan will show you."

"Sounds exclusive!"

I snorted. "That's right. Fountain Court is the most exclusive slum on the Aventine." And he had not yet seen Rodan. I wouldn't spoil the surprise.

"Best you can do?"

"I am only a poor widow." Never imply you have money.

"Oh is that so?" scoffed Andronicus. He sized up my outfit pointedly. I like a man who sees through banter. Indeed, I like a man who notices that you have dressed nicely to meet him. Still, he had not gained the full measure of me. Not yet. "And what is your name when I ask for you?"

"Flavia Albia. Just ask for Albia. Everyone knows me." A lot of people did, though "everyone" was pushing it. This was another ploy for protection that I had learned; it gave the impression there might be many people looking out for me.

I said I had to be going. He said he had enjoyed meeting me. More people were now arriving for official reasons, so I saw myself out, which seemed to be procedure in that office. In mine, I like to be quite sure visitors have left, but Andronicus did not need such precautions.

So, no aedile. That had been a wasted trip, like so many others. I was used to it. In the street I paused, turning up my face to the Roman sky. Heard the hubbub surrounding me on the Aventine and also coming from far away all over the city. Smelt hot oil on lunchtime griddles. Felt the oppression of the Temple of Ceres, gloomily shadowing the street.

Mentally I apologised to my romantic little sisters. Despite my smart get-up I would not be meeting the love of my life this afternoon. Nevertheless I had just had an extremely pleasant experience. That was an improvement on normal.

In any case, I had met the love of my life already, met him long, long ago. You will not be surprised, any more than I was at the wise age of seventeen, that the man toyed with me, then dropped me when he feared it might be serious. The pain had not lasted; I soon met and married Farm Boy, and if people thought that was love on the rebound, they understood nothing about me. There was nothing fake in my affection for him.

He was still around. Not Farm Boy; Farm Boy died. The other one. For family reasons I saw him at social gatherings and sometimes

I even worked with him. These days, our past seemed to bother him far more than me.

There had been one result from visiting the aediles' office. If the rapport I had built with the archivist today ever came to anything, that would be fun.

Something would happen with Andronicus. Hades, I was an informer. I could tell that.

III

The surly man they called Tiberius was standing at a bar counter further up the main street. Most people would have passed without remembering the aediles' runner, but my job needs good observation. I walked by quietly on the other side of the street, making no eye-contact. I bet *he* did not notice *me*.

Whatever kind of running the aediles employed him to do must make few demands. He had a beaker and the bar's draughtboard in front of him; he looked set there for the afternoon. I was tempted to march up and exclaim, "Three radishes says I can thrash you!" I knew I could. Farm Boy, my late husband, had taught me draughts, sweetly allowing me to beat *him* on a regular basis. He never cared who won; he just liked us to play. He liked most things we did together and, as the uncle of mine he worked for used to say, he had a heart as big as Parthia.

I was at a loose end myself now, but a presentable woman of twenty-eight may not take herself to bars alone, apart from the speedy-breakfast kind where you can have a pastry and a hot drink before most members of the public are up. Even then, you have to look as if you keep a salad stall; riding in on a donkey at dawn from a market garden way out on the Campagna gives even a woman a legitimate cause for sustenance. Otherwise, it is obvious to everyone you must be touting for paid sex. The men with randy propositions are bad enough; the furious grannies hurling curses at you soon become unbearable. Roman grannies really know how to hustle a flighty bit off their street by giving her the evil eye. The worst of them do it to everyone, just in case they miss one.

Considering unpleasant old dames led naturally to thoughts of my client.

I had to grit my teeth to make me visit her, but in my career of nearly twelve years as a solo informer, that had been my feeling about many people who employed me. It's not a job where you meet the cream of society. Indeed, if you want to see the worst manners, filthiest motives and saddest ethics, this is the profession. Informers deal in hopelessness at every level.

Salvidia, as I mentioned before, had inherited the construction firm when her husband died. Nobody had much to say about him, but I sensed that originally he had been typical of a builder with his own business: sometimes hard-working but more often lazy, and always a poor manager with money troubles. Salvidia soon toughened him up. She stormed in and buffed the firm into an extortion machine until Metellus and Nepos became the high-quality renovation shysters they were now. Nepos vanished, probably squeezed out deliberately, while her husband Metellus expired after a few years in the face of Salvidia's driving efficiency.

Salvidia was running the firm at a huge profit, but you would not know it from the untidy builder's yard they still used and the cramped living quarters she maintained alongside. They had always operated out of premises on the Vicus Loreti Minoris, Lesser Laurel Street. Like most of the roads that passed among the great cluster of temples on the Aventine, it thought itself superior yet had its bad smells and seedy side. It ran from near the Temple of Ceres, so was in the north-west corner of the hill above the barbers' quarter and the corn dole building; it climbed slightly towards the once open area where Remus took the auguries in the contest to see who would found a new city, Rome. You know the story. He lost out to his twin brother Romulus, who had all a great leader's ideal qualities—by which I mean he cheated. Nowadays, the Aventine high tops were completely built up. From most vantage points you could barely see the sky, let alone count enough birds to foretell the rise of a great nation.

Lesser Laurel Street ran into Greater Laurel Street at the crossroads with Box Hill and the Street of the Armilustrium, a long byway that passed close to where I lived. These were some of the earliest roads I learned when I first moved up to live in Fountain Court. They all occupied the part of the hill right above where my parents had their town house on the river embankment. That was downstream of the salt warehouses and the Trigeminal Porticus. When life was hard, I could head for the steps, scamper down the steep escarpment and hide away at home. Often I went just to see them. They were good people.

No need of a refuge today, however: I was fired up, in full professional mode. I had decided it was time to tell Salvidia she could keep her commission. "Keep" was a more polite word than the one in my prepared speech.

I was all the more impolite when my plan was thwarted.

I had gone to the yard first because my client was usually there, making miseries of her workmen's lives. It was a jumble of planks, sheets of marble (mostly broken), handcarts and old buckets full of set concrete. A pall of dust over everything made it an asthmatic's graveyard. Two labourers in ripped tunics were squatting on a horizontal column; a chained, skinny guard dog pretended he would bite my leg off if I came within reach. The men seemed too depressed to speak and the hound shrank against a piece of dismantled partition when I glared his way. I refused to give the men the time of day, but I spoke to the dog, who then remembered me and whined hopefully. Last time I had given him the end of a rather poor meatball I regretted buying, but today I had nothing for him. At least it would save him a bellyache.

I picked my way to the office, trying unsuccessfully to keep my sandals clean. A runt who called himself a clerk-of-works was hiding in a cubbyhole amongst mounds of filthy dustsheets. He told me the bad news. There was no chance of me being paid, even for the work I had already done. Salvidia was dead.

Now I was glum. I said, "I've had clients who go to abnormal lengths to avoid paying, but expiring on me is extreme."

"She just came home from market, took to her bed and stopped breathing."

"Whatever caused that? She wasn't old."

"Forty-six," he groaned. The workman, gnarled by disappointment and a poor diet, was probably forty-five; today he had suddenly become nervous that life might be transient. He probably hadn't bet on as many dud horses and screwed as many altar boys as he was hoping for.

I cursed in a genteel fashion ("Oh what a nuisance!"—approximately), then since he had no more to tell me, I went to the house. Pretending I wanted to pay my respects, I meant to double check. The thought did strike me that Salvidia might not be dead at all, but had arranged for me to be told a yarn in order to get rid of me. I even wondered if she was avoiding all her creditors, intending to shimmy off to a secret retirement villa. Anyone else in Rome who had money passing through their hands would have acquired a second property by a lake, at the coast, or on an island.

Anyone else in Rome who had money and their own building firm would have lived somewhere better than a run-down hovel on Lesser Laurel Street, with its porch propped up on a scaffold pole and broken roof tiles in teetering piles either side of the doorstep. A neglected oleander in a tub would have convinced a more excitable informer than me that Salvidia died of botanical poisoning, but I stayed calm.

Inside the house there was slightly less dust but it was crammed with almost as many building materials as at the yard next door. In what passed for an atrium, which had no tasteful pool or mosaic, stood quite a lot of garden statues that had clearly been removed from other people's houses. A maid confirmed her mistress was indeed dead. She had passed away that afternoon. If I wanted, I could see the body.

You might have sidestepped that invitation; not me. It's true Salvidia was almost a stranger. I had only met her twice and I hadn't liked her either time. As far as I was concerned, I owed this woman no respect and I might as well cut my losses.

Yet my papa really was the excitable kind of informer I alluded to above; he saw mischief in everything and had a lifelong habit of stumbling into situations where persons died suspiciously. It was one way to earn a few sesterces, by exposing what had happened. There was no reason for me to suppose anything unusual had happened to Salvidia; she was an unfriendly woman who probably expired from her own bile. Even so, I had been taught always to invent an excuse to inspect a corpse. To be *invited* to view one was a welcome privilege: I was in there like a louse up a tramp's tunic.

IV

As I had been told, the woman lay in her bedroom, one of the few places in her house that was furnished normally. Years before, she and Metellus must have invested in a pretty solid marriage bed, though the webbing under the mattress was now sagging too much for my taste. I guessed she had never taken a lover, or they would have constantly rolled into each other awkwardly during moments of rest. Why do people who are surrounded by their own workmen never get them to do repairs?

The room had the usual cupboards and chests. There were no windows, so although it did not smell particularly sour, the lack of fresh air was oppressive.

"She was just like that when I found her," the maid quavered from the doorway. I saw no reason to comment. I was wondering how long I had to stand looking solemn at the bedside before I could leave politely.

Salvidia lay on her back. Her arms were straight by her sides, she looked relaxed; either she died in her sleep or someone had closed her eyelids. With all the life gone, she was a shell, middle-aged in actual years but now sunken like an old woman; certainly a woman who would have claimed she led a hard life.

Salvidia had had a heavy build, the kind of weight that arrives with the menopause. Her hair was wound up in a simple bun, which she probably did herself. She had flabby arms and a lined, sunken face. She wore day clothes, the same kind of bunched tunic I had seen her in, with a girdle cinched tightly as if to hold in her constant anger at everything. Her wedding ring and one other plain ring gripped her fingers; her earrings were dull gold drops which somehow gave the impression she just put the same pair on daily and had done so for the past twenty years. There was no other jewellery on her, and no gem boxes in the room that I could see; no cream or cosmetic pots either. She wasted no cash on self-adornment.

I assumed her heart had suddenly stopped, or something similar. That was how it looked. There was nothing to suggest any kind of interference. Her skin had a few shapeless brown spots you would expect in a woman of her age, that's all. No bruising. I did notice a short, fine scratch on her left arm, with faint reddening around it, but it was like a graze anyone could pick up brushing clumsily against something. Salvidia had not been an elegant mover.

Even a lifeless body can give off an aura. This woman's endless agitation was over, yet her corpse signalled permanent disappointment. I felt her unhappy submission to death after a life that was in my terms, and probably her own, mainly wasted. Had she ever known contentment? I doubted it.

Depressed, I left the bedroom. The maid stayed there to watch over her mistress, with more loyalty than I had expected. Staff would forget she had been annoying, it seemed. They would feel normal sadness at her early parting. It should have given me faith in human decency but I felt unsettled. Needing to recover, I made my way to a small outside area beyond the atrium that I had spotted earlier.

With better owners, this space could have been made into a natty little courtyard garden. Salvidia had almost filled it with a huge stone basin of the kind used in public baths, though this was rough and unattractive, not fine-grained alabaster or porphyry. Lolling at an angle, the monster was so unwieldy and heavy-looking I could not imagine how they manoeuvred it in—nor why they bothered. It was stored, no use to anyone, and ruining what could have been a pleasant sitting-out place.

I found a bench, upturned against a low wall. Nobody could have used it for years. With effort, I turned the seat right way up in a tiny patch of sunlight, then perched on it, trying to avoid the mossy parts. I was reflecting thoughtfully in a way that generally means someone is upset—and so I was. I was furious that because of Salvidia's inconvenient death I had probably lost my payment.

I assumed no one would bother me as I sat brooding there. From the surrounding house came only silence, as if even the maid might have left. I had seen no other staff and wondered if either the mistress had been too mean to have any, or if when she died they took their chance and ran away. Most homes have cooking smells, woofing dogs, distant knocks and footsteps, snatches of indecipherable conversation. This place lay still, seemingly deserted. Not even a pigeon shared my nook. It all gave the impression nothing much had ever gone on here. Even calling it a "home" seemed an exaggeration.

At least it was peaceful. Eventually my annoyance and melancholy settled. Just as I was ready to leave, surprisingly someone turned up. I never heard him coming and he was equally surprised to see me.

The new arrival was in his late thirties, lean build, unremarkable face, clothes decent but not expensive. I could tell he was not, and never had been, a slave. Neither muscle-bound nor dusty, he looked more like a stationer than one of the construction workers. If I really thought Salvidia had had a lover, I might have suspected this was he, but although he had an air of ownership, I doubted that. Instinct again.

The way the man crept up, he could have been a walk-in thief, trying his luck. If so, he would presumably have gone through the atrium to search indoors for items he could quickly pilfer, not come out here and slumped on the little wall between the peristyle columns, looking as low-spirited as me. Perhaps he felt grim for similar reasons. Had he too come from viewing the corpse? Once he noticed me, he made no move to absent himself. Nor, oddly, did he turn me out. He just nodded once, like a stranger sitting down nearby in a public park, then he lost himself in brooding thoughts. So, I stayed and waited to see what would happen. My father would say that kind of curiosity had got him into plenty of trouble. But you have to trust your intuition. (That idea too, as my mother would dryly remark, had often landed dear Papa ankle-deep in donkey-shit.)

Eventually the stranger roused and introduced himself. He was called Metellus Nepos and he was the sole heir and executor. I asked about his name, because I knew "Nepos" was Latin for "nephew."

"It's just a name," he answered brusquely, like a man who had been asked the same question far too many times. "*My* name!" Fine.

Romans pride themselves on their wonderful organisation, but when it comes to assigning names to babies, they tend to lack logic. Never try to tell anyone this at a dinner party, especially if they have a stupid name.

He relaxed enough to explain that the original Metellus who founded the company was his father, while Salvidia had been a second wife, his stepmother. Nepos told me he now had no intention of carrying on the business, but would sell up. He said that with enough bitterness to convince me I was right about the stepmother edging him out. At least he had gone off and done what he had always wanted; he became a cheesemaker. I said that was different. He said not really, if you like cheese.

I do. We had a meeting of minds, though not extravagantly.

He decided to become official. "May I ask what you are doing here?"

I had been waiting for this and saw no reason to prevaricate. "My name is Flavia Albia. I work as an informer. Salvidia hired me to apply legal pressure against some compensation-seekers."

"After a botched job?" Clearly he knew the family firm. I related the sad story of little Lucius Bassus being run over. Nepos asked what settlement the parents wanted; when I told him he immediately offered, "Fair enough. Tell them once I've sold up here, I'll pay them."

I was amazed. "To be honest, my commission was to fend them off!"

"Despite the drunken driver and overloading?"

"Metellus Nepos, I don't like all the jobs I have to do."

"The family deserve something. I am overruling Salvidia. I never saw eye to eye with her. And you would have been due something?"

Still bemused by his attitude, I said what I had hoped to charge Salvidia, plus expenses; Nepos agreed to honour that as well. I saw no reason to mention it had been no win, no fee.

I did not suppose this man had turned benevolent in the throes of grief. More likely, he was just lying to get rid of creditors. While they were lulled by his promises, he would grab his inheritance and make off. He had not told me where his dairy farm was. Out of Rome, I could bank on it.

Still, he might be unusually honest. If he wanted to be good-natured as some kind of moral cleansing, it was his own business. I don't meet a lot of that, but I was open-minded.

Then Metellus Nepos leaned back against a pillar, turned up his face to the tiny patch of sky that was visible above us, and let out the kind of ponderous sigh that was all too familiar to me.

"That sigh sounds like one of my clients, at an initial consultation," I said. He certainly looked troubled. "When they half wonder if their intended commission will sound like madness—which it often does, apart from 'I think my wife is sleeping with the butcher.' That's usually true. A sudden effusion of escalopes at the dinner table tends to be the giveaway."

"Tell me what work you do," urged Nepos. It was not a social question.

I gave him my professional biography. I stressed the mundane side: chasing runaway adolescents for anxious parents, routine hunts for missing birth certificates or army discharge diplomas, or for missing heirs, or missing chickens that naughty neighbours had already cooked up in tarragon . . . I mentioned other aspects of my strangely mixed portfolio. The time I investigated the quack doctor who raped female patients after giving them sleeping draughts. How I sometimes eliminated innocent suspects from vigiles enquiries, when our fair-minded lawmen went for an easy option, regardless of proof. Then there was work I did occasionally for the Camillus brothers, two rising prosecution lawyers who might need a woman's assistance when they were gathering evidence.

"Impressed?"

"You work mainly for women?"

"I do." Female clients trusted me. They shied off male informers, who had a reputation for groping and worse indecency. Besides, many male informers were simply no good. "Why do you ask, Nepos?" I had a glum premonition.

"Do something for this woman!" Nepos was short. "I shall hire you. I want someone to check my stepmother's sudden death."

This was a shock. My guess would have been that he sought an informer because he believed a devious rival had stolen his best cheese recipe. "Nepos, if I had not needed the money I wouldn't have given her a cold, in life."

"Help her in death, Albia."

Startled, I ran through all the reasons I had previously produced for myself as to why Salvidia's demise was of no interest at all. "Just because somebody dies unexpectedly does not mean their death was unnatural. It happens. Happens all the time. Many people die for reasons that are never explained. Ask any funeral director."

"No," he disagreed. "This death is not right."

"Why? What's bothering you?"

Nepos moved restlessly. "The old lady was completely tough, she was not even fifty, she was thriving. Her people say she was herself this morning—yet apparently she comes in, dumps her shopping in the hall, and just passes out for no reason. I don't believe it. That's impossible. I didn't get on with her, but I'm not having that."

"Nepos, there is no evidence of foul play. Keep the commission." I decided he was not the only person in Rome who could make gestures. Besides, I had that terrible sense of gloom that you experience when you think a tiresome case is safely over, then it bobs right back at you. "You would be wasting your money, hiring me."

"That's for me to decide," replied Metellus Nepos in a grim tone. "Either you look into it for me, or I'll hire someone else."

So I took the job. If the stepson was set on wasting his newly inherited cash, why should some other informer benefit? I was here in position, so I stepped up obligingly, took on the task and said a polite thank you.

He had to be wrong.

But then, there is always that little niggle that won't go away. It always gets you. What if his daft suspicions were not daft at all? What if he was right?

V

I did not believe I had a case to investigate, but I still looked into the facts. There was a routine; I followed it. Nepos dogged me like a hungry hound so I could not be desultory. Anyway, I really did want my final report to reassure him. Sometimes that is the point— telling your client that they do not need to worry.

Occasionally, when it's best to protect them from the awkward truth, you have to say that everything is fine even though you have proved their suspicions are well-founded—but I did not expect that to be the result here.

I rechecked the corpse, this time with the stepson standing beside me so I could point out its sad normality to him. He sniffed, unconvinced.

I then spent several hours retracing Salvidia's movements earlier that day. I interviewed the maid and a few other household staff whom Nepos winkled out of back rooms for me. I ascertained that their mistress had shown no signs of being suicidal. I talked to the workmen at the yard. They said she was definitely full of plans, enjoyable plans to do customers out of money. The maid then escorted me round all the market stalls where Salvidia habitually bought provisions; we identified those where she had been that morning, matching the produce that still lay in her shopping baskets. Nobody in the markets told me anything unusual.

I pondered motive. Suppose Nepos was right. Unnatural death has a cause, which we could not identify here, and it has a perpetrator. If the woman really had been sent on her way deliberately, who would want to do it? The picture that emerged matched my own previous experience of Salvidia; she was an ill-natured character you wouldn't share a fish supper with yet, after all, she had been a businesswoman so it was never in her interests to fall out with people completely. She ordered her house slaves about, but not unbearably; she rampaged around the yard, but the workers were used to it; she let down customers almost on principle, but they rarely bothered to complain. That was the limit of her aggression. When she dealt with me she had had a testy attitude, but not so bad that I refused her case. I had decided I could work with her. So when I now asked the usual question—did she have any enemies?—the answer was, not particularly. Rome was stuffed with women who were just as unlikeable.

I pointed out to Nepos that the one person who benefited from Salvidia's death was him: he inherited. We agreed that if *he* had finished her off in some undetectable way, it would be very stupid of him to draw attention to it. If he had, hiring me could be a smoke-screen. But unless someone else had become suspicious of the death, there was no need at all for him to set the wood smouldering.

I made sure we considered the family of the toddler, Lucius Bassus. Salvidia's drunken driver and overloaded cart had killed the child. Nevertheless, she had brazenly tried to avoid paying compensation. That meant the bereaved parents might harbour real loathing of her. But they stood to gain a large amount of cash soon—because, being realistic, they had an unbeatable claim for negligence which my best efforts would not have thwarted. It was in their interest to keep her alive, so she could pay. Anyway, I went and saw them. They all had alibis.

Reluctantly, Nepos accepted that no misadventure was indicated. He still wanted to bring in a doctor to look at the body; I persuaded him to keep the money and ask an opinion of a funeral director, who had to be hired anyway. They see enough to give the best assessment of what has happened to a dead person.

The undertaker who came seemed competent. He surveyed the body and refused to excite himself. He did take notice of the mark that I myself had noticed on Salvidia's arm, though like me he thought it was some accidental scrape. He claimed that women were quietly passing away all over Rome for no obvious reason that spring. It might mean some kind of invisible disease was claiming them, but more likely it was just a statistical coincidence. His verdict was that old saying, "There's a lot of it about."

He took the corpse. I promised Nepos I would go to the funeral. It's a good time to claim fees, before the heirs disperse.

I finished up much later in the day than I had expected when I set out earlier to visit the aediles. But that is common in the work I do. Dusk was falling and I needed food, so I went to see my family; they would ply me with supper, in a real home full of warmth, light, comfort and lively conversation. It would improve my mood. I could consult about Salvidia too—not that anyone was able to add any useful thoughts, it turned out. We all agreed I had made the only possible enquiries. If that produced nothing, there must be nothing to find.

VI

When I rolled up back at my own building, it was seriously late. Much of Rome was sleeping. Those awake were sick, making love, committing suicide or burglarising. I would leave them to it.

We had a routine. After dark, moneyed families send home their visiting daughters by carrying chair, with burly slaves and blazing torches. I went along with that. The lurching made me queasy but accepting an escort kept the peace at home. Once the chair reached Fountain Court, we were in my territory and I made the rules. The bearers knew to drop me by the kitchenware potter's. His lock-up shop was diagonally opposite the entrance to my building and he left a flickery taper to show his display. One night the taper would burn down the premises, cindering his lopsided stacks of grape-drainers and grit-bottomed mortars, but in the meantime it gave one faint point of light. I hopped out and stood in silence, listening and making sure that no prowler was likely to jump me.

At the corner, before they left the alley, the bearers always looked back; if I signalled all clear, they would go on their way. If anything in the street felt wrong, I recalled them. I never took chances. This was Rome. Half the people who are mugged at midnight are attacked on their own doorstep.

You may think the bearers could have seen me all the way indoors. Oh yes—and tell every Aventine villain which doorway was mine? A lone female, finely dressed on this occasion, coming back exhausted and a little tipsy . . . I was ready for bed. I didn't want to have to stick a carving knife in some thief or rapist.

Own up, Albia: all right, I could have coped with that. I just couldn't face having to sit until dawn in some cold interview room at the vigiles station house, being driven mad by a barely literate bonehead trying to spell "self-defence." Rufinianus, no doubt. The man was straight, but indisputably a halfwit.

Yes, I had once stabbed an intruder and stupidly reported it.

Yes, after lingering a little, he died.

No, I do not regret it.

The Eagle Building, Fountain Court. Everyone still called it the old laundry, though it had not been a wash house for years and nobody knew what had become of the proprietor. Some would have retired on the profits, but it was rumoured ours had drunk them.

I gazed up at the hulking apartment block, half unoccupied as usual these days, though barely a crack of light showed, even from parts that I knew were lived in. Tenants who had work would be up at first light for their back-breaking labours; skivers and the otherwise destitute could not afford lamp oil. Six storeys of ramshackle misery loomed over me, therefore, like a hideous black fortress where prisoners-of-war were being tortured all night. Maybe it was a trick of the darkness, but the whole lump sometimes seemed to lean over the alley as if on the verge of crumpling. It was the kind of building where solitary people died, then their bodies lay undiscovered for weeks. If someone was not seen for a while, we just assumed they were hiding from an estranged spouse or from the authorities. What was one bad smell among so many?

A typically rancid slum landlord had owned this place for many years, until he was bought out by people with consciences. Well-intentioned plans to renovate had come to nothing, defeated by structural failings that were discovered to go right down into the foundations, such as the foundations were. The new owner employed a builder; the builder summoned an architect; the architect brought an engineer; the engineer said stuff it, keep the fee, because even with danger-money he wouldn't touch this place.

So far, the Eagle Building was still there, just about holding itself up. If any tenant had a bad cough, they were asked to go and stay with friends in case reverberation dislodged a crucial structural element.

I lived in the building rent-free. My nostalgia-prone father saw this ghastly building as the home of his carefree youth. My unusual mother humoured him. So it was my crazy family who had bought the lease.

Originally, they had benevolent dreams of filling the apartments with deserving tenants who would be grateful; this crackpot idealism foundered when the first layabouts "forgot" to pay their rent and used the stairs as a lavatory. Now the intention was to demolish the teetering wreck, then sell the empty plot to a millionaire senator, duping him with claims it had potential for a private home. It would happen. An ambitious general from the provinces would be bamboozled by smooth talk of how secluded the Aventine was, a little-known refuge from the city bustle, a historic Roman district where this prime land was ripe for development at a reasonable cost, a rarely available opportunity to build a custom-designed town house . . .

Don't think we had smoke in our eyes with this plan. We had someone lined up. His name was Trajanus.

Yes, you may have heard of him, and yes, nowadays he does possess a discreet private mansion on the Aventine. My father may look like a barking-mad fantasist, but he comes from a brazen line of hucksters who can sell nuts to people who own their own almond orchards. My grandfather, for example, was a rich auctioneer which— allowing the customary discretion when listing his income for taxation purposes—meant he was as well off as anybody ever needs to be. After he died we all benefited, even me.

Available cash did not help the Eagle Building. Investment

34

would have been wasted on it. A flank wall was shifting and the dirt grew blacker annually. It was no longer safe to use the balcony outside my upstairs office, even though that was the only good feature of the rooms I had there. I ought to move, but lived here because I was used to it. The hideaway at the top had always been an informer's office, so would-be clients had heard of it and could find it. Once they staggered up six flights of stairs, even the ones who thought they were coming to see my father gave in and settled for me.

Hidden away—*much* lower down, believe me—I had my own apartment, a refuge most people never knew existed. It was where I had lived for the three happy years of my marriage. I stayed there alone afterwards because although life went on, I never thought that fate would favour me a second time. I stopped there with my memories. This was all I had. Happiness had been and gone.

My husband was killed in an accident. I was already an informer by then, earning my own living as a gesture of independence, even though Grandfather's legacy had left my family comfortably off. I was only twenty when I was widowed. The family offered me security back at home; I refused the offer gently. I was rooted here. Before I was adopted, my childhood had been harsh. It mattered that during my short marriage I had made a good life for myself. I had lived alone for eight years now, and I coped well enough.

Many people would settle for an easy time. I continued to work because finding solutions to problems had a logical appeal. I could, sometimes, direct other people towards peace of mind. You need goals, when you have already had all your joy and expect destiny to grant nothing further.

I must be more tired than I had realised. It was making me maudlin.

Time to move. I knew how to melt into shadows, and there were plenty of those. Luckily nobody here put out street lanterns, so any prowlers would have to look very hard to see me.

I crossed the road. From experience, I moved cautiously. In

Fountain Court at night, I generally found my way by smell. Even with practice, I could end up stepping into something in my gold sandals. Perhaps putting bare toes against something that was still moving, even though it was half dead . . .

The building had a crumbling fire porch, attached to a portico that ran along the street. Inside the porch an iron grille had been added a few years back. I was not surprised to find Rodan had stupidly left it unlocked.

Either side of the vestibule were a couple of rooms that guarded old stone stairs which pretty well held up the block. Little more than cubbyholes, in one room we stored brooms and buckets and in the other my father had installed a porter-cum-bouncer who was supposed to scrutinise visitors while using the brooms and buckets. As usual, someone he felt sorry for had pleaded for work. Rodan. Not one of Father's best appointments—but he was hopeless at selecting staff and it was by no means his worst.

One dim lamp stood on the floor outside the nook where Rodan was allowed to live. I think it had once been where the laundress hid from angry women whose saffron yellow tunics had been accidentally dyed streaky green; there she swigged from her flagon to keep back the grim reality of life. Even now, occasionally some vague customer turned up and asked Rodan about a sheet they had left for washing five years ago.

"Not so fast!"

"Oh bloody hell, Rodan!" I had been stopped by my own concierge. He popped out of his cubicle and shoved me backwards out of the porch. Pointless to hope he was as efficient as this when strangers came. He was large, but looked sleepy and stupefied. "What are you doing up in the middle of the night, you idiot?"

Rodan was an ex-gladiator. He couldn't frighten a housefly. He must be the oldest ex-gladiator in the world. Normally even those who gain their freedom are so worn out by the arena they don't survive long in retirement, but if he kept eating his lentils Rodan was going to reach ninety. He did have a hideously broken nose, but he'd got that from a tenant who hit him in the face with a mallet. The truth was he had lasted precisely because he had never sustained any injuries professionally. As a gladiator he was so useless, the trainer he worked for would not put him into fights. For most of his life, Rodan had just ambled about the Aventine, acting as a bodyguard and rent collector. Now he was dwindling into natural senility, too bleary-eyed to see when he was barring the woman who handed over his wages. Father should do it, but he loathed having to deal directly with Rodan.

"Oh it's you," he muttered. The furious way I kicked his ankle when he tried to shoulder me out of the porch should have told him that. "It's been a right night of it. Some fellow came to see you."

"One visitor? You call that a night?"

"I was having my dinner," Rodan complained pathetically. "I had to take him all the way up to the office, and then bring him down again. My chitterlings got properly cold but after all that, he wouldn't even tip me for my trouble."

"Who was he, a client? Works late and can't come in office hours? I can wait in tomorrow for him; I hope you said so. What is he called?"

Rodan sniffed. Not hard enough. He wiped his nose on his arm. "He never told me."

Dear gods. This was why in family tradition Rodan was a creature to despise. How simple is it to enquire, "who shall I say visited?" Especially after several years of me kindly explaining how to do it? He didn't even have to write down names. Rodan could not write.

A thought struck. Could this be the archivist from the aediles' office? If so, he was really keen. Almost too keen, a cynic might say. I described Andronicus. "Friendly fellow. Bright-eyed and gingery." Rodan gave me his vague look. "Wore a white tunic with blue braid?"

Sometimes I wondered if he was irritating on purpose. "He might have done."

I said if the man came back, Rodan was to bring him straight up to the office and be nice to him. "If I am not there, make a proper appointment." I would be there. I would hang around on purpose, in case this was the archivist.

The idiot doorman finally owned up that the visitor had promised to return tomorrow. This made me so cheerful I made no attempt to kick him again as I said goodnight.

Rodan may never have had his brain pulped in the arena, but he was born addled. I was pretty sure he had never noticed my living arrangements. If so, that was good, because he could not reveal them to anybody else.

I lived on the second floor. I had a front door. It was blocked by dusty flower troughs, with the plants dying as though the last tenant had done a moonlit flit. It was feasible to climb over the troughs, but I rarely went in or out that way.

Instead, I walked up only one flight, turning out of the sight of Rodan or anybody else in the entrance. They would hear me go into an apartment that was occupied by a North African family, immigrants from Mauretania. Well, most of the family. The mother lived there, with increasing numbers of little ragged children, who came in a variety of skin colours. None of them could speak a word of our language, which saved me ever having to ask after their father.

They had four rooms, arranged along a corridor, but they only lived in three; using my prerogative as the landlord's daughter, I myself used the last room. I even kept a couch and other things there. But its main purpose was to give me access out onto a decrepit wooden walkway that had been built as a fire escape. Back when this place was a laundry, the lowest steps descended to a cluttered drying area at ground level; now that was a derelict courtyard with access to both the street and a back lane. Anyone who ever followed me into the Africans' apartment would find my room empty and assume I had gone out and escaped downstairs.

It may sound as if I was obsessed with fears of being followed home. That was the legacy of the intruder I stabbed. Home invasion leaves permanent damage. You never really recover from it.

Like most Roman tenements, the Eagle Building had minimal safety provisions. Apart from the first level which had been constructed more robustly, the fire-escape stairs to upper floors had rotted and not been replaced. In a fire, everyone upstairs would be trapped. But the old walkway gave me more than my personal flight route. If I popped along it a short distance, an old screen leaned against the wall. Secreted behind it were steep, narrow steps. They led inside, up to my real home.

This haven of mine had always been the best apartment in the block. It was small, just three good rooms, one with a firebox which I used for heating drinks, though I rarely cooked properly because for one thing I had never learned, and anyway I did not want the place to end up full of smoke. I had equipped it over the years with quite fine and comfortable furnishings thanks to my family's trade in antiques. When I came home after any trying day, it gave me peace, refreshment for the soul and solace. It was my place of happy memories.

I went in, fastened the door behind me, threw off my clothes and fell on the bed to sleep. Very few people would know where I was. Only nightmares would ever trouble me, and that night thankfully there were none.

VII

Next morning I was upstairs in my office bright and early. My heart felt a small patter of excitement. I did the silly things that fill in time, like emptying the rubbish bucket, tidying the letters you cannot be bothered to answer, and playing dice solitaire.

I heard Rodan and the visitor coming. From several floors down, Rodan was grumbling breathlessly and giving the impression he was likely to pass out. If ever he brought up some undesirable who turned out to need manhandling, I would have to do the heavy work. I would have to expel the troublemaker myself then climb back up and tow the wheezing Rodan down.

Luckily this visitor was friendly. Like everyone, he had failed to pace his climb upstairs so I heard him exclaim with relief as he reached the top level. There he would have passed an ancient collection of empty amphorae, before arriving at the battered door. I whipped it open. My heart bumped at the slim figure and eager expression of the charmer I met yesterday.

Andronicus was still looking at the indicator tile, with its mystic crescent moon. People around here thought I was a Druid. They were stupid, but I let them. Clients admire an exotic background.

"Andronicus! What a surprise—thanks, Rodan—you can go now . . ." I shoved Rodan out as fast as possible, while the archivist stood in the doorway and stared around my outer room.

I had made it a very different boudoir from the crude masculine den I inherited. You can do so much with soft furnishings. An informer should not interview people in a bare hole like some bar's back room where the pimps and gamblers congregate. Well, not unless all your clients are gamblers and pimps. That can happen. Ours is a low trade.

The tiny space was now arranged for cosy discussions. I had my own high-backed chair, a basketwork throne which showed clearly who would be in charge. A couch where agitated clients could slump and pour their hearts out had a colourful spread, with loose cushions they could hug nervously as they told their tales. There was a small round wooden table with an inlaid top, on which refreshments could be served, once we had agreed those important little details about my payment. On a shelf stood carefully chosen pieces of Greek art. Loans from the auction house, these were regularly rotated. Art always implies taste and trust. Art suggests you may have received these lovely things as gifts from previous clients, who had cause to be very grateful. It is much more subtle than nailing up written commendations, which people always imagine are fakes you wrote yourself.

Art, if sufficiently solid, can also be used to thump the heads of any crass men who molest you.

"How good to see you." I took my seat and indicated the couch for him. "Somebody called last night when I was unavailable . . ."

"Not me." I thought Andronicus wanted to hide how keen he was. "Where were you then?"

He had a slight frown between those wide-set, almost over-intense eyes. I felt too cheerful to worry. It was just conversation anyway. "With family."

"No lover?" This man took the direct approach. He gave me a twinkle to show he knew it was an impudent thing to ask.

Long practised, I parried with humour. "Oh, the one with the yacht is out of town, detained for customs infringements last I heard, and they reckon he won't get away with it this time. The actor let me down as well; he was getting all frothed up with a group of rich old widows. He's given himself a hernia, lifting the contents of their jewel caskets . . ."

"You read a lot of satirical poetry?"

"No, I write my own lines."

I had no lover at the moment. I had had no one for a long time, but a girl should never sound too available. Not on a first tryst. I had my self-respect.

Andronicus abandoned the grilling. Opposite me, he settled in a relaxed pose, one arm along the couch's backrest. I liked the way he had made himself at home. We assessed one another, both pretending not to. I still found him delightful.

"Sorry," he said, reading my mind. "Of course you ask the questions here!"

I kept it light. "Indeed I do. I would not want to waste my carefully learned interrogation skills . . . What brings you?"

"She goes straight to the point!" He leaned forward earnestly. "There has been a development. I wanted to be first to tell you."

"You care! I'm thrilled . . . So what's the news?"

"Salvidia is dead. Someone from her family—a nephew—came to inform Faustus yesterday evening."

I chose not to enlighten my new friend that I knew of the woman's death already, nor did I correct him on the real status of Metellus Nepos. I liked Andronicus, but did not know him well enough—yet—to break my rules. Say nothing that you need not say.

"That's shocking, Andronicus. She was hardly old. What happened?"

"Just reached the end of her thread, apparently. Must be annoying for you to lose a client. That's why I thought you would like to know—no point wasting any more of your time on her."

"Yes, thank you." I thought he could not have been present when Nepos and Manlius Faustus were talking. The Nepos I met would undoubtedly have mentioned to a magistrate his nagging doubts about how his stepmother died. I wondered how Faustus had reacted. Tried to put him off?

"This 'nephew' came to the aedile's house? How did you come to be there?"

"I live there." He had been a slave there, presumably. You can deduce a lot from what family freedmen prefer not to tell you. Some are brazen about their origins; well, slavery is not their fault. Yet I could tell Andronicus was quite sensitive. He was never going to say the words "slave" or "freedman" in connection with himself. "It is his uncle's house; on and off, Faustus has lived with his uncle since boyhood."

"He is not married?"

"Divorced."

"A parting for mutual convenience, or was he caught out with a kitchen maid?"

"There were rumours . . . He left his wife rather quickly, and had to surrender the dowry. I've never been able to squeeze out of him anything to explain what happened; there's a conspiracy of silence in the family."

"Read his diary?"

"Bastard doesn't write one."

"The man's a disgrace—tell him he has responsibilities to clarify matters for his caring household!"

"Well, if he strayed from the marriage, he behaves like a sanctimonious prig now," Andronicus grumbled.

"No mistress then?"

"Never even fingers the girl who makes his bed."

"So she thinks he has lovely manners—but she'd rather he tried it, so she would get a big Saturnalia present! And the uncle?"

"Oh a different mullet entirely. Tullius is a bit too randy in his habits to be tied down to marriage. You know the type—jumps any slave of any age, male or female; has even been known to stand up after the appetisers, leave the room with a serving boy, hump the lad in the anteroom and saunter back for the main course as if nothing has happened, taking up the conversation where he left off . . . Flavia Albia, you do rack the questions up. I am impressed!"

"Just habit. I apologise."

"Oh I don't care if you want the scandal on Faustus . . ."

"You haven't told me any scandal about Faustus," I corrected him.

"No, he's a cold fish."

"If I ever have to meet him, I would like to be primed with some salacious background!" I had now confirmed that Andronicus really disliked Manlius Faustus. His manner with me generally was so open that I could tell he was being reticent about his poor relationship with the aedile. Of course, that aroused my interest, though I let it pass, temporarily. Andronicus thought me direct, but I could be very patient. "So, Andronicus—last night?"

"Faustus had this visitor—people sometimes bother him on business after dinner."

"He is good about it? Doesn't mind being cornered at home, when he's relaxing?"

"I've never known him to relax! He takes a pious attitude to 'duty.' He loves to suffer. And I expect he was curious."

"Whereas you didn't care at all what Salvidia's nephew wanted?" I teased.

Andronicus raised his eyebrows so his forehead wrinkled, looking fake-innocent. "When Faustus gets up and abandons a nutmeg custard for a mystery caller, I do tend to follow and put my ear to the door."

"You need to know what he's up to?"

"I like to keep a kindly eye on him."

In some homes, freedmen take that much interest for dubious reasons, hopeful of causing friction between family members, planning blackmail even. Luckily the good-natured way Andronicus joked about it would have reassured even Faustus.

He suddenly became more serious. "I did have an interest, Albia. The fact is, I myself had had a grisly run-in with that awful woman. I can hardly bear to remember it. Salvidia came to see Faustus, but he was out of the office. I had to deal with her. She was furious about the wall poster, the one asking for witnesses to the child's death. She laid into me something terrible. Left me shaking."

"Oh poor you!"

"As if it was my fault!" Andronicus still seemed upset. Having met Salvidia, I could imagine why. "She was a pest. Her arrogance was simply unacceptable. I thought she was going to attack me physically."

"I expect she was afraid there would be consequences after the accident." Manlius Faustus could come down heavily on her building firm, to punish them for negligence. Overloading carts and having drunken drivers were areas of interest for aediles. "Had you told Faustus about how she confronted you? Was he sympathetic?"

"According to him, my job is always to be helpful to members of the public."

"He doesn't know much about the public."

"Albia, how true! When her nephew arrived to speak to him, Faustus ordered me to sit tight. I wasn't having that. He went to speak to the visitor; I sneakily followed him."

"You thought there was some trouble arising from your altercation? Why would a relative feel he ought to inform a magistrate Salvidia had died, Andronicus?"

"No idea." The archivist shrugged.

"Maybe," I suggested disingenuously, "he is prepared to pay the compensation that has been demanded for little Lucius Bassus. So he thinks the poster calling for witnesses should be taken down now? Hush things up? If he means to carry on the construction business, being named as an organisation that has killed a child besmirches its reputation. And if he wants to sell up, he has even more need to hide what happened so he can ask a good price for a going concern."

"I can think of another motive for him paying the compensation. He wants to prevent the company being fined for negligence," retorted Andronicus.

"That's possible." Since Nepos was my client, I felt obliged to keep my tone neutral.

"Oh you have such a trusting nature!" smiled my companion, unaware that I had simply preferred not to sound too clever. He composed compliments like many men: clichés I found embarrassing. "So where does that leave you regarding Salvidia? You can stop working on her case now?"

What a generous friend. He seemed so keen to spare me unnecessary labour. "If the compensation is paid, I am redundant. Unluckily for me, Salvidia had tied me to a no win, no fee contract."

Andronicus cocked his head on one side. "Upset?"

"No. A child was killed. I never liked the case."

The archivist rose to his feet, looking pleased with my answer. "So! Since that vile termagant is out of the way and your work is over," he offered, "maybe you might come out and have lunch with me?"

I had work. But I knew how to pace it. Suddenly I became the kind of woman who goes out to lunch with a man she only met yesterday.

I let him choose where. Juno be praised he did not go for my aunt's place, though we did walk past it.

He picked an eatery with an interior courtyard, secluded from street noise and well run, so it was pleasantly busy with a clientele of commercial customers. We had a light lunch, fried fish and salad, water with it. We talked and laughed. He made no moves. I valiantly refrained from making moves on him, though I was tempted. A woman has needs. Mine had not been met for a long time. Too long. I really liked him and was ready for adventure.

Afterwards he went back to the aediles' office. He had a nice line in looking regretful that he had to leave.

Left alone, I walked to an ancient piazza called the Armilustrium, where I sat for a long time, thinking about life.

VIII

The Armilustrium was the shared name of a festival and a sanctuary. The place was an old walled enclosure, sacred to Mars, the Roman god of war. From time immemorial, it had been where weapons were ritually purified in March and October, the start and end of the fighting season. After each ceremony there would be a big parade down to the Circus Maximus: all noise and triumphalism. Romans love to make a racket.

Since the enclosure served as a parade ground during the spring and autumn ceremonies, it was kept mainly bare, although there was a shrine at one end, a permanent stone altar in the centre and a couple of benches for the benefit of old ladies. In one corner was alleged to be the ancient tomb of Titus Tatius, a Sabine king who had ruled jointly with Romulus for a period, thousands of years ago. As a foreigner, he had been buried here on what was then the outsiders' hill; an oak tree shaded his resting place. It must have been renewed. Even oaks don't last that long.

In between festivals, the Armilustrium often lay deserted. I liked to come into the enclosure and sit out here. It was better than a public park where you were constantly irritated by lovers and rampaging schoolboys, beggars and mad people pretending to be lost as an excuse to engage strangers in conversation. There was hardly any litter here because the populace never wandered about with food in their hands, and nor was there that worrying smell of old dog dirt that tends to waft over even the most formal gardens if people are allowed to exercise their pets.

Don't misunderstand me. I like dogs. At one terrible time of my young life, I had lived on the streets of the town I was born in, scavenging with the feral dogs; they were kinder to me than most humans. I became as wild as they were. Maybe at heart I still was. If ever I paused quietly to consider my origins and character, the fear of having an unRoman nature unsettled me. It positively scared other people. Men, particularly. Not that I minded upsetting men.

The ideal Roman matron was supposed to be docile, but I had noticed how few of them were. It seemed to me, Roman men had devised their prescriptive regime for their women precisely because the women really held domestic power. We let them think they were in charge. But in many homes they were wrong.

I liked the Armilustrium because even without dog dirt it did harbour a smell, a musky odour near any undergrowth, a rank scent of wildlife that deterred many people: foxes frequented the area. When sitting still and silent I had often seen them. To me, since I had never kept ducks or chickens, foxes were a wilder, more intriguing kind of dog.

The Aventine foxes were currently causing me anxiety. It was April. In the middle of the month would come one of the numerous festivals that cluttered the Roman calendar, this one dedicated to Ceres, the Cerialia. Like the Armilustrium, it always had several days of public events down in the Circus, but with one extra feature that I found loathsome. On the first night, live foxes would be driven down the hill, with lit torches tied to their tails. Whooping celebrants would herd them into the Circus, where they died in agony.

Some years I went away. My family owned a villa on the coast.

This year there was a big auction in which Father was involved, so the others were not going to the sea until later, and they wanted me to stay in Rome too. Ever since I was widowed, it had been understood I would be with them at this time. Our family had almost as many ritual days as the city had festivals, and the Ides of April was a compulsory engagement for me. In an unstated way, they had made it conditional on their allowing me to be independent the rest of the time. The thirteenth day of April, during the Cerialia, was my birthday. On the Ides, I had to be with them.

Oh let's get this out of the way.

Nobody really knows when I was born, nor who my parents were. No one will ever know. Being an informer now, in a family of investigators, made no difference. I could never find out. Even I had accepted years ago that a search would be a waste of time. I would never go back to Britain. There was nothing for me there. Not even the truth.

I was discovered as a crying baby in the streets of Londinium, that ramshackle shanty town at the mist-covered end of the world. I had been abandoned, or perhaps hidden for safety, when the Boudiccan tribes attacked and burned the Roman settlement. There were few important officials in Britannia in Nero's day; it was a new, very remote, province. I was unlikely to be an official's baby or my loss would have been noted. There were soldiers, but soldiers were not supposed to have families and in a rebellious frontier province that rule tended to be enforced. The most likely possibility is that I was a trader's child, which meant I could be of any nationality, or half and half, with my mother possibly British though just as likely not.

Orphaned babies plucked from horror tend to be hailed as miracles. They give hope at a time of chaos and grief. People fostered me. My childhood was spent among shopkeepers. These slipshod, uneducated people, emigrants from mainland Europe, were decent to me, until caring for an extra infant and feeding an extra mouth became burdensome. I began to sense they had ideas of selling me into one kind of slavery or another, so I ran away. I was a skinny, bitter, unwanted street-child who slept in chilly colonnades, handed as many blows as curses.

Finally, more compassionate people saw me there and saved me.

Didius Falco and Helena Justina, my new, cultured, adventurous, warm-hearted and eccentric parents, certainly did not object to a challenge; by then I was undomesticated, vermin-ridden and although we never talked about it afterwards, I had been targeted by a brothel-owner and raped. I was aggressive and angry, too—moods I never really lost. But I also yearned for survival. I recognised a chance. Never stupid, I took it.

I came to Rome. A diploma of Roman citizenship had been arranged for me. I agreed to be formally adopted (my rescuers had principles; they gave me the choice). Birthdays are important in Roman families and I was encouraged to choose a date we could call my own. Since the Boudiccan Rebellion had happened in the autumn, and by then I had survived without a mother, spring seemed a likely time for me to have been born. Father's birthday was in March; I selected a date three weeks after his, time for us to recover from one family party and arrange the next. I chose the Ides of April before ever I knew anything about the foxes.

They came in from the country, following the great highways, sneaking at dusk up through the roadside ditches along the Via Latina, the Via Appia and the Via Ostiensis. They came to raid rubbish piles and detritus in gutters. They knew the places in the city where poultry was kept in cages, ready for butchers' shops or market stalls: ducks, hens, pheasants, geese, even occasional exotics like peacocks or flamingos. They ate mice. Occasionally they snatched puppies or kittens, or tame doves; certainly they carried off the corpses of dead pets, and also rats and pigeons. Perhaps sometimes they would scoop a fancy lamprey from a garden pond. They licked fish skins and skeletons; picked through rabbit bones; ran off, weighed down lopsidedly with meat carcasses in their mouths; skulked around butchers' stalls, licking the blood on the streets; snatched the remains of religious offerings from outdoor altars.

After a night's foraging, most probably scampered back to their dens on the open Campagna, the agricultural plain surrounding Rome. Others stayed. I knew that because I recognised at least one animal at the Armilustrium. I had seen him a few times; I knew the size and shape of him, and his regular habits. The time of evening when he visited the walled enclosure. How he paused, ears up, to check for safety. How he slipped along in shadow, almost impossible to see unless your eyes were keenly used to the darkness and spotted slight movements. He must have made a lair somewhere. I called him Robigo. It's the name for wheat rust.

Some nights I slipped out to the Armilustrium with a bowl of scraps and fed him. He had learned that I would come. If I stayed long enough, I might see him. I had learned to look for his ears, pricked up as he crouched on the top of the enclosure wall, waiting and watching until he felt secure. Then he slid down the full height of the wall, tail at full stretch, vanishing into shadow. I had to strain my eyes to find his movements. Keeping close to the wall, he would approach the bowl, with his neat tread and constant hesitation. He sniffed, he ate. The way he took food was surprisingly dainty. He made domestic dogs look like untidy gluttons.

Any slight sound would send him silently melting back into cover. But soon he would creep out again, returning until the whole bowl of food was eaten.

He liked pies, with gravy, or other broths. He thought dry grains were an insult. In many ways his appetite was the same as mine.

Once, a piece of fish I put out for him must have been dangerously rotten. Robigo lifted it out delicately and laid it on the grass a stride away, before returning to the bowl and finishing the other scraps.

He never acknowledged my presence. I knew I was communing with Nature, while Nature remained aloof.

Maybe the fact that I had been nearly burned alive myself in the fire-storm that destroyed Londinium made me so angry about the torches and terror that the devotees of Ceres perpetrated on the Aventine foxes. The foxes were like me. Private, ruthless and self-sufficient. Intelligent and untameable, yet capable of strong loyalty. Loners who could socialise, joyously and playfully, but afterwards slip back into being reclusive.

We all lived within the city community, yet surreptitiously. We were never truly part of it.

IX

Informers have ridiculous rituals. One is that if anyone connected with a case dies, especially if it is your client, you must go to the funeral. Everyone pretends this action symbolises our good nature and fine feelings. Diligent nurses brought us up from the cradle to have elegant manners. We not only sympathise with the bereaved, we ourselves are troubled souls who share their sorrow . . .

The real reason is a myth—nothing more, believe me—the myth that you chance seeing the perpetrator wailing beside the pyre. Sometimes they are indeed present, if only because most murders are committed by a member of the victim's family. If so, you can give up immediately. The person you are looking for has exactly the same snub nose and bad breath as all of their innocent relatives, and the same gormless expression. If they brazen it out, you will never home in on the guilty and catch them.

The funeral myth presupposes your killer is an idiot, who will be drawn to the scene, yearning to witness the grim results of their crime and daring you to identify her or him. It also implies informers have powers of prophecy and can tell, without using spells or magic talismans, exactly which of the off-putting mourners is really going crazy with guilt.

I have never met any informer who has achieved this feat of recognition. I go, but I never expect results.

_____

Roman funerals comprise two events, over a week apart. Tradition-ally, informers attend the gloomy outdoor interment, not the jollier feast nine days later. Whoever wrote our rulebook must have been depressing—although, let's be fair; if you were to wait nine days and enjoy the feast, all the villains would have got their acts straight and any evidence would have vanished; also, anyone who might have paid you to investigate has learned they will inherit an olive grove, so they have lost interest in causing upsets.

The will is supposed to be read on the day of the feast, but any-one who hopes for a legacy has already popped the seal off the scroll by lamplight and peeked. You, the unlucky informer, will be granted no opportunity to spot a suspicious reaction. If anyone is going to froth with rabid rage at an outrageous bequest, it happened several nights ago, in the library, with no witnesses but moths.

Perhaps there is nothing to cause offence in any case. Most wills have been put together by lawyers, and some lawyers can do a de-cent job of advising a client (I know it hurts to hear that). Besides, people planning for their deaths have a besotted wish to be well thought of, so many wills adopt a shamelessly conciliatory tone. The slave who expected to be riven with disappointment because the horrid master fails to give him his freedom has in fact been freed, with an almost adequate pension and enough money to put up a dear little plaque praising the master's liberality. The pinched sister tormented by fears of neglect has acquired the villa at Laurentium. The disgruntled wife is praised as the most deserving of women. Business partners are delirious because they will now get their hands on the legendary wine cellar . . .

All these thoughts ran through my head as we said farewell to Sal-vidia. It was the next evening, out in the necropolis on the Ostia Road. Roman funerals involve a long period of standing about; un-less you roll up late, exclaiming that the roads from Tarentum are terrible, you have to wait for hours, from the arrival of the bier until the body burns sufficiently for some sad mourner to scrape up the ashes. Winter is worst, but even in April the wood at this funeral was green and claggy. Although undertakers have covert ways of making fire take hold quickly, it seemed as if Salvidia was reluctant to go.

Metellus Nepos was there of course, carrying out the offices of chief mourner. Most of the mourners appeared to be Salvidia's home and business workforce, rather than friends or neighbours. It did not surprise me that she had no real social circle. I identified the stepson's wife, younger than him and about six months pregnant; she stood among a small group of women of a similar age, probably her own friends coming to support her, rather than people showing respect to the dead woman. They talked inanely of their houses and children, until I moved away.

I ended up alongside one of those old ladies who loves going to funerals. She could have been my grandma. A tiny, frail figure wrapped in swathes of black, she had had her mourning garments out of the clothes-chest regularly and knew how to keep a head-veil in place, even on a breezy day. She looked vague, and as sweet as honeycake, but without doubt had a vicious tongue when it suited her. I hoped she would be better value than the young housewives.

"Nothing like a good funeral to get you out of the house!" I said, striking up conversation. She looked interested in my frank attitude. "I am Flavia Albia; I had business dealings with the deceased. Did you know Salvidia well?" There was a chance this treasure had not known Salvidia at all, but just hung around the necropolis every day, attaching herself to any procession that came by; she could gloat at having herself outlived the corpse, whoever it was, and I bet she was adept at tagging along when the chosen few went back to the house for refreshments. Nobody ever likes to challenge an old lady. Gran managed to look inside plenty of strangers' houses that way.

"Oh I knew her for years. You're the investigator, aren't you?" That told me she did have prior connections, or she would not have known what I did. And as I expected, she took a nosy interest.

"Neighbour?" I guessed. I wanted to place her before I gave too much away myself.

She wasn't having it. She ignored my question with the selective deafness old ladies apply so readily. "Such a good son. It's right that he asked you."

I gave up on the first question and lightly posed another. "So do *you* think something odd happened?"

"Ooh, I couldn't say!" That's a trick they like to use. None of them are self-effacing really. She pursed her lips to show there was much she *could* say, but she clung on to pretending she was too insignificant to comment. "Nobody wants my opinion."

"I do," I challenged her, looking earnest. "It doesn't seem I will be able to do much more than reassure Metellus Nepos, but I'll try my best. I would welcome the views of someone with your common sense."

The old dame gave me a half-reproving look, to say she recognised blatant flattery and it would not work on an owl-wise being like her. I grinned, unfazed.

I knew she was assessing me. Trying to decide whether she condemned me as a flighty piece, or could just about concede that I was experienced and capable. Clearly, she did not mind me working. She came from low enough in society to accept that many women had to help their husbands earn a living in the family shop, bakery or forge; she understood how some of us had no male head of family, so must find our own way to avoid prostitution yet to bring in money for rent and food. I guessed I would be categorised with manicurists and hairdressers, women who knew about herbal creams and traditional medicines, freed slaves who were literate enough to read or write letters and documents for other people. And yes, the local abortionist.

I categorised her as a widow of course. Women either die young in childbirth or they tough it out for decades and long survive their husbands.

The undertaker's musicians broke into a burst of determined fluting and wailing, so we had to stay silent for a while.

Afterwards, the moment was lost. I extracted no more from the old lady, who then had to leave early. As she went, she patted my hand and encouraged me. "You do what you can for her, dearie." She definitely implied that Salvidia had gone before her time.

As the ancient one departed, someone who must know her remarked that she could not stay because of obligations at home. So she did not, as I had assumed, live alone, but had a close relative she must care for; who, was unclear. I could guess. Either a drooling husband, too demented nowadays to know her, or some great lummock of a son or daughter who had been damaged in the birth canal. A daily burden and a responsibility, for whom the exhausted old body had to stay alive because they would be helpless without her. This half-sighting of a hard life made me melancholy.

With nothing to do but think during another hour or so of chilly pyre-watching, I ended up considering yet again what she obviously believed about Salvidia's death.

I walked over to the undertaker. His previous contribution when asked for an opinion had just not been good enough; I asked him again about that comment he had made when he came to view the corpse.

"You said, 'There's a lot of it about.' Did you mean people keeling over, for no reason? I have to admit it has stayed in my mind. Would you mind telling me what made you say that?"

He was a big-bellied pompous type, who was accustomed to patronising bereaved people. He must be a particular trial to defenceless new widows. All the man could come up with for me was that he "had a vague feeling." He still believed it might be nothing more than coincidence.

"Were these people all women?" I asked, pushing him.

"No, all sorts. Just a few more sudden deaths than usual—possibly. I haven't been counting. Don't ask me for names."

"Any rumours?" I wondered. The public can be good at picking up illegal activity.

The funeral director gave me a swift glance. He did not look nervous or hunted. He did not brush me aside like a silly young thing. Instead, he appeared to consider my question fairly and to honestly say no, there were not. If he was hushing up a scandal, he was good. I had to believe him.

I was to develop more doubts about Metellus Nepos. In a quiet moment while he waited to do his duty gathering the ashes into a ceramic urn, he approached and thanked me for coming. I took the opportunity to mention that I knew he had visited the aedile. He confirmed that he went to say he was paying compensation for the child's death, and make it plain that the family were satisfied with what he offered them. He made no mention of the wall poster; Nepos seemed too decent to demand its removal, or even to think of doing so.

Nepos volunteered that he told the magistrate about his suspicions regarding his stepmother's death. He had discussed hiring me. (I wished my friend the archivist had thought to warn me about this.) "I discussed with Faustus all the aspects you had checked so carefully, Albia, and admitted that you found no evidence." Nepos seemed concerned that I might be annoyed. Certainly, if the case had been live, I would have wanted any client to consult me before he involved the authorities. "The aedile is not the same as the vigiles, but he does have responsibility for aspects of law and order. It seemed right to let him know my concerns."

I reassured him. "That is perfectly reasonable. I would not have stopped you . . . So what did you think of him? According to my contacts, Manlius Faustus sounds—let's say, unsympathetic."

Nepos stared at me for a moment, seeming surprised. "No, I found him very straightforward. He doesn't say much, but he listens. A good, intelligent choice for the job."

"That's rare."

"Exactly!" replied Nepos. He sounded annoyed, as if I had insulted a friend of his.

I did not let this alter the picture of the aedile I had previously from Andronicus. Plenty of men behave quite differently with a one-time business visitor from how they treat members of their household. In that case, how they are at home tends to be their true character. Manlius Faustus must have social skills; he needed votes to win election to his office. In short, he must know how to schmooze. It was quite possible for him to act polite to Nepos two nights ago, and yet be a pernicious swine to his own slaves and freedmen on a daily basis.

"And did he react to your unease about Salvidia's death?"

Nepos was gazing at the spitting flames. "Not specifically."

"I presume he is not intending any follow-up action?"

Nepos spoke a little abstractedly. "No. No, he won't be doing that."

Like the undertaker, Nepos made it casual and seemingly sincere. But his acting was less good. He was a cheesemaker and seller. He did not spend his professional life putting on a show of false emotion, as any funeral director has to. Nepos seemed so honest that if a piece of cheese had a spot of mould, he would point it out and advise you to slice off the worst before you served it. So in his case, I saw through him: as he tried to deflect me, a curtain came down. More had been discussed with Faustus than he was prepared to tell. He was blotting out a topic he did not want to discuss with me.

Something was going on. Something that was being kept from the public in general and me in particular.

X

The death squads were out that evening.

When I first came to Rome it was the reign of the Emperor Vespasian, tough but decent. My parents knew him. They knew his elder son Titus as well, but Titus only survived his father by a couple of years, years that were dominated by the disastrous volcanic eruption of Mount Vesuvius. Even in that dark moment, Rome was well-run and thriving. But when Titus died unexpectedly, rumours that he had been poisoned by his jealous brother Domitian indicated just what kind of rule would follow. Eight years later, we were used to suspicion and fear. Praetorian Guards were regularly sent out to search for those whose low opinion of their emperor had aroused his loathing for them.

Failure to flatter that podgy despot Domitian was a deadly mistake. Many people inadvertently made the error; the slightest thing could offend him. So, as I returned wearily to the city from the necropolis, I was not surprised to glimpse a small group of soldiers passing the end of a dark street; there was no doubt of their sinister intent. As they tramped into the neighbourhood, everyone disappeared from the streets. Even a cat fled, yowling. It realised the soldiers were pitiless men who, if it strayed within their reach, would grab its tail and dash its brains out.

The night was dark by then, moonless and starless, though almost too early for the imperial guards to arrive. Normally, they liked to surprise victims with sudden and thunderous knocking at the door while everyone was sleeping. Just before dawn, a bleary porter would find set-faced men with drawn swords, bringing punishment, often for a crime the victim had not even known he had committed. If the soldiers turned up during hours of darkness, there was less chance of resistance; less chance, too, of angry neighbours raising a public outcry. Tyrants are petrified of riots. Come the pale light of morning, word of a new death in the upper classes would infiltrate basilicas and emporia, though such brutal deletions of humanity were never formally listed in the *Daily Gazette*.

That night the first warning of their presence was their torches. Guards always carried rather good torches, and plenty of them. Trained killers need big, long-lasting flames; only the very best tar for Domitian's punishers. These heavyweights are crack troops; they don't want to march out on a mission to murder some measly senator only to be jumped by one of the petty muggers who hang about at night. It would be just too, too shameful to creep back to the Praetorian Camp and have to admit that they had been held up and had their medals and fancy daggers stolen by one of the moth-eaten larcenists on Chickenbone Alley.

We were used to the execution squads. That was the worst part; we now accepted it. Children were growing up in Rome who had never known an ordinary, safe existence. Even adults who remembered better times rarely questioned the way things were.

For someone like me, who worked among deceivers and double-crossers, the new atmosphere of dread was an appropriate backdrop. We had reached a grim period when Domitian was clearly becoming more cruel. He believed his wife had betrayed him with an actor; his foreign wars were derided; he had just survived a rebellion in Germany headed by a man he trusted; and his beloved niece Julia had died. He took it out on us, his helpless subjects. Probably he had realised that, much as he wanted to be adored, nobody liked him. The more he executed people who showed their hostility, and the feebler his excuses, the less our charmless tyrant would be loved . . . Neither he nor we could escape the cycle of misery.

Constant executions had affected the public. Political uncertainty led to desperation. People lost their morality—where they had had any in the first place. A cynic would say it gave more work for informers—the emperor, for one, certainly used spies, spies at all levels of society, spies who were good, bad or absolutely indifferent these days to the faint concept of honesty that had once existed in some of us. As well as the emperor himself wanting to destroy the personal enemies he saw behind every palace pillar, informers could find plenty of ordinary people who were ready to betray others. Picking a fight with your neighbour over a boundary dispute or insulting a shopkeeper who served rotten leeks were now dangerous exploits. You could end up in court, with some unscrupulous informant-turned-prosecutor accusing you of treason or that wonderfully nebulous concept, "atheism"—all with sworn statements to "prove" the crime that had in fact never happened.

I never worked for the state. I had relatives who had done so in the past, but it was now too dangerous. No dubious practices, bedroom or religious, would be exposed by me to further the emperor's morality campaign and make him look good to the gods. No bearded philosopher who foolishly lectured on historic tyrants would spot me sitting in the back row, scribbling notes that would earn him exile to a very uncomfortable island. No silly woman casting horoscopes need fear me reporting her for prophesying Domitian's death.

Any clairvoyant who was any good at foreseeing knives and poisonings was safe from me. Like everyone else, I would be too interested in knowing exactly when we could hope for a decent coup with a well-organised assassination. I knew what I thought about Domitian, but I hid my opinions.

I had nothing to fear from the Guards in theory, yet, like anyone, when I heard them coming I kept out of their way. I did not want a bad-tempered officer to decide any lone woman on the streets after dark must be a whore. I would be at his mercy. Pleading that you have just "come from a funeral" sounds a lame excuse. So I stood carefully in a dark shop doorway while they marched by.

Once again, as I waited, I became depressed. I had been unsettled by Nepos admitting he had discussed me and my work with the aedile. That could lead to bother. And the issue of Salvidia's death gnawed disturbingly. You could say that compared with the problems some brave opponent of the emperor was about to have this night when the Guards arrived at his home, the unexplained death of a middle-aged woman who probably suffered from a bad heart hardly mattered. But that magistrate Manlius Faustus, the supposedly intelligent man Metellus Nepos had taken a shine to, had obviously instructed Nepos to stop talking to me—Nepos, with whom I had previously enjoyed a frank professional relationship. I hated that: the impression that my client and an official had entered some male compact, from which they were high-handedly excluding me.

In these dark streets, full of the menace that trailed behind the Praetorians, I started to think all sorts of things. After they had gone, people kept in their homes, with shutters drawn. I heard neither music nor laughter nearby. Stillness descended. In this unusual, uneasy quietness, an insidious cover-up of strange crimes began to seem almost plausible.

I cursed Nepos again—but this time my irritation was practical. I remembered that I had forgotten to ask him to pay my fees as he had promised.

XI

I had no energy that night to work myself into a frazzle. I was too tired and had had little to eat all day; it was easier to ignore my fretful thoughts. It would not be the first time that work I had already completed had to be written off. Losses splattered my ledger as if some damaging weevil had got in and left little droppings all over the scroll.

Next morning I devoted time to the ordinary things a girl has to do. I went through my apartment gathering laundry, bundled it neatly, and hauled the bundle to be washed. People think an informer's life is all exposing frauds in court and beating up stubborn witnesses, but you need clean sheets and tunics. Clients are put off by bad hygiene. Anyway, I hate itching.

I often ate breakfast at a bar called the Stargazer, but on days when I attended to chores I just munched whatever stale bread roll I found at home. I took one out with me when I went to the laundry. I chewed slowly; it was so old and hard, I risked breaking a tooth.

I picked up the previous bundle and went straight to Prisca's bath house, a civilised all-female establishment, where I was able to gain admittance even when they were closed. None of them are supposed to open in the morning, but I was a regular and welcome to use either the gymnasium or the library at any hour. Prisca herself let me in, with one of her pleasant greetings: "I see your hairdresser's on strike again! And if you don't mind me mentioning this, Flavia Albia, it could be time now to start tucking yourself up in a bustband."

What is it about baths that makes people think they have a right to be insulting?

She just wanted to sell me a band. There was nothing wrong with my figure, any man would agree. I was shorter than I might have been if I had had a better childhood, but by the time my chest grew, I had been adopted by the Didii and given a decent diet. Physically, I developed late, but enough. I seemed to be still growing well into my twenties. Fully mature now, I kept trim; everything was in the right place, whatever Prisca implied.

I tossed my quadrans onto the money bowl, made a gesture that could pass for friendly if Prisca was exceedingly short-sighted, then with her cackling after me I barged through into the changing room, hurled off what I was wearing, grabbed a modesty towel and headed for the main facilities.

The bath suite was on the right; it was a simple row of tepid room, steam room and cold room with a plunge bath. On the left, a small court opened out with colonnades where people could relax sensibly or work themselves into a froth with exercise. A couple of hard-bitten women dressed in combat gear were huffing about with fancy little bucklers and wooden swords, making themselves a spectacle. I don't object to female gladiators, but if such hopefuls must adopt butch sports I expect them to have enough self-respect to fight decently; these were hopeless. I refused to gawp because I figured that was what the silly madams wanted.

Prisca had followed me. "You should be able to find a bit of warmish water left from last night. Why don't you come at a sensible hour? Do you want someone to scrape you down?"

"I'll manage."

This was hard on the girls who tried to earn a few coppers wielding a strigil for customers who could not drag off their own bathing oil, but Prisca had known me long enough; I don't know why she asked. I always brought my personal strigil, a nicely curved, comfortable bone one, and at the moment I was using up a little flask of plain almond oil I had had from one of my sisters last Saturnalia.

Prisca made no money from merchandise with me. But she knew I was no trouble and if she kept on my good side, I would keep paying the entrance fee. She was a good businesswoman.

She sat down on the ledge in the steam room with me; when things were quiet she liked a chat. I put up with it because she could be a useful source of gossip.

She was a sparely built woman in her late middle years, always in a long sleeveless tunic, permanently damp and clinging, and with rope-soled toe-post sandals. I had only ever seen her in the same jewellery: a gold chain with a greenish tinge and heavy hoop earrings. Despite regular attempts to discover her background, I still had no idea how she came to be running this bathhouse. It would not surprise me to find she had jumped some male owner, whether her husband or someone unrelated, holding his head under the water in the plunge pool until she drowned him, then she just quietly took over. It was her decision to make it women-only. Most baths had sessions for both sexes, kept separate by different times.

Although Prisca remained fully clothed, I did not object to her watching me at my ablutions. She saw enough bodies to be indifferent. My sisters always giggled about this place, claiming it was a club for lesbians. They were fourteen and sixteen, so found that idea dangerous and thrilling. In fact most other customers were working women, some not even prostitutes, but honestly employed as freelance embroiderers, midwives or fish-scalers. Mothers of schoolchildren came here for some peace and quiet. Worn old aunties muttered over their oil flasks, trying to use as little as possible to save money. Any of these could possibly belong to the Grecian sisterhood, or flirt with it, but at Prisca's there was no higher proportion than in ordinary society, and they were no more visible.

"Who are the two toughs in the garden?"

"Zoe and Chloe. They're harmless—even though they think they terrify everyone. What you working on? Anything interesting?" Prisca knew what I did. Sometimes she shuffled clients my way.

"Nothing special." I was always discreet. "My last employer just died on me."

She laughed. "You do know how to pick 'em!"

"Apparently people are dropping dead before their time, for no reason."

"Is that so?" Prisca showed no interest. If there was a crisis, clearly news had not reached the bathhouse circuit. I was interested, because baths are where most rumours first pop into life.

I finished my routine and Prisca left me to it. I dried off, put on one of the clean tunics I had fetched from the laundry, then sat by myself in the colonnade. The show-offs with swords and shields had gone, so I was alone. That suited me. I liked certain people, but otherwise was naturally reclusive. I could hear Prisca and her various slaves moving about and occasionally speaking to each other, but no one bothered me. I did not think about my work, I just restored my spirits peacefully.

If I had come later, I would have had a session with Serena, the best physical manipulator on the Aventine, but she tended to work in the evening when the baths were officially open. Combing my hair dry in a patch of sunshine served to calm me almost as much as a massage. The long slow strokes always reminded me of those first months after I was brought to Rome. I very quickly got to know all of my new female relatives; they were numerous, and I learned to dread the heavy-handed ones. Every time any of them visited our house, I would be passed across to be worked on. Most women in Rome own a nit-comb and are adept at using it.

I have dark hair which, unfortunately, gives no clue to my original nationality. I will always remember the first time Helena washed it for me: her firm but kindly touch as she made me endure the warm water on my tender scalp, while I whimpered and wriggled, then the wonderful clean scent of rosemary as she rinsed and untangled everything. She could have had a slave look after me, but she had chosen to foster me, so she herself carried out all the unpleasant tasks of cleaning me up and taming my wild habits. I wanted so desperately to be mothered, at first I could hardly bear to trust her in case our new relationship abruptly ended. It took me years to re-alise that motherhood did not come to her naturally; she saw it as a duty and would much rather have been reading, or spending time with her husband.

She loved us now. No, that sounds wrong; she had always given us love, willingly and amply, but she *enjoyed* us more, now we were older and she could talk to us as equals.

She had hated it when I left home to make my own life as an in-former, seeing my exit as her own failure. But she too was a dogged, independent spirit; I had learned that from her. Undoubtedly, she was proud of me now. I often went home and consulted her about my work.

Thinking about her, I decided to have lunch with Mother today.

The girls were out, visiting friends, and our brother was having les-sons, so I stayed for hours, talking and not talking, just spending time together. Just when I was thinking I should leave, the girls reap-peared, full of excitement; then Father came home from the auction house, so we all adjourned to the roof terrace for the ceremony of hearing about his day. Many bowls of olives later, I declined the offer of dinner, and made my way back up the Hill to Fountain Court.

I was in a good mood. Most of the day had gone by, but who cared? That is the bonus of being freelance. You can make your own hours—always an excuse for working no hours at all.

My mood improved even more when Rodan emerged to tell me that Metellus Nepos had called while I was away, and had left something for me. He had brought my payment for the work I did for Salvidia, plus extra for when he hired me himself. He had even presented me with a sample of his cheese too. Such a civilised man. Immediately my benign feelings towards him reasserted themselves.

It was too late to apply myself to work, and since I didn't know how long Nepos would remain in Rome now the funeral was over, I decided to trip around to Lesser Laurel Street, tell him his offerings had been safely received and say thank you.

That was when I found him in a terrible tizzy. He was about to visit the house of a neighbour who had died, just after she attended his stepmother's funeral. Celendina was her name. I had not known that previously, but I gathered she was the old woman I had talked to at the necropolis. That alone gave me a reason to accompany Nepos and pay my own respects—even though he and I both knew I was going along out of professional curiosity. Celendina had been perfectly well yesterday, a self-sufficient body who had stood at the side of the pyre without complaint until she had to leave. I could still see her in my mind's eye, as she toddled off home at a good pace. Although she was elderly, Nepos and I were both amazed to learn she had died barely hours afterwards.

Nepos was very upset. I could not blame him. There seemed a striking similarity to what happened with his stepmother. Neither of us thought it was a coincidence.

Celendina had lived just around the corner. As I walked there with Metellus Nepos, I tried calming him, to little avail.

Some well-disposed neighbour had supplied a couple of small cypress trees to stand either side of the doorway. People who lived locally were keeping a sharp eye out for visitors, as they do when something odd has happened and they don't want to miss what follows. We soon had several helpful persons presenting us with information.

It was a night and a day since the old woman had been found dead. Her body was no longer at the house but had been taken away by the undertaker—an officially supplied one. Somehow the vigiles had become involved at the scene. From what we heard, I realised their removing the body was for a corpse-inspection, in a case of presumed foul play. But this sounded different to what occurred before with Salvidia, at least in the neighbours' version—a sorry tale that only emerged slowly as people started to feel uncomfortable about it.

It was her son Celendina had lived with and vigiles' suspicions centred on him. As I had deduced, he had been not right from birth; we were told that only people who knew him very well could communicate with him. He was never able to go out, and had grown into a strange, heavy lump who became upset if he was alone for too long, so that was why his mother left the funeral early. Sometimes in the past a neighbour had minded him for Celendina, but I could tell they had never liked doing it. No one wanted to take over full-time care of him now. Motherless, his future was uncertain.

The son, Kylo, was no longer at the house. The neighbours said people had been drawn there last night by him screaming and shouting. They broke in and found him with his mother's lifeless body, violently shaking her. Everyone at once assumed something had gone wrong between them and he must have killed her. In such circumstances, people easily turn against a man with mental difficulties. Uproar ensued. The vigiles arrived. Now Kylo was in custody, accused of his mother's murder.

One peculiarity of the events was that, although no one could make sense of most things Kylo said, when they found him he distinctly said several times: "Flavia Albia." My name.

XII

I made sure I got to the vigiles before they came looking for me.

Our local cohort was the Fourth. Their headquarters was in the Twelfth District, over in the Piscina Publica, by the Aqua Marcia. They had sub-barracks too, one of which covered the Thirteenth, here on the Aventine. I knew it well. I had been coming here as long as I had lived in Rome, so it held no terrors for me.

You could tell you were approaching the barracks by the number of gloomy drinking bars. The complex had a pair of huge gates, which led into a courtyard stacked with equipment for firefighting, which was the vigiles' primary purpose. Their other interest, in crime, had developed when the patrols who went out sniffing for smoke at night kept running into muggers and burglars as those evil-doers carried out their own nightly patrols. The vigiles started to arrest them. So law and order became an additional function. It would be nice to think that made Rome a safer place, but only halfwits would believe it.

The force was composed of ex-slaves, volunteers who each served six hard years then gained the privilege of citizenship—if they survived. They were led by ex-soldiers, one of whom in the Fourth had been an uncle of mine. He was now officially retired, though whenever he managed to give my aunt the slip, he still hung around the station house like a disapproving ghost, on the excuse of unfinished business; there was a particular gangster he had failed to catch. It continued to obsess him.

Like many community organisations, there was never enough money allowed for the vigiles' upkeep, while they also had no prestige and so no incentive to excel. This gave the men a hangdog, shabby air; they could often be seen lolling against a siphon engine in some quiet alley, pretending to wait for a call-out, but eating snacks and chatting up loose women. They had a humourless tribune, who roosted in the main building in the Twelfth, while Titus Morellus was now in charge of investigations in our local depot. He was typical— overweight, shaved head, lazy attitude. He was not quite as sweaty as some of the others, though they all smelled.

"Flavia Albia! Don't you come here begging for favours."

He knew who I was. That is to say, in vigiles' terms, he knew who my father and uncle were (best pals, who had cooperated on many a case in their day—a day that was past now, though not according to them). I would hardly have counted here, but for a lucky break-through on an old inquiry: my own reputation rested on that time I exposed a doctor who drugged his women patients and then inter-fered with them. A couple of them had got together afterwards and asked me for help. Unfortunately, that was ten years ago and we were running out of men who remembered it. The vigiles have short memories. Although in theory they build up local expertise and a detailed record of previous cases, in fact their interest only extends to this week's tasks. Half the time they are not even interested in those.

I told Morellus why I had come. He spat. The vigiles were all crude.

"Yes, we've got the lad here. I call him a lad; he must be over thirty but he's like a big baby. And big he is; his poor old mother must have struggled to deal with him."

"So what's the verdict?" I asked, attempting a show of respect for his opinion.

"He can pee in a pot. We don't have to change his loincloth."

"Don't be a pain, Morellus. What's the verdict about his mama?"

"The obvious one. He killed her."

"True?"

"No, convenient," Morellus admitted. "You know us, we're very public-spirited. We just want a good clear-up rate." If he had been more sophisticated, this would pass for a joke. In him, it was a curious mix of mild shame at their failings and real couldn't-care-less.

I told him I had heard a rumour that there were many mysterious deaths happening. He shrugged. "Nobody has told us. But nobody ever tells us anything."

I thought, there could be a good reason for that . . . "There is an aedile involved now."

"There would be!" He spoke with contempt.

I grinned to show I shared it. "Can I see this Kylo?"

"In the cells. One of my boys is looking after him, one who has a child of his own that was born simple. You know. Big head and squinty eyes. According to her father, his little girl needs help, but has a wonderful personality. She's vulnerable, but completely loving."

"What do you think?"

"I think he's right," Morellus replied immediately, giving me back a level stare. "She does."

"Have a wonderful personality?"

"That's what I said."

"But is Kylo different? Do you believe he is capable of violence?"

"He is odd." Morellus mimicked Celendina's son, holding one arm across his chest, with the hand dropped, and hitching up one hip. "Someone like that might be feared locally, especially as he is so big and powerful. Say a group of neighbours responded to a commotion, found her dead with her son shouting wildly and holding her corpse—what happens? It would be instinct for them all to assume he had shaken the old woman to death."

"So?"

Morellus might be fat and lazy, but he had a brain when he bothered to use it. "Could be something different. What if in fact Kylo had panicked? He *found* her dead, became upset, then just shook her as hard as he could in a hopeless attempt to wake her up again?"

I said that was remarkably fair-minded, to which Morellus—blushing—replied that I was not to quote him.

The prisoner was sitting on the ground in the second courtyard. The vigilis who was on guard had him feeding crumbs to pigeons. Physically, he looked no more dumb than any barrow boy or household messenger, though the brain damage was obvious in his vacant eyes and the way he held himself. Morellus had done a good mime.

Kylo was tall, powerfully built and deeply uncommunicative. He had loose curls like a little boy but was indeed over thirty; despite that, you could see at a glance that he could not take care of himself. His mother must have managed everything: food, dress, hygiene, keeping him occupied, keeping his sexuality in check. She would have had a lifetime of defending him from other people's ignorance, and of pleading with people to accept him.

I explained who I was. Although it seemed rude to talk about Kylo in his presence, he was taking absolutely no notice of us. The vigilis agreed that without his mother, Kylo was lost. "And he knows it."

Even though Kylo appeared not to be listening in, he glanced up when we mentioned his mother. I saw the fear and sadness in his eyes. Yes, he knew. The only person who had ever cared for and looked after him was gone. He was alone; nobody wanted him; he was finished.

I managed to get his attention for a moment and said clearly, "I am Albia." It seemed to mean nothing to him. I said it again. "My name is Flavia Albia. Somebody said you wanted me."

There was no response. I explained to the vigilis how Kylo was supposed to have spoken my name to the neighbours. If so, he had already forgotten why. Maybe his mother had come home and told him about Salvidia's funeral, mentioning that she had met me. In his first moments of terror after Celendina died, he might have clung on to her last words. Now, there was no way we would get him to explain. He had completely forgotten all about it.

Since the vigilis had a daughter with disabilities, even if hers were different from Kylo's, I thought his advice was worth having. "He doesn't look like a murderer. He's just a great lopsided lump who seems happy enough feeding pigeons. Do you think he killed his mother?"

With regret in his voice, the man answered, "I think we have to proceed as if he may have done."

"Would it have been accidentally?"

"I can imagine that."

"Really? Some little thing upset him and he suddenly lashed out? Then Celendina was not strong enough, or not quick enough, to get out of the way safely?"

"Could be."

"I met the mother at a funeral. I suppose she may have been tired after that, and let her attention wander . . . Or perhaps Kylo was piqued by her leaving him alone. But he seems docile now."

"We'll have him here a few more days before we charge him. I am supposed to watch and assess him."

I was unhappy about it. "There is no witness to what he is supposed to have done, no proper evidence. You call this justice?"

"No," said the man quietly. "The neighbours were throwing rocks at the house. They were all set to tear him apart. We call it protective custody."

As I left, Morellus emerged from an interview room and called out to me. "His Eminence wants a word with you. I have orders to take you over to the Twelfth."

He meant Cassius Scaurus, the tribune, the humourless one. Scaurus ran his cohort the same way as his predecessors did; the method was to put up his feet in the main station house over in the

Piscina Publica while he thought up ways to cream off the budget for his personal use. He ruled this outstation by the fine tradition of leaving it to look after itself.

I knew a truly serious interview would entail me being tied to a bench or chair and subjected to endless shouted questions in a very violent atmosphere. It was unlikely they would use their heated metal implements to inflict unbearable pain, though it could not be ruled out. The aim was to force a confession. Any confession. It did not have to be true. Why niggle about details?

"What does he want?"

"The proverbial few questions."

"Help with your enquiries? Is he authorising the full torture package?"

"He has to get a chit from the Prefect for that," Morellus admitted, as if he thought I might find this comforting. "I had the impression your interview will be limited to basics—horrible threats and mental cruelty."

"Delightful! So when are you coming to collect me?" I asked thoughtfully.

"When I get around to it," Morellus told me. His tone was heavy with the suggestion that it would never happen. I hoped he did not expect a reward for "forgetting" to do it—especially sexual favours. Perhaps he took a lenient attitude out of respect for my father and uncle. That may have figured partly, but the real reason was that he loathed the tribune.

"Right. Don't expect me to come quietly."

"No, I'll arrive mob-handed."

"I don't suppose there is any point in me asking what I am supposed to have done, Morellus?"

He laughed.

Hunching my shoulders, I threw my stole round them angrily. "And you still expect me to believe you when you say that there is no funny business going on?"

Morellus paused. The flabby, lackadaisical brute really did hate that tribune to a horrid degree. "I suppose, Flavia Albia, if I wanted to upset the old man by taking the initiative, I could start asking around about mysterious deaths."

I was satisfied. I despised him, but the dregs of being a good officer had somehow survived in him. He could do a decent job when he chose. He would also be deeply annoyed if he discovered that his superior had been keeping him in the dark. If Morellus did uncover any funny business happening on the Aventine, which the tribune had failed to mention to him, then because of his deep-seated loathing of Cassius Scaurus, there was a good chance Morellus would pass on the details to me.

XIII

W ell, Flavia Albia—you're hiding quite a history!"
    There was only one way to offset my depression: lunch. I
had come to the Stargazer, the neighbourhood snack-bar my relatives had owned for years, where the aediles' archivist now discovered me. Rodan probably told Andronicus where I would be and, as
I greeted my new friend with a lightly pattering heart, for once I
blessed the porter.

Andronicus flopped on a bench opposite. Junillus, the young waiter,
came to see what he wanted. Being Junillus, he just stood silently,
with a waxed tablet poised for writing orders. He had an apron. He
had cocked his head. It was obvious why he was there.

When Andronicus said nothing, Junillus walked off, presumably
thinking the customer needed more time. I noticed the archivist
moved the purse on his belt to a more central position, instead of on
his hip. That conveniently told Trinius the pickpocket where to find
it, once Trinius had finished glugging his mulsum and wanted to lift
the price of tomorrow's drink before he left. "The waiter seems a
bit off . . ."

"Deaf." Still upset after the vigiles, I was terse.

"All right! I only meant all waiters can be odd."

"Junillus is deaf. Which means he grew up dumb. And in case
you are thinking of moving us on to some dump where the staff pass
for normal but they spit in your pottage and cheat on the bill, he is
my cousin."

The archivist waved a hand airily around the caupona. "Ah! A family business?" I could see him thinking what a shabby dive it was. At the Stargazer, even the cobwebs had cobwebs. Sometimes they wafted in a breeze, as if the spirits of old customers were crying out for rest.

Andronicus looked serious—his way of announcing a joke. "I presume that even if it doesn't get you a discount, they flick the flies out of the dish before serving you?"

"If they remember." I finally calmed down. "Never order the special here; it means specially burned." I signed to Junillus that Andronicus would have the same as me: dish of the day (chickpeas, it was always chickpeas), with lettuce on the side, a hard-boiled egg crumbled over the lettuce and a beaker of their not-exactly-Falernian. "See—that was easy."

"Of course. Albia, I understand. He is only deaf. It doesn't make him stupid."

Junillus, who could lip-read or at least interpret moods, gave us an irritated look and loafed off to the kitchen. He was a handsome boy of maybe seventeen, with a tolerant personality. I had a special bond with him. He too had been adopted into the Didii, after his disability must have become apparent and his birth-parents dumped their deaf baby in a rubbish skip. At least they chose a well-maintained one. He survived. My father found him. My childless aunt took him. She needed somebody to dote on; her husband was useless.

It was Junillus who had renamed the place the Stargazer. He was right that there was no point calling it Flora's—its previous incarnation—now that nobody remembered who Flora had been. He had acquired a wall painting of an ugly fish with its eyes on the top of its head and a big mouth, to advertise. I thought it looked rather like Uncle Gaius, Junillus' father, though I never said so.

"In fact he is extremely intelligent," I stated, still defensive.

"Presumably he needs to be," returned Andronicus in a quiet, sensible voice. He was diligently winning back my friendship. I saw no need to make that difficult.

To justify my bad mood, I mentioned my problems today with the law and order boobies. "Just a technicality. But when they flaunt their power, they are a menace . . ." His food came. I waited while he sized it up and had a taste. At the Stargazer they were not ambitious, but they could manage hard-boiled eggs. "So! What did you mean about my 'history,' Andronicus? Has someone been spreading malicious rumours?"

As Junillus retreated to the counter, he executed a silly dance, for my benefit; he was indicating that Andronicus was of an even worse standard than my usual class of follower. Andronicus happened to catch this from the corner of his eye. In his most teasing manner he commented, "I suppose it's inevitable your family will mock any man-friend they see you with!"

"Saturnalia will be fun," I agreed, not disputing his definition of himself. "By then sisters, aunties, Mother's dressmaker and the pet monkey should all have seen us around together. My life won't be worth a nutshell."

"I think you'll cope." Andronicus had laid down his spoon, probably with relief, as the sour chickpeas hit his tastebuds; my aunt was still using up a sackful she must have bought the year Vesuvius erupted. He spoke in a low, more intense voice. "From what I heard this morning, you are tough. And an interesting character . . . You don't seem perturbed that you have been discussed by people?"

I smiled gently. "I always wait until I know exactly which colourful anecdote—or which fanciful lie—has been told about me." We tussled in silence for a while, with him resisting in order to tease me, then I added in a murmur: "And to whom the lie was told."

Andronicus projected his wide-eyed amazed look, eyebrows up and forehead wrinkled.

"Give!" I commanded more sternly. To help him out, I said, "I've learned that Metellus Nepos told Manlius Faustus that he was hiring an informer." I did not explore why Andronicus had not mentioned to me what Nepos said. Perhaps I should have, but I was more interested in knowing what had happened today. "Does that have something to do with this talk of my 'history'?"

Andronicus then confessed readily enough. "It was only a matter of time, Albia, before Faustus asked for the background on you."

"You were right before. He *is* an interfering bastard."

"Routine. All he did was to call up the vigiles register."

"And he found I wasn't there."

"Ah! Yes, he did."

The vigiles keep lists of characters the government chooses to monitor. That's people with low careers, or people who follow foreign religions that encourage lofty morals, certain types of which the authorities find highly dangerous. Among a ragbag of prostitutes and astrologers, these registers include informers.

"It must be difficult," Andronicus suggested. "Being on that kind of list?"

"But I'm not! I couldn't object; after all, it's perfectly true we informers follow curious rituals, speculate on ethical questions, and above all, sell ourselves. We try to solve puzzles, like mathematicians. We sit in bars, philosophising—though, thank the gods, it's not compulsory for informers to grow beards."

"Not even when you operate in disguise?" tried Andronicus wickedly. The way he said it verged on flirting. Very pleasant.

My father's name was on the vigiles' list. He thought that was hilarious. They never came to search our house these days, nor bothered to arrest him. His name probably had a "Do Not Disturb" mark alongside, to indicate that he was too pally with the old Emperor Vespasian.

My name had never been added. When I first became an informer, Uncle Lucius fixed that, claiming old-fashionedly that all I did was write love letters for the illiterate.

I did those sometimes. When the tear-jerkers were too banal, I passed them on to Father's Egyptian secretary. Clients liked it. His handwriting was beautiful.

"So I suppose," Andronicus pried gently, "you arranged to be erased from the registers with perhaps a hefty pay-off?"

"No, my uncle in the vigiles never listed me to begin with."

He whistled. "So you do have friends in all the right places!"

I asked Andronicus what the aedile did when he heard my name was missing. I should have guessed: he raised the level and sent for Cassius Scaurus. Although they worked in separate branches of law and order, Faustus would presume that as a magistrate he outranked a cohort commander. Scaurus wouldn't think so, but he would certainly not refuse the summons. Now I knew why that morning Morellus had told me I was in bother with his tribune.

One thing was certain. As soon as Scaurus returned to the station house after a stiff wigging from Manlius Faustus, he would have summoned his clerk. I had escaped for twelve years, but I was definitely on the damned list now.

"Actually," Andronicus assured me, "you emerged rather well from their discussion. Cassius Scaurus came to our headquarters, very nervous, expecting a stink. He wanted to make Faustus overlook their omission by providing as much detail as possible, so it would seem as if they did know all about you. After what he told my master, Faustus was well impressed."

"Educate me. What am I reckoned to have done?"

It was in the tribune's interest to paint me as virtuous, in order to explain why I had never been listed. Apparently I was a pleasant widow, determined and intelligent (and with the aforementioned excellent social connections), who had aided the vigiles with a tenaciously difficult medical fraud. The implication was that I had put myself in danger then, acting as a lure.

"In fact," I told Andronicus, "the one condition my parents laid on me when I started this work was that I must never, ever act as bait. It always goes wrong. Any woman who puts herself in jeopardy with a criminal is a fool."

"I am delighted you are so sensible, Albia."

"Of course I have done it. I just don't tell them in advance." That, needless to say, is the main reason this ridiculous ploy fails. Nobody knows where you are, so how can they provide backup, or come rushing to rescue you?

Andronicus leaned forwards across the table. He abandoned his food bowl. He was a fast eater, one who probably never consciously noticed the taste of his food; when he had had enough he stopped, not bothering to clean up the bowl. "Please be careful!" he pleaded, at his most earnest.

"I'm still here."

Just.

He had become too close to me; he cared too keenly about my welfare. I had no intention of scaring him by mentioning any narrow escapes I had had.

I made Andronicus tell me more of what had been said.

Cassius Scaurus had painted me to Faustus as an exotic specimen; he dwelt on the fact I had come to Rome from Britain, with all the usual nonsensical flourishes that holds. I groaned. "The remote and mysterious island, hidden in the mists, where red-haired, be-trousered inhabitants, every one wearing a huge gold torc, are permanently painted blue . . . Believe me, there is nothing romantic about mist if you live in it."

"Are they blue?"

"Of course not! Well, occasionally—but the great freckled lumps want to wear togas nowadays, and earn a fortune swindling all comers in some dodgy import–export business. If going to the baths means a life of ease and underfloor heating can be yours, the average go-getting British tribesman is up for it. Why live in a hut, when a subsidised forum has been provided at imperial expense? Why farm, when international trade is such a doddle? They rush from their fields, dying to sell Rutupiae oysters to Rome."

"While we eagerly buy them!" Andronicus grinned. Clearly he had heard that British delicacy outrivalled others.

"Allowing the Britons to drink themselves silly in Londinium bars."

"By the way—you, dear girl, may look like a neat little Roman matron who has a distaff in one hand and household accounts in the other, but you have a muddy provincial background and may be a druid."

My heart sank again. "I solve my cases by waving a mistletoe bough over the evidence? Ridiculous. I did let people spread that rumour years ago, though believe me I never started it. Actually, all druids are devious old men. Uncombed beards and mystic secrets. They never write anything down, because then people could check on what dirty cheats they are. Then it was explained to me by a sharp lawyer that in Rome dabbling in magic is a capital offence."

"Faustus was told that you do indeed know some sharp lawyers." Andronicus was watching me keenly, but there was enough fun in his gaze for me to enjoy it.

"More uncles. I consult them for free, every time we have a family party."

"So handy! . . . The well-known Camilli, I believe?" Oh joy! Cassius Scaurus really had gone into detail. "Up-and-coming barristers—and both of them are in the Senate. *That* news was disconcerting to a plebeian aedile, I can tell you, Albia. He thinks himself so lofty—then he found out you were way above his level socially."

"You really do not like Faustus!"

I asked him straight: what had the aedile done to him? Since we were exchanging personal information so openly today, Andronicus told me.

Manlius Faustus was plebeian nobility, the kind that had a long history of confrontation with the Senate because their wealth made them so powerful they refused to be told what to do by the traditional aristocracy. Princes in trade and commerce. As Rome became a great empire, they had seen and exploited the possibilities: Faustus' family commissioned, built and hired out warehouses. Through this, they had become extremely rich. Although they lived in modest style on the Aventine, it was thought they had chests of money, and they certainly owned a battalion of slaves, all high-priced ones, selected by the aedile's uncle because they were beautiful or talented. These were groomed and educated with the same attention to detail with which the Fausti looked after their warehouses. A clerical freedman with this background could consider himself a highly desirable commodity.

So, after being brought up and trained in the uncle's house, once he was granted his freedom from slavery (now he did finally acknowledge his status), Andronicus had expected to be promoted. He had wanted a position as Manlius Faustus' personal secretary. Faustus thought otherwise. He would not grant Andronicus that kind of access to his private papers. Andronicus felt the nephew should have fallen upon him gratefully as an assistant and confidant. Instead, Faustus not only refused, but arranged for him to work outside the house as an archivist at the Temple of Ceres.

"I can just about put up with that—but then this year the swine gets himself elected as aedile. Of course Uncle Tullius fixed that, with vigorous wheeling and dealing, in the usual way. So now, I'm stuck with his godforsaken nephew on a daily basis, yet without the job I wanted—which in a just world was mine for the asking."

"Poor you."

"Thank you. I am indeed unfairly wretched."

Junillus had despaired of us ordering anything else we might actually pay for. Since we continued to occupy his best table, he dumped a pair of free drinks in front of us. He glared. We ignored that.

"So," I said, as we raised our beakers together, "while Faustus and the miserable tribune were gossiping, what cunning fly-on-the-fresco position were you occupying?"

"They were sitting outside in the courtyard. I placed myself by an open door in a room across the colonnade. Cassius Scaurus has a booming voice; Faustus is softly spoken—"

"But tends only to listen?"

"I thought you had never met him?" Andronicus looked hurt that I had other sources of information.

"Someone just happened to describe him. Maybe I *should* meet him—since he is so interested in me."

"No. Don't have anything to do with him."

"Why not? What's dangerous about Faustus?"

"Listen to me. Just don't."

Andronicus was so insistent, I feigned agreement. Of course, he only spurred my curiosity.

To sidetrack him, I directed the talk back to my origins in Britain. I explained about being a miracle baby plucked from the ashes of ruined Londinium. As an archivist, Andronicus was fascinated. "So you do not have a birth certificate?"

"That's the least of my worries! Somewhere I may well have done. It was probably destroyed in the Rebellion—though if it survived, it would be useless because nobody knows it is mine."

"So you really are British?"

"Probably not. I could be anything. Most slaves know more about themselves than I do."

"That's hard. Is this something that an aedile could use against you, Albia?"

"No." I spoke dispassionately. "I have full Roman citizenship. I have a properly executed diploma granting me that. As a citizen, I was formally adopted. Your man cannot touch me—even should he want to. And why would he, Andronicus?"

"He can be vindictive if he's crossed."

"What have I ever done to offend him?"

"You are poking around."

"In what? If I have touched on something confidential, all Manlius Faustus has to do is explain. I am a reasonable woman—look, can't you see, this is why I feel maybe I should come and talk to him."

"He won't see you."

"This is the second time someone has said that so adamantly. Why? Does the pompous being believe he is too phenomenally busy or—" I was passionate now—"is he just terrified of women?"

Andronicus gave thought to this. Eventually he said, as if light had suddenly beamed in through a shutter, "I think you just nailed it, Albia!"

XIV

We sat on in the caupona.

Customers thinned out. Junillus mopped a cloth around, then sat by himself with some building plans. He was a bright boy. At various times my aunt had paid for him to have lessons, when she could root out an understanding teacher. He had studied geography and, I seemed to remember, mathematics. He particularly shone at geometry. Wrestling had preserved him from being bullied.

Recently his parents had downsized to a new home after his father retired from government service; Junillus had grabbed the floorplans to put a stop to the kind of ghastly remodelling Junia and Gaius had imposed on their previous apartment. Gaius Baebius was a man who could not tell which end of a nail should be banged in. Nevertheless, he was always attempting to create a sophisticated sun terrace. His projects usually came to a standstill when he fell off a ladder and hurt his back.

Andronicus and I talked, or sometimes did not talk. He seemed to have no need to return to the aediles' office that afternoon. I could tell he had a maverick attitude; he came and went as he chose. This might displease a pernickety master.

The weather was sunny, but not yet hot. April is one of the most pleasant months in many countries. I felt myself sliding into a dreamy state, not all of it caused by wine.

The rest of the day passed easily. After a time, Andronicus and I, and my cousin, were the only people there. My dear cousin saw no reason to disappear and leave us in private. Despite being adopted, he possessed all the most annoying traits that ran in our family. It was interesting that he had absorbed the others' bad points, whereas I remained so unquarrelsome and discreet.

When people started dropping in on their way from work, Junillus stood up and began making pork nuggets to grill on skewers.

I glanced at Andronicus. Meat dishes were banned in bars. His master, the aedile, would punish my aunt if this crime ever caught his eye. Andronicus grinned; he held no brief for Faustus in his official role. Junillus signalled forcefully that he would give us take-away nuggets gratis, if we would just stop hogging his best table. (There were only two tables in the tiny indoor space: the best and the one on the way to the latrine.) Most customers leant on the counter during daylight hours, but in the evening there was more demand for seating. Men who dropped in then were more likely to relax for longer; they liked to play dice and board games too. If they were sitting down with a table between them, there was a split second longer for intervention when they fell out over the game and tried to kill each other.

So, we accepted a long kebab skewer and, you guessed it, took the nuggets home to mine.

As we walked, the level of excitement between Andronicus and me rose significantly.

I looked in on Rodan in case there were messages. The useless bundle was not there.

Andronicus bounded ahead, going straight upstairs towards the office. Had he been slower, I was seriously intending to take him to my private apartment. By the time I caught up, my over-keen admirer had lost his chance. That did not mean he had lost altogether. He and I were extremely happy together by this stage. On one of the landings, Andronicus pulled me to him and we kissed. His kissing was light and fluttery, compared with how I really liked it, but naturally he was just making overtures for more serious work later . . .

Up in the office, I ignored the armed chair and we settled side by side on the couch. It seemed the natural place to be. When Andronicus relaxed, with one arm along the back of the furniture, it seemed natural, too, that in due course the arm should slide down around my shoulders. I pretended not to regard it as significant. He pretended not to know he was doing it.

Like anyone who has ever spent a long period as an unloved starveling, I ate my full share. I never waste food. Like any freedman from a privileged home, the archivist had been spoiled all his life. Whatever the miseries of slavery and of patronage after formal manumission, he had never had to earn his keep. Rome was full of people like him, who knew there would always be free food at home and who gave no thought to waste. He snatched at enough of the pork nuggets to keep him going, then concerned himself with other things.

This meant, first the sliding of the arm. Then, stroking the back of my neck. Then, engaging more closely. He had one hand moving up my left arm, with his fingers encroaching well under my tunic; he had one hand cupping my chin for a kiss. Although my real concentration was elsewhere, I was fumbling with fasteners, to assist him. He was preparing to fondle where I was desperate to be fondled . . .

I became reacquainted with that thrilling but slightly awkward moment when you adjust to a brand new lover. You are wondering what he will be like. Not quite in tune yet. Not absolutely certain that you have an understanding. Not wanting to admit your own desperate interest, in case you have misjudged his, and end up looking foolish . . .

Of course I knew. Andronicus was my kind of hero: attractive, amusing, nice-looking, around my own age, of low-class origins and hungry for self-improvement. He made me laugh; how badly I had been missing that. He seemed devoted. We discussed my work, we ate and enjoyed wine together, we were plainly soulmates. I had fallen for him just about as hard as it is possible to fall. The fact that all my family would cluck that I had not known him long enough, and would warn me to be careful, only made the situation swooningly attractive.

As we approached the final moment of full commitment, we were completely wrapped up in each other—yet not too much to be unaware of our surroundings. At exactly the same instant we both heard somebody coming. We pulled apart and tried to look nonchalant.

Normally I heard visitors. Shoes or boots are noticeable if you are an alert person, and after six flights, most people arrived breathless and stumbling noisily. Someone who had managed not to do that was now outside, at the top of the stairs. This person had approached so quietly it could only be on purpose. They had crept up on us and were right outside my door, shamelessly fiddling with the latch.

XV

Irecognised the man who broke in. I had despised him at our first encounter, the time he barged into me at the aediles' office; I took against him furiously now. It was the fellow called Tiberius, who was supposed to act as a runner for the magistrates.

He was stocky, the way my plebeian grandfather had been—not overweight, yet strong in the body, with sturdy legs. His shoulders could have broken down my door had he not successfully manoeuvred the latch instead. Today he was in a porridge-coloured tunic in some rough material that must be itchy; he kept scratching absentmindedly, though I saw no fleas hop off. A wide, crude belt held him in. The same cloak as last time was folded over one shoulder; this must be his informal indoors mode.

If the aedile's uncle chose his slaves for their beauty, he must have sent a short-sighted steward the day this man was first purchased, assuming he had once been bought in the slave market. The unshaven face gave him the classic look of any worker on the Roman streets. He could be a driver or a rent collector. More than a manual labourer, however: a man doing some job that called for competence, with considerable trust from whoever employed him. There was nothing timid in his manner.

"Cosy!" he commented sourly. He had sized up the situation between Andronicus and me, even though we were acting unflustered. It was the first time I had heard him speak. His accent was more refined than his appearance suggested. Like the archivist, he was presumably a freedman now. He would have been encouraged to develop a diction to suit their well-off home.

I glared. "Most people knock," I stated in a cold voice. "Most people think they should let a householder believe that the right to admit visitors lies in their own control."

Tiberius gave me a steady, half-amused stare. He had grey eyes. I always notice that. Mine are the same. His were a chillier colour; mine had been blue when I was younger.

The general crowd in Rome have brown eyes, though there are many of blue and grey. Nero had blue eyes. Grey is not significant. I was never going to fantasise that this fellow might be related to me. All the same, I do notice.

"You are Flavia Albia!" He did not wait for a snappy retort. It was just as well, because I was so surprised at the way he burst in that no ideas were flowing. Inevitably, I would find plenty of thoughts to sum him up later. The wit would not be complimentary.

He turned his attention to Andronicus. "You have been missed—at work and at home." Andronicus showed no reaction. Tiberius snapped back to me. "I need to speak with you—not now. It's too late and, frankly, it's inconvenient. I am putting you on notice. I shall call tomorrow morning. Be in—if you can manage that for once." I gathered he had tried to find me previously. Once more, he spoke to Andronicus. "I am going to the house for dinner. You can walk with me."

It was not exactly an order. Still, the way he spoke left little choice. As a "runner" he was no more than a messenger, even if the errands he was sent on meant his master trusted him. He was several years older, though hardly superior to an archivist, least of all one who had been assigned that role in a major temple. As his equal, therefore, I half expected Andronicus to argue. Instead, he shot me one of his rueful looks and swung to his feet, ready to leave with the other man.

I tried to understand. Andronicus might be reluctant to admit that there was something between him and me. I knew better than to question the dynamics of a strange household, but if he left meekly,

I was bound to start wondering if I had been wrong. If, after all, we were *not* soulmates.

They did leave together. I heard their feet clattering downstairs, this time even Tiberius making a noise as he went. As far as I could tell, they were not speaking.

I was furious, tantalised, passionately disappointed.

I did what women have to do: I tidied the office; took the Stargazer's titbit skewer downstairs to wash and return to the caupona tomorrow; retreated glumly to my apartment; went to bed alone.

That night I heard the terrible, near-human screams that I knew to be the foxes. It was unlikely anyone else noticed. Violence and fear were commonplace in the hours of darkness and few would want to investigate.

It reminded me that soon officials of the Temple of Ceres would be setting traps to catch the necessary animals for their horrible ritual. That plebeian aedile, Manlius Faustus, would be supervising the Games, so he must have an interest in the ritual with the torches. It made another reason for me to dislike him.

XVI

I woke feeling groggy. Though sluggish and bitter, I was determined to rebel against the abominable Tiberius. No stubbly factotum would command me to stay in for an appointment. Nor would I ever forgive his interruption of my tryst. It was clearly malicious; he broke us up last night deliberately.

I lay for a while in the arid mood of a physically frustrated woman. I looked around the apartment, remembering how my husband and I had made love here together with such energetic young joy.

I had brought no man here since I lost him. This had been our place. After eight years, it was unsentimentally *my* place, where I could do as I chose; even so, only a really good love affair would make me break the chaste regime I had imposed on these rooms after Lentullus died.

I was now ready to allow a new man in; I knew that.

It would have been, could have been Andronicus last night, even though my head said it was too soon in our relationship to open my home to him. I was half glad he had pre-empted me by rushing up to the office. On the other hand, if we had been secreted here in my apartment, Tiberius would never have found us . . . Although Andronicus was a vibrantly intelligent man, he had apparently not noticed there was no proper bed up in my office. He cannot ever have wondered where I usually slept. No informer would have missed that point.

There had been men before. I was no Vestal. Well, these days not even the Vestals were Virgins. If the rumours were true, all those hard-faced venerated women took lovers. As for me, I had on–off affairs, occasionally with people I liked a lot. None lasted. Being truthful, none so far had been connections I really wanted to last. I took one or two of the least dopey to family occasions, though that was never a success. Their deficiencies were soon exposed because Manlius Faustus was not the only person in Rome who used background checks; I had my personal scrutineer, whether I wanted it or not. Once our loving father scented any male interest in one of his daughters, he soon prepared an informer's dossier on her suspect friend. He had been doing this professionally for a lifetime, so he was brutally good at discovering faults.

That tended to kill the passion. Most lovers soon ran off, petrified. Sometimes the dossier contents made me keen to dump the lover anyway.

Hey ho.

To thwart the runner and the high-handed "appointment" he thought he had made with me, I scrambled out of bed early, gathered my things and went out to Prisca's bathhouse, ready to lounge there all morning. I could take a bite of breakfast from the pedlar who circulated with a snack tray. During official opening times he had palatable warm sausages; in the morning all he could produce were last night's offerings—but I think that on occasions a mature cold sausage, congealed in its fat, is an end in itself.

Prisca let me in and had her usual moan about me turning up before lunch. I told her anyone with a love life was likely to do that. You have to plan ahead. She offered to recommend a trepanist who drilled holes in skulls, a good one who mostly managed not to kill people, because if I was getting a love life I needed my brain seeing to.

I went through the cleansing rooms, taking my time. Serena happened to be there so I placed myself in her hands for a renovating massage. Some baths employ huge masseurs, mountains of flab who give powerful workouts. Serena was so slim and tiny it seemed impossible she could manipulate anybody, yet she would spring up onto the platform where she laid out her victims and kneel right on you with her whole weight, crunching tight muscles magnificently. I liked the fact she never wanted to talk. Who wants gossip while you are being forcefully tied in knots?

All I desired today was to flop while she did whatever was necessary, leaving me to dream of the archivist, with his bright eyes and appealing expression, and what I knew had been his plan last night, to have his wonderful way with me . . .

It was a short dream. While I was lying there naked on the slab, we heard a male voice angrily arguing with staff out in the anteroom. I was shocked. The aedile's runner had tracked me down and was even attempting to interview me *here*. I shot an appalled glance at Serena. She was an astute young woman and always conscious of clients' modesty. By the time the obnoxious Tiberius shouldered his way into the treatment room, Serena had dropped a towel across my midriff—though baths are notoriously mean, so it was a small towel.

My privates stayed private. All the rest was clean, oiled, toned, and on display. He had a good view. At least that unsettled him. Reddening up, he backed out, while rudely ordering me to get dressed and come to speak to him. Serena took him on without even consulting me, pushing him from the room ahead of her, with the flat of her hand against his chest. She called to me from the corridor that she would collect my things for me from the manger in the changing room.

"Let the repulsive bastard wait!" I snarled loudly.

I was up off the slab already. My tunic and sandals, as Serena well knew, were hanging from a wooden hook here in the massage room. I wriggled into the tunic, before dragging the treatment slab sideways, including the trestle it rested on. When it was close to the wall, I scrambled up on it, climbing towards a high, square unglazed window that lit the room. I could reach it, but the opening was very small. This needed planning.

I could go out the obvious way, squeezing through headfirst, but that was the fool's choice. The exterior wall of the building was smooth, with nothing I could grasp and I would have to drop down outside headfirst too, inevitably breaking both arms and cracking my head open when I landed. A man might try that way, stupidly hoping for the best, but I made myself struggle with the sensible method: stayed inside and pushed my feet out first, so I could then shimmy over the sill, clinging on to it while I twisted to face the wall and lowered myself as far as possible. Eventually I could land more safely.

I did this. I was proud of myself. The window was so small that the tunic I hoped would shield me runkled up as I squeezed out; the wooden frame then scraped my skin like a cheese-grater. As I descended, I was also treated to admiring whoops from the courtyard, where the two women who played at being gladiators had been knocking about. They had been alerted when I threw out my sandals. If they were lesbians, they were receiving a big treat as they watched me emerge, bared from the armpits down and backside first. I slithered out, pulling my tunic after me as best I could. They had the kindness to catch me; I dropped to ground level, without too much indecent groping.

I thanked them for their assistance. They were leering unashamedly. As I shook down my garment, I reckoned they deserved that thrill.

Zoe and Chloe introduced themselves. They already knew who I was.

They rushed me to a back exit that we all knew. They forced the locked gate by leaning on it (they were hefty girls and unafraid of strain), while I hopped about strapping my sandals on.

I thanked them again. I shot off down the alley. They cheered and I heard the gate close after they went inside again.

That was good. It meant they did not see the disappointing end to my madcap escape: I ran straight into Morellus, from the Fourth Cohort. The podgy swine was leaning on a corner, chewing his thumb, waiting for me to scamper away from Prisca's and into his arms so he could escort me for the promised interview with his tribune.

"Flavia Albia! What's your hurry?"

"Oh spit, Morellus! How did you trace me?"

"Rodan mentioned where you might be." I don't know why I bothered asking. "That charmless turd from the aediles' office was ahead of me, but I reckoned you were capable of giving him the slip. So here I am. The twerp is still waiting for you pointlessly out front but, sweetie, you are all mine for the foreseeable."

"Soldier, I admire your reasoning." I was cursing it.

Morellus asked if I would come quietly, or should he fasten a collar and chain on my pretty neck? I assured him that was unnecessary, so he could forget any erotic thrill. Bondage was out; the only formality needed was to drop in at the home of a mature female relative who could come and be my chaperone. He said there was no time for that. Surprise! At least it saved two women having to endure abuse in the interview. I would not want an auntie to see this.

On principle I asked, would he send for my father then, since he was my male head of household, who ought to speak for me legally? Morellus said request noted, but no he would not, and did I think he was stupid? Surprise again.

So far, this was banter, almost routine. But I assumed what happened next with the tribune would be very different.

XVII

The Fourth Cohort's main barracks was conveniently positioned right at the end of the Marcian Aqueduct, from which they could draw water. One corner of the building abutted onto the Street of the Public Fishponds (an amenity which no longer existed), with the station house entrance on the road that came up the Aventine through the Ardeatine Gate, at that point called the Clivus Triarius. The barracks was the usual forbidding edifice, with two-storey interior courtyards where the men on call hung about "preparing equipment"; they took an unnatural interest in an unchaperoned woman. I had expected that. Morellus fielded most of the suggestive remarks. I played deaf.

The vigiles were unarmed in the conventional sense. However, since they were hefty ex-slaves, kitted out with axes, grapplers, ropes and other heavy implements, they were never to be trifled with. Morellus gave me theoretical protection, but I kept my eyes downcast. I think of myself as spirited, but I never enjoy situations like that. Once we came in through the mighty gates there was nowhere to run. I won't say nobody would hear you scream, but screaming was so normal here, nobody would investigate.

Down at the fancy end of the three massive courtyards was a shrine, and to one side of it a hidey-hole in which the cohort tribune ensconced himself when he wasn't out to lunch. Morellus had appointed himself my guardian in this masculine environment. He asked squeamishly if I wanted him to come in with me.

"No, thanks. Don't interfere with your darling tribune's technique, Morellus. So much easier for him to frighten me silly if I am trapped alone among strange men!"

Morellus, who had always been a baby about torture, looked relieved to miss the pain and terror, though he claimed he would wait outside only because the tribune had a rather small office. He promised to walk me home afterwards, and I replied cruelly, he was assuming I could still walk. He winced. I took a deep breath. He knocked. I marched in.

Inside the sparsely furnished office in fact there was sufficient space for four other men as well as Scaurus. I managed not to let the number of interrogators worry me. As soon as I stepped into the room, I felt disconcerted. I was staring at a low serving table they had probably borrowed from a tavern, upon which were placed several small bowls overflowing with olives and fancy pastries.

I managed not to show a smile. Once I grasped what these were for, I saw that Cassius Scaurus and his brutes were about to be thoroughly underhand. Their intimidation tactics took the form of fingersnacks.

They placed me on a folding stool, the ceremonial X-shaped kind used by important officials, with a cushion (it was rather lumpy but I was astonished to get it), then asked solicitously if I was comfortable there. The tribune must have given me his own stool. What an honour. I wondered if I could manage to wee on it with terror.

Before beginning, we had a short, awkward chat about the weather that day. So far, the attempt to intimidate me worked, because I hate that kind of small-talk.

The five men assembled in a circle, with Scaurus directly opposite me, so he could lead the soft bargaining. They were all standing up. I did not find that menacing, because there were simply no other seats in the office and, anyway, they all looked sheepish.

Cassius Scaurus had a big nose, straggles of grey hair and the self-satisfaction of a man who is playing out his time at public expense in a dead-end job. He had beaten the system. He must have been a centurion in the legions, but that didn't mean he was sharp, merely sly at manoeuvring. Thrown out by the army proper on "age" grounds, he had wangled himself to Rome, but the man would never make it past the vigiles into the more coveted Urban Cohorts or Praetorians. That was regrettable, because in the vigiles he could probably do more damage to the general public.

"So, you are Flavia Albia, Falco's daughter. I have heard a lot about you." I decided not to show any encouragement. Obviously he was wondering if he dared ask, "Any chance you'll get your titties out?" They are all the same, right down to the ghastly vocabulary. He only stopped himself because all the rest would have wanted a grope too. He was too mean to let his men have a go. "So you work in the community, as an informer? That's an unusual occupation for a woman. What are your interesting investigations at the moment, Flavia?"

No one I like ever calls me Flavia. I let him do it, without comment. He thought he was being intimate, not seeing how my hackles rose.

"Oh you know, sir . . ." I would never tell him what cases I really had. "One can always get by. Approach any bathhouse and offer to catch the peeper who keeps squinting through a hole he's made into the women's changing room. There is bound to be one. I help out."

"Fascinating!" His vigiles ought to apprehend the peepers, and he knew it. As an excuse why they didn't, he would claim shortage of manpower, but the real problem was total lack of interest in stopping the problem. Half his men would themselves squint through the hole at the women undressing, given the chance. I bet he would too. "Can we get you anything, Flavia? Something to drink, perhaps?"

"No, thanks. You don't want to waste time sending out a boy for peppermint teas all round—it's such a hassle working out how many with honey, how many without. And there's always one awkward customer who wants borage instead . . ."

Determined to be a gracious host, Scaurus gestured eagerly to the almond cakes. I made no move. My taste is savoury. Scaurus, who must have the usual male sweet tooth, was desperately trying not to slaver.

He could no longer resist the bounty spread so close, and awkwardly pulled a comport nearer. He snatched his hand back like a boy who heard his mother coming. He resisted some more, but then reached again and began munching. The other men watched longingly while their superior tucked in. I gave them a pitying smile as I wondered which had been sent out with coins from the kitty to buy the goodies. Somebody had passed off some extremely stale-looking custards on the errand boy. You know how after three days on the platter, they shrivel and the skin goes leathery.

"Very unusual—" Scaurus was gobbling too fast. He nearly choked on his cake and had to pause to sort himself out. He had crumbs all round his mouth. The others looked anxious. They were trained to revive people from smoke inhalation but, unless they were fathers of small children, might have little expertise in choking. When the tribune stopped coughing, he carried on wheezily, "—having someone like you come in to visit us."

"I imagine so," I answered gravely. "Successful and admired in the community. A nicely brought up equestrian's daughter and senators' niece." I would never normally have used such pressure, but felt inspired by my conversation with Andronicus about how my family's status had impressed the aedile. I gazed at Scaurus mildly: "Instead of the usual back-of-the-arena whores, poor girls, all ready to open their hairy legs so your troops will let them leave with only a black eye and a big fine."

All five men looked embarrassed. I heard one or two intakes of breath. It was nerves, rather than regret.

I gave Cassius Scaurus a longer, even more direct stare. "This is fun, but shall we be straight? I know why you have brought me in. A decision has been taken, involving people who consider themselves important, that you—unfortunate man—should be given the task of deterring me from something I was doing. First, you are supposed to deny that anything odd is going on in Rome. Then you will plead with me, will I please stop taking an interest in this hypothetical crime that nobody will admit is happening?"

The tribune had stopped eating. "Flavia, you are a very astute woman!"

He had changed his tone, not much, just slightly. I did feel a shiver slide down my spine inside my tunic. Scaurus knew how to seed a compliment with just enough threat. We both knew he had reached his rank through the normal application of bribery mixed with brutality. Vigiles officers were often poor quality, but he was by no means the lowest grade; he packed enough power to frighten me.

"I was very well taught," I said simply.

That was enough reminder of where my expertise came from. But I stood no real chance of blackmailing this man with my family connections. Under Domitian, both Father and my uncles were keeping their heads down. My parents regularly spent long periods out of Rome. Scaurus probably knew all that.

We reached the crux of the interview. Scaurus writhed, as he attempted to put into words some delicate concept. "Suppose," he began carefully after a while. "Just suppose there had been one or two similar episodes."

"'Episodes.'" I savoured the word, as if impressed by his subtle vocabulary. "You mean, the strange rash of dead people?"

"I do not want to say that, Flavia."

"I know you don't, Cassius, my friend. That is why I am helpfully saying the words for you. I can spell out the unmentionable because I am not bound by your official code of confidentiality—though don't panic; I am always discreet."

The tribune looked as relieved as he was also torn. "I'll be perfectly honest with you, Flavia—" I doubted that! "There may have been one or two odd events that are causing concern. My men are on it, working all hours. We expect to contain the situation very soon. Until that happens, there will be no public announcement. That is absolutely normal procedure," he insisted.

"Absolutely," I concurred.

It made him anxious that I seemed to be compliant. I could see he felt he could not trust a young woman who sweetly agreed with him. He may have had deceitful girlfriends who robbed him blind, though I did not suppose there had ever been many. "The people at a high level who understand how to manage these things have said we must do nothing at this stage that could inflame the situation."

"Until you know what you are dealing with," I spelled out, as if we were cronies. He liked me knowing this standard jargon. "My family has always worked closely with the government. Cassius Scaurus, why don't you let me help you, by way of my enquiries?"

"Now then! You are not to be involved in this, Flavia!" The tribune panicked. My disingenuous offer scared him. He had been told to get rid of me, but here I was, smiling and moving in closer. "We have got to keep it professional. The powers above do not want any wild rumours that could shake public confidence."

"I would never encourage rumours."

"Oh *we* know that!" exclaimed Scaurus. All the rest moved about and shook their heads, keen to demonstrate to me that I was famous for being diplomatic and public-spirited.

I sighed. "You have been very frank, Tribune, whilst also being absolutely as discreet as your superiors could require. I appreciate all this."

"We can rely on you?"

"Of course you can." I even relented and took one of the neglected olives daintily between two fingers, shaking off the brine before eating it so none would drip onto the far-from-clean serving table. One of the braver men grabbed a cake while I was doing it. The rest were keyed up, ready to fall on the sweetmeats as soon as they could.

"Any time," swore Scaurus earnestly. "Any time the vigiles can help you with your work, Flavia Albia, you only have to come and ask. Titus Morellus—you know Morellus, don't you—"

"I do, I do. Wonderful fellow. Good family man, hugely experienced officer."

"Morellus has instructions to help you all you want."

"That is so good to know, Scaurus." If he wanted to believe he was winning me over, I could let him have his delusions. "But not on this?" I gurgled playfully, as if we were all pals now, sharing a joke.

"But not on this!" pleaded the tribune, his eyes dark with distress in case he had failed to coerce me as he had been ordered.

"Rely on me." I could be kind. I could tell lies too.

Rising to my feet, I shook hands very formally with each of them, then I made my escape. Behind me I heard the gasps of men who had been placed in an unfamiliar position that had made them very nervous, finally relieving their tension by snatching the almond cakes.

XVIII

When I emerged into the courtyard with its untidy piles of smoky rope mats, Morellus was talking and laughing with some of the vigiles. Flitting from pillar to pillar, I managed to tiptoe down a colonnade without him or any other men noticing, and started back to the other side of the Aventine by myself. He caught me up, unfortunately.

"Holy hermaphrodites, Morellus! That man you work for is dog-shit. Still, I am glad to report he told me I should liaise with you. We are to share information—and to start off nicely, you are going to tell me everything I need to hear about these unexplained kill-ings."

"Did Scaurus say that?" asked the enquirer warily.

"Of course. You don't think I would work a flanker on you—especially over something this important? Just when Scaurus has impressed on me the need to do things right?"

"I suppose so . . . not that I have been told much."

I took pity and seeded him with starter-facts: "Let's begin with, there seems to be an outbreak of strange, unexplained deaths. People arrive home from some perfectly ordinary local expedition, but they feel odd, have a lie down, then shortly afterwards are found dead. No explanation, and no marks on them."

Morellus nodded. We walked on.

"Are all the victims women, Morellus, and all middle-aged or elderly?"

"I don't know. That would be peculiar. Normally, the trend is for us to be chasing killers of young girls. The perps do it for . . ." Morellus paused awkwardly.

"Sexual excitement." I was brisk with him. The man was a vigiles investigator. He must know what serial killers did. "Sad bastards spewing their seed on corpses, who can't answer them back. Or, if these perverts can actually manage to operate their pricks, actual sex."

"Rape," he agreed, boot-faced. "Whether before or after death."

"Nobody raped Salvidia or Celendina. As far as we know, there was no attempt to so much as get their attention. No robbery occurred. No assault at all, in fact . . . And if nobody realises there has been a murder, there can't be any excitement for the killer in waiting for the news to get out. No, Morellus, it won't do."

"It's a real puzzle, Albia."

"Is he merely thrilled by the fact he gets away with it?"

"He could be the type who enjoys thinking he is *so* clever, he completely fools the authorities."

"No anonymous notes thrown through the gates saying, *I've done it again, you idiots!*"

"Oh plenty of those!" Morellus grinned. "All from Nonnius, about him stealing little girls' loincloths off washing lines."

"Are these deaths just happening here?" I asked, staying serious. "In our district? Or on a wider scale?"

"All across Rome," Morellus admitted. "If it's real."

"So what is being done to find out?"

"Hard to say. Where can we start? It seems to be completely random. Not just an invisible killer, but invisible deaths too. How are we to keep decent records, if nobody notices trouble and makes a complaint?"

"No, that is very inconsiderate of the public! *Is* anybody keeping records? What are the figures?"

"I've just been told to start." He sounded troubled by the instruction, and I didn't blame him. It would be tedious, probably pointless work.

"How will you go about it?"

"Check with funeral directors." He indicated a tablet stuck in his belt. "Scaurus presented me with a dirty great list."

"Oh," I said. I wish I was ashamed of my tactics when I went on innocently: "That must be the list Cassius Scaurus mentioned when he was burbling about cooperation—hand it here for a moment, and then I'll know which ones you are meant to be covering."

He handed it over. The man was so malleable. His wife must be having the time of her life. I bet she owned more snake rings and triple pearl earrings than any other woman on the Aventine, and when she wanted him to drive her bad-tempered mother to the country for a holiday, he just did it.

There were too many names and addresses to memorise, so I told Morellus the easiest procedure would be if I took the tablet home with me, made a fair copy then sent back his original. You guessed. The dumbo fell for it.

I did not bother writing out the tablet, but used it neat. I spent the rest of that day going round the funeral directors, to get at them ahead of the vigiles.

By dinnertime, my clothes reeked of myrrh and funeral cake but otherwise I had little to show. I talked to them all, pretending I had been hired to assist because the vigiles were overworked and also needed to disguise these enquiries by using a civilian. Calling my-self an undercover consultant, I quoted Cassius Scaurus on the need to maintain public confidence. "He means, prevent panic and riots."

Everyone wants to avoid that. Funeral directors hate behaviour that interferes with their processions through the streets. The only ri-ots they like are glorious ones that end with the Urban Cohorts rush-ing in to calm things down by beating people up, and doing it so hard they produce massed corpses. Even in Domitian's Rome such riots were rare.

The undertakers all swore it was impossible to identify for certain any victims of the random killer. However, all agreed there were increasing rumours. Those in the trade generally believed that people were dying of some undetectable malady, most times without even suspecting that something odd had happened to them. Some did wonder if foul play might be involved.

Undetectable maladies meant magic or poison in Rome. Both, possibly. I refused to believe in magic, but I might be dealing with people who did. I knew that according to vigiles lore, poison invariably meant any killer must be a woman, though I did not suggest that to anyone I spoke to. Male enquiry agents would seize on the idea, but I was cautious. There was no evidence. I prefer to make deductions based on material fact, not bend the facts to fit some pre-formed forensic theory. Especially when rather conservative paramilitary men had first devised the theory.

I ended up with just two likely-sounding cases. One was a lad, the other some rich woman's maid. Both died in March. I obtained addresses. It was really too late to turn up and ask questions, but I tried the mansion anyway.

A door porter who thought his job called for awkwardness refused me admittance. I accepted it quietly, knowing the best tactic was to turn up here again in daylight, when the staff would have changed. If I insisted now on making a fuss, this intransigent swine would mention my visit to his relief when they swapped places; if I held back, I stood more chance of charming my way past the relief slave tomorrow.

I took back the tablet to Morellus, who had gone off duty anyway. I respect "liaison." Considerately, I drew stars beside the undertakers who had been helpful.

I went home, hoping perhaps the archivist would visit again. Rodan said he had not seen him. I decided Andronicus was being heavily supervised by Faustus, the spoilsport magistrate.

I had picked up bread as I came home. I ate a simple supper, with the cheese Metellus Nepos gave me. I liked it. There were two kinds, both piquant and sustaining.

As my exhaustion faded, I began mulling. Sitting quietly at home, I reviewed what I knew and whether it was worth continuing. I was now sure a random street killer was on the loose, possibly with accomplices who ranged over a wide area. News was being censored from the sensational parts of the *Daily Gazette*. The aedile and the tribune had put their heads together and decided to keep me out of this. Scaurus had been deputed to warn me off, with orders to keep it civil: no open threats or violence. Hence he ridiculously tried olives and cake. Could I owe that courtesy to the aedile? It failed to make me like him.

Did these men really imagine a millefeuille and a fingerbowl of mint tea would buy my obedience? They were ridiculous. All they had done was to tell me that there really was something wrong. That instantly made me determined to plunge right in there, exploring.

Since my love life, though still promising, had lurched to a halt, I wrapped myself in a dark stole and took out food to leave for the fox I called Robigo. I did not see him or any of the others when I visited the Armilustrium. But later that night when the city grew quiet, I noticed an animal calling. The cry came from somewhere over towards the river. This time it was not screaming, but a single bark, repeated several times. Most people would have taken it for a domestic dog, but I could tell it was hoarser. I knew it was one of the foxes.

XIX

Next day I pursued the other possible case.

Lupus had been a fishmonger's boy working at a busy stall at the Trigeminal Porticus, down where you could hear the boats and smell the Tiber. He was fifteen, very fit, a little cheeky, the middle one of five brothers; his job was shucking oysters. According to his father, he was loveable and popular; everyone had liked him. That might be true. On the basis that no one was angrily pointing the finger of blame at anybody else, it seemed reasonable to believe the boy had had no enemies.

The father also reckoned Lupus had had no girlfriends. Since I noticed how the father's eyes followed, each time a woman passed the stall on her way to a nearby fountain, I did wonder if the allegedly pure Lupus had inherited any lustful tendencies, but I was prepared to accept that his life held no amours that might have caused a slighted girl to have it in for him.

The father seemed a shifty type; he and his clothes stank irretrievably of fish. Lupus himself may possibly have looked like a gilded demigod when viewed from the end of an alley by a girl who was optimistic, but I guessed that the dead boy had had a hard time attracting anyone to squeeze in close. He had probably died a virgin; the father was the kind who would regret that on his son's behalf.

People do surprise you though. The father had somehow persuaded some woman to bear him at least five children. The surviving four brothers, who all worked at the stall, looked alike, as if they shared one mother. I decided that poor soul must be a slave, who was not allowed to say no.

I knew it was the father who had raised with the undertaker the strange way Lupus died. I asked what had brought him to question his son's death.

Until that point the father alone had dealt with my enquiries, but now the four boys all left what they were doing and gathered round as well. I guessed this had been the subject of many family conversations. Their mood now was quiet; none of them clamoured stridently for justice, as some bereaved relatives would do. I quickly gained the impression they had never expected anyone to take the issue seriously. They had discussed their suspicions with the undertaker, but had not reported a crime to the vigiles. That was worrying. It could mean there were other cases which despondent families who distrusted the authorities were keeping to themselves.

I surveyed all members of the family while we were talking, in case one behaved differently from the rest, indicating he had harboured a reason to attack his brother. I saw no such behaviour.

The day Lupus died had seemed like any other day. He had been squatting on his low wooden stool, head bent over a bucket, shucking. He let out a yell and said something had nicked him. His brothers told me he was right because, being a close-knit, affectionate family, they all converged to take a look; they had seen a big bright bead of blood welling up on the back of his neck. He had been wearing a tunic with a wide, loose opening. I was shown this very garment. His younger brother Titus was now wearing it. There was even a rusty mark on the facing that they all said was a bloodstain. There seemed more blood than would normally happen after, say, an insect bite.

My young sisters would not take over a tunic worn by somebody who died, let alone wear it unwashed for the next three weeks, but when your skin, hair, sandals and every other thing about you stinks of your trade, I dare say you are not fastidious. I myself would now be carrying the odour of fishscales on my shoes for days, just from crossing the street to get here.

"So what happened next?"

Lupus carried on with his work for a short time. He complained of feeling dizzy. He was told to rest in the shade. When they closed up the stall that evening and called him, his family found him dead.

That was the whole story, really. They all always ate the same meals together, and no one else had been affected by illness. They assured me that if Lupus had swallowed a bad oyster, distinct symptoms would have followed, symptoms he had definitely not shown. There were no links any of them knew of to either Salvidia or Celendina. On the day, people had been passing who would have been close enough to touch Lupus, as he squatted on his stool by the stall, right on the street. No one had appeared to stop or speak to him, however; the father had been serving one customer, but a good six feet away. There had been no reason for the others to notice or remember any particular passers-by.

Reliving events, the father and sons all became upset. This was the first time they let themselves see the full implications of their previous vague unease about what happened: the first time someone directly put into words the possibility that Lupus had been murdered— and murdered right there in front of them. Anything I asked, they answered. They were open, all concerned to have justice for Lupus. I let them see me gravely writing notes, hoping to reassure them that now someone *was* taking their boy's death seriously and that, if possible, whoever killed him would eventually be found and apprehended.

After I took my leave, I glanced back. Titus, the brother in the inherited tunic, had turned away and was obviously weeping at the back of the stall; one of the others was comforting him. The father was simply standing still, lost, helpless in his misery. Another brother occupied himself kicking pebbles into the gutter angrily.

They had said little to me of their grief, yet their private poses and gestures told me everything. It was three weeks since their loss. They were still swamped by unhappiness. Whoever killed their lad had broken all their hearts. Lupus the oyster-shucker would not easily be forgotten; I thought never.

The fish stall was down on the Embankment, close to the salt warehouses, en route to the Trigeminal Gate. When I left, it would have been an easy stroll along on the flat to my family home, but I was too depressed to socialise. I had just witnessed another good family overwhelmed by sorrow. It seemed wrong to enjoy myself with mine.

I climbed the Hill, slowly flogging up the steep Stairs of Cassius, my usual route home. I returned to the apartment, felt restless, wandered out again. I knew where I was going. I called out to Rodan, but don't know if he heard. My steps took me to the Stargazer. It was mid-morning so there were no customers, and would be none for at least another hour when the lunch crowd began trickling in. "Crowd" was over-gilding the anticipated scenario. They had about four daytime regulars, of whom two were occasional and one could only come if his son was not using the false leg that day. Assume I'm joking, if that comforts you.

I told Junillus to take a breather. I would sit there and look after the place. They had an old waiter called Apollonius who would turn up eventually but in the meantime I knew how things were run. I needed a quiet place to think.

My cousin gave me a small tot of wine in a big beaker and a large jug of water. He indicated that if I was hungry I could help myself to food. I gestured back that I chose not to live dangerously. I kissed his cheek and let him go off for a stroll.

Before I sat down I sloshed copious amounts of water into my wine cup, then fetched the herb pot to add some flavouring. At the Stargazer, any flavour was better than the wine itself. Perching at a table, I took one sip, then sat with my head in my hands, studying my notes. Whatever clue I was searching for failed to leap out.

What did happen, infuriated me. Someone came in and sat down opposite me. It was the aedile's runner, Tiberius.

He was sturdy, a man of unobtrusive movements, subtly confident. I had recognised his shape and approach from the corner of my eye. I did not bother to look up. "We are closed."

"I am not here for refreshments. I've come to see you." He pulled his bench closer in to the table.

I raised my head and scowled at him. Every aspect of this meeting annoyed me. He had broken into my quiet time. He was hounding me on a daily basis; he had disturbed my tryst with Andronicus; his master had had me taken in by the vigiles and pathetic attempts made to bamboozle me. "I don't want to see you, Tiberius—is that your name?"

"Shut up and listen."

"Get lost."

The man had seen my note tablet. Without warning he reached across and took it. I was enraged, though I made no move to retrieve it, confident that what I had written would make no sense to him. I always used shorthand. On a sensitive case, I would write up the notes in a cypher.

For a man of the streets, he looked oddly studious while he read. "Impressive!" I reckon he meant to be patronising. The fact that he could read what I had written—and indeed had read it, taking his time and not skipping—increased my irritation. "Were you not told to abandon all this?"

I snatched back the tablet. "Listen!" I was seriously angry. "Don't tell me there is no silent killer. Don't tell me nobody has died in peculiar circumstances. There is, they have, and I will carry on looking into this until I prove what has been going on. I have just interviewed members of a stricken family in need of assistance—assistance the authorities, including your filthy master the aedile, have refused to give to victims because they are too busy fabricating a farcical cover-up using stale pastries."

There was a change in his face which in a better man would have been amusement about the vigiles' hospitality. But he made no comment.

"Stuff you," I said. "I will not talk to you. Get out of this caupona while you still have legs to walk on."

Tiberius leaned back, hands linked behind his head, observing me.

He said, in a measured tone that did not impress me, "Let us agree there appears to be a silent killer. More perhaps. If so, you, Flavia Albia, had a connection with at least two of the victims. I am considering the possibility that you are one of the perpetrators."

I don't know what came over me. When the moron said that, I jumped up. I think I intended to storm out of the eating-place. He stood up too. His move was quiet, but deliberate. He clearly intended to block me, even if it meant physical intervention. He was solid. I was slight. If we grappled it would be an unequal contest.

"I am not listening to this!"

"You will do what I tell you."

When I came here this morning I had brought back the metal skewer from my aborted supper with Andronicus. I snatched it. After Tiberius swung himself upright, for a moment he was leaning with one hand on the table while he moved the bench to climb out. I was very, very angry. I lifted the skewer and stabbed it down hard. I speared his hand, right through the palm, pinning him to the wooden table.

XX

As soon as the runner tried to move, pain kicked in and blood welled out. At that point he yelled. I thought I had probably missed damaging tendons, by sheer luck, but the situation was now tricky. He was still stuck to the table, for one thing. If I left him, my aunt would have something to say about that.

I switched moods. "Stand still," I ordered, adopting a sympathetic tone. "Don't worry. I got you into this, I'll get you out of it."

Tiberius had had time to react; he became incandescent. "Don't come any closer. Flavia Albia, go for a doctor, go fast, bring the nearest you can find. Otherwise, if you come within range, I will bite through your spinal column so you drop and die in this hole with me."

That was lively. I paused as if to admire his bravado, then exclaimed, "No doctor worth trusting will come to the Stargazer. And I'm certainly not carrying you to a surgery, stapled to the table . . . Oh no! Look!" As I pointed to a spot on the wall behind him, instinct betrayed him and he turned his head. I dragged out the skewer. He yowked with pain again. I grabbed a sponge Junillus used to mop up spills and pressed it hard on one side of his wound.

While Tiberius jerked away from me and jammed the sponge against the upper side of his hand, I found what looked like a clean drying-cloth to staunch the blood from his palm. I seized his wrist. He protested again, but I pressed against both the skewer's exit holes, with his hand caught between the pair of mine. It was not like the touch of lovers, believe me.

He had gone very white. With one elbow, I pushed him back onto the bench. He was pressing the wounds for himself now. "Sit down. Don't faint on me. Don't tell me you can't stand the sight of blood."

"There was no need to be vicious. I had to ask the question."

"Then you took your chance of a bad reaction."

"I am getting the feeling you dislike me, Albia."

I ignored that. "You need to get this cleaned."

"What has been on the skewer?"

"Pork nuggets. Lovely honey glaze with rosemary. Don't worry; I washed up. Anyway, they were thoroughly cooked; this caupona specialises in charring . . ."

The runner shoved himself back to his feet. He tossed away the sponge and cloth; he would regret that, as blood continued flowing. He was leaving. I let him go.

I sat down on my own bench, feeling squeamish myself, frankly. It was years since I had inflicted that kind of damage on anyone. Years since I had had to. Suddenly I was back in that dark period, a waif on the streets, fighting for her life. At the time, it was just the way I lived. In retrospect, I went weak with the misery of it.

I wanted to be respectable. I wanted to come from a nice Roman family, and lead a decent life.

I was still reminiscing bleakly, when the runner lurched back. Leaning on one of the counters, he stared down at me with an odd look as if he saw I had dark thoughts. If he knew, he made no attempt to discover them. "So answer the damned question, Albia. I don't want to be skewered a second time. Are you, or are you not one of the killers?"

"Logic, man! Why would I admit it, if I was?" Facing him down, I growled, "I am not."

"Keep saying that," he replied coldly. "Believe me, you want me to think you are innocent." He turned and disappeared again. I did walk out to the street in case there was a blood trail I could follow to check he was all right, but he must have stopped dripping.

I thought, I can't wait to tell Andronicus about this! Then something changed my eagerness so I knew I would not mention it. Too much of my past would have to be explained. Andronicus was not ready to hear what kind of woman I could be. I was not ready to tell him. Maybe I never would be. I was too used to concealing my old background.

I was shaken by what I did to Tiberius. I had not been filled with that much aggression since the old days, not since I came here to Rome to be civilised. Such violence belonged in the history that I wanted to forget. I hated this man for making me go back there.

XXI

I was too disturbed to work any more that day. I took my notes home, went up to the office, tossed aside the tablet and lay on the visitors' couch with a rug on my legs. The grazes I acquired when climbing out of the window at Prisca's had now become raw weals; I had soothed them somewhat with an olive oil balm that had a lot of use in my life, but I was still stiff and sore. I rested, feeling sorry for myself. I almost drifted off to sleep.

The runner came after me again.

I had hoped to hear Andronicus mounting the six flights, but I was not surprised it was only Tiberius. I had the door partly open, with the balcony leaf ajar too, so a breeze wafted through the room. It was a mild day and this was my effort at spring-cleaning.

Tiberius now sported a huge, padded white bandage on his left hand and wrist for which some medico must have charged the earth; he had even been given a sling. Even though he had open access, this time he did knock first, tapping the doorpost sombrely. From my couch I just looked at him.

I watched him walk across to look out at the balcony; I was willing him to step outside and make the whole thing crash off the building, taking him with it, but sadly he could see it was dangerous. My father and Uncle Lucius had fixed up ropes to stop anyone opening the door fully, and I had been instructed never to go out there again.

Tiberius surveyed the safety measures, tugging a rope in a desultory way to test its hold, then turned back into the office. He strode across to look in the second room. He was one of those men who never asked permission, just nosed where he wanted as if he had every right.

When he pulled open the curtain, the sight beyond startled him. What had once been a bedroom was now unfurnished, its battered floorboards graced only by an artistic installation of bowls and buckets. These caught any rain that dripped through missing roof tiles, which were numerous. The walls, being dry except in cataclysmic downpours, had been equipped for me some years ago with big wooden pigeonholes. Nets slung across the ceiling kept out real pigeons. The shelves housed my extensive library—my reference books and old case notes. One benefit of writing up investigations on waxed tablets was that they were cheaper than papyrus and much more durable. Damp did not affect them.

Tiberius blinked. He put the curtain back where it had been, twitching it quite tidily into place again.

I stayed put. He therefore took my usual throne. He pulled out the cushion from the small of his back and held it on his lap instead, resting his wounded arm on it.

"Flavia Albia, you are not a nice young lady!"

Tiberius wagged one finger slowly, a finger sticking out of his bandages. He was older than me, though not enough to behave so paternally. Ticking me off was not my father's style, in any case. He never wasted energy. He would call me an idiot then leave me to reform myself, assuming we both felt reform was called for.

"Thanks for the 'young.' I'm twenty-nine next week. It's just a puncture, stop whining. Take my advice—peel off the fancy wraps and let the wounds breathe in the air every day. The wadding looks good, but if you don't do that, you will fester underneath."

The hole I had made might be small, but the way he was nursing his arm suggested his hand was burning. He kept up the pompous rebuke: "Maybe you should remember, Flavia Albia, that Manlius Faustus could have your aunt's bar closed down."

"Oh—on what grounds?"

"Unruly behaviour. Attacking an aedile's servant—"

I scoffed quietly. "Magnificent! I'll have my day in court on that. Your aedile has had me harassed by paramilitaries, and you, his nasty servant, have been following me about. Imagine how a good defence lawyer would work that up—*'Members of the jury, this poor woman, a respectable widow of fragile build and honest background, still grieving for her husband, has been subjected to appalling indecencies'*—" I folded my hands, gazed down at my lap, and played the part of a demure matron, silent in a court of law while clever men talked about her. "—*'The man Tiberius, a rough creature of the streets, even burst in on her when she was undressed in the private massage room of an all-female bathhouse! How would you react if this was your noble niece or daughter?'*—Oh just take me to the judge, Tiberius!"

He went red when I referred to him seeing me nude. I was pleased to make him uncomfortable, but dropped the reference, since I felt a little awkward at the memory myself. After a moment, he demanded unexpectedly, "*Are* you still grieving your husband? I thought he died some time ago."

I was startled. "Eight years. Nine, I suppose. Yes, I miss him. We had a good marriage."

"That's rare." The runner seemed intrigued, though he spoke ruefully.

"Cassius Scaurus must have been ridiculously detailed when he reported on me to your master. Do I assume you were present when Faustus grilled him?"

He looked shifty. "I was there, yes."

"Have you any idea how unpleasant it is for a woman to have men clustered together, picking through her life?"

"Yes, I see that," Tiberius agreed briefly.

"I have a right to dignity."

"You keep your dignity very well, in the circumstances." I was startled. It didn't even sound as if he was scoffing. "I apologise." I wondered if that was on his own behalf, or included the aediles, the tribune, Morellus and all the other members of the vigiles who had tried to unnerve me. The runner had become subdued. "Shall we have a truce?"

"Suits me." I was not vindictive. "Anyway, I want to know why you keep chasing after me."

We had a short pause for readjustment. I bestirred myself to serve refreshments. Basics. Just two sturdy beakers, my green Syrian glass ones, and a water jug. Tiberius weighed his glass in his unhurt right hand, still looking around at the room and its trappings, as if my set-up appeared unusual. He noticed the shelf of sculptures. I saw his eyebrows rise. Maybe he had heard that informers inhabit sordid surroundings, full of empty wine amphorae, cockroaches and the smell of old sandals.

Eventually he settled back, signalling time for conversation.

I made it clear that if anyone was going to give, it must be him. He opened up; I was surprised how much. He knew how to lay out facts logically too. I wouldn't call him surly, just plain-speaking. It should be mentioned that I was never alarmed in his presence and, given the job he did, I thought the man honest.

According to him, he had been working as the aedile's eyes and ears on the streets ever since Faustus entered office. I knew that Faustus would have been elected last July, starting the job officially four months ago in January. There were four aediles, two of them plebeian, who divided up the city among themselves and cared for a quarter each. So Faustus must have charge of more than just the Aventine peaks. His various tasks covered the repair of temples; sewers and aqueducts; street cleansing and paving; traffic regulation; dangerous animals; dilapidated buildings; fire precautions in all kinds of property; superintending baths and taverns (hence his genuine ability to blight the life of my Aunt Junia, who owned the Stargazer); anti-gambling and usury laws; plus, if this list was not enough excuse for interfering in people's daily lives, the care of public morals, including prevention of foreign superstitions. Aediles' market duties involved overseeing the storage of commodities; they were trading standards officers; they checked weights and measures. On top of all that, they were responsible for aspects of the public games, not least the Games of Ceres with its ritual of the foxes.

"Having an undercover spy on the job must boost the fines Faustus levies," I said, "handily fuelling his personal ambition."

"He is not unduly ambitious," Tiberius disagreed.

"So how do you see him?"

"A decent man, trying to do his public duty."

I whooped with derision, freely letting rip.

"You are wrong," argued his runner, in a patient tone. "It's true he grew up a rich boy who never had to do anything. He lost both parents, one after another, when he was sixteen. He came to live with Tullius, his mother's brother, and although there has always been a pretence of teaching him the business, in reality, Tullius rules. Standing for aedile was the uncle's idea, of course, with the aim of increasing their joint prestige—but that doesn't prevent Faustus seeing it as his opportunity to achieve something useful at last."

"Well, Tiberius, you are a good advocate. But he sounds a typical politician, with an added snort of piety."

Tiberius shrugged.

We moved on to discuss the peculiar deaths. Tiberius wanted me to know that Faustus had always been taking these seriously. He, Tiberius, had been redeployed from his previous forays investigating dishonest street traders. Now he was out full-time, trying to spot the killer. He even claimed that was what he had been doing when he came across the accident, when little Lucius Bassus was killed by the runaway cart.

"Of course if the perpetrator concentrated on one area, it would be easy to flood the street with manpower. But he moves about— assuming it's just one person. These attacks seem to have a random nature. It makes our task impossible."

"Some incidents happened up here on the tops, but the oyster-shucker was down on the Embankment . . ." I smiled slightly. "I assume you know about the oyster boy? You have conspired with Morellus today?"

Tiberius shared my grin. "He told me you filched his list, Albia."

"Borrowed."

"Whatever you call it. Morellus is now scrambling around after you, doing follow-up interviews to those you were not supposed to do yesterday." Cocking his head on one side, the runner then asked in a changed voice, "Have you looked into the murdered maid?"

"Not yet. Don't try to stop me!"

"Calm down. Not the intention. Manlius Faustus has had a change of heart about you."

"Oh really?" I sneered. "Highly unlikely, so soon after he tried to get rid of me!"

"Yes really, girl." He leaned forward a little. "Look, do try to give him credit. He is a good man." He made no attempt to say why Faustus changed his mind. Still, magistrates are above explaining themselves. This would not be the first time one of them was confused and contradictory.

"That's not the impression I gain from my friend Andronicus." Now our relationship was in the open. Why not? Andronicus and I were free people.

Tiberius looked troubled. He seemed to be trying to decide how much to say. "Be very careful, Albia."

"What does that mean?"

"It means I realise there is no point trying to influence you, regarding him. You won't listen to me. But please, do not trust everything Andronicus may say."

"You don't like him."

"It's mutual," stated Tiberius, even more curt than usual.

"Do you want to explain?"

"No."

To avoid meeting my gaze, the runner poured himself more water, managing the jug and beaker carefully, one-handed. Conversation had jerked to a halt. I reversed, going back and asking him about this so-called change of heart he credited to Faustus.

It had to do with the other suspicious death I had heard about when questioning funeral directors, that of a wealthy woman's maid. Tiberius knew something about it already. Mistress and maid had been out walking. They were jostled in the street. The maid was struck so hard she nearly fell over; shortly after returning home, she died.

Morellus had been given orders not to involve himself in this, because of the mistress' standing. Manlius Faustus had decided that sending a woman to take a formal statement would be both more discreet and reassuring. I would have that privilege. I would be armed with a letter of introduction and was even offered a fee.

This was some change of heart. After instructing his runner to find me and block me from investigating Salvidia or Celendina, then ordering the vigiles to menace me too, the aedile had had a complete turnaround. No longer was I to be harassed. Now he wanted to commission me.

XXII

I saw no reason to hide my ridicule: "So let's be clear, Tiberius: one moment your aedile is determined to sour my relationships with clients and prevent me working, yet suddenly he wants to hire me himself?"

"Not 'hire.' It implies too much permanence." Tiberius flashed teeth irritatingly. "One interview. It is in your interests to help."

"Yet more threats! Why doesn't he question this woman himself? He is her rank. He could have her husband, who is no doubt a crony of his, duly sitting in—"

"He believes a woman's approach could be beneficial; now that he is satisfied you are professional—" He could see I was raging at that. Tiberius held up his unbandaged hand in an almost, though not quite, pacifying gesture. "Don't dig your heels in." I remained hostile. "It is marginally tricky, Albia."

"Oh? What's his game?"

"The issue is not about Faustus—"

"Why not? The man is trying to choreograph this investigation in a very odd way. Justify his motives."

"We already discussed what Faustus is attempting in his role as a magistrate. Just conduct the interview, Albia, and see what you think. Then, if necessary, I will explain the rest."

Since I had wanted to do the interview anyway, I caved in. May as well be paid for it. I could have asked for a higher fee than normal, but I kept my integrity.

Marcia Balbilla was another member of wealthy plebeian society. She and her husband lived in a big two-storey mansion on the Street of the Plane Trees. She enjoyed river views and the nearby amenity of the old grove of planes. Yesterday evening I had been turned away. Though it was now late afternoon, I thought it was worth trying again for an interview today.

The introductory letter worked, so this time I was admitted. Once in, they kept me waiting. I expected that.

The matron who had lost her maid was in her early thirties, beautifully dressed and bejewelled. Under this flash, she was ordinary. Possibly she knew it. Two surviving maids, undoubtedly part of a much larger complement, accompanied her when she saw me. They were dressed much more plainly and wore no decorations. There was no indication that Balbilla beat them, but they were too subdued for me to tell if they had any character. I was interested in them, because the dead young woman must have been a colleague.

I assumed she had been young, though in fact the two others were no longer girls. As slaves, they were probably starting to hope for their release at thirty.

Marcia Balbilla thought she was conducting the interview, but I had more practice so I managed to steer it my way. While we conversed, she lay gracefully on a couch laden with cushions, while I was stuck on a backless divan. Still, I have no problems with posture and note-taking is easier when you perch on a hard seat.

Marcia had been out with a friend, not previously mentioned in the story as I knew it. Each woman had a maid as chaperone, though they had not taken bodyguards. The party was marching along the Vicus Altus, with the maids behind, where they would not overhear what their mistresses said. All four were well shrouded in stoles to be respectable, which I came to believe was significant.

Ino had let out a scream. Marcia Balbilla and her friend spun around, probably intending to chastise her, only to see the girl floundering. She would have tumbled to the ground had not the other maid grabbed hold of her and kept her upright. Both girls thought someone had banged into Ino from behind, hard, and they were sure it was deliberate. Although there were other people in the street, it was not particularly crowded. All the women decided it must have been a malicious lower-class person's prank.

Feeling vulnerable, they hurried home. Ino was crying and upset, but there was no reason to expect that she would then be found dead in her cubicle.

Marcia Balbilla had had a stone plaque made as a sweet memento of Ino. She insisted someone fetch it down from the wall (it was quite small) so she could show it to me. I commented on how beautiful the maid had been. Apparently not so beautiful, nor so young, as the portrait on the plaque, but Marcia Balbilla had thought it would be more pleasant to remember her looking soulful and artistic.

"Tell me, did Ino have a male follower you are aware of?"

"Certainly not! I never allow anything like that!"

I did persuade the mistress to let me have a few quick words with the other maids, who admitted without much pressure that Ino did have a boyfriend. He was a slave in the same household, the husband's wardrobe keeper, but he had a clear alibi; everyone was able to say he was at home when the street incident happened, and he had done nothing but sob since Ino died.

There had been much mention of Marcia Balbilla's friend. Both women were senior members of the cult at the Temple of Ceres, Marcia told me; a much older woman was chief priestess though I could tell these two had their eyes on the position. The friend was a wonderful woman. The friend came from an important family of plebeian nobility, very wealthy; a leading figure in the ladies' cult, she was religiously devoted, and a model of self-sacrificing service to the community. The friend was called Laia Gratiana. I had already met her, the first time I went to the Temple of Ceres. I had thought her a right menace.

I would have to visit the woman, nonetheless. Marcia Balbilla told me her dear cultured religious friend had thought at the time that she glimpsed the person who had bumped into Ino.

"Did you report this to the vigiles?"

"Oh no. People like us never have contact with them. Laia Gratiana said she would pass a note to the aediles' office."

Great.

So Manlius Faustus had already known everything about this.

I met up with Tiberius at a prearranged rendezvous next day. I had promised to report back at the Stargazer. When I arrived, the runner was ordering a drink from Junillus. I prepared to interpret, but he seemed to be managing. I was not ready to approve of him just because he could communicate calmly with my deaf cousin.

Junillus must have seen that I was frazzled, because he gave me a hug and then brought me a bowl of pistachios. I kept them on my side of the table, so Tiberius could not reach them.

"I'm bloody annoyed with you, Tiberius. Would it have hurt you to mention that there was a second high-and-mighty mistress and a second downtrodden maid, and that I would end up having to endure a second interview—with Laia Gratiana?"

He looked surprised. "You know her?"

"We met. I am not going to enjoy this."

"Why?"

Although I was gobbling nuts furiously, I screwed up my mouth as if they tasted of aloes. But until I learned the situation here, I held back on too many insults. "Not my type."

I spotted that the runner's surprise changed to a faint gleam of humour. However, he said nothing.

"Explain!" I commanded. As his expression became positively

whimsical, I kept nagging: "This is ridiculous. Laia Gratiana has enough connections with the aediles to notify them directly of her experience. So why not? What held her back and why doesn't Faustus simply trot along in person to ask questions? Why involve me?"

"It is nothing untoward."

"So?"

"He prefers not to interview Laia Gratiana himself." Tiberius then owned up, watching my reaction: "They have not spoken for years. Laia Gratiana is his ex-wife."

I admit I laughed.

XXIII

After a pause, Tiberius asked nervously, "So are you going to see her?"

"I would not miss this for the world!" I would never have asked intimate questions of the aedile himself, but staff can be useful. Many a confidence shared by a slave or freedman has opened up a case, so I pressed Tiberius: "Brief me."

He raised one eyebrow.

"I need to know what I am walking into, Tiberius. Exactly why won't Faustus take this statement himself?" The runner still looked blank. "Something odd must have happened. People get divorced all the time, but without being estranged for years. Plebeian plutocrats are a small circle. Every time someone throws a poetry recital, keeping Faustus and Gratiana apart must be an inconvenience to the hostess. Tell me about the marriage and divorce."

He was scowling so much, I thought he would clam up. "This is confidential, Albia."

"Do you want me to ask madame herself? What was it—did she sleep with charioteers? Or was it actors and their understudies?"

"Don't say that to her!" He seemed horrified.

"She's too prudish to have it suggested?"

"She is a respectable woman."

"Oh I see! So it was him at fault?" Tiberius remained silent. "Something happened. Even my friend Andronicus, who likes to know everything, seems not to know the story. But I can tell he senses that there *was* a story. He wonders, so I wonder too . . . Do *you* know?" Tiberius nodded slightly. I settled back. I wondered why he came to be favoured with the privileged information. "How is that? What's your own background, Tiberius? Did you grow up in the uncle's household?"

"No."

I took a guess. "You arrived there along with Faustus? From his parents' home after they died?" That was a difference between Tiberius and Andronicus, who seemed to have been a slave belonging to Tullius. "When Faustus married, did you move out with him then too?"

"Where he goes, I go." Tiberius suddenly took a breath as if cutting me off from that line of enquiry, then launched into the briefing I had requested. "Faustus was married when he was twenty-five, the age for a man to take his place in society. His uncle arranged it, for business and social reasons—"

I chortled. "I know how that works: *Young man, it's time you spawned an heir. Couple up with this woman you have never met, but we owe her father money; she's a nice sheltered virgin, only twelve years old—*' Wonderful beings, the important classes!"

"Laia Gratiana was at least eighteen."

"Then I take back that detail. But the rest holds good!" Tiberius did not deny it. "So Faustus and the imperious Laia were heaved into a union by the puppeteer uncle. What next?"

"The marriage progressed for some years in a polite fashion."

"I note how you phrase that! Children?"

"No."

"Did they share a bedroom? Or have a room each, like the stately rich?"

"Separate," said Tiberius, giving me a look; I ignored the reprimand. "But everything that was supposed to happen happened."

"Not very spontaneously! When intercourse was wanted, one of them had to make an appointment. I bet I know which one expected to do it. Demanding his rights would be the man's prerogative . . .

So, which of them looked elsewhere for passion? Who broke the marriage?"

Having posed that critical question, I just sat and let Tiberius struggle with his conscience. He spoke, eventually, as if I had dragged it out of him using the vigiles' torturer. "What happened was entirely the fault of Manlius Faustus."

He was terse, yet he gave me all I needed. It was an unedifying story. Faustus not only had his uncle looking out for him, but in those days he had attracted the interest of a distinguished man, a decade and a half his senior, who had had a connection with Faustus' late father and who offered him friendship and patronage. As Tiberius told it, the older man was childless and influential, the younger attractive, talented, a social asset. It was the kind of situation where formal adoption might have been considered. There was even talk of sponsoring Faustus to enter the Senate.

The patron had a much younger, very beautiful wife.

"Voluptuous?"

"Free-spirited."

"That was what I meant—spilling over the front of provocative frocks."

"Not shy," conceded Tiberius, in his dour way.

Sometimes, when his patron was away on business, Faustus was entertained at their house by the beautiful wife alone. On the surface, his relationship in his patron's home was that of a favoured relative, a young cousin or nephew, say, who might come and go without question—though of course such freedom is dangerous. Although his own wife was always made welcome, she did not generally accompany him. Throughout their marriage, she spent much time with her own friends. Too much time, probably. "You can guess the rest," said Tiberius, his voice dry. "One evening when they were alone together, the atmosphere became intense. The beautiful young woman felt unsatisfied by her ageing husband. He loved and admired her—"

"But rarely made demands in bed?"

"Who knows? . . . A younger man had obvious attractions, and maybe the tempted couple even convinced themselves the older man had left them together on purpose."

"Who made the move, do you know?"

"She offered. Faustus took."

"So they enjoyed a wild conjunction, during which these two bored, spoiled people were thrilled by the risks involved . . . And what happened next?" I asked quietly.

"Naturally, the liaison was discovered—very soon; barely a week passed from first to last. A slave reported on Faustus to Laia Gratiana. She left him and went back to her father's house within an hour. Uncle Tullius had to rush in and salvage the situation, at some cost. This was when we had Vespasian as emperor, when affairs were regarded more indulgently than Domitian treats them now; if it happened now, the straying wife and her lover would be prosecuted, lose everything and be exiled. Even at that time, the situation was horrible. A wronged husband is compelled to divorce his wife, as you know."

"And once slaves start piping up about adultery, situations get ugly."

"As you say. Faustus had wasted his own potential, hurt people terribly, and destroyed two marriages. Worse, he had betrayed a most deserving man, who had given him great friendship."

"He did it for love?"

"No."

The runner was harsh. He swallowed water, looking as if he had bellyache.

"I bet she had done it before," I mused.

Tiberius seemed intrigued. "Possibly . . . She died. She died in childbirth."

"Was Faustus the father?"

"No. Absolutely not. He never saw her again. It happened a couple of years later."

"Some other robust lover! So, Tiberius, what then? Faustus returned to Uncle Tullius in disgrace, having to endure a barrage of blame, I'm sure—especially since the scandal had cost money. He kept his head down. Did what he was told. Knew that any promise or ambition he once possessed had been aborted by his own stupidity . . . If he's an aedile he has to be thirty-six now, according to the rules. Has he ever remarried?"

Tiberius shook his head. "The man lives with guilt."

I thought ten years of guilt was no use to anyone. I also realised that even if those events had hit the scandal column of the *Daily Gazette*, that most disreputable noticeboard in the Forum for the doings of celebrities, I would not have noticed at the time. But it sounded as if everything had been covered up successfully.

Tiberius and I had become downcast. All we had done was discuss this sordid little tale of a young man's idiocy, a decade ago, but the effect on us was gloomy enough to bring Junillus over, anxious that some worse tragedy had affected us. I reassured him, then got up to go and take Laia Gratiana's statement. I left Tiberius at the Stargazer; last I saw, Junillus had brought him the draughtboard.

He was not playing. I knew Junillus would have given him a game, or he could have played solitaire. Perhaps the draughtboard was his standard cover when he was on observation.

The runner had told me the address. Laia Gratiana had remarried after her furious split from Faustus, but her next husband died, then her father. She had since moved from what had no doubt been an enormous family home to a lesser, but still large, apartment owned by a brother. It too was on the Street of the Plane Trees, where her friend Marcia lived. Yet more splendid views. Yet more heavy marble tables with gilded capricorn legs. The statuettes were better than at Marcia Balbilla's house, the frescos not so good. The same fashionable designer had sold both women their wobbly bronze hanging lamps. So that was two homes where oil got spilled on the mosaic below every time the slaves tried filling the reservoirs.

The fact that you know something about someone's history that could make you feel sorry for them does not inevitably alter your attitude: I still thought Laia Gratiana was a snobbish bitch. For her part, she was interested enough in who I was, and why I was working for the aediles, to remember she had encountered me before. She did not say so; I just saw it in her eyes. I wondered if she knew how rude she had been to me the first time.

I did not ask her anything about her marriage or her ex-husband. I am not stupid.

All the same, this time I took a harder look at her. She appeared to be around my age (though her manner added years); she was my height (less toned); a blonde (natural); with brown eyes (painted, but very subtly). I regret to say, she was decent looking. Knowing that her ex-husband had been lured astray by a brooch-buster (my husband's term for big-bosomed), was it significant that Laia Gratiana was very flat-chested? Also key was that Tiberius had told me the woman with whom Faustus had his affair was "a free spirit." That usually means vivacious, witty, and more likely to hang admiringly on a man's every word than to slap him down. Gratiana was a slapper-down. She could no more curb this habit than avoid believing herself special because of her role in the cult of Ceres.

When I was taken in to see her, an old female slave quietly left the room. Laia Gratiana did not reckon she needed a chaperone or support. She was a powerful character. Everyone around her knew it.

Was she like that when she was first married at eighteen? Or did the shock of her husband's betrayal toughen her up?

I took out my note tablet and explained my task. "My first question is this: Marcia Balbilla said the incident with her maid, Ino, happened in the Vicus Altus. That is some way from here; can you explain why you were there, please?"

With a trace of impatience, Gratiana said, "It is on the way back from the Temple of Ceres. Marcia and I regularly walk home if the weather is fine, after we have been attending to cult business. Normally we walk down the Street of the Armilustrium, but that is tediously straight and long. That day, we chose to take a detour through the quieter back streets. So," she finished triumphantly, "if someone deliberately wanted to attack Ino, he would not have known we would change our usual route. He cannot have been lying in wait—he must have followed us."

She was sharp. And she did *so* enjoy pointing this out before I could say it myself.

I sat quiet, making a note of the detail. "Tell me about what happened."

"Marcia Balbilla must have described it to you." Gratiana was a little petulant, annoyed by being visited second.

I stayed calm. "She said you saw something."

"I *think* I did."

"Even if it happened quickly, any fleeting perception may be helpful."

"Well. The maid cried out. Dear Marcia and I at once turned back to see what the matter was and to assist." That was not the impression I had gained from dear Marcia; she implied the cult ladies had been annoyed at the girls' public squealing. "My own maid was just catching Ino as she staggered off balance. If somebody pushed her, it must have been extremely hard. Before I went to comfort them, I had the impression I glimpsed a man, with his face hidden as he was turning away from me. I had a momentary sense that he had been involved, that he had just made a movement aimed at Ino."

"What kind of movement?" I gestured with the flat of my hand as if pushing a door open.

"No." Next, I mimed a dagger thrust, fist raised and plunging downwards. "Not that either. More like this—" Laia Gratiana made a different move, underarm, at waist height: a quick jerk.

"Interesting. Do you think he had a weapon?"

"It is illegal to be armed!"

"That rule might not stop a killer," I said dryly.

"If he did, the weapon was extremely small." Laia Gratiana bunched her thumb and two fingers. "Like a musician's plectrum."

Were we looking for a crazed harpist?

"But when Ino passed away, no wounds were noticed on her, I believe."

"She had a bruised arm," Laia Gratiana corrected me. "Where somebody had shoved her. Hard enough on her arm to spin her right around. A vicious blow, in fact."

"She was turned around towards him? So did she say she recognised the assailant? Or might it have been somebody she knew, but would not want to admit to knowing, in case Marcia Balbilla was angry about that?"

"I see what you mean. No. Marcia Balbilla's staff are clean-living and respectable. Ino thought she had been awkwardly jostled, by someone who may not even have known they had knocked against her. We all thought it was an accident—until later, when she died so unexpectedly. Then some of us—" she meant herself, but was feigning modesty, "—put two and two together."

"And you yourself felt no recognition of the person you had glimpsed?"

"I would not know anybody one encounters in a street!"

"No, of course not." This woman was so pure, she would not even say hello to her own brother in a public place. That's assuming he had not spotted her first and fled to avoid talking to her. "So can you describe the man you saw?"

"Ordinary." No serial killer would like that! They tend to believe they are exceptional.

"Height? Build? Colouring?" She had no idea. It was a member of the public, one of the mob, anonymous.

"A slave?"

"No, not a slave."

"Long hair?"

"No, not like a boy. Older."

"Beard?"

"No. No, I don't think so."

"A workman? A soldier?"

"How would I know?"

"Someone in imperial livery?"

"No."

"Is there anything else you can tell me?"

"That is all I saw." I was putting away my note tablet when Gratiana suddenly added in a troubled voice, "She dropped her stole." I looked at her enquiringly. "Ino. I wonder if it had been tugged off her during the collision? While Marcia Balbilla and my maid were comforting the girl, I picked it up."

Although Laia Gratiana was clearly troubled by this detail, it hardly seemed significant. I was ready to leave. Now, she could no longer help herself. "So—do you work closely with the aedile Faustus?"

"We have never met." I gave her a bright smile. Bright enough to worry her, if she was jealous. "I take my instructions from his staff. I presume you must know him socially?"

"His uncle is on friendly terms with my brother," replied Gratiana dismissively. Women like that are practiced at denying unpleasant history. She had blotted out her failed marriage.

She knew I knew. She hated me for it. I am never unreasonable. I did not altogether blame her.

XXIV

I walked over and had a look at the Vicus Altus. Just a street. Nothing unusual or significant. I walked back.

When I finally returned to the Stargazer, Tiberius was still there, with the draughtboard unused in front of him. The counters were still in their leather bag, as if he had never taken them out. He looked as if he had been depressing himself, perhaps continuing to think about the aedile's failed marriage.

In the moment before he glanced up and spotted me, I had a chance to assess him. Some customers in bars are clearly vulnerable, especially if they are preoccupied; not him. I noticed, for instance, that Trinius the pickpocket made no attempt to sidle up, and I thought it unlikely any drunks would be troublesome.

In the few days I had known the runner, he can never have visited a barber; that unpleasant stubble of his had become full-face untended growth. Andronicus was bearded too—Hades, they must have more beards at their house than an academy of Greek philosophers. Andronicus' light gingery hair was carefully trimmed. From a short distance away, it was undetectable. In no way did it hide his features. The runner was darker. I could see nothing of Tiberius but those wary grey eyes.

"Sorry it took a while. I am surprised you are still here."

"I knew you would come."

I explained about going over to the other side of the hill to inspect the crime scene. "You know the Vicus Altus?" Tiberius bluffed, but I could see he was unable to place it. I enjoyed laying out my expertise: "It's a short, narrow street, above and parallel with the Embankment, back of the big Temple of Juno the Queen." Still no reaction. "It runs off the bend in Lesser Laurel Street." Tiberius sat up. "That's right," I told him quietly. "If we are looking for the same killer for the four odd deaths we have identified, this is his beat. Right by where Salvidia and Celendina lived. We don't know exactly where either of them was attacked, but the location is significant. They too may have been jostled by him in the Vicus Altus."

"But what about the oyster-shucker?"

"Still nearby. The stall is down on the flat, it's true—but it's in the Trigeminal Porticus—that's right below the Temple of Ceres. Every event we have identified happened in the Aventine's north-west area. It narrows the search."

While Tiberius was looking thoughtful, I told him I had warned Laia Gratiana that she and the other cult ladies should not walk about unless they had bodyguards present; she claimed they were using chairs or litters now. Inevitably, she said it as if I was exceeding my authority in giving her advice, especially as she had thought up the safety measure first.

The runner was drawn to murmur, "Sounds like her!" He made the comment to himself; there was no sharing with me.

I said what Laia Gratiana had told me about the incident with Ino. Tiberius let me talk in full, never interrupting. I finished. He remained silent.

"How did I do?" I queried, mildly satirical because I thought I had handled things excellently.

He sucked his teeth. "Did you question Laia Gratiana's own maid?"

Privately, I cursed. When I suggested this, Gratiana had snapped that it was unnecessary. "Oh, *you* would have insisted!" Tiberius nodded, so I felt unprofessional. He was right; we had so few witnesses that I should have interviewed the girl as well, whatever her mistress wanted, just in case she saw something additional.

Some informers would have dashed this aside, but I admitted immediately that I was at fault. I said I could go back and do it.

He seemed to lose interest. I could tell by the way he was holding his hand that the wound I gave him with the skewer was hurting. I told him he should go home and rest up.

He stood up. For a tough man, he was visibly demoralised this evening. "Yes, this is sore. Don't trouble to apologise, Albia."

"I am not sorry."

Tiberius overruled me with one of his knowing looks. "You are!" he said.

He abruptly left the caupona without a goodbye. I thanked the gods I was not obliged to have a lot to do with him.

XXV

In view of the scepticism the aedile's man showed, I was determined to prove myself. The following morning, I did return to Laia Gratiana's apartment and asked to see her maid, whose name I learned was Venusia. She was out with her mistress. The older slave, the one who had left the room when Gratiana saw me, came and talked. She seemed sensible. (This impression can be *so* deceptive!) She wanted to say that she had tackled Venusia about what happened, and the maid insisted she had not noticed any assailant.

"Is she a good girl?"

The elderly woman looked torn. Still, she was a good sixty herself and would probably distrust anybody under thirty. "She has always been very loyal to the mistress."

"Oh?"

"She speaks up, if she sees anything wrong . . ." It sounded as though this referred to some old incident or a trait that might be deplored perhaps, but if so, the woman was not telling. I could imagine a scenario where the older woman was tight-lipped and conservative, while the younger one babbled more thoughtlessly.

I mentioned how Marcia Balbilla's maid, Ino, had a follower.

"I'm not surprised—you know what young girls like Ino are like."

I said I did. I tried not to think about Andronicus while we were speaking.

"Fools for the men, so many of them!"

"Oh yes!" *Me too, me too . . .* "Tell me—is Venusia like that?"

"Not unless the silly thing has managed to keep her cupid well hidden."

Privately, I could see why Venusia would do that, and not just because she worked in an environment where the habits of slaves were minutely scrutinised by their elders, with stern rules prescribed by mean-minded owners. It's not only slaves who need to be discreet. Any woman who talks about her lover before she has known him for at least five years is asking to finish up by finding she's a fool.

I did pursue the issue of Venusia further, dutifully trotting over the Hill to the Temple of Ceres where the old woman said Gratiana had gone with the maid, but I just missed her there too. A certain class of witness can be guaranteed to be annoying. Rich blondes, for instance.

Time to write up my report.

For this, I did not return to Fountain Court as usual, but went to my parents' house and dictated it to Katutis, Father's highly trained Egyptian secretary. Often underused at home, he was thrilled. He penned it in ink on papyrus, to look good—perhaps the most expensive client report ever. Father saw the work in progress and almost laughed himself sick.

I climbed back up the Aventine, carrying the elaborate scroll, which Katutis had labelled on the outside *Highly Confidential*, tying it up with strings, to which he appended wax security seals. Luckily, I have a seal. It's an old coin set on a finger ring. It shows a British king, with horrible clumps of spiky hair, looking as if he can't wait for helpful Roman invaders to ship in some decent barbers.

By taking the Stairs of Cassius, I was able to walk down the Vicus Altus on my next errand: delivering the report. I was well swathed that day, since I had known I was visiting women who made much of being respectable. That morning I had even wondered whether to borrow the eldest daughter of the Mauretanians who lived on the first floor of the Eagle Building; I did pass off this silent ten-year-old as a chaperone occasionally. Today, I decided, as usual, that it was too much bother. Instead I had just lumbered myself with a huge stole, the kind that's as big and as warm to wear as a toga but shows oodles of respect when you visit smart women. Out on the streets I could snuggle in it unrecognisably—head covered, face and body attractions all neutralised, nothing but fingertips showing.

So, as I slipped up the Vicus discreetly, I was able to spot Tiberius, lurking. He had abandoned last night's noticeable white bandage and sling, and instead had his wounded hand in a grubby-looking, frayed piece of material, perhaps torn from a worn-out tunic. He was mooching, no doubt looking for our killer, just as I was. We had both made ourselves seem like slaves going about our business in the invisible way slaves do on Roman streets. Nobody else would have given either of us a second glance, though of course I saw him.

I could have handed my report to the runner, but I had better ideas. I wanted to go to the aedile's office in the hope of finding Andronicus.

Thrills! He was there.

We were both delighted at finally meeting up again. Andronicus amused me with choice words about Manlius Faustus, who had been keeping him on a short rein these past few days. I saw that my friend had the freedman's dilemma: on being manumitted from slavery, he could take himself off and be his own man, with whatever love life he chose, but then he would have to take big financial risks. Go into business with very little start-up capital. Face possible failure. If, instead, he wanted to remain in secure employment with people who knew him, he was stuck with the fact that his patrons, as they now were, expected to order him about. He had some rights to their protection, but in return his duty to them meant he must be obedient. I could see that Andronicus did not possess the necessary humble character to accept this. He found his position extremely frustrating.

I unwound my hot person from the confining folds of my stole. He greeted the process with the excitement of a child unwrapping a present. As soon as he saw the scroll, he seized it from me, chuckling over the confidentiality notice and the seals.

I explained: "Although your Faustus ordered the vigiles to deter me from my private assignments, the confused man has now hired me himself. That is my formal report for him."

"And you have given it," joked Andronicus, "to the one person who is capable of undoing the strings, reading the secrets, and replacing the seals undetectably!"

"Ah yes." I did have second thoughts, though briefly. But I trusted him. "I suppose counterfeiting legal seals is the first thing an archivist learns!"

"No, the first is how to hide your beaker of posca in a scroll-box quickly, if your master walks in."

Posca, which is little more than vinegar or wine spoiled by bad storage, is a slave's drink. I did not comment. I knew he would hate being reminded—and would hate me being too aware of his past.

Taking my right hand, he examined my seal ring. After comparing it to the marks in the wax, he kept hold of my hand. I like a masterful lover, but felt awkwardly conscious that we were in a public office. In Rome, only very low-grade people—or very drunk nobles—make love in public. For his part, Andronicus seemed to enjoy the danger of being discovered.

"Luckily," he said, gazing into my eyes from a rather close position, "I do know what is going on. People are being attacked in the street. There have been high-powered meetings involving all the aediles, occurring for some time now. Three out of four of them are hoping they can delay any action until their term of office ends, sticking the problem onto next year's stooges. Our Faustus has to be different. He has made this his personal mission. He wants to catch the Aventine killer, and if he fails, the idiot will be brokenhearted."

"Maybe he is right. Don't the public deserve protection?"

"Of course." Andronicus had his distracted look, almost as if he had been intending to give a different reply. I reckoned he had a low opinion of the public—for which I could not entirely blame him. The more of them I met, the more I despaired.

"Is Faustus here today?"

"No, thank Jupiter."

"Any of the other three?"

"Naturally not. You don't think these golden boys *work*, do you, Albia?" Andronicus pulled me close, beginning some gentle neck-nuzzling. He smelt of an attar that must be expensive; I was amused to find he liked such luxuries and had money to buy them. "So what have you discovered for the sad man?"

"Oh it's all there," I murmured back, still trying to keep one eye on the door in case someone came in. I do have standards. I have never liked smooching in public. I want to relax and give my all. I like comfort too. I was certainly willing to give my all to Andronicus, but not backed up against the money-chests in a magistrates' public office. Who wants a rusty old hasp in the ribs? "You will see, if you do break the seals . . . I was asked to interrogate Laia Gratiana."

"Over that incident where her friend's maid died?"

I was glad Andronicus had heard about it, without me needing to reveal a confidence. "Yes, I get all the wonderful jobs . . . I had to force myself to be polite."

"Poor you! She's a cow. I can't bear taking documents to the temple when she's swanning about in her Queen of Heaven mode."

"I managed."

Andronicus then mused, "Laia Gratiana, eh?—You know she and Faustus share a murky past?"

"Hence me being sent for her statement." Wonderful though it felt to be in his arms again, I had no intention of telling Andronicus that Laia Gratiana may have seen the killer. Nor would I pass on what Tiberius had confided in me regarding that ancient divorce.

"Yes, he will run vast circles to avoid any contact with the haughty Laia—and she won't ever approach him either. Something went on there, Albia. I would give a lot to know exactly what it was!"

To sidetrack my inquisitive friend (and to try to ignore where his hands were wandering), I mentioned my wise theory that if either of the maids had a secret liaison, she would have kept it to herself, given my view that any woman should avoid boasting about her lover. We fantasised comically: "You know—either he's on the verge of dumping her unexpectedly, to fulfil his real ambition of joining the legions or of going on a long sea voyage—"

"—Or else," Andronicus finished for me, "her confidante, who was previously her best friend, turns out to be a deceitful bitch, the very woman with whom sonny has been two-timing her . . ."

We laughed. It was wonderful to have someone to share such zany moments in the midst of serious work. Andronicus was the master of the art of light flirting, of easy friendship. He made me feel safe. I sank into this pleasant sensation, even though I knew that much trust could be dangerous.

"So . . ." he suggested. "I gather you won't be boasting about me?" He couldn't help it. He was a man; he needed to be the centre of everything. I just smiled wisely.

We returned to the topic of my investigations.

"Are you supposing a boyfriend made this attack on the maids, Albia?"

"There is no evidence of that."

Footsteps sounded outside in the colonnade. By the time the damned runner entered, Andronicus and I were innocently sitting apart on separate stools.

"You ditched the feeble disguise, I see," jeered Tiberius, nodding at my discarded stole. He had to let me know he really did see me earlier, in the Vicus Altus. I wondered if he then followed me here deliberately, to interrupt any fun with Andronicus. "When you two have stopped giving each other the glad eye . . . I presume that is your report? Shall I take it?" He glared pointedly at Andronicus, who had to part with my scroll.

"I pretty well covered everything," I intervened, trying to distract them from their mutual hostility. "I have still not spoken directly to the second maid, but a source told me she claims she saw nothing. Of course I want to check that. I will keep trying for a proper follow-up."

"Keep me informed."

I did not reprise my opinion about women and their lovers. Tiberius was not a man to joke.

Tiberius left us, clutching my scroll, and took himself off somewhere else in the building.

I mentioned to Andronicus how I had seen the runner patrolling the street where incidents had happened. "He seems obsessed."

"Of course, there could be another explanation," said Andronicus sombrely.

"What?"

"Does it never strike you that Tiberius is an odd character himself? A loner. A prowler. A cold, friendless, arrogant, unsocial person who cannot make anybody like him, even if he tries to—most times he does not bother to try. A man who has been given the task of moving among the public, exercising his judgement about their characters and their behaviour . . . So, might he have decided to impose a personal punishment on those he regards as being at fault?"

"Go on." I felt unhappy with where this was leading, but I let him add his finale.

"What a coincidence, Flavia Albia, if *he* turned out to be involved in what you are investigating! Suppose Tiberius is your villain."

XXVI

Romans were marinaded in suspicion these days. Our paranoid emperor had made us all too ready to distrust people. I said that I would think carefully about Andronicus' suggestion. I meant it. Normally I like to exercise my own judgement. But this idea about the runner had struck me too.

Tiberius had certainly known of Salvidia, because it was he who chalked up the advertisement for witnesses after her driver's accident. I knew of no connection between him and the old woman, Celendina, nor was I aware that he had ever met the oyster boy, though it was by no means impossible. He certainly knew a lot about Laia Gratiana. Given the official links between the aediles' office and the Temple of Ceres, which must include the cult, he probably knew her friend Marcia too. A trusted runner was not too disreputable to engage with such women, nor too lofty to have spoken to their maids.

Roaming the streets on the excuse of looking for public misdemeanours, Tiberius was perfectly placed to make attacks on pedestrians. He looked shifty. I had always felt something about him was wrong.

I began to discuss this with Andronicus, who was eager to share his own thoughts on the subject. We had to stop when Tiberius reappeared.

"A good report," he commented. Although I had had the scroll addressed to the aedile personally, the uppity swine had taken it upon himself to open and read it. Then, to my surprise, he added, "I am meeting up with Morellus tonight to review a plan of action. You could join us."

I said I would. Immediately I noticed Andronicus signalling that I ought not to. Tiberius naturally noticed too; he waited, sneering, for me to do what the archivist said. If they thought I was likely to be influenced, they were both wrong. I asked what time to arrive at the station house and since the appointment coincided with the normal hour for dinner, I advised Tiberius to bring his own food. "The vigiles have a terrible habit of sending out to Xero's for hot pies."

"Aren't they famous?"

"Legendary. Everyone goes to Xero's, has done for years. If your master ever wants to set up a public health investigation of pie shops, he could prevent a lot of food poisoning."

Andronicus looked as if he wished I had not given Tiberius the warning.

I saw no future in hanging around while the two of them locked horns. The runner had spoiled the moment for me and my friend. Giving Andronicus a polite goodbye kiss on the cheek, I managed to squeeze in close enough to whisper to him that the best way to monitor Tiberius was to watch what he was up to. Then I went home.

That evening, after the baths, I walked to the vigiles' local barracks. The last watch party was going out on patrol, so the building was silent and empty yet to me felt much safer than when the troops were there. I found Morellus in his interrogation room. This was the luxury suite at the station house—a grubby nook with a table that bore suspicious burn marks, a couple of three-legged stools that had had their fourth legs pulled off for hitting suspects, and an old cloak on a peg. The table was for Morellus to put his boots up on while he cleaned his nails with a knife he had once taken off a prisoner.

Morellus seemed puzzled to see me, so as I fitted back a leg on one of the stools to make it usable, I explained I had an invitation.

"Really? Has Tiberius taken a fancy to you, or something?"

"No, he thinks I'm a useless amateur. I've no idea why I was favoured tonight—unless he knew I would come with a packet of garlic squids." I placed it on the table. Morellus immediately swung more upright so he could have a look. The vigiles respond to very simple stimuli.

"I didn't know it was a bring-an-amphora party." He need not have worried because in fact nobody did bring one.

Since the runner had yet to arrive, I asked how well they knew each other. According to Morellus, he and Tiberius regularly shared information, and had done since Manlius Faustus took up his post in January.

"I'm finding this runner a baleful presence," I commented.

Morellus gave me a sharp look. "Oh, Tiberius is all right!" Normally I found the enquiry officer quite astute, so this surprised me.

We heard steps approaching across the yard outside and Tiberius turned up. "Quiet tonight!"

"I've got them all out looking. Even the ones who are off-shift."

"On a bonus?"

"No, I just promised *not* to punch their heads in." Morellus lowered his voice. "Funds are tight."

"I might be able to help?" offered the runner, as he went through the routine of temporary repairs to a stool. Presumably he could ask to break into the aediles' fines box for some petty cash.

Morellus waved this away. "No, no. The devious Scaurus is putting together a budget. Maybe for once our tribune will make himself useful."

At that time of night in April, the room was already dark; Morellus lit pottery oil lamps, most with pornographic scenes, of course. We gathered round the table. We munched as we worked.

Tiberius had brought a fancy little picnic basket containing bread rolls, enough for all of us, and cheese, which he said Metellus Nepos had supplied. I presumed this was a gift to the aedile but Tiberius had snaffled it.

I grinned. "I suppose if you live in a large household, especially if it's a bachelor den, there must be competition to snaffle titbits from the kitchen staff . . ."

"I find appearing in person with a starved look generally works," Tiberius conceded.

As I had feared, Morellus had equipped himself with a big rabbit pie, from Xero's. With an obvious wrench, he offered it round. Tiberius took a sliver politely. I was tempted, but held back.

Ignoring the danger of dripping gravy from the pie still in his hand, Morellus stretched out a crackly map skin of streets in our area. It looked decades old; I pointed out where parts were out of date.

"Oh it gets us from Alpha to Omega," Morellus mumbled.

"Well, maybe from Alpha to Phi . . ." suggested Tiberius, almost letting himself smile.

I have to say that the next hour of three-way collaboration was an unusual session. It went better than I expected. The two men accepted me; I could work with them. Nevertheless, they seemed a slightly mismatched couple and it was unheard of for such men to consult with a woman. But we all approached the problem with the same level of seriousness.

First we had a round-up of known facts. Morellus contributed surprisingly useful background: "I have found out this is happening in other districts of Rome, and the word is, in other parts of the Empire. That might mean a global conspiracy, if you like such theories. Myself, I don't reckon to that. More likely, some pervert commits a rash of random street attacks in one place, then however much those at the top think they are in control, word gets out because the public are not fools."

"And a rumour gives some other madman the same idea?" I put in.

"Copycats?" Apart from this question, Tiberius was letting Morellus lead, or at least he was so far. Somehow I failed to see Tiberius as a hang-back subordinate.

"It's a known phenomenon. Well, if we can catch ours, that will still leave the others, but to be frank, I just want to clean up my own patch. I really do think," Morellus said defensively, though at his most convincing in fact, "if we concentrate on our particular perp, if we apply sound procedure directly to him and do manage to cop him, it will be more useful than haring about pointlessly, trying to tackle a whole city-wide scare and, let's face it, getting nowhere."

Tiberius nodded. As I watched him, I thought what an irony it would be if Andronicus was right and he was the killer. Andronicus had been lively and convincing about this, yet now it seemed a crazy idea. Tiberius looked up, perhaps saw I was considering him with a dark interest, and bit into a bread roll with his most unpleasant expression. This man could win the grimacing competition at the Olympic Games.

We debated my theory that the Aventine killer was a local. I showed Morellus on his map the Y-shaped junction of the Vicus Altus and Vicus Loreti Minoris. The map skin was probably a valuable antique, but the vigiles investigator pulled out an inkpot and marked it up with incident spots. Morellus spent half his working life chasing after stolen property; it had left him with no respect for treasures.

The other half of his time was given to victims of violence. I was unsure whether he had lost his respect for human life too, but tonight he theoretically paid it the right attention. "As far as we know," he pointed out, "all attacks have been in broad daylight."

"Wouldn't it make more sense to use the hours of darkness?" I asked. "Don't most repeat killers do that?"

"Yes, but there's two things against it," Morellus mused. "Fewer people about, so less crowd-cover when he attacks. And once dusk falls, the streets are full of vigiles. He may get the squits at the thought of meeting up with us."

Tiberius and I for the first time joined forces, as we rolled our eyes at that idea.

"He likes to go home for dinner," I decided. We were calling him a man, on the basis of Laia Gratiana's possible sighting. "Perhaps he is *obliged* to go—can he have a bullying wife? She picks on him; he dares not stand up to her. He avenges himself by attacking members of the public, instead of dealing with the woman at home he's scared of?"

"Or he has a nagging *mother*," Morellus corrected me. "Two of his victims are not young."

"Doesn't explain the oyster boy."

"If he is getting his thrills sexually, it doesn't rule the boy out," Morellus answered, cynically. Tiberius looked uncomfortable.

Although he had made no comment while Morellus and I were talking, he had been paying attention. The runner was quietly eating his cheese, cutting off thin slices and savouring the taste. He used the knife Morellus had been cleaning his nails with; I had seen Tiberius wipe it first very carefully on the hem of his tunic. The tunic was the scratchy one he wore a couple of days ago, though he had a softer-looking undertunic this time, showing beneath the bottom hem and sleeves: his layered look. Generals have it on their statues, to signify they can afford a big wardrobe.

I found myself staring at that cheese. Without a word he cut several slices and put them within my reach. Its texture looked unpromising, but Metellus Nepos must have smoked it. The result was wonderful. I chewed slowly, showing that I liked it, while not extending myself to say thank you.

My garlic squids had gone. They vanished early; it always was best to have them while some warmth remained, but between the three of us we had had a bit of a race to grab them.

"He could be a slave," I said, still gently chewing.

Morellus liked that. "Sent out on daily errands—?"

"—And does something vindictive while he is out of the house."

Tiberius just listened in, but he pulled a face to agree it was plausible.

With no more available evidence to help define our killer, the talk turned to measures for catching him. This degenerated into them planning manpower rotas, which I found boring. I merely sat, lolling forwards on the table. Tiberius and Morellus were exercised about the coming Cerialia Games. The Aventine would be taken over with seven days of public events, which could offer this man cover and new opportunities. Even if we broke the silence about the killings and warned locals to be careful, our district would be visited by many strangers who knew nothing about the warnings.

At one point when we were taking a breather from hard thought, Morellus looked at me and exclaimed to Tiberius, "She loves this!"

"Conspiring in dark little rooms full of lamp smoke? She does," agreed the runner. Although normally I would have kicked against two men discussing me that way, somehow it was neither exclusive nor patronising. We were all friends tonight.

"Beats interviewing supercilious women," I said easily. "Persuading those ladies who run the cult of Ceres to tell me anything useful had all the attraction of scraping up vomit."

Morellus chortled. "Someone has to do it. Albia, some jobs are just too filthy for us men!"

"Wimps. The trick is not to let them notice that I'm steering them into actually giving answers."

"She's Falco's daughter," Morellus mentioned to Tiberius, as if explaining my tradecraft. "Do you know him?"

"I know who he is."

Morellus nodded. "She can hold her own." Tiberius must have been starting to get the traditional pain in the guts from his sliver of Xero's rabbit pie; he must be distracted, because he too nodded. Morellus then asked, "What does your pa think, Albia?"

"Oh don't give me the old song, Morellus. I've been doing my job for twelve years now and I do not need you throwing out that stale line, *'Should we ask someone more experienced—and male—to come in on this?'* He keeps his head down nowadays, in case Domitian remembers they are enemies. Anyway, my whole family is entirely obsessed this month with the upcoming Viator auction."

Tiberius raised one eyebrow. He put down the knife. "That wouldn't be Julius Viator? The fur importer?"

I nodded. "It's a huge estate being sold off by the heirs. Why—did you know the deceased?"

"If it's the same man, Tullius does business with him—*did*, I suppose I should say. Viator was even at our house once. He was young, younger than me certainly." Although it was hard to be exact with all that facial whisker, Tiberius looked in his middle thirties. "I am very surprised to hear you say he is dead, Albia. When did that happen?"

"Must have been March. I first heard about the auction at a family party." Father's birthday. That reminded me: mine was fast coming up.

Tiberius was silent for a moment, then went on, "I didn't take to him—he was one of those fellows who spends his whole day exercising . . . No conversation, unless you wanted to hear how many weights he had lifted, and a complete drag at dinner because he was so careful about his diet."

"Fit?" asked Morellus—a throwaway comment, but he soon realised it could be significant. "Shit! Young and healthy?"

Tiberius looked thoughtful. "Fittest man I ever met. Too fit to die! It looks as if I had better make discreet enquiries about this tomorrow."

Morellus and I caught each other's gaze. Then we too fell quiet.

The possibility that we might have accidentally noticed another death to count in made us all low-spirited. The meeting broke up.

I gathered the remaining crumbs and remnants of piecrust into the packet I brought the squids in.

"Midnight supper?" jeered Morellus.

"Stray dog." I was taking it to my foxes.

In view of the hour, the investigator suggested that the runner should escort me home. I sensed what that was: a male hint that Tiberius might be in with a chance. Morellus himself was married with three young children; that would never have stopped him trying it on, but he knew I had met his wife. A nice woman. She had married a bum, though what choice did most women have? But if he played up, Morellus could expect Pullia to hear about it from me.

Knowing that he himself was ruled out, Morellus was signalling to the runner that the track was clear for him. He would think he was being generous. I don't know if the grubby matchmaker actually winked, but it was well implied. Tiberius looked unimpressed— thank you, Juno! I rejected the offer.

I strode off alone from the station house, moving fast to make sure I shed the runner. I was making my way to the Armilustrium. There, Robigo must have been hungry. Almost as soon as I put down the food and stepped away, I sensed his presence. On top of the boundary wall I saw his head come up, ears pricked. Soon he came slipping down the wall and was nosing what I had brought him.

I did not stay. I felt suddenly nervous, as if someone was watching me. Robigo, too, seemed to be listening more than usual.

Luckily Fountain Court was near. I walked fast. When I reached home, Rodan had for once locked the grille. I knew how to pick the padlock, though it was tricky and always took some moments. Once I was inside and fumbling to relock it in a hurry, I looked out through the metalwork.

Tiberius was standing a few strides away. His feet were planted apart, his arms folded. When he knew I had seen him, he jerked his head, apparently reproving me for taking risks. In a moment, he was gone.

Of course he would claim he was just seeing I reached home safely. I could not judge his true motives, and felt outraged. I was more unnerved to be followed home by him, than if a stranger had secretly tracked me. I knew that women are most often attacked by men with whom they have a previous acquaintance.

Tiberius must have seen me with the fox. I really hated anyone from the aediles' office knowing I had that interest. The Cerialia, with its abominable ritual, was close now. And I was planning to do something to prevent them setting fire to any foxes.

XXVII

I had breakfast with my parents. If they were surprised by my early arrival, they hid it well, apart from the customary "Darling, you are always welcome—but don't eat all the olive paste!" After that, "Confess then—what are you up to?" soon surfaced. I didn't keep them in suspense. Nor did I pretend it was sheer love that brought me to share their white bread rolls, cold meats and refreshing cucumber dip. I admitted at once that I wanted the background on the big Viator auction.

By the time I left, equipped with facts, Pa's assessment and the dead man's home address, I knew that he had sold furs from all over the Empire, which no doubt explained why he was acquainted with the plebeian aedile's uncle, a man who hired out warehouses. Importers bring home their gains, then Rome has the cleverest negotiators in the world; these slick leeches never sell to the first comer, but while they haggle their way to the most extortionate deal, the produce has to be put somewhere and kept in good condition.

I had learned in a brief seminar that even in a country as hot as Italy, there was money in fur. Not only were live animals prized in the arena, the rarity and luxury of skins from big cats, bears, wolves, ermine and even rabbits easily found a market. Julius Viator's grandfather had personally travelled to many provinces; so, too, the next generation as they became more and more specialised and prosperous. More recently, Viator had been able to lead a life of leisure in Rome and instead used troops of agents who went out for him. He could spend all day in a gymnasium because he owned many well-packed stores of pelts. He was a stay-in-Rome young man who, had he lived, was about to start his own family.

The house sale on his death had made my auctioneering relatives extremely happy. The profits from fur had paid for an enormous collection of exotic furniture, ancient bronzes, gorgeous silverware—plus a remarkable amount of what was, in my father's expert opinion, horrible reproduction Greek statuary. Pa was confidently intending to sell even the fakes. People will buy anything, and a hint of fraud just adds to the excitement for some punters. They hope the auctioneer is wrong and they can pull a fast one on him.

Those who think that don't know the Didius family.

It seemed odd to visit a house in the course of my enquiries and find it full of my own people. Julius Viator had lived in a sprawling villa, over the Tiber and in one of the better parts of the Janiculan—I mean, not the teeming favela we call the Transtiberina, which is full of dubious immigrants and criminals huddling out of sight of the authorities, but further along, up on the hillside slopes, with elegant views over to the city. My family has a villa, even better placed than Viator's. It's a quiet area. Imperial freedmen retire there to live off their loot. Successful gangsters and fraudsters have big mansions, heavily shuttered and guarded by mean-looking dogs. Retired senators and impresarios lurk, looking over at the city and mourning their lost glory.

Viator's house had almost been stripped. Our porters came and went in their respectful fashion, carrying out the final pieces to be sold in the Porticus of Pompey, always a favourite auction spot with my late grandfather, Didius Favonius. Supervising was Gornia, who must be ninety now. He had been forced to retire at one point, but when the Saepta Julia burned down a decade ago and a sudden death reduced the family, Gornia wangled himself back in as cover and had never left again. I greeted him, as he tottered about on spindly legs like a stick-insect. He introduced me to one of Viator's staff. Gornia was pretending to let him write notes, though our chief porter always carried lists and costs in his head.

The fellow Gornia brought to meet me, Porphyrius, was a junior secretary, now redundant. He was a slave, not old enough to be granted his freedom, even if Viator's will had provided for it. He must be facing sale to strangers in the near future, though tried to hide his natural anxiety about what fate might await him. Quietly saddened by the loss of his master, he spoke to me freely and was, I thought, trustworthy.

I learned that there were no close family members, which normally guarantees that staff like Porphyrius will be reassigned to them. In Viator's case, after brief provision for his wife, his legacies were all left to distant acquaintances, none of whom wanted any of the household slaves. They were also breaking up the family firm and selling its stock, so there would be more disruption for other workers too. An established home and a thriving business, both created over three generations, would become extinct.

Julius Viator had been married, but recently. The widow had borne him no children and was thought not to be pregnant. This had slashed the amount left to provide for her. She would take away little more than her dowry. Another result of this young man's death, therefore, was that a woman who had never done anyone any harm had to return to her father's house, where she would probably be regarded as a failure for coming home with nothing to show from such a very short marriage.

Porphyrius said Julius Viator, though not intellectual, had been a good master. He was rich enough to be an idle playboy if he wanted, but he did take an interest in the business. He had had many social connections, if few close friends. Everyone liked him. He seemed to have made no enemies. On the day he died, he came in from the gymnasium as normal, went to his room to change his clothes, and was soon afterwards found lifeless on his bed. He had not complained of feeling unwell and did not call out for help. His sudden death, at twenty-three, was regarded as a tragedy.

"What do you think caused that death, Porphyrius?"

"Nobody knows."

"Did a doctor examine him?"

"He had not been ill."

"Was no doctor called to examine the corpse?"

"There was no reason."

"Did the funeral director say anything about his abrupt death at so young an age?"

"Only that there is a lot of it about."

As I left the house, Tiberius turned up. It really riled him that I beat him to it. Furious, he ordered me not to interfere when he had made it plain *he* intended to take action. Clearly he was unused to having a rival on a case.

"Tough. Here's the situation: it fits the pattern. He had been in perfect health. There was no time to call a doctor and the funeral director only spouted the usual pointless platitudes. There is a young widow. I have been told she is devastated. You know perfectly well, Tiberius, I should do that interview."

"I can handle young widows!"

"Oh I don't think so."

We compromised that we would go together. He would wait outside the room, while I went in to put our questions gently to the heartbroken girl.

She wept a lot. She was only nineteen, completely flummoxed to find herself with such a close bereavement. I interviewed her at her father's house, of course. From running her own large establishment, she had to accept becoming just the little girl at home again, with no real position. Her parents were elderly and though probably kind, they were not up to helping her readjust. She could barely cope with losing her perfectly decent husband, let alone being flung back on the marriage market when she had thought her life's pattern was fixed.

She was not dim. I told her straight that we feared foul play. She became hysterical at my news, but eventually rallied and thought about it more calmly. I could tell that once she was alone, she would continue to brood. It was another aspect of the tragedy. This simple young woman would never escape the horror of her husband's murder.

From the start, I assumed a third party was responsible. I entertained no thought that the wife herself might have killed Viator (normally this is the first issue to investigate). She would have had no idea how to do it. Besides, there seemed genuine affection there—or at least, regret to have lost him. She gained nothing from his death. In fact, she had lost a lot of freedom as the wife of a very rich man—especially (being cynical) one who was out at the gym all day.

I could not deduce how much she had loved her husband, but I saw she felt responsibility towards him. In marriage, what more can anybody ask? She would mourn Julius Viator. She would pick over her memory of their life together, rue they had not taken better advantage of the time they had—even, if she loved him enough, wish she had a child by him. He was a man whose only conversation was athletics, described as a dire dinner companion, yet ample tears would be shed in his memory.

Because the widow could think of no one who had hated Viator, she was now also anxious that the apparently motiveless assailant might home in on her. The killer had not only destroyed her home and shattered her life, he had terrified her.

XXVIII

Viator's widow was only a year younger than I was when I lost Farm Boy. Her bereavement echoed mine. Normally I see that coming, but this caught me out. Unexpectedly emotional, I strode from the room where I left the girl weeping.

Tiberius was waiting outside. I just summarised the facts, as tersely as possible. "She knows nothing new. She never even saw him when he came home. She heard the wailing begin, then they took her to his corpse. She had never seen anyone dead before. All she remembers is her terror. The event fits the pattern. That's all."

A new wave of feeling overcame me. "Her life is wrecked. She is little more than a child. I was that age when I lost my husband just as suddenly. I know what she still has to go through . . . Don't speak to me. Don't follow me. I've had enough of you!"

I cannot say what showed in my face, but the way I stormed off must have made a big impression. Tiberius let me go without a word of protest. After I decamped, he must have returned to the aediles' office and ordered Andronicus straight out to find me.

I was not in the Eagle Building, nor at the Stargazer. Rodan must have suggested where else I might be lurking. I cannot imagine it was Tiberius who told Andronicus, although after the other night the runner did know I had another local haunt: I was sitting

167

hunched in the Armilustrium, on one of the benches, with my stole wrapped tightly round me.

I had not cried, but my mood was so black it startled even me. I knew I should have been more controlled at the widow's house. That made it worse.

"Do I dare?" Andronicus spoke softly, as he joined me. I managed not to be annoyed that he asked permission to join me, and did it so tentatively. First he perched on the bench end; then he shuffled closer and simply kept me company. He seemed to understand it was what I needed. Sometimes you run away by yourself purely so someone who cares will come to find you. Half the time nobody does. That's the tragedy of life.

When, finally, I looked directly at him, those brown eyes were so sympathetic, I nearly did break down and weep. He pulled a wry face at me. He knew I could be a fury, but I could see it did not frighten him.

I wondered if he knew it was me who stabbed Tiberius through the hand.

After a time I murmured, "I appreciate your kindness. Will you be in trouble? Can they spare you from your work?"

"I'm under orders. I dread to imagine what you must have done to Tiberius. He thinks he's tough, but he looked properly scared."

"I was unprofessional. I let myself be upset, instead of staying neutral."

"Want to tell me?"

"Thanks, but no. My stupidity is not your problem."

"You think?" Andronicus gave me his wide-eyed, rueful look. "I have been grabbed by the scruff of the neck, marched out of the archive room, informed that Flavia Albia sees me in a friendly light and may not eat my liver and lights therefore—and so despatched to comfort you. Had I not moved like a startled flea, I would have his boot print on my tunic arse."

I laughed slightly, thinking I would have liked to witness that little scene.

"You seem to be spending a lot of time with him," muttered my friend, with that edge of complaint he sometimes showed.

"Jealous?"

"Absolutely!"

I shuddered. "Horrible thought. Don't be bird-brained. It was work. He thought he could use my female skills. He will not repeat the experiment."

"He means to plunder your expertise, then steal the kudos," Andronicus warned me. "Everything with him is about how *he* appears."

"I see that."

"So did you help him?"

"Not enough to be of any value."

I sighed and relaxed, glad to be with someone I trusted. This was why I had been so badly affected earlier. The lonely young widow reminded me how I used to share my concerns with Farm Boy. Talking my cases through with Lentullus had clarified puzzles for me. He loved listening; I was like a storyteller for him. I had had nothing like that since, which was why I identified so closely with the isolation Viator's widow felt.

Still, I had someone to confide in now. "It's hopeless, Andronicus. We are trying to solve a series of seemingly unrelated deaths, where even the stricken victims themselves often don't realise anything bad has happened." I paused. "Except perhaps one old woman. Celendina. She said my name; she may have been telling her son to involve me."

"Did she say anything else?" asked Andronicus, drawing out the story to help me re-evaluate the evidence. I loved the thoughtful way he was listening.

"I don't think so. Even if she did, the son, the only person she spoke to, is unable to remember."

"What's happened to him?"

"Locked up by the vigiles?"

"They think *he* killed her?"

"Possibly. But he could not have killed the others. He never went out of the house."

"And otherwise you have no clue about who is doing this?"

I turned my head and gazed at him again. "No."

"You would never tell me anyway!" Andronicus grinned.

"That's right," I agreed, smiling back because I was glad to acknowledge openly that sometimes I had to be discreet. Andronicus shrugged his shoulders. If there were any secrets between us, we were easy with that.

Instead, he begged me to say why I was so upset. Since it was personal, no case-constraints applied, so I chose to tell. I explained about the rush of memory I had when the soft, unformed features of Viator's bereaved wife and the way she crumpled into tears made me remember my own youth. She had gone past the first stage, refusal to accept what happened, moving on into bewilderment. I knew all that. I knew her panic, finding herself so unexpectedly alone.

"When it happened to me, I had tripped home innocently from buying garlands for a family event, to find people in the apartment waiting for me. They said there had been a street accident. Lentullus was dead. The next months were terrible—the complete isolation, however much other people sympathise. The fear of being unable to cope with life by yourself, after you have grown used to sharing everything." My good friend nodded, full of kindliness. It made me wonder what griefs, if any, he had known himself. Bereaved slaves are often not allowed to show their sorrow, but must continue their duties impassively. "Those simple things he would have done, Andronicus—because even a rich fellow must surely sometimes find his wife's lost earring for her, or take a decision about calling in the carpenter, or settle on cold meats for lunch when she can't choose. Julius Viator spent all day at the gym, but he must have been home for meals and bedtime, even if all he did was grunt when she spoke to him."

When I finally stopped, shaken by so much revelation on a subject I never talked about, Andronicus asked in a subdued tone, "You think they had a good relationship?"

"I know they did. It was obvious when I talked to her."

"She is young. She will marry again."

"She cannot imagine that now."

Andronicus smiled. "And of course *you* did *not* remarry."

"I was a breakaway character. Viator's widow comes from a very conventional family. She is conventional herself. Her parents will come up with some new husband, suggesting that will be a consolation. I suppose she will go along with it. She is soft dough. They will push her into it before she is ready, long before she has stabilised. She will believe that is the right thing for her to do."

"You seem more upset about this young woman who at least is still alive than about the dead man," Andronicus pointed out.

"He is gone beyond the living world. He feels no pain."

"How did you know the widow is young?" I asked abruptly, though in fact it stood to reason.

"She came to our house when Viator had dinner with Tullius."

"Did she?" Tiberius had not mentioned that detail. I supposed he called himself a man's man. All he said was that he met Julius Viator. An accompanying wife was beneath his notice. "You saw her?"

"Pretty thing, not exactly stupid, but out of her depth when the men got talking. I discovered her moping in the peristyle, all dressed up in her rich clothes and fancy jewellery, dabbling her fingers in a fountain, bored to tears. You know—the men discuss contracts interminably, she's eyed up the pretty serving boys for long enough, she makes an excuse to use the facilities, then lingers in the garden for as long as she can."

"Oh I know that scene!" I, too, had enjoyed a breath of cold night air in a scented colonnade, on occasions when I wanted to go home, but had to stay at some grim dinner for what passes as politeness. I would amuse myself thinking up hideous ways to cause other guests' downfall—though in my assessment, Viator's wife lacked that much imagination.

"Luckily, along comes a handsome, debonair archivist to take pity and have a chat with her."

It was my turn to be jealous, though I was better than him at hiding it. "You think such a lot of yourself, Andronicus! Did you meet Viator too? Tiberius says he didn't care for him. What was your verdict?"

"Thick neck, even thicker brain. Big thighs, big biceps, even bigger opinion of himself. A bully."

"What makes you say that? Did he bully her?"

"No, I wouldn't say that. But he roared out from the dining room to see what was keeping her."

"Was she frightened of him? That was not the impression she gave me."

"Your judgement is ever perfect," Andronicus flattered me. I basked in his admiration, all too easily perhaps. I was used to people who gave compliments more teasingly, and who shaded them with irony. "She was definitely not scared. She returned happily enough to the dining room with him. He slung his hairy arm around her shoulders, she slipped hers round his waist." I nodded, reassured. After a moment Andronicus added, "Faustus then sent for the flute-player to lighten the mood at the party. Viator and wifey did not stay late. He'd had a drink, he'd concluded some matters with Tullius. I expect he dragged her home for a good shagging."

"You can be very crude!"

"I know these people," replied Andronicus. He made it plain he intended it as no compliment.

Not long afterwards, cold and stiffness convinced me it was time to move. Before Andronicus found me. I had worked through my rage and grief; talking to him had helped. I stood up—then quickly sat down again because I had spotted two pert ears above the boundary wall; Robigo, my favourite fox, was sitting there, as perhaps he had been for some time.

Andronicus noticed, and in his astute way, could tell I had a special interest. He too resumed his seat. We said nothing, while I waited to see what Robigo would do. I had put no food out for him, so felt surprised when he came down and rooted round; then there was no sign of movement for some time, yet I had not seen him leave. Eventually I walked over to the spot by the altar where I generally left scraps for him, and discovered the reason. A large animal trap had been positioned where I usually put his food bowl. Robigo was inside, going demented.

Squatting down nearby, I began to speak to him quietly. He froze against the far side of the trap. Andronicus came up behind me to see what was happening. He dropped to his haunches alongside. "They are catching foxes for the Cerialia."

"Well they are not having this one!"

Although he worked for the aediles, so closely connected with the Temple of Ceres, my friend was sufficiently maverick in his attitude to authority for me not to fear betrayal.

Speaking in a low voice to keep the trapped fox quiet, I told Andronicus about my hatred of the ritual with the burning torches, and my regular feeding of the animals here. "Someone must have known! They have played on his trust of me. It's my fault."

"What are you going to do?"

"Release him, of course. I need to calm him down first. They can give you a bad bite."

I stood and walked to the trap, still murmuring to Robigo. He now trembled violently, rolling the whites of his eyes at my approach. He jerked once, but did not run up and down in his prison as he had been doing before I found him. His beautiful coat was wet with frothy saliva; there was blood on his muzzle. He must have tried to bite his way free.

The trap was a long box-shaped wire cage. It looked old and rusty; they must use the same ones, year after year. They put raw meat in one end. When Robigo entered, which he had probably done only after much wary investigation, he stepped on a flap which sprang the door behind him. I had to pull a wire so the door could be drawn up again. I needed to stand to one side and back from the entrance, leaving his escape route clear.

When I ordered Andronicus to stay out of the way, he said, "Do you want me to do it?"

"No need."

"I deduce you have played with animal traps before?"

"I'll never admit that!"

This year and previously, yes, I had done it. I would wander the Aventine searching for the traps, and I set free as many captured animals as possible. If I found any traps empty, I left them with their doors safely shut.

"Their ritual is wicked. I do everything I can to stop them."

"They don't just trap creatures locally," Andronicus told me. He would be familiar with the arrangements. "A grisly old yokel, who sweats and stinks of pigsties, comes in from the Campagna in April, bringing a cartload."

"I know. It happens every year. They pay him a bounty for every live fox he supplies. If I can find out where they keep those, I will release them too."

"You mean it!" marvelled Andronicus.

"I trust you over this," I warned.

I did not ask him to help. That would have been a step too far. But he said of his own accord that he would see if he could find out where the Campagna foxes were being closeted by the aediles. They must be in Rome by now.

I had worked up the flap in Robigo's cage, and could open the door. The dog-fox watched what I was doing, soundlessly. As soon as he knew the way out was free, he streaked through the opening and fled, tail streaming behind him. As always when I set free a trapped animal, I felt the same rush of panic he must have, but then happy relief.

XXIX

I spent much of the next day leading my own life. I had not abandoned the murders, but there were no obvious leads to follow and I had no wish to subject myself to more disparagement from Tiberius, so I was determined to avoid him. I collated my notes about various other cases for private clients; they had been neglected lately. I carried out domestic chores. That included even sewing braid around the neck of a tunic, one with a square neck that had developed the traditional run in the material, from the weak point at the corner. I was covering up the ladders by stitching on braid, which would also strengthen the neck and give the garment a longer life. It had been a good tunic, blue, which was always a favourite colour of mine, though it is expensive and fades terribly.

I quite liked sewing. I enjoyed the quiet push and tug of the needle as I pressed into the layers of tunic and facing, then jerked the thread through, and the satisfaction of smoothing the work well, so it lay flat as I made progress.

This task calmed me after another experience that had left me horrified: I had walked around the Aventine all morning, looking for more fox cages. I found several. All but one were empty and I made them safe. The last contained a young fox, dead. At some point before or after he collapsed, crows had managed to insert their beaks through the wires and peck out his eyes. I shooed them off, but then could only walk away.

Just as I finished sewing, Andronicus came. I was up in the office, seated in the balcony doorway to use the best light. At his cheery greeting, I bit the thread on the last stitch then carefully docked my needle in the tunic braid; needles are not cheap.

"Not far off weaving at a loom like a traditional wife!" I mocked myself as I tidied my work and gathered up my sewing box. My friend took that from me, inspecting the elegant casket which had been a present from my parents: fine fragrant cedarwood, with patterned ivory inlays and silver fitments. My younger sisters had enjoyed themselves finding contents: a bronze thimble, shears, hole-punch, carved bone needle-case. I had filled up the box with remnants of braid and threads, buttons and beads. To anyone else it was a jumble of untidiness, though to me each cheap treasure represented past history.

"Somebody loves you!" As he placed the decorative box on my table, Andronicus had his suspicious look. My nut-brown lovely stood there, slim and trim, with no idea how little need he had to be jealous with regard to me.

"Not a man!" I growled, knowing how he thought. "Generous parents."

"You stay close to your family."

"People who know my history never expect that—but why not?"

"You live alone," Andronicus said. "But there seems to be a great deal in the background that you hide."

"I hide nothing."

"You live in this horrible place, although you have a rich father."

"This was my father's office before me. He made his own way in the world, and so do I."

"You fell on your feet, yet you turn your back on a fortune." Andronicus seemed unable to comprehend the situation I had chosen. I suppose to a freedman money mattered too much. "You told me you came from nothing. If that is true—" His implied suggestion that I might have invented my story for effect startled me. My past was hard; why would anyone burden themselves with a miserable past unnecessarily? "–why don't you now take advantage of what is available?"

"It would seem obvious to most people. And I expect it is my father's biggest fear that any men his daughters like will adopt that attitude." As I explained the alternative, I felt my chin come up. "I don't. I never will. I appreciate good fortune, but I make my own way when I can. Anyone who is my friend will see it my way."

"I just wanted to understand." Now Andronicus had his wide eyes, his seriousness about the mouth, his manner earnest and trustworthy. "I love the way you see things, Albia!"

As if to prove it, he told me why he came. He had learned where the aediles were keeping the Cerialia foxes. That news certainly won my affection and gratitude.

What we did in the next hour was dangerous, and could have brought down public wrath on both of us. Andronicus was eager not just to show me where to go, but to join in and help me. Sometimes I did crazy things, but never before with a partner. Since our destination was the Temple of Ceres, so familiar to him yet so alien to me, it would have been pointless to quibble. Anyway, our friendship easily extended to sharing this rash adventure.

As we walked there, he asked, "What would your wonderful family think about this?"

"They would very strongly advise against it!"

Clearly the right answer. He laughed gently.

I in turn asked how he came to be allowed out. He said Faustus was chairing a big meeting about arrangements for the Cerialia Games, a duty he could not neglect, while his uncle had gone to some drunken banquet, a normal night out for Tullius. The household was unregulated. Slaves and freedmen came and went.

It was a fine evening, though cool. People were on the streets though not in great numbers. We went side by side like strolling lovers. It was too early, and still too light, for most robbers to be active, while the old ladies who maintained moral standards had gone home for mean suppers with their cats. Families who spilled out of shops and workshops took no notice of us, since we were clearly not window-shopping. Nobody would remember us. Nobody could have imagined our illegal errand.

We reached the temple. One of so many on the Aventine, its isolated position in the northwest corner overlooking the Circus Maximus meant this particular temple was turning towards the city opposite as if offering some upstart rivalry to Rome's grand official gods on the Capitol.

Ceres was benign to humans. Ceres gave us agriculture, and with it the habit of a regulated life. How could the goddess who taught mankind to plough, who discovered wheat for us, who reigned as a patroness of decent human values, of peace and justice, require the torturing of foxes? One of her companions in this ancient temple was Liber, Father Freedom, a god of wine and male virility, but— perhaps because liquor will loosen the tongue—also a champion of free speech. This temple represented a longstanding centre of rebellion against restrictive social order. What Andronicus and I intended to do at least fell within that spirit.

Not that the plebeian authorities would approve. If we were seen with the foxes—if we were caught—it would count as "an insult to Ceres." Traditionally, the penalty for that was hanging.

That night my friend was so fired up it was wonderful. He dragged me up the worn steps and through the wide-set stubby columns beneath their bleached wooden pediments, then headed into the sanctuary. I had never been inside before. In Rome most religious life takes place outside, where the altars for sacrifices stand in the open air. On the eve of the festival there was more public presence than usual. Old women were selling cakes and honeycombs from little tables set among the columns.

We slipped past them, to enter the interior unchallenged. Another old woman, in white Grecian dress, clearly the chief priestess, was tending the statue of Ceres. Her movements were creaky but she straightened the goddess's wheatsheaves and torch to her satisfaction before turning. She recognised Andronicus and perhaps looked disapproving, but made no attempt to shoo him out. She ignored me. Women were allowed here.

Andronicus was a fine actor. As if to explain our presence, in a grave voice, he began giving me a lecture about the cult statues playing guide to a curious tourist. Each in their own sanctum were three extremely handsome bronze gods, paid for from fines the aediles extracted: Ceres seated on the snake-wreathed box which contained secret items used in her mysteries, Liber with his Dionysian wineskin, Libera, associated with Proserpina, the daughter Ceres lost to the god of the Underworld, but rescued . . .

Unlike so many stories of the official pantheon's gods and goddesses—that randy, amoral group who seemed concerned mainly with love affairs—Mother and Maiden had a special appeal for me. Their story was the core of the festival. In a few nights' time white-robed women would be running all over the Aventine with torches, to represent the desolate goddess's desperate search for her missing daughter, when the earth dies in the dead dark of winter before the mother is reunited with her child in the light, and green shoots are allowed to sprout again. Even in the city—*especially* in the city where there were so many mouths to feed—the renewal of the life-sustaining grain was celebrated.

Once, according to legend, a boy found a fox stealing chickens. When he tried to burn the fox alive, it escaped; as it ran away ablaze, its burning tail fired the fields and destroyed the precious cereal crops. Forever after, foxes had been punished in the name of Ceres . . .

The incense-scented hall became deserted but for us. A few hanging lamps burned, keeping the gods company. Andronicus winked at me, yet refrained from disrespect for the deities. He led me back outside; we sneaked through the columns and down off the podium, now with our hearts bumping. He was undoubtedly the leader, as we made our way from the main street, keeping in the shadows along one side of the temple, to a discreet doorway. Most temples have these, generally the entrances to underground vaults where treasure can be banked. Here, the Senate archive for which Andronicus was responsible had its location, a store of decrees kept at the heart of plebeian Rome, tended by commoners as if snubbing the aristocracy. He took me inside and showed me the array of columbaria, the endless banks of dovecote-style holders for scrolls, that formed his domain.

He snatched a kiss. He was highly excited, and I could tell he wanted more and would have taken it, defying propriety there among the banks of scrolls, had I not been single-minded about our mission. "Later!" I hissed, letting him know I wished we did not have to wait.

Further along the street, still beneath the temple, was a store. Untidy but functional, it was like any hiding place for equipment. Here they kept cleaning materials and lamps, cult items, and a pile of unlit torches ready for the festival. Andronicus showed me a phallic herm, an attribute of Liber, dumped here to gather dust. According to him, the priestesses of the cult were a sanctimonious collection of matrons who had thrown out the huge erect member in one of their many spring-cleans. He fingered it suggestively; we both giggled.

Unlike the archive, to which Andronicus had a special key, we had found this store unlocked. Andronicus told me two public slaves were supposed to guard it, the same sad lags who used the brooms to sweep the temple steps and the buckets to fetch water from fountains for washing the shrine daily. Every evening they went out to supper, and since they served at a temple housing a wine-god, they were known to take the attitude that Liber would want them to enhance their meal with the joys of fermented grape juice. It would be some time before the pair rolled back, stupefied.

They had left a lantern to stop themselves stumbling into things on their return—and to give some light to their current charges: four stricken and mange-ridden country foxes.

We acted fast.

The animals were all housed in one big cage. They had water, but no food that I could see. They were snarling, unhappy creatures whose stink had filled the storeroom. I could not imagine how it was intended to catch them and control them enough to fix burning torches to their tails. The thought was hideous. Andronicus said men would come from the imperial menagerie.

"I know what foxes do," I admitted. "My husband was born on a farm. He always hated foxes because they slaughter poultry. Tearing off chickens' heads, regardless of their actual need for food. Every year, while I hid at home, deploring the ritual, he would go out and join in, whooping down to the Circus with the crowd."

"So you and he had nothing in common?"

"Love is when you stick with someone despite disagreements."

"I don't see it," said Andronicus.

"Then just shut up and help me do this."

We had to be careful. Loose foxes in this store would cause havoc and be pointless. We needed the creatures to go straight out into the street and run away. To make sure they did, we manoeuvred that big cage to the doorway before we opened it. The foxes cowered, afraid we intended to harm them. At first they just stared at the open door, assessing the new situation. We shooed, trying not to make much noise in case we attracted attention. At last one edged forwards and put his nose out, then made a crouching run for safety; the rest followed. The third waited for the fourth as if they were mates or siblings. Once in the street, they all slunk into shadow and were quickly lost from sight. I heard a harsh bark, then nothing.

We moved the cage to make space for us to leave. I wanted to get away from there as fast as possible; Andronicus now decided to cause even more disruption to the rites. He carried out the pile of torches and dumped them in the roadway. He poured a bucket of tar over them. While I watched admiringly, scarcely able to believe his rashness, he lit a piece of matchwood at the lantern. Cupping the flame, eyes bright, he brought his taper outside and dropped it onto the pile of brands. They flared alight, bringing a sudden warm glow to our rapt faces. He kicked a loose torch onto this bonfire, causing a stream of sparks. I ran indoors for more torches to add to the pile, until the whole side street filled with light and fire.

The smell of the smoke must have travelled. As a vigiles whistle sounded close by, Andronicus grasped my hand and, both laughing out loud, we finally turned the other way and made a run for it. So we vanished from the Temple area, shooting away into the night, just like the foxes.

XXX

We had scampered north because the shouts told us the vigiles were coming from the street on the temple's entrance side. Heading away from them took us down off the hill near the corn dole station, after which our footsteps naturally led us to the Tiber Embankment. We walked, hand tightly in hand, through the long Porticus of the Trigeminal Gate. Its stalls had been closed up for the night, some of them actually towed away; although we passed the family stall of Lupus, the murdered oyster-shucker, no one was there and we did not mention it.

We had calmed down, though were still prone to bumping our heads together, my dark crown against his ginger sideburns, and bursting into giggles. We were like naughty children, though what we had done made us far worse than scallywags. The consequences could have been dire, and not only for us. We might have wreaked terrible destruction; the hundred-year-old timbers on the temple's roof would have gone up in an instant if a loose spark had flown to pediment height. Then who knows how far the flames would have spread? It was barely ten years since a huge fire had destroyed half of Rome; rebuilding still continued.

We looked at the river. We sauntered along the Embankment by the old salt stores and moored boats, listening to the water lapping close, hearing noises from warehouse and tavern on both waterfronts. It was dark now, though only just. Rome was a mass of mysterious shapes and hidden buildings all around, with most of the remaining light suffusing the sky above us, where only a few shreds of cloud scudded slowly and as yet there were no stars. In mid-April, the weather was cool but bearable, an impetuous breeze carrying a faint hint of summer heat to come. Tiny lights had begun appearing, mere pinpoints. Where humans gathered for entertainment, occasional strings hung like beads in a goddess's necklace in the heavens. Isolated spots high in buildings marked a scholar's vigil or the restless sick.

Andronicus and I were silent now. It grew colder close to the water; we had cloaks; we stopped holding hands and each gathered our outerwear around us, standing separate. At that moment the spot could have been romantic; later tonight it would become a disreputable haunt, favoured by prostitutes of all sexes and their clients, not to mention the purse-snatchers who preyed on them, generally in league with the whores. So far, sidewalks and roadways had been virtually clear. But now the daylight ban on wheeled vehicles lifted, so carts began to rattle up from the port into Rome. Pretty soon the streets would be hectic. With one accord we moved, turning back to home in again on the Aventine.

We climbed the hill the same way we came down. Alone, I would not have done that, but I was letting Andronicus lead. He seemed to enjoy danger; he even took us past the back wall of the Temple again, to look down that narrow side street, the scene of our crime. The vigiles must have doused the bonfire and cleared the debris. We could hear voices from inside the store, though we could not see inside.

"They will catch more foxes. They will bring in more torches. But we have caused them wonderful inconvenience—" Andronicus winked at me. "And Faustus will hate this interfering with his festival management."

"You like that," I commented. Upsetting his master was probably why Andronicus had helped tonight.

"Oh I do! We made him look useless. He will be livid!"

He seemed to entertain no thought that what we had done was

wrong. This was a big difference between us. A civilised society has to have rules (thank you, Ceres, for bringing mankind out of barbarian ways of living!). I was very aware we had broken those rules. To me, that was justified because a civilised *person* must always be ready to exercise choice. An individual must have, and use, a conscience. I looked wild, but these days it was an illusion; Andronicus looked respectable, but maybe with him that was deceptive. Tonight he seemingly had no conscience.

The daft daredevil would have walked down the side street for a closer look, but I refused to go. I was perfectly capable of strolling up like an innocent passer-by, but why invite notice? I insisted we walked on a couple of blocks, turning in past the Temples of Flora and Luna, then worked our way to my home ground through a few secluded back streets, then the Street of the Armilustrium.

We ended up at the Stargazer. It was a classic case of being desperate for wine, to heighten our mood again in the anti-climax after a wild adventure. Anyone who noticed the pair of us arrive, bright-eyed and breathless, must have thought we had come straight from a bed of hot passion. There were no free tables so we leaned on the counter. That was where we were, toying with nibbles and gulping *vinum primitivum* (the only palatable house wine my aunt stocked, which she swore was misnamed), when Tiberius and Morellus arrived. Neither was happy.

Enough time had passed for them to have been summoned to the scene by the patrol that found the fire, to have surveyed the damage and to work up a theory. Well done, lads. Tiberius must have remembered me feeding Robigo; he knew I liked foxes. Now he and the vigiles investigator were here, looking for me. Seeing Andronicus with me just gave them more ideas.

Morellus sombrely spelled out what had happened, with the air of a man who believed he was wasting effort on people who already knew. He was in his evening workwear: his ordinary daywear over his loose gut, plus a fire-axe through the back of his belt and a hefty nightstick in front. He looked as if he had neither for effect, but regularly used them. Tiberius sported the best tunic I had seen him wear, a pristine white effort; he looked short-tempered, as if he had been summoned from an evening of leisure he was sorry to miss. Andronicus might hope we had made Manlius Faustus livid, but the aedile himself would not be out tiptoeing through fetid alleyways at night-time, where drunks might insult him or sluts make indecent grabs under his toga. He had sent his man-in-the-street to suffer for him.

"Look, Albia, we know you take a kind-hearted interest in wildlife." Morellus addressed me in his officially patronising voice. Tiberius just stood with his arms folded.

"I see." I spat out an olive stone. "Of course I love animals. I was born in a province full of horses, where the barbarians worship hares—even when I came to Rome, it was me who walked the family dog. So, to a moron, that makes it obvious. Why bother looking for evidence, Morellus, when you can attack such an easy target?"

"Where have you been this evening?" he demanded patiently. Tiberius said nothing. Those grey eyes moved between us, observing, assessing, reaching bad conclusions. I found him more worrying than Morellus.

"Here!" Andronicus barged in, though I had been trying to leave him out of the conversation. "We were here, having supper and snuggles, all evening. Anyone can tell you."

Anyone could really have said he was lying—but nobody would. The usual moves had already taken place among the other customers: as soon as the vigiles arrived, they slid coins on to the counter for what they had consumed (underestimating heavily), and vanished. Morellus had brought a couple of his men with him, but they had conducted their own traditional moves; they stood by, looking gormless, while potential witnesses all made their exit.

Time was, back in Londinium, I would have been the first to slide away. Now I was respectable and had to stand my ground. To Tiberius and Morellus running away would prove my guilt.

The Stargazer had suddenly emptied, except for my cousin.

Since the bar had been rather busy until now, Junillus had not cleared the counter. It was the night the other server took off to attend his club; Apollonius went to a weekly gathering of geometry puzzlers, a gentle hobby that had to remain unmentioned in front of anyone from the aediles' office or the vigiles, especially in Rome's current paranoid climate. Mathematics is a suspicious activity. All those hypotenuse drawings must be plans for assassination attempts. Algebra is treacherous code. When did you ever meet a student of infinitesimal calculus who didn't harbour rabid ambitions to rule the world? And anyone who tells you Archimedes was killed at the capture of Syracuse by a soldier who didn't know who he was, is ignorant of how military forces work. There will have been a secret order: *man making diagrams in the dust equals number one target.*

The runner's expression said *his* target was me.

So. Apollonius, who kept a meticulously neat bar counter, was not here. Junillus presided cheerily over honest mess. At my side, Andronicus waved his arm above the used bowls and beakers on the crude marble slabs. That should be enough. Nevertheless, a mime ensued where Andronicus asked Junillus if he had been serving us all evening. Morellus joined in, wagging his finger to notify Junillus that this was a matter of exorbitant importance.

I watched apprehensively. Junillus leaned on his forearms. Pushing aside a long lock of hair that had drooped in his eyes, he frowned, to show he wanted to be sure he understood. He gestured to the food bowls, like a bad actor in a very tedious tragedy. In fact he had known me long enough to be sure I would never have ordered polenta at all, and if the stewed leeks with lentils had been mine, I would have cleaned up the gravy with my finger before finishing. I never leave my crockery full of crud.

Junillus was a bright, humorous lad with a wicked side to him, who suffered from a disadvantage. He stood on his own feet. He took what came in life. But he had been adopted into the Didii, so he was ours. We all looked after him. I felt uncomfortable over this.

Junillus lied to Morellus and the runner without thinking twice. "All night!" he carolled, with characteristic heaviness in the syllables. His mother had laboriously taught him how to say words, but he overstressed his consonants and his vowels were too long. His speech always sounded odd, though when he kept it simple he was intelligible. "Albia at Stargazer." He signed to the fish picture. Then he beamed, looking around those standing at the counter like a particularly irritating acrobat seeking applause. The naughty boy was playing on his weakness. It worked just fine.

Andronicus ought to have left it there, but he was carried away by the fun of invention. "You can tell the truth, Junillus—there was a long gap, when we went upstairs."

"Upstairs?" demanded Morellus, who had known me a few years and rightly saw this as unusual. "What for?"

"What do you think?" scoffed Andronicus. Light from a small oil lamp glinted on his hair and beard as he responded. "This is a bar, they have rooms, customers break off from their meals for playtime."

I felt myself blush. It was routine in bars for sex to accompany the drink, a service usually sold by the waitress, though tired waitresses were often glad if customers just hired the rooms and made their own arrangements.

The Stargazer had never had a waitress and I happened to know that despite various dubious events taking place in its two upstairs rooms, at present they were innocuously rented to a gang of jobbing builders from Gaul. They came to Rome to earn money and worked all hours, mixing concrete at the docks which is heavy labour; when they were here, they lined up like sardines in a trug and slept. Even my aunt said they caused no trouble.

"Listen, Junillus! Did Flavia Albia spend this evening having bedroom fun upstairs?" Morellus made a crude gesture to illustrate. I saw Junillus' gaze waver because he knew I would give him trouble for this but, trying to please everyone, he gravely nodded. "Oh very good!" Morellus groaned, adding to Tiberius that they could never put Junillus in court. "Nice alibi!" he muttered to me. Of course he knew I was perfectly willing to sleep with Andronicus, though would prefer him not to boast in public. Tiberius' disgusted face said he, for one, despised me.

I cannot say my reputation was tarnished, but my dignity was distinctly affronted.

Morellus did make one last pathetic attempt at an enquiry. He leaned suddenly towards me, sniffed at my cloak and announced, "You know, Albia, to an expert you smell distinctly of smoke!"

Once again Andronicus produced a neat excuse. "That will be because she has been standing next to the grilling meat for hours."

"Meat!" growled Morellus to the aedile's man, suggesting this at least was a reason to arrest someone, but Tiberius just shook his head wearily. He had no heart for bar-food laws tonight. The Stargazer was safe.

Junillus, who routinely used his deafness to assist in over-selling, pretended he thought "Meat" was a food order, so he started laying out dishes of mutton morsels on beds of lettuce. The vigiles Morellus had brought with him reached for these, of course. Before long, drinks were being ordered. It was hard to tell that any law and order issue had been under debate. Even Tiberius was pecking at the mutton, sprinkling the charred cubes with oil to make them palatable, while he slowly unwound the bandage from his hand as if it was hurting him. Tonight's bandage was another perfect white one to match his tunic; coordinating his accessories seemed an unlikely touch. Anyone would take him for a toff with a wardrobe keeper.

Morellus and his men looked at the wound and winced. The

scars each side of the runner's hand were weeping, red and angry; the man himself looked a little feverish. The vigiles all came to inspect him like experts. Someone was sent to fetch their medical orderly with mastic salves.

Andronicus and I were standing off to one side; it seemed best not to leave too precipitously, after we had made so much of our having been at the bar for the long term. He gave me a sideways look. "Would you happen to know how he acquired that?"

"Why are you asking me? I'm not his mother. What does he say?"

"He leant on a nail."

I chuckled. "Really? Has he always been an idiot?"

Out of the corner of my eye I saw Junillus slyly tidy away the skewers on which he had kebabbed that night's titbits. My young cousin was needle-sharp. I loved that boy, and my sour feeling about him being persuaded to lie renewed itself.

Not long afterwards I made my way out through the kitchen to what passed for a customers' lavatory. As I went I winked at Junillus. He flashed me thanks for bringing so much custom. Behind me, the bar was humming.

The latrine was a health hazard in a lean-to shack at the back. Most men ignored it and peed in the alley, so anyone in open sandals needed to step carefully. I did what I had to, then slipped away from the Stargazer without saying goodbye to anyone. The rest were now all men together and I had felt excluded. Even Andronicus was guffawing over some low joke with one of the vigiles. He seemed unlikely to notice I had gone.

I went home.

As I entered the Eagle Building, I caught a glimpse of some animal slinking away on the far side of the yard. It could have been a dog or cat. I hoped it was the vixen I had once watched bring her four cubs to exercise. She had lain under the steps on guard, looking exhausted by motherhood, while her boisterous offspring spent a good hour playing tag together, jumping on and off old washtubs delightedly.

I told Rodan to lock up the grille and not allow anyone to come in tonight unless they lived here. "Does that include friends of yours?"

"I have no friends, Rodan." This was a myth I liked to project: informers are moody, lonely folk. What informer can expect clients, if she is known for frittering away her time in a cheery social circle? "If one of my lovers turns up, I'm not in the mood. Snubbing him will just make him more keen tomorrow, won't it?"

"What lovers?" asked Rodan, looking puzzled.

Later, and not unexpectedly, I did hear Andronicus calling out. He sounded none too sober. Despite him rattling at the grille, Rodan must have been snoring on his pallet and never answered. One way and another, I was not ready for a first night of passion. Setting free the foxes together had thrilled me, but I was piqued by events at the Stargazer. I buried my head under the pillow until what passed for silence fell on Fountain Court.

I knew I had acted against my own interest. That surely proved I was in love, or at least in lust. Tiffs and tussles are mandatory. I was old enough to know how it works. This is how you test whether an affair is serious, as it provides the meat and muscle for the anguished poetry. You have to have pointless separations in the mating process, don't you?

XXXI

I awoke knowing it was now twelve days into April, which the Roman calendar describes as the day before the Ides. This was the start of the Cerialia festival. The organisers would hold sacrifices at the temple and a great horse race in the Circus; tonight would end with the ritual of the burning foxes. There was no longer much I could do about that.

I tried. I never give up.

I walked about the Aventine, searching for traps. They had placed more, presumably because they were now desperate. Each trap had a member of the vigiles on guard unobtrusively nearby, pretending to drink at a bar counter or leaning against a wall and using a twig as a toothpick.

I was returning home despondently when I met Morellus. He bore me no hard feelings for yesterday, if only because he was too lazy to want to create a charge-sheet. He was convinced of my guilt, but realistic; without witnesses, his case was weak—not that that counted too much in a Roman court. He knew I could call on good people to speak for me, so whatever theatricals a prosecutor came up with, once my defence heavies began their sweet-talk, the case would be thrown out. My lawyers were the kind who would then demand remuneration for the "false" accusation . . . Of course they would. The people I knew specialised in compensation claims.

He was so forgiving towards me this morning, I even wondered if Morellus, or maybe his wife, sympathised with my feelings about the fox ritual. Conceivably, an urban couple might take no joy in horrible old traditions that were rooted in agricultural prehistory. But I would not push it with a vigiles officer. When challenged about any aspect of religion, most people go along with the establishment.

"Leave it alone, Albia," Morellus chided, proving my point. "You will only make it worse. The aedile's agents are collecting dogs with pointy noses now, to act as understudies. Kindly give up, woman! My children have just acquired a puppy with rusty-coloured fur. While we're having to keep him in so the dog-catchers don't snaffle the poor little beggar, he's peeing on the floor rugs and driving my wife crazy."

I gave him a wry, defeated smile.

The atmosphere on the streets had changed overnight. Visitors flooded into Rome, wandering about the Aventine not so much because it was a cultural high spot for travellers but because the Temple of Ceres stood here, the festival's focal point. Workers were starting their holiday. There were more people than usual even this morning and by tonight everywhere would be packed. Bars were open. Hawkers with trays of dubious snacks were roaming about. Garland-girls sat on kerbs, surrounded by mounds of greenery and flowers that were too heavy to carry. Only the race in the Circus Maximus would suck the neighbourhood dry of crowds again. At that point, Morellus would face double anxiety: needing to police the racetrack down in the valley, yet also to keep watch over homes and businesses on the heights that would fall prey to robbers taking advantage of owners' absence. He was used to it, but he loved complaining.

We stood on a street corner, gossiping. Inevitably, we talked about our big preoccupation, the random killings. He told me there had been no further street attacks locally, or none he knew about. The authorities had brought in extra manpower, to police the crowds. Morellus was not convinced by the gesture. His instinct told him this madman made his moves for some as yet unknown personal motive, which I agreed. Crowds alone would not draw him. Only if someone he already had in his sights went to the racecourse would he go after them. Even then, it would break his pattern, which was to take his victims while they were engaged in the most ordinary daily occupations.

Before we parted, Morellus could not help asking, "So are you having it away with that scroll-shoveller?"

"I might be."

"Bit of a character."

"In vigiles' parlance, that's an insult?"

"Too clever. Cocky. I hate that."

I was hurt that my judgement was being maligned. "You're a misery. He suits me. Andronicus is bright, witty, appreciative—"

"A lightweight." Morellus would not be swayed. He was the worst kind of stubborn, self-opinionated man. "Wandering eyes. I bet he two-times you, gal."

Stubborn myself, I walked off, burying myself in thoughts of work in order to blot out the annoying conversation.

There were two things I wished I had done better in this case. One was to speak directly with Laia Gratiana's maid, Venusia. The other was my mishandled interview with Julius Viator's widow. Finding myself not too far from her parents' house, I went back to revisit her.

Facts: Her name was Cassiana Clara. She had a round face, with solemn eyes, though when she managed the ghost of a smile it was attractive. Neat of figure and well groomed; oils had been lovingly massaged in by maids. Judging by her perfect eyebrows, she tidied away superfluous hair routinely, kept herself nice for the man in her life. There would only be one of course. Well, one at a time. But well-off widows don't stay lonely.

I could imagine that Viator would have been happy when his prospective bride was introduced and he stayed content with the marriage.

The widow was the youngest child of affluent parents, though not so wealthy as her husband's family. Whatever older siblings she had, they were all married and settling down to lead good lives and produce grandchildren, as parents think they have a right to expect. Clara, who had probably always been seen as less reliable just because she was the baby, had now fluttered back home, in grief and in trouble, unsettling everyone and unsettled herself.

I apologised for my abruptness last time. I decided to tell her why, frankly mentioning my own bereavement though I kept quiet about how long ago it was. It gave us a bond. We settled down and talked; she was glad of my company. When you suffer a major loss, people treat it like an illness, even though physically you are undamaged. Cassiana Clara, now loitering as a subordinate in her mother's house, was restricted in her social life. Too sweet to mutter about it, she was secretly bored.

She seemed at ease in my company this time. Any strangeness about being interviewed by an informer and any shock that her husband had been murdered were over. She had had time to think about Viator's death, quietly on her own.

I had anticipated correctly. She had brooded. Then she had been to talk to the slaves who saw her husband that day, in the moments after he came home from the gymnasium. One of them had told her Viator kept slapping at his arm as if he had some irritation; he mentioned that something had scratched him. "Like a fish-hook, the slave told me." Although Clara seemed to believe it, I had doubts about the fish-hook; by design, it would have remained in the flesh. They leave a big and bleeding tear if they pull out. None of our victims had had a mark of that type.

I took the slave's name, though Clara said she doubted he would know much more.

We talked about the redundant slaves and their plight. Cassiana Clara had now seen for herself how anxious they were about their coming fate, a new consideration for this young and privileged matron. She told me she was trying to find positions for as many as possible in homes she knew, rather than have them consigned to the slave market. She knew enough of the world to understand how evil that would be. A few loyal staff were being absorbed into her parents' household, one or two were going to her sister. I could not tell how energetically she had applied herself to this task, but I could see the reallocation of labour gave her an interest. I was surprised a girl with that background did it at all.

I was right about something else: Clara had agreed to be remarried. She was betrothed already to one of the legatees of Viator's estate, an older man; she had met him and thought him good-hearted. It was not my place to feel saddened.

I told her to let him know what she was doing about the slaves. "He will be impressed by your kindness—a good basis for your marriage." She was puzzled. The girl was without guile. "Stand up for yourself, Cassiana Clara. You may be much younger than your new husband, but *you* want to control the keys to the store-cupboard, not some sneery freedman who has worked there for years. Make it plain that you expect to have your place as the mistress. You want a role. You mean to lead a worthwhile life." She made no response, but I could see the idea seriously taking root.

I asked about her marriage to Viator. She spoke about it openly. Yes, his obsession with exercise had placed limitations on their domestic life, but we agreed there were worse things a man could do. Business affairs can be deadly. Drink is bad. She mentioned gambling as a hideous possibility. I alluded to pornography, though when she blushed I did not stress it. I made sure we discussed these things, hoping in vain for a clue to the motive for Viator's murder.

Then I broached a new subject: "Do you mind if I ask about a particular social occasion? I believe you went to dinner once at the house of a warehouse owner called Tullius and his nephew. The nephew is now a plebeian aedile, though he may not have been then."

A guarded look appeared on Clara's face. She nodded; she said she remembered the dinner. "We went once. It was not long before my husband died." Her husband died last month, or not long before, going by when my family was commissioned for the auction: March, or late February at the latest. "We never went again."

"Why was that?" No answer. "Well," I suggested, "men often like to do business in their own settings—by the rostra in the Forum, dinky spots in private cloisters, hidden little eating places beside the Emporium . . ." Clara nodded. I waited, then asked gently, "Did something happen? Will you tell me about that evening?"

"Is this important, Albia?"

I could hardly admit, *I want to find out if your husband bullied you.* "To be honest, I don't know. Odd things turn out to matter sometimes . . . I have attended dinners like that myself, and not enjoyed them. While the men busy themselves with their politics or work affairs, any female who has accompanied them can feel like an unwanted outsider. And from what I have heard of the aedile's uncle, he sounds frightful."

Clara was lured into confiding that no, she had not found Tullius congenial. "Nothing blatantly obvious, Albia. You know; the sort of old man who greets you just a little too warmly, makes you share his dining couch as if the honour of your company is all his . . ."

"Too feely?"

"Not crudely obvious."

"Oh yes. They paw you just enough to make you seem like a bad sport for not liking it, but all the same, you spend the whole time feeling very uncomfortable, struggling to edge away from them. Meanwhile all the other men present appear not to notice what is going on, because none of them wants to upset the randy old bastard by taking him to task."

"He would just laugh it off." Clara knew the score. "Anyway, it was his house."

"And of course, in that situation, a wife is obliged to assist her husband's business interests by putting up with it . . . All you can do is skip off to the facilities and take your time over coming back to the dinner couches." No reaction. "Were you the only woman guest? Who else was there? Was it formal, with the full nine places set?"

"No, just an informal supper really. Tullius and his nephew. Julius and me."

"No one from their staff included at table?"

"Not that I recall." Tiberius, who had said he was there, would hate that!

"I have never met the nephew, Manlius Faustus."

"He is quite nice."

"Good-mannered?"

"We had a nice conversation about music."

"How was the food?"

"Very nice," said Clara. We laughed. Clara showed a glimmer of realisation that her vocabulary was bland.

"Not nice enough for you to want a second tasting?"

"No, my husband apologised to me afterwards and said we would not visit again."

"He sounds a decent man."

Bad move. The widow creased up, suddenly in tears. "He was. He was a wonderful husband. We were not married very long, but Julius was loving and protective and I miss him."

We sat quiet while she composed herself.

"What did he have to protect you against?" I murmured gently. "Or whom?"

"Nothing," answered the widow quickly. If she had a moment of panic, she was hiding it successfully. "No one. That was just a manner of speaking."

"I heard you were in the garden and he came and fetched you?"

"He had missed me."

"How wonderful." Innocuously I slipped in, "Did anything else happen?"

"What do you mean?" asked Clara. I left it, mainly because I was not sure what I did mean.

Instead, I said brightly, "Changing the subject, I believe you met a good friend of mine that evening! Did you run into their lovely archivist, name of Andronicus?"

Just as she had over Tiberius being present, Cassiana Clara blanked this. "Possibly. I don't remember."

I supposed the memory failure must be because Clara had been so preoccupied with her attempts to evade the grabby Uncle Tullius.

"I wonder about this household," I mused. "All male, and from what I have heard, rather a lot of unhappiness. Old guilt and current resentment. Did you find the atmosphere seethed—"

"It was fine." Clara interrupted as if she could no longer bear to remember the evening. "A perfectly ordinary dinner!" At least that made a change from calling it nice.

Something had happened. Something she was refusing to discuss with me.

At that point her damned mother had to intervene. She was elderly, upright, pleasant but firm, and she came into the room on purpose, aiming to get rid of me: Mama thought helpless little Clara had given me enough of her time. She was still grief-stricken and suffering; I ought to be more considerate. There could not possibly be anything else I needed to know; I should say goodbye now.

A brief glance passed between Cassiana Clara and me, like two girlfriends mildly deploring the older generation. She did not argue with her mother. Perhaps she really was glad to shed me—though I still thought she had been relieved to have a visitor to talk to. Someone who had come to see *her* specifically, as if she mattered. While she was married, she had mattered to her husband. I believed that now.

We embraced and kissed, just like old friends; after so much confiding, it had become a necessary ritual. I have little patience for that charade. I would not want her for a friend. I could not dislike her, but I agreed with what Andronicus had said: she was not exactly stupid, but out of her depth. He meant out of her depth when men talked business in front of her, but with ten years between us I felt she was out of her depth with me too. Not enough character or experience on her side to make us equals.

Perhaps I was snobbish. I certainly felt sorry for her. Before I left, I remembered how anxious Clara had been before, afraid that her husband's killer might pursue her too.

"I should have reassured you more. Let me do it now. From what we have worked out, he selects his victims randomly. Afterwards he moves on. He never seeks out anyone connected with his previous crimes." Well, not apart from Celendina after Salvidia's funeral, but I had no idea how or why that happened.

Cassiana Clara gave me an oddly fixed stare. "Unless you know who he is, and why he is doing this, how can you be sure, Albia?"

I did not protest that I was sure because I was the expert and she was just an innocent. She might be right. Sometimes an outsider can be perceptive just because they view an event with new eyes. I would think about what she had said.

XXXII

I had no appetite for lunch. I had no interest in anything, obsessed only with what was about to happen that evening with the foxes.

The Aventine's mood degenerated. Outsiders, here for the festival, had taken over. Locals were struggling to find places in their regular haunts. We were jostled on our own streets by visitors who seemed to have no sense that they had invaded our ground. Why do tourists never allow space to other people on pavements? Why are they so loud, why be such disrespectful idiots? Do they all leave their brains at home, sitting on a shelf with their good manners, when they pack their travel bags? They climb out of their carrying chairs, right in your way, then stand about, gaping vacantly. They don't ignore us; they simply do not see us.

I was not even a Roman but I loathed this influx of grockles. The impact would be temporary but, as every year, it unsettled us.

A killer who didn't care who he attacked would find these morons easy pickings, but I doubted ours would take one. They posed no challenge. It would be someone local, someone who had drawn his notice in some way.

How long since he last struck? Too long, I thought. He must be in need of excitement again. Such killers had regular patterns of behaviour. Assuming he planned in advance, he would certainly be planning a new death now.

If he did not plan, but acted on sudden urges, the desire for power, the callous sense of power that repeat murderers enjoy, might agitate him at any moment. He could be jabbing at his next victim while I stood here in the Vicus Armilustrium, scowling as I was buffeted by braying idiots in their best tunics, just in from Campania without their brains.

I went home. I stomped moodily up to my office, as if I wanted to distance myself from the crowds that way. It was not entirely successful, since noise rose between the narrow buildings and seemed amplified when it reached me. For the next few hours, even when I stayed indoors and refused to look out over the balcony, I was increasingly aware of large numbers of people moving about below. For the most part they were quiet so far. The festival involved sacrifice and solemn rites, with a deep religious purpose. And most had yet to find a hole they liked, in which to dig in for the evening and drink themselves silly.

In any case, there was the race. It was a big event. Horses and riders had been training for a long while. This was the first outing of the season; owners hoped their horses would become this season's famous winner. Jockeys, too, were eager for fame. Public gambling was illegal—yet big money rode on the outcome.

My local neighbourhood grew still as everyone flocked to the Circus. The bulk of the Aventine's main peak lay between Fountain Court and the Circus Maximus, muffling sound partially; yet when surrounding buildings lay quiet on great occasions, we could always make out the distant roar. It started with snatches of distant music as the religious procession entered through the ceremonial gates at the apsidal end further from us, passing under the new triple arches built in honour of the Emperor Titus. Then a slight surge of vocal approval might cover the arrival of our current emperor in his official box, though Domitian's new elaborate viewing platform, high on the edge of the Palatine in his grand palace, made him almost invisible to the crowd so far below.

On legal advice I retract that. People had supposedly been

thrown to the arena beasts for insulting the emperor in his hearing at the Games. Writing about him critically was as bad.

There came a lull in the noise, which would be when white-robed women carried out mysterious rites for Ceres; those rites were reserved for female initiates, though one of Rome's cadre of senior priests, the Flamen Cerialis, would officiate in his cape and pronged headdress, while the plebeian aediles also had a traditional role in the prayers. This would be important for the ambitious Manlius Faustus. Aediles who managed the Games well and won the crowd's approval could later use their public support to help them gain more important positions. It was not easy to impress a Roman crowd. Indifferent to his glory, many in the predominantly male audience would be still gathering, talking among themselves and assessing their surroundings during this part of the proceedings. They had to endure the rites, but would be bored. You can't make bets on the sacrifice of a pregnant sow. Indeed, even for a suave audience of hard-nosed Romans who would gamble away their grandmothers, placing bets during this solemn moment is generally frowned upon. Their upright grandmas would have taught them that.

Next came a long, steady noise as the audience settled in their seats for the race, a steady hum that broke into a strident crescendo once the runners emerged. This outburst was always heard loud on the Aventine, because the twelve brightly painted starting gates stood at our end of the track. A burst of sound marked the moment when they opened. As the horses completed each circuit, the noise swelled. You could follow the progress of each lap, without needing to be there. You knew each time the leaders passed the turning points at the ends of the central barrier, that curious construction dividing the tracks that bore big marble eggs for counting laps, among dolphin statues, obelisks, refuges for assistants, small temples and shrines.

A race in the Circus was seven laps. The finish came with a full-throated roar that resonated even up here, through the unstable fabric of my building. The audience would have thrown themselves to their feet in ecstasy. Enormous gusts of garlic- and cabbage-laden farting would billow above the stadium, a ripe miasma that was barely contained by competing breath pastilles and hair pomades. The ovation for the winner would be the high spot of the jockey's life; even the exhausted horse would toss his head and enjoy the glory.

After the race finished, normally the many exits would empty the Circus in moments. Tonight, though, people would not leave. Tonight, they would wait in their seats for more entertainment. The snack-vendors would run up and down the steps handing out beakers and bundles of food for the peckish. Marshals would try to order people about, just to show they had that privilege. In a crowd of that size—it was estimated to be a quarter of a million, though boy cousins of mine once did the sums and claimed it was only two thirds of that—someone was bound to have fainted. Someone would have keeled over and not come round, exciting rumours that they had died. Nosy folk would crane their necks to gawp at the stretcher-bearers, until new lights flickered at one end of the stadium, where whoops and wild cries announced that the foxes had arrived.

I went downstairs, so any screams of pain and smells of burning flesh were less likely to reach me.

I tried not to imagine how the terrified, wriggling foxes would have been grabbed, grappled, fastened down and encumbered with the torches that were tied to their beautiful brushes. I tried to blot out thoughts of their agony, as flames were given to those torches, then as the foxes bounded free, men whistled and yelled, driving them away from the temple, running headlong down the lower slopes to the great valley of the Circus, headed off, herded in through the starting gates, shocked by the cruel uproar their arrival caused, and then subjected to slaughter amidst screams of delight from the crowd.

Then, only those of us with compassion in our souls understood it was a cause for shame. And every year I wondered, was not living decently supposed to be a gift to humans from the generous goddess Ceres?

XXXIII

Next morning was the thirteenth day of April, the Ides. It was a long day for me, and in due course I was to see that it was the pivotal point of my enquiries. It was also my birthday, although when I woke in the morning I had forgotten about that. When you live alone, all days are equal.

It began mundanely. A domestic day. I made life hell for the boy who swept the stairs, the water carrier, the lamp provider and Rodan. Supervision of lacklustre male staff is the traditional role of a Roman woman, in a business, on a farm, in the home. We hold the keys. We organise the rota. We know where to lay hands on equipment when it is needed. We keep things running smoothly, while the half-baked and the blatantly bone-idle mess about. Men are convinced they run the Empire. The Empire would collapse without us.

Throwing my weight around perked me up. I then changed the covers on my bed, sorted my wardrobe, tidied my jewellery box. I went to the baths, scrubbed myself harder than usual, layered on moisturising oils, let a girl arrange my hair exotically, invested in a manicure, let myself be lured into a pedicure as well, had some over-due depilatory work done, and slowly relaxed.

Prisca appeared. "I've heard all about those murders you're involved with!"

"Ah, word has got out now?"

"I'll say! When are you going to catch him?"

If I knew that, I thought glumly, I would be out putting a neck-collar on the bastard right now. The bathhouse owner did not want to hear me speaking reason. Public hysteria was now rife and according to Prisca there were hundreds of victims. For once, I felt a mild sympathy with Manlius Faustus for having wanted to keep this epidemic of deaths a secret.

The killer was a mad poet, I was curious to learn. He had a grudge against anyone born on Thursdays, whom he stabbed with specially made silver stilettos. Prisca had been told this nonsense by an ointment-seller on Lupin Street whose nephew worked in the tax office.

"Are you telling me murderers are notorious for not turning up to be taxed?" I scoffed. "And I suppose he has a harelip, a crooked toe and his star sign is Aquarius? Oh, come off it. None of the victims had a stab wound, Prisca. I think he must use poison." I decided right at that moment. His weapon was too small to inflict noticeable damage; he must use a small piercing device of some sort and coat it with a deadly paste like that used on hunters' arrows. The poison was what eventually finished off the victims. But it was not the same as hunters used, because theirs paralysed before death and we had no reports of that. All we knew was that it must be swift-acting.

"Poison!" Prisca rushed off, brimming over with excitement that she had a chance to tell other people something new.

By this evening, the mad murderer would have a golden alabastron containing a deadly potion made by Cappadocian dwarfs from a recipe handed down through thirty generations, to which there was no antidote except moonbeams, and he would identify himself by etching a Greek letter onto the foreheads of all his victims as they twitched and gasped their last. The Omega Killer had been born, and it was my fault.

I slipped into a clean tunic and laced shoes, then disappeared from the baths to apply myself to proper enquiries.

When evidence is sparse, you have to dig, dig, dig away at what little you have. Once again, I trudged to the apartment of Laia Gratiana and attempted to see her maid, the elusive Venusia.

They had set their hearts on disappointing me. This time I was told that Venusia was no longer there. She had been sent away "for a rest" to one of her mistress's estates in the country. I could not tell whether this was a disguised punishment, or a reward for good service. In a week when her mistress was taking part in an important festival, it seemed odd that anyone on Laia's staff whose duties involved such personal care should leave Rome. What woman lets her maid vanish the very moment she herself will be on public display at ceremonies in the Circus Maximus? Come to that, what maid wants to miss such an occasion? The chance of receiving a festival thank-you present, or better still a cash-in-hand gratuity, must be hard to pass up.

Apart from the usual reluctance to allow me indoors, the situation at Laia's apartment did not favour casual visitors today. During the Cerialia it was a custom in plebeian high society to issue dinner invitations to other swanks. Laia Gratiana and her brother were to host a large dinner party that evening, so the entrance was full of flustered slaves wielding long poles to sweep spiders' webs from the ceiling and plaster cornices, while others sponged the floor at the same time, causing everyone to be at risk of falling off stepladders, slipping on the wet marble, or having a pole land on their heads. Meanwhile a bunch of effete contractors were mincing around with dining-room decorations and having a quarrel with a steward about their bill.

When somebody screamed, "Who sat on the poppies and the wheat-ear crowns?" I thought it time to leave.

It was the wrong time of year for poppies. Even wheat, that other traditional symbol of Ceres, would be at planting stage, not harvest. The items must be fakes.

The professional decorators ("thematic banquet designers' as they called themselves) had had an exciting idea of using snakes, like the twin serpents that pulled Ceres' chariot as she searched for Proserpina, her kidnapped daughter. Nobody of taste and social standing wants live snakes in their lovely home, so fake ones had been created by a tousle-haired young man who enjoyed crafts.

Oh dear.

Nevertheless I made an attempt to talk to him, helping him lay out his structures, which I admired politely because I knew he would be desperate for approval and nobody else would have troubled. We had a conversation about making the display floats for military triumphs. We talked about the Cerialia chariot, which would have even larger snakes. I asked about his hopes for the future. I wrote down his name on a note tablet in case I could ever put a commission his way. At least, I said that was the reason.

Then I told him I myself felt a little rebuffed and a great deal frustrated because of the Venusia problem. And he told me he had overheard somebody mention that she had gone to Aricia, where there was an ancient shrine to Ceres.

Too far to travel, unfortunately. Still, it might be handy to know.

I needed to be cheered up by seeing Andronicus. I badly wanted to be chased around a small room by a man with a determined gleam in his eye.

I went to the aedile's office, but a public slave who was very slowly picking up leaves in the courtyard told me nobody was there. I left the slave collecting his leaves individually, then placing them in a bucket one by one as if they were very thin-shelled eggs.

I could ask for Andronicus at the aedile's house. He was a free citizen. His friends could call round. I had never been closely involved with a freedman before, but surely that was one point of being freed? A freedman's friend might have to go in through a side entrance, but visiting him was surely possible . . .

I decided against. Manlius Faustus remained an unknown quantity and I felt diffident about straying too close. But the idea was tempting. Worm my way into somebody's house? I tried not to imagine members of my family urging me to do it. Hades, I had been trained to take that kind of risk as an informer.

XXXIV

I met him. Io Saturnalia!

That light frame and his thick, swept-back hair gave me a pang. Andronicus came jauntily along the Street of the Armilustrium, swinging a small glass flagon on a leather string from his left wrist. It looked like a bath-oil jar. I met him as I returned homewards in a grumpy mood, which instantly lightened. He conducted a farce about pretending he couldn't remember knowing me. I lapped it up, overjoyed by his happy silliness.

We then kissed cheeks, with extreme formality, to respect our position in public on a main street. His breath felt warm and tantalising on my face. He nuzzled around me, not touching, just growling under his breath with suppressed desire. It drove me wild, as he intended.

We walked.

He had lost his beard. The effect was not too striking because it had been so light-coloured, never hiding his features; to begin with, I didn't even notice the difference, but he was conscious of it. They had had a cull of facial hair, he said. Even though the rites of Ceres were famously Greek, Faustus had ordered patriotic Roman clean-shaven chins all round. A barber had even been specially brought in to scrape everyone.

"Even Tiberius?"

"Even the bristly kitchenmaid. Albia, you wouldn't recognise Tiberius."

Andronicus said that Manlius Faustus expected everyone in his household to be spruced up every evening, to attend as a group whatever festival ceremonies he organised. They were all on show. There could be no skiving.

"Dutiful support?"

"Showing off how rich he is by the size of his retinue!" complained my friend. "Most of the others are stupidly thrilled because he hands out free tickets. Of course he does. If an aedile can't pack the Circus seats with his own people cheering him, what's the point of the job? I'd like to bunk off and see you sometime, but any absence will be noted and reported to him by some mean spy in the cringing entourage."

"Don't get into trouble on my account, Andronicus."

"You are so sweet!"

Not sweet; diplomatic. Andronicus' well-being mattered and I had some self-interest. I did not want Manlius Faustus to decide I was luring one of his staff away from proper duties. I had not even met this man, yet I felt we had a prickly relationship.

I told Andronicus how pleased I was to have found him by chance today. Perhaps foolishly, I mentioned how I had toyed with visiting his home and asking to see him. As usual, my mischievous friend immediately picked up this rash suggestion. He said the aedile's house was close nearby, so he would take me there at once and show me round.

Of course it could be a bad idea. And I fell for it.

Why do I take such risks? Well, if nothing else, my Aventine granny would have been proud of me. As I said in connection with Salvidia's funeral, Junilla Tacita seized any opportunity to inspect her neighbour's houses. An aedile's home? Thrills! She would expect me to check the sheets for moth holes and run a finger along shelves, looking for dust.

XXXV

In Rome, the homes of the great are as well-protected from intrusion as it is possible to be. They have high walls, no windows on the exterior, the most hostile door porters in the world, and often troops of taciturn guards from strange overseas provinces, in charge of snarling dogs who also don't respond to Latin—or not unless someone orders "Kill!" They all know that one. In daylight at least, these houses are also notoriously chock-a-block with inquisitive outsiders, invited in for a look around by members of the staff. In a house of this status, everyone thinks they are a cheeky slave in a play. Kitchen hands' out-of-work brothers-in-law lounge around the storerooms, pinching commodities. Maids' giggling friends come and try out the beds, still warm from members of the family. Factotums are pitifully keen to ingratiate themselves with people they drink with at fish restaurants on Fridays. Even the snootiest stewards love a chance to impress; fine fellows who claim to have been trained in etiquette at some minor villa owned by a relation of Julius Caesar's can easily be inveigled into showing off to total strangers the mansion where they work. It's a sad fact that only when a hardworking informer has a genuine reason to call at one of these places does entry seem difficult.

Manlius Faustus and his uncle were bound to have forbidden casual visits. But I knew they were probably resigned to it happening.

They lived on the western side of the Hill, close to the main bank of warehouses they owned. They were in the triangle of large properties that lay to the west of the Street of the Plane Trees, so they were close to Laia Gratiana and Marcia Balbilla; it was clearly an enclave of plebeian aristocracy. Tullius owned half a block of typical urban mansion, of some grandeur, with an atrium just inside the main door, beyond which your eyes were drawn to an enclosed garden. A typical formal vista. Sightlines developed to impress.

All the public rooms were placed directly beside the entrance. People came here on business, probably on a daily basis. Only the few who were permitted close intimacy with the masters would ever penetrate as far as private snugs and bedrooms. I sensed that plenty of those existed, off discreet downstairs corridors and upstairs on a second floor. In a city where most people lived crammed against other people's halitosis and smelly armpits, the lucky occupants here had space.

Andronicus marched straight in through the double front doors, which opened at the top of a couple of marble steps, each tread adorned with standard rose trees in matching urns. An elderly porter, who had probably lived there for years, put out his head from a cubicle; he looked surprised, but made no objection to me being brought indoors by the archivist. Perhaps he thought I had come about ink supplies, though I doubt it.

Just inside the atrium was a lararium, a family shrine against a wall, with signs that the household gods were tended daily with offerings. The flowers and wheat cakes looked fresh. "Tullius," said Andronicus. I nodded; it would not be the first time a man who showed casual disrespect to women gave heavy reverence to the gods. As head of the household, he would make the offerings himself. He would call himself "an old-fashioned traditionalist." I bet if I met him I would want to thrust his old-fashioned attitudes down his old-fashioned throat before he had time to say what a pretty little backside I had, and feverishly make a grab for it. I hoped we would not run into him.

I was led around the main areas, feeling nervous. There was an inside dining room, with convenient kitchen areas to the right-hand side of the garden. Salons with seating and a few display cases for statuettes lay on another side, along with a small library; there was no time for me to pull out scrolls and see what authors they read. Everywhere was decorated with wall frescos that had been painted in the not too distant past, as if they had a routine maintenance programme. I suppose I expected pornographic scenes, though if they existed I saw none. It was all minor myths, stylised architectural views and pleasant garlands, well executed but in unexciting colour schemes.

Where the aedile lived with his uncle was neat, and not particularly ostentatious. You could tell they had money, but the money was used with a light hand, so the place had simple elegance. I was surprised by its calm atmosphere. This house was well run, in a casual way that I found rather remarkable. Even though I was uninvited, I soon felt comfortable. The easygoing mood did not fit the antagonism I had witnessed between Andronicus and Tiberius, or the sharp way Andronicus spoke about the aedile and his uncle; still, that shows how human nature can fester, even in a good environment.

Andronicus had asked a serving boy to bring us refreshments in the garden. As a family freedman, he could order himself snacks; as his guest, I just kept trying to look as if I had come about stationery and Andronicus was trying to persuade me to give them a bulk discount. We established ourselves on a bench, with a little portable table carrying man-size cups and miniature dishes, as if we owned the house.

I never ascertained if Tullius was on the premises. The young master definitely was at home, I was told. After his late night running the festival, the aedile was still dead asleep in his bedroom; given that he had more to do this evening and for several nights to follow, nobody was disturbing him. To know he was so close gave me an odd feeling, though Andronicus seemed unfazed by any thought that Faustus might emerge, yawning.

It is always intriguing to see someone at home when you have only met them outside before. Here, Andronicus was the most relaxed I had ever known him. He lost that spiky, restless edge. Occasionally a slave would pass, giving him a nod and a quiet greeting. He returned it, seeming on good terms with all of them.

I was pleased. I liked to know he could be like this.

Soon we were talking avidly. Naturally our conversation turned to the aedile, when I made it plain I felt shy being in his house without his knowledge or permission. "So does he always lie in until lunchtime? Is he exhausted by organising the festival?"

"In fairness, the Cerialia has meant a lot of work for him." It was probably the first time Andronicus had ever shown such understanding when talking about Faustus. "He has never been used to working hard. It matters so much to him that he comes out of it well, and he has been a bit off-colour."

"Nerves?"

"Not him. But he is desperate to look brilliant."

"So what was it like last night?"

"Oh you know, the usual. A lot of parading in white, hymns, torches, complicated rituals performed inaudibly on special altars."

"Fun with the gods."

"Fannying with the female college—they bag most of the ceremonies. Unless they want to be Vestal Virgins, women have no other chance to be domineering priestesses."

"Laia Gratiana loves it?"

"And behaves as if she leads the cult—since she is currently single, she's deluding herself. The chief priestess of Ceres is always a wife, and fertile, to enhance the myth of everything in abundance. Having twins is good—triplets is better; triplets who all survived the birth is a clincher."

"Though somewhat rare! That's the old biddy we saw the other night in the temple?"

"The same. 'A mature woman from a good family,' or rather, a bad-tempered old bat who can't remember her lines in the ceremonies because her wellborn brain is going. Gratiana always pushes forwards to help her, but last night was demoted among the ranks all prancing like ancient Greeks."

I had been to this kind of festival. "Give a cult devotee a big flaming torch and she'll just adore pointing it at something in a ritual manner."

Andronicus did a hilarious mime for me. "Terrible posing and slow-motion solemnity. *Really* embarrassing dances by young people who had been made to dress up in fake Hellenic costumes. Horrible little playlets, with truly gruesome dialogue."

"Oh, you had a good time then!" I grinned and Andronicus snorted.

"Yes, I had a good time." He was obviously waiting for me to question the statement, but I teasingly refused.

We were silent for a moment. I was enjoying the bread that had been supplied with our refreshments. It was a good, fresh, crusty loaf torn up into its eight portions and served in a basket lined with a crisp white napkin. It came with a small silver platter of cheese which, unless I was mistaken, had been made by Metellus Nepos, Salvidia's stepson. I was sure I recognised the flavours, though sadly there was none of the smoked cheese; perhaps Tiberius had devoured it all. At least tragedy had brought Nepos custom.

The thought struck me that since this appeared to be the only enclosed garden in the house, it must be where Cassiana Clara had lingered that night she came here to dinner with Viator. I tried to imagine the place, lit by a few oil lamps flickering along the colonnades. There were festoons of jasmine where sparrows played, small statues of young dryads and a bubbling fountain that actually worked. It would make a pleasant place to hide away—though not if you then had some kind of unfortunate encounter. She had. I was certain now.

I noted that if Clara had cried out in distress, people in the dining room would easily have heard her and come running to assist. A few strides would have brought Viator, angry that in some way his young wife had been affronted. I visualised how he must have strode out here, slung that muscled arm around Clara and steered her back to a couch for the dessert course, the flautist and her polite conversation with Faustus about music . . .

"What really made Cassiana Clara so upset?" I asked. "From talking to her, she clearly was."

Andronicus looked startled. "Why do you ask?"

"Mild curiosity."

"She's a silly girl."

"All girls are silly. I was silly myself once. She comes from a sheltered environment, she's young, she is probably easily bored by long conversations about retail space and storage conditions."

"Personally," Andronicus joked, "I can never get enough of the iugerum-to-denarius ratio, and the free flow of air currents for optimal mould prevention."

I loved his sense of humour. "You're giving me a fine glimpse of the breakfast dialogue in this home."

"You're right. From early dawn, one is expected to enjoy a symposium on underfloor granary aeration, with the latest anxieties about mice and beetle damage. Tullius is a *very* successful warehouse owner, Albia."

"It's gained him a lovely house to hold beetle symposiums in . . . So," I persisted, "what did happen when Clara was bored with the space-to-hire-cost ratio?"

Andronicus shrugged. "As I said, I found her here and talked to her, aiming to cheer her up if I could. Hard work, I must say! When I could see it was making her uneasy to be on her own with someone, of course I quit the scene."

"Perfect manners," I murmured. I had not found Cassiana Clara hard to talk to, even now she was grieving, but I was a woman.

He pretended to preen. "I didn't go for her anyway."

"Would that have made a difference?"

"Why not?" he demanded lightly. I felt a lurch in the pit of my stomach, but reminded myself he was a man. Surely he had no idea this caused me a pang of jealousy? Or maybe he did know. What he said next came as a shock. "Faustus must have come along immediately afterwards, when she was still moping alone, and could not believe his luck."

"Faustus?"

"He lives here, you know!"

"But 'couldn't believe his luck,' Andronicus?"

"He grabbed. She screamed. Out rushes everybody, her maddened husband in the lead."

"Hey, steady on for a moment! . . ." I had to readjust. This was a possibility that had never occurred to me. Up until now I had not imagined the supposedly priggish aedile as a man who would set upon a young female visitor to his home, let alone when her husband was toying with the nuts and peaches dessert course only a few yards away.

"The girl was to blame," said Andronicus.

"Why? All Cassiana Clara did was put herself in the wrong place briefly, while she needed a breather from a stultifying dinner."

I could accept Clara was inexperienced enough to have secretly been excited by an older man mildly flirting (any aedile must be thirty-six by the rules, against her nineteen, a significant difference). But anything serious would have shocked and alarmed her, I was sure. She would not have known how to handle it. Anyway, she was devoted to Julius Viator—unless her devotion now was guilt after the event.

"She wound him up." I stiffened instinctively, at which Andronicus immediately dropped the hard attitude. "Oh, just testing! I realise you are bursting to accuse me of every kind of masculine hypocrisy, dear Albia. You are quite right. A woman should be able to sit by herself in the garden of a private house—"

"Or anywhere!" I snarled.

"Without every hot-blooded male who spots her taking it as an open signal to stick his prick in."

"You're saying Manlius Faustus is the same lousy type as his uncle?"

Andronicus just pulled a face and left me to think as I chose.

I put this in context with what Tiberius had told me about the aedile's old affair. Imagine it: back then, Faustus, when left alone with his patron's trophy brooch-buster, assumed the beauty was there for the taking. "She offered. He took," Tiberius had said. But presumably that woman liked and wanted his attention.

For some reason, I suddenly felt I would like to ask Tiberius for his opinion about this story of Cassiana Clara's assault.

"You can imagine the furore when the silly thing started yelling. The girl was to blame," repeated Andronicus, matter-of-factly. Then he said, "So you know, Albia, there is a good reason to say it was Faustus who got his revenge by taking out Viator afterwards—revenge for spoiling his fun and showing him up."

XXXVI

"Took out *Viator*?" I drew a sharp breath. "You are accusing *Faustus* of killing the fur magnate? Oh come on! Let me remind you, Andronicus, last time you had anything to say about this, you pointed to Tiberius."

"Yes, I do seem rather changeable." He smiled, unabashed. I had a weakness for his pretended amoral streak. A girl likes the unpredictable. Then he explained, "Fact is, Albia, something happened last night that made me see things differently."

"What? What happened? What did you find out?"

Andronicus leaned back, with his hands linked behind his ginger-brown head. I had never been in any doubt he enjoyed being the sole focus of my attention. I hoped it did not make him exaggerate for effect. "Something happened after the horse race."

I took myself in hand, playing calm. "Tell me."

"Come on. You are excited. Admit it."

"I am excited. Now show me whether you are a full player or your dice box is empty, you abominable tease."

Andronicus, who had as usual been picky about the food we were brought, now stopped to take a slice of cheese and savour it. What he was really revelling in was the suspense. I let him.

"My dice box is never empty." He had a way of speaking sometimes that could sound over-serious. But he gazed at me with his confiding expression. I grew up watching people who worked in a close, loving partnership, and his manner at that moment gave me a warm feeling of promise for our own relationship. People ought to work like this.

"Oh come on, friend!"

He leaned forwards confidingly. "This is it. At the end of last night's proceedings there was a big social shock. A gathering had been arranged at the chief priestess's house; Faustus went, naturally. A lot of our people had to go home, but I managed to get taken along." I couldn't help thinking wistfully that that was the moment when Andronicus could have escaped and come to see me. But one must not be selfish. "We all trooped to the old woman's house, where we mingled in a stilted fashion with spiced wine and oatcakes, most people wishing they had not bothered to go. Faustus was lapping up compliments, but the night had taken a toll; he looked about finished. Then it happened. While people were beginning to drop out and leave, Laia Gratiana actually came up and spoke to Faustus."

I blinked. "From what I know, that must have startled everyone."

"Especially him! Normally they would ignore each other. It was the kind of do where she could easily have kept out of his way. She hates him. He can't bear to deal with her. Yet she marched up and confronted him without any foreplay. He, poor dog, did not know where to look!"

"So what did Laia want?"

"A word with him—*in private!*"

I sucked my teeth. "That's annoying."

"Trust me, Albia."

"You bug! You listened?"

"I was not going to miss it. You would have been in there with me."

"Oh I would!"

"You would have had to disguise yourself as a small bay tree, but fortunately the planting pots where I was obliged to lurk were large."

"And?"

"He said, *'This is a surprise!'* She said, *'Shut up and listen. I just wondered if you had realised who Venusia was.'* Annoyingly, he then—

the bastard—only said, *'Surely not* that *Venusia?'* Anybody would think he knew I was watching."

If he was at all alert, there was a good chance Manlius Faustus suspected Andronicus was spying on him. Any of his staff might do it. In Domitian's Rome, this was inevitable, whether or not people really had secrets. In fact, to stand near any plant tub or statue when you could not see behind it was extremely foolish. Some would say even laurel leaves had ears these days.

"So Faustus knows something about Venusia, even if he has to be reminded by Laia? *She* thinks it so important she has broken her fierce ten-year vow of Faustus-avoidance?" My mind was racing. "Andronicus, Venusia was the other maid, that time Marcia Balbilla's girl was attacked in the Vicus Altus."

Andronicus whistled quietly.

"And we do know what she once did to Faustus," he corrected me.

"You found out?"

"Oh I learned a lot from their merry banter, Albia. Details I have wanted to know for years. Apparently he may be a moraliser now but he was degenerate then. I finally discovered what happened to end their marriage."

"So?" I asked cautiously.

"Fortunately, Laia Gratiana is the type who likes to be theatrical when she has a chance to wallow in unpleasantness. *'Yes, Faustus. Venusia—who, when you had your filthy affair with that terrible woman, loyally came and told me.'* To which he could only answer, *'Oh!'* His repartee is extraordinarily tedious."

I swung my legs out, kicking my feet restlessly.

"Well, that's interesting, but I fail to see why it makes you say Faustus may have killed Ino."

"Don't you see—wrong maid!"

"What?"

"Faustus knows perfectly well it was Venusia who broke up his marriage. Naturally he has never forgiven her for snitching. Who would? He intended to get his revenge by killing her, but seen from behind, two maids all wrapped up in stoles look identical. Suppose instead of each following her own mistress as you would expect, they had inconveniently swapped places?"

"With a group of people going along together in a bunch, it can easily happen," I agreed.

"Yes—so he attacked Ino by mistake."

"Good theory. But it's guesswork. How can you be sure they swapped positions?"

"I can't," agreed Andronicus. "But I bet if you ask any of the survivors, they will confirm I'm right."

I had another reason to believe it. "That could explain something I learned today: Laia has sent Venusia off to the country. I thought it peculiar, but not if it is for protection. So could the two maids be misidentified? I wonder what Venusia looks like?"

"An old Greek gargoyle."

"You know her?"

"Seen her with Laia at the temple."

Andronicus was probably exaggerating and anyway, the marriage ended ten years ago. I thought it was unlikely Faustus had ever taken much notice of his wife's maid. He might well fail to recognise her now.

"She's gone away to save her skin, in case he goes after her again." Andronicus was definite. "Do you know where they have sent her?"

"No, I don't. Look, killing a maid who betrayed him would be rather obvious—and also rather late in the day, don't you think? Ten years later?" I heard myself becoming stern. "I have to say that this is a far-fetched theory, Andronicus. For a man in his position to go around causing people's deaths is—"

"Feasible, if he's crazy."

"You live in his house. Is he crazy?"

"Why do you think," explained Andronicus gently, "I have always been so keen to keep you away from him?"

I smiled back into his loving eyes.

"But are you suggesting Faustus was responsible for the other deaths as well?" I asked, struggling to keep to business, while Andronicus kept being affectionate. "Salvidia, for instance?"

"He knew about Salvidia causing the little boy's death. He hated that. He put up the wall poster calling for witnesses."

"I thought that was Tiberius."

"Did it or did it not have Faustus' name on it? I seem to remember you coming to our office asking for him, Albia."

I nodded. "All right. Suppose in that instance, the aedile took his role as a public official way too far. He hated Salvidia causing a child's death through negligence, so instead of just fining her company, he took it upon himself to impose harsh justice. But what happened with the old lady? Celendina had done nothing to upset him."

"Ah, that I don't know. There must be a reason. We simply have not seen it yet. Maybe that son you mentioned really did for her . . . As for the oyster boy," Andronicus rushed on, hopping in ahead of me, "Faustus often buys special provisions. He loves his food. He enjoys oysters and is particular who supplies them. He must have gone to that stall and somehow the lad annoyed him."

It was routine for heads of household to shop for the home in that way. Men, particularly, saw themselves as retail experts. Killing a boy who, say, shucked his oysters incorrectly seemed unlikely, but once you start thinking that someone is crazy, normal rules fail. Andronicus was right about that. We all struggle to identify motives, yet killers are a feckless, inconsistent breed.

This was bizarre. Here I was, sitting in the man's house without his knowledge, while one of his staff attempted to prove to me that he was a serial murderer. Andronicus seemed almost blasé about it. I was increasingly uncomfortable.

"We had decided," I demurred, "the killer must live in the area where the deaths, or at least the attacks on victims, all occurred."

Andronicus shrugged. "Lives nearby—or works?"

He was right. Sited beside the Temple of Ceres, the aediles' office was right there.

I watched a slave, burdened with a large tray of silverware, including bowls with crisp napkins like the ones we had had, walk along the upper balcony as if taking this to one of the bedrooms. The boy was staggering. He had to steady himself against a column. That was an important tray.

I jumped to my feet. "I can't sit here discussing him. I'm going home."

Andronicus asked, almost excitedly, "Are you frightened of the man?"

"No." Perhaps I should be. Informers have to look tough, however. "I don't want him to pop out from his room and see us analysing what he may have done. It's premature. We have to assemble evidence that connects him to the crimes. Most of what you have said could equally apply to your old suspect, Tiberius."

Not the maid, though. The maid destroyed the Faustus marriage. Taking revenge on her gave a motive for murder only to Manlius Faustus.

Andronicus followed up my suggestion. "And you are no doubt thinking it's Tiberius who is regularly out on the streets."

I had not progressed that far, but I nodded.

"Think about this. Yes, Tiberius is sent out under cover, but don't be misled. You know what Faustus is like. He wants to conduct his job better than any aedile ever. The one thing anyone must say for him is that he does not sit on his togate backside in the office, waiting for news. He makes himself familiar with what happens in his area."

"Knows his own patch?"

Andronicus clapped his hands. "Exactly."

"He gets out there? He knows places like the Vicus Altus and Lesser Laurel Street? He regularly walks in the Trigeminal Porticus?"

"He goes to the Porticus to buy Rutupiae oysters. Thinks them much tastier than Lucrine."

Andronicus was starting to convince me. All the more reason to vanish from here. I repeated that I was going home, and this time did gather myself to leave.

I was not surprised when Andronicus decided that he would come with me. And, with a lift of the heart, I knew how he intended that to end. Even in public, he made that obvious. When we left the house and walked together, he had us entwined like lovers on their way to bed.

XXXVII

From the Street of the Plane Trees, it was a shorter distance to Fountain Court from the Tullius and Faustus house than from the other side of the hill, and my previous visits to the Temple of Ceres area. Even this stroll gave some reflection time.

I rarely feel triumphal when I may have identified a wrongdoer. More often, it seems such a waste. The cleverer a criminal, the more that applies.

Andronicus and I did not speak much. He had his mind fixed on lovemaking, as if discussing death held an erotic charge. Although pleasure had its attractions for me, which on any other occasion would have been urgent, I was lost in the case temporarily. It was not a moment for collaboration. I was not even sure I wanted that. At a critical juncture, I prefer to mull over enquiries on my own. Although Andronicus and I were close, his method of jumping to immediate conclusions every time there was a twist did not fit mine. I dwell on results. I go back and test all the clues and facts, in case of mistakes or missing links. What's more, I do it when I am ready. For me that afternoon, being silent only meant I was clearing my brain in readiness for when I *did* ponder. I wanted to sit alone on my own couch in a silent room, a cup of wine untouched beside me, a note tablet in my lap.

Well, that was how I would tackle the enquiry later, after Andronicus and I had fallen into each other's arms and spent delicious time together . . . I was human.

Two things worked their way to the front of my consciousness right then. I needed to ask Cassiana Clara to confirm if, that night at dinner, Manlius Faustus assaulted her. If he did, it was a clincher.

I wanted to ask Laia Gratiana's maid Venusia about Faustus too. Specifically: how had she known about his affair and what (if it wasn't simply her unpleasant character) drove her to say something? Was it really loyalty to Laia? A true friend might have kept the young wife in the dark and tried to preserve her happiness—or, if you are cynical about marriage, preserve it for as long as possible.

One idea I now developed was this: while Faustus and Laia were wed, had he dallied with the maid? Plenty of husbands make a grab for the wife's attendants. Venusia might have enjoyed his covert attentions, even convinced herself she was special; she would then have hated him starting an affair elsewhere, so she snitched to her mistress as an act of spite, a thwarted lover herself.

As I walked with Andronicus, I asked whether Faustus might do that. Andronicus claimed the man was notoriously fresh with female slaves. According to him, when Manlius Faustus visited other houses, people knew he was a risk and took steps to keep their good-looking girls out of his way.

"He is not the only man in Rome who has that reputation," Andronicus concluded.

"Agreed. But you are making him out to be very different from all I have heard before. Didn't you yourself once tell me he never even lays a finger on the girl who makes his bed? I hope you are not embroidering!"

"His bedroom slave is a boy, come to think of it," Andronicus replied gravely. "I never do sewing. Even when we need to have papyrus lengths stitched together in the archive office, I delegate."

"Nothing wrong with needlework," I disagreed, smiling. "It's not as dainty as people think. Stabbing the cloth, you have to use a lot of force sometimes."

"Really?"

The embroidery nonsense filled time while we moved from the end of the alley to the Eagle Building, where we were so ready to rip our clothes off and fall on each other. Even I had regained my interest. Instead, at the entrance we met an agitated Rodan.

"Oh thank the gods, Albia—I can't deal with this! It's an animal! It's on the stairs. Nobody can get past. Somebody has to get rid of it."

The great lump was nearly in tears, he was so upset at having to catch and remove a wild creature that had entered the building. I supposed it was a rat or even a mouse. Even when supplied with mousetraps, our janitor was too squeamish to empty them. He brought them to me.

"Calm down, Rodan."

When I came home with a lover, I did not want to find a domestic emergency. It looks bad. It wastes time. It spoils the mood. So, yes, I was furious. Rodan was so used to people being annoyed, he barely noticed.

Andronicus was openly chuckling. "What is this thing, an escaped lion?"

"You're a gladiator, Rodan," I grumbled. "Find a spear and deal with it." I knew Rodan had never killed anything. Faced with a serious predator, he would expire himself, of cowardice. Fortunately we did not live in the kind of area that was constantly beset with exotic pets escaping from wealthy people's show-off menageries.

Rodan passed me a broom. Accepting it, I assumed responsibility. He made the broom a baton in some kind of relay race, the wild beast sprint. I had to run with the problem now.

I cursed. With Andronicus excitedly jostling at my shoulder, I shoved past Rodan, who fled into his cubicle, covering his ears until it was over. I entered the lobby. At first I saw and heard nothing. Then came disorderly scrabbling sounds. As I inched up the first stairs, a terrible sight lay ahead. A vixen used in last night's ritual had survived the Circus and escaped. Horrifically burned in the hindquarters, she had dragged herself partway over the Aventine and into our building. Although she had managed to shed the torch they tied to her, the damage was dire: the exhausted creature had almost no tail, her flesh was charred, her long back legs hung useless.

She lay cowering in a corner of the first landing. Her amber eyes were dull and full of dread. As I approached, she struggled as best she could, too weak even to spit or snarl.

"Stop. Don't go near!" Andronicus made a grab for me.

I could see why Rodan was so upset. It was my turn to become hysterical. "What can we do? We must help her!"

"She cannot be saved, Albia. It's hopeless."

"I must put her out of her misery then. I can't leave her like this!"

The scene worsened, as the African children who lived on the first floor heard our voices and looked out of their door, where they must have been hiding. Now that there were adults to pay them attention, they started screaming. They were spooking the vixen. They were spooking me. I directed them to go indoors, but they only screamed louder.

"Right. Stand back." Andronicus took control. He was wonderful. I was a jelly. Every time the pathetic fox quivered and jerked, panic swept through me. I hid my face in my hands, hardly able to look, and could hear myself whimpering. While I dithered, Andronicus was assessing the situation. "This will not be easy . . ." He took the broom from me. "Go back down to Rodan. Fetch me a decent knife. Find me something—go, Albia!"

Fighting sobs, I obeyed. I would have fetched one of my own knives, but could not pass the wounded animal to reach either my apartment or the office. Behind me I heard Andronicus sternly ordering the children back indoors; this time the subsiding noise indicated the little ones obeyed.

Part of me was prepared to tackle the wounded vixen myself, part was relieved that although he clearly did not like it, Andronicus was willing to take over.

It took a long time to make Rodan come up with a suitable knife. He was unhappy about me going inside his smelly cubicle, and when I shouldered my way past him, he seemed unable to remember where he kept things. He had so few possessions it was easy to see most of them. Some had started out belonging to other people, by the looks of it. The rest was junk. Cracked pots and flywhisks with no feathers. A lumpy mattress. A loincloth hung on an old spear—lacking its head or I would have taken it. Finally, the porter produced a vicious dagger that must pass for dainty dinner-cutlery on rare days when he did not eat with his fingers.

I stumbled back up the stairs. To my huge relief, I found that everything was over.

The vixen lay motionless. Andronicus was leaning against the wall, looking pale and breathing fast. He had dropped the broom on the steps. Everything was silent and still.

"Don't ask." His eyes turned to me with a tired expression. "Don't be upset. She's gone. She passed away, dear tender-hearted one, that's all you need to think about." He stopped me questioning, then held me back from going closer. "She just ran out of strength and stopped breathing, without fear or suffering."

He would not tell me. Perhaps he was right and she simply collapsed from exhaustion and blood loss, or perhaps he had somehow helped her. I suspected he had sent me down to Rodan to get rid of me while he ended her pain.

I felt convinced Andronicus took some action, though could not imagine what. I saw no new marks on the dead animal. He was unarmed. If he had hit her with the broom, it would not have worked and I would have heard the commotion. Besides, my friend lacked that kind of cruelty.

As I hugged him, Rodan came up with a sack to remove the tragic corpse, playing the big man now somebody else had completed the hard task. He bent down to gather the vixen's mangled body, gasping with effort as he doubled up. I looked away. Andronicus shielded me, holding me against his shoulder.

I was still shaking when the porter straightened up, sack in hand. His knees cracked loudly. In a prim voice, he said, "I don't know if you are expecting it, Albia—but your father has sent a carrying-chair to fetch you."

Hades. I *should* have been expecting it. I had quite forgotten. Today was the Ides of April. My compulsory birthday.

XXXVIII

I was in shock over the dead vixen. Otherwise, I might have handled the situation better.

I could have invited Andronicus to come home with me. Why didn't I? Mainly because I had not known him long enough. I still wanted to keep him to myself. As soon as you introduce any friend to your family, they take over. My parents would interrogate him in their separate ways, discreet but determined; my sisters would ask inane questions about us in front of him; even my little brother, a difficult child at the best of times, would stare disconcertingly. We were not ready for that.

Mentioning that it was my birthday seemed unnecessary. I would feel embarrassed. So, looking back, I must have given Andronicus an unfortunate impression that this was a pre-arranged occasion of no great significance, from which I might escape at an early hour. It was only lunchtime now.

"Will you be all right?" he murmured lovingly. I was in a tizzy, which he must have thought was still the fox's fault.

"I shall be with my own folk, don't worry."

"Oh, they will look after her!" Rodan put in, though nobody had asked him. "That Falco is a nasty piece of work, but the rest are quite a nice family in their funny way."

"Thank you, Rodan!" Andronicus seemed more amused by the mixed commendation than annoyed at losing me.

I reassured him that he could dutifully attend the aedile's festival that evening, under no obligation to me. We were no longer in the mood to go to bed together, even if I had been free. The dying vixen had drained our desire. I was distressed and he was disturbed by whatever happened when he was on his own with the fox. It would take a while for either of us to recover.

I apologised for rushing off; he mentioned he might come along to Fountain Court to see me again later. The half-promise was not serious enough for me to mention that my return could be in the early hours.

I was too numb to think clearly. I could still hardly speak.

Andronicus exchanged sweet-talk with me, then sauntered off. He would have seen the chair, with its patient bearers, stood outside waiting. He probably thought if I was summoned in the morning, it would be for a light luncheon and perhaps an afternoon of gossip. I remained shy about explaining that today was my anniversary.

After he left, I went right upstairs to the office to fetch the blue gown on which I had sewn the braid the other day, especially to wear now. It still had the needle in the neck facing, where I had parked it when Andronicus visited. I intended to put away the needle in the bone case that I kept in my sewing box, but maddeningly could not find it. The box was crammed so its contents overflowed if I rummaged too much, and I was hurrying. I assumed I simply failed to see the case, the way you do sometimes even when an object is right in front of you. In the end, I had to stab the needle into a spare end of ribbon. Grabbing the box and the dress, I locked up the office and returned downstairs.

By the time I had made my way back to my apartment, I had become annoyed with myself for bungling. I like to keep equipment neat. I was now in a clumsy state where even putting on earrings was awkward; I could not find the hole in one lobe, which must have been made at an angle and was always elusive when in haste. Once I had changed into the dress and tidied my appearance, I calmed down. Before I left, I upturned the sewing box onto a low table and systematically sorted through its contents, determined not to be beaten. The needle-case was not there.

It could have dropped out on the floor of the office, but I had no time now to return and look. Anyway, I was sure I would have noticed. I hate the feeling something is not right. I particularly hate any hint that someone has tampered with my things. The needle-case was pretty and useful, but not exquisite; the office contained other items to attract a walk-in thief, all perfectly portable. Not many can be bothered to intrude so far up inside a building, with added risks to them at every storey; my apartment downstairs was far more at risk of burglary. So what trickery was this?

Eventually, I was ready to leave, in my blue dress, gold sandals and best earrings, knowing that Mother would comment I was looking tired, as mothers are obliged to do apparently. Tiredness, when it derives from the trials of life, cannot be altered. Nor can a mother be thwarted from looking at you narrow-eyed, even though you know it is her way to show you she cares. The first thing my sisters would shriek would be, "Horrible hair, Albia!" Those two madcaps, Julia and Favonia, would fall on me with combs and ornaments, carrying me off to remedy at least that perceived defect.

Suddenly I wanted to be there. I wanted to be pampered by my sisters and feted as the queen of the day. I wanted familiarity. I would relax—indeed, I was starting to relax already. I would emerge from the girls' patting and primping at once more bright-eyed and fun-loving, and quite willing to enjoy my birthday. I even wanted, marginally, relief from Andronicus, because there is a subtle strain when you are with a new man, whose reactions remain uncertain. With him, I still felt constantly wary.

At home, I could simply be myself. They all knew and happily deplored me. That, as I had learned since my teens, was the point of a family.

Departing, I saw Rodan and demanded, "Have you let anyone up to the office in the past few days without telling me?"

"No." He was bound to say that. Who wants trouble?

"What about the other night? That man called Tiberius was looking for me, with Morellus from the vigiles."

"They came to my cubicle. I knew you weren't here."

"They believed you?"

"Why not?"

"Because anyone who knows you doesn't trust you to remember anything!"

Rodan looked at me and said slowly, "They never went up. They seemed to think they knew where you were that evening. They just danced off somewhere else."

I too spoke more levelly. "Rodan, I think someone has been in my room."

"Not that I know, Albia."

I gave up. "Well, keep your eyes peeled."

Rodan looked sheepish. "Happy birthday, by the way."

"Thank you, Rodan."

Yes, I had a wonderful birthday. My relatives can throw a party. As was traditional, it was so good, darkness fell before I realised. Admittedly bleary, I intended to call up the chair and toddle home, but was delayed at the last minute. Nobody was making good decisions at that point. I was prevailed upon to have a comforting word in private with my little brother.

Postumus was eleven now. We all knew his birth mother, a colourful character who ran a large entertainment company. Thalia might be maternal with baby lions, but had shrunk from ownership of a human child and handed him over to us. There were doubts over his paternity, but the story we all stuck with was that my grandfather had fathered him, just before he died. It was certainly what Grandpa in his vanity had wanted to believe.

My parents took the baby and because he too was adopted, it was always assumed he and I had a special bond. In truth, we shared neither blood nor sympathy. I felt sorry for him in some ways, but if I had to be honest (and I hoped this did not show to Postumus) I could never warm to him. He was none too keen on me either. Mind you, he was no lover of other people. My parents and sisters treated him kindly and fairly, but he endured it with suspicion, aware from the start that his existence obliged my father to share with him, as a half-brother, a major legacy; anyone who loved my father would therefore view Postumus as a cuckoo in the nest. Anyone who saw my pa as a much more wily operator would in fact suspect he only adopted the boy because, as his son, the legacy provision no longer applied . . . That was probably what my brother thought.

Postumus made few friends, within the family or outside, and seemed to enjoy his isolation. He had the kind of personality that makes you think a boy will grow up to be a public torturer. However, he harboured genuine anxieties. He had worried about his security during all his little life. Now, I was told, he felt convinced that his birth mother had her eye on him. He had reached an age when he could be useful to her in her work. Postumus feared she would be coming to claim him (he was a bright child, because not long after this she did).

"Cheer up," I told him, when I was asked to probe and intervene like a big sister. "Then you can be the only boy in history who, instead of running away from home to join a circus, has to run away from a circus to go home."

My brother bestowed on me his most baleful look. I would say he was going through a difficult phase, but with him, one difficult phase simply flowed into the next without a kink. "How would you feel, Albia, if those cabbage-sellers came from Londinium and fetched you back?"

"Trust me, child; life with the Didii has taught me to make exciting decisions. I would run away from the cabbages and become a lion-tamer."

I admitted to myself that I had been drinking wine for so long I might be viewing his unhappiness too flippantly. My brother stomped off, then I was so guilty I felt the need to drink more wine with my parents, who were similarly depressed by their helplessness in handling him. I abandoned any thought of returning to Fountain Court that day. They kept my old room there for me; as on many previous occasions, I stayed overnight.

I did pop home next morning, but only for a flying visit. I needed to pick up things because, at intervals during the party, we had had discussions about work. On the mysterious killings, everyone decided there was only one thing to do next. As relatives do, mine handed me their orders; as you do to avoid arguing, I caved in. So I was being despatched to Aricia where Laia Gratiana had sent her maid, Venusia.

Venusia had to be interviewed. Neither the vigiles nor the aediles' office would ever get around to it and, even if they did, we could be sure they would botch it. Morellus was a deadbeat; Faustus and his runner were implicated. I was not only a neutral party but female. I could bamboozle a maid. Crucially, unlike everybody else, I was efficient. Father would lend me a cart and driver next morning, so I could do it.

Someone I normally thought well of had the bright idea that the sullen one, my brother, could come along on the trip, to take him out of himself.

Thank you, Mother.

XXXIX

Some informers lead different lives from mine. Those big names will be insulted by satirists and historians, but hardly care because they retire on their profits to luxury villas with delicious cliff-top settings above gem-like azure seas. I mean the famous faces who prosecute in notorious court cases. True, they are despicable tools of despotic emperors, but they can balance public loathing against the simple joy of fine working conditions. Their offices are elegant. Discreet staff pad about, carrying silver salvers. Their hours are short and convenient. When they have to travel, assuming an emergency where no agents can be sent on the errand for them, it is in immense style and comfort, all plush litters and an enormous entourage, with many stops for sustenance, which will include vintage wines and potted lobster, served by naked Numidian boys under a demountable canopy. With tassels.

As a one-woman outfit, this was not my way. But for my father stepping in to loan me a ride, I would have been standing at the roadside on the Via Appia, trying to hitch a lift in a haycart. Those haycart drivers are all beasts, believe me.

Instead I was graced with a certain Felix and his mule, Kicker, the deathless team that made up the auction house's secret money-moving cart. This was by definition ramshackle. It had to look fifty years old with a rickety axle, a vehicle so unsophisticated nobody could be using it for anything other than transporting three chickens and a very smelly woolsack. In reality, the axle was well-oiled and the wheels were new. It had a false floor, beneath which lay a reinforced compartment to hold treasure and/or coinage in bulk. Kicker had knock-knees, but if you fed her as much fodder and water as she wanted, she could be a deceptively smooth mover. Felix was the most inappropriate person ever named Happy or Fortunate, living proof that nobody can tell how a babe-in-arms will turn out when they are imposing its lifetime label. We used him because he could be relied on in roadside inns; everyone would shun this glum-face, so he never got sozzled in the wrong company and told prospecting highway robbers he was carrying money. The hens, who had been named by my sisters, were called Piddle, Diddle and Willykins. They were devils for pecking passengers.

Felix collected me from the old laundry, with Postumus already looking unhappy in the cart. Wheeled vehicles were not supposed to work in Rome in daylight hours, but exceptions were made for builders' carts so Felix had long mastered the art of keeping a plank in the back to look legal. I told my brother this was so we had a handy plank with us, ready to lay down across any marshy ground when we stopped on the journey to pee behind a bush. Postumus was horrified; he could not bear teasing.

Some boys would have brought their toy charioteers to play with harmlessly. He had his ferret. It was called Ferret. That was the kind of wild imagination my little brother not only had, but was proud to own.

I asked Felix, who confirmed my fears that ferrets and chickens do not mix. Indeed they don't. We spent the entire trip with Ferret going crazy as he tried to get at the three hens.

I remember visiting Aricia as a young girl. My parents had gone to the shrine of Diana at Nemi, during one of their official top-secret missions. Nobody can talk about some of their mad adventures. My pa won't be able to publish his memoirs for about two thousand years.

When we stayed there before, it was a grim mid-December stopover at a hideous inn. This had given me a poor impression of a place that I now found to be extremely prosperous. As the first staging-post on the well-travelled route between Rome and southern Italy, Aricia was in a prime position to persuade folks to part with cash while they were still in a good mood. Hanging up on the outer rim of the Alban Hills, its climate was airy. Its situation was equally fine, with gorgeous views down a sweet valley that must be an old volcanic crater, views that extended away to the sea in the misty distance. These benefits, combined with its closeness to the city, had drawn many Roman families of good name and even better finances to have second homes in the area. For their culinary delight, rich volcanic soil furnished the market stalls with excellent vegetables, there was a fabulous local dish of pork cooked with fennel, wine was made and the mountain strawberries were justly famous. A further bonus was the start of a three-mile sacred way through the woods to Nemi, with its beautifully sited lakeside shrine to Diana in her role as the goddess of painless childbirth. Fashionable medical services on offer included conception guidance for the freeborn rich, who flocked in droves.

Obviously much advice at this shrine involved intercession with the goddess and prayer, expensive processes to buy, but possibly supplicants were also told, "Have more sex," which made the visit worth the money. I bet it worked too. Nemi certainly had a wonderful reputation, plus an income to match.

My father reckoned if they were bribed an extra fee by the childless, the priests would help out. He's appalling.

But so often right.

At Aricia was a virtually forgotten shrine to Ceres. Also a fertility divinity, although unlike Diana specifically not virginal, Ceres in her wheat-stalk crown was honoured with busts and seated statues, nursing two young children. Abundant motherhood depressed the couples struggling to have babies who came to Nemi, so this shrine

241

was short of benefactors. It lacked all the elegant facilities at Diana's nearby complex.

Nor did being dumped among its dilapidated acolytes hold much appeal for the spinsterish maid of Laia Gratiana. I found her moping. If she had been dumped here for her own safety, she was certainly not grateful.

I had left Felix and our luggage at what I hoped was a different travellers' mansio from the one my parents cursed previously. I had to bring Postumus with me. You can't leave a boy with a ferret on his own at an inn. With his surly, insulting attitude, he was bound to be grabbed by kidnappers in mistake for a consul's son and shipped off to a village in Sardinia. The bandits would be stuck with him, as he complained about the conditions they held him in and criticised their inefficiency at negotiations. We would pay no ransom. The crestfallen gang would end up desperately pleading for us to take my brother off their hands. Worse, Postumus would soon be running the racket, a task that would suit him, but that was no life for a ferret and, as a convinced animal lover, I had to think about Ferret's future.

Postumus said nothing during my interview; even Ferret stayed down inside his tunic and rarely poked his head out. My brother was never any trouble at work. He liked to watch whatever was going on and decide how much better he himself would have done it.

Venusia flapped around, trying to distract me by querying whether my dear little boy would like some fruit juice or a bowl of raisins. Postumus had never been a child who accepted juice from nagging ladies who treated him like a three-year-old. Even when he was actually three, he behaved like an old man, an old man who had several wives buried out under the woodhouse floor with hatchets in their heads. He gave Venusia his stare, the one that asked openly why did this stupid woman not know all he wanted was to be allowed to go into the sacred woods and find a hedgehog to dismember as bloodily as possible?

During their tussle over the juice, I had a chance to look at Venusia. I was shocked that she was no longer a girl. You tend to assume a lady's maid is a young person, whose conversation will be more fun for the lady and who can be bossed about or even beaten; the plaque I had been shown of Marcia Balbilla's had certainly portrayed *her* as youthful. Mind you, Marcia had freely admitted she had that depiction of Ino made more attractive for the salon wall than true-to-life.

Venusia was a woman of a certain age, that age being in my estimate forty-five. Not quite due for retirement (because maids have to flog away for years, patting the pimples of mistresses who are determined never to lose their assistants), but verging on loss of hope, I thought. Andronicus' description of her as a gargoyle went too far, but that was a man's dismissal of any older woman who was no flirty honeycake. She had an awkward body, a face spoiled by a prominent wart, and an uncompromising manner. From what I knew, Laia Gratiana was a match for her, but with other employers Venusia would have been a bully.

I explained I had come to ask about the incident with Ino. Venusia looked hostile. In the usual getting-to-know-you session, I slyly slipped in questions about when Laia and Faustus were married. "What did you think about that?"

"She could have done a lot better."

"You were not keen?"

"I never liked him."

Now I had seen her, I wondered if this was because Faustus for his part had not cared for Venusia? Any young husband may resent a maid who is too close to his wife, exercising an influence on her that he may see as unhelpful to him, especially if he and the wife are none too compatible in the first place. Venusia would be older than Laia by around ten years, possibly first trained by Laia's mother; she was a woman who had been placed in charge of a bride when the bride herself was still a girl. She might have deep-seated bonds to Laia's family that overrode the new bonds she should have to the marriage.

Personally, I would have got rid of her. I don't only mean, if I had been Manlius Faustus. I would have done it if I had been Laia.

I decided immediately that there had been no relationship between Faustus and this woman. Even now, nearly a decade after the divorce, her dark eyes burned with contempt when she mentioned him. Just supposing at some early point she had thought him good-looking and nursed a passion for him, it must have been one-sided and had ended abortively. "I am told you have always been tremendously loyal to your mistress?"

Venusia sneered. "You mean, when he cheated, and I found out, I made sure she knew about it?"

"Yes, I did mean that. *How* did you find out, incidentally?"

"I noticed he was behaving as if he was up to something. I smelled the woman's perfume on him. I marched along and talked to the slaves at the other house. They soon told me."

"So they were fully aware of the illicit goings-on?"

Venusia scoffed. "Of course! You don't think it is ever hidden from the staff? People are fools to believe what they get up to on a couch never gets noticed."

"Oh, people are fools all right! . . . Did Faustus make eyes at anybody else?"

"Not that I know."

"Never?"

"Once was enough. Laia Gratiana was too good to be messed about that way."

"You didn't regard him as a predator? He never made a move on you?"

"You are joking!"

"Believe me, it has been suggested."

"By idiots!"

"Well, he does have supporters. His people make out his affair was a single, stupid mistake."

"Then he did it to the wrong person. She had me to look after her." Even now, Venusia was unforgiving. Laia too, presumably. I wondered how far, then and now, the maid's insistence on punishing Faustus had leached into the wronged wife's perception.

"Venusia, do you think Manlius Faustus blames you for the loss of his marriage?"

"We have nothing to do with him, so I wouldn't care to say." She said it anyway. "But no, I reckon he blames himself. Which is right. It was his own fault."

"So would he be harbouring a grudge against you still?"

"Oh, I don't suppose he likes me!" proclaimed Venusia proudly. "But I don't expect he ever thinks about it."

"He would not be a man to brood over revenge for many years?"

"Hardly!" Again, the woman sneered. "Too much effort. He never had that much staying power."

"A friend of mine suggested Faustus may have intended to harm you, but made a mistake and attacked Ino."

"It's rubbish. Who said that?"

"Someone from the aedile's office."

"Your fancy man!"

"You know Andronicus?" I was startled.

"I do not! I've seen him. The office is right by the temple. We recognise men who work there. I know he goes around with you." The maid sounded scornful. "It's the talk of the place."

I hate being the subject of gossip, though I kept my temper. I felt a strong need to move on. "Well, we were discussing Faustus. Are you frightened of him?"

"I certainly am not."

"So who are you frightened of, Venusia?"

"I am not frightened of anybody."

"Then why," I asked, "are you stuck out here in these thickets, a day's journey from Rome, in a run-down shrine with no passing trade? While your mistress is taking part in the year's most sacred ceremonies and must have a need for you?" There was not a flicker. "Tell me, Venusia, who are you hiding from?"

XL

I don't understand your question!" Venusia was bluffing brazenly. "It is a shrine to Ceres, our goddess. My mistress is a member of the cult of Ceres; she will be the chief priestess one day, mark my words."

I retorted, "She will have to remarry first! . . . This is a distraction, Venusia. I repeat, why are you here?"

"I was very upset over what happened to poor little Ino, so my mistress very kindly sent me here for a while to recuperate."

"Where nobody could get at you?"

"I don't understand."

"Oh, that again! All right." I had no patience with her stubborn resistance. "Tell me facts instead. What happened exactly when Ino was attacked?"

Now the woman showed she felt pressurised; sweat gleamed as she began to mop her forehead. Even so, she coolly described the walk in the Vicus Altus, Ino being jostled hard, and then stumbling—all according to accounts I had heard already. When I checked, she confirmed that, for no particular reason, she had been walking behind Marcia Balbilla, with Ino behind Laia Gratiana.

"Laia thought she glimpsed someone assaulting Ino."

"I don't know about that. My mistress is not obliged to tell me everything." I thought privately, *but I bet you consider that she should!* The tussle for control in Laia's house must be wearying. Only Laia's own forceful personality can have kept her independent.

"Did you see this man?"

"No."

"Did you notice anybody melting back in slyly among the other passers-by?"

"I told you, no."

"Did you recognise anybody in the street at the time?"

"No."

"Did Ino say anything about him?"

"No."

"How did she come to lose her stole?"

"What?"

"Her stole. She dropped it, Laia told me."

"I don't know. It must have been slippery material. She was wearing it pulled over her head like a good girl." Automatically, Venusia mimed the way a respectable woman grips her stole with one graceful hand at the throat, to keep it anchored on her hair as she is walking. "She must have lost her hold when she fell over."

"How tall was she? About your height? Taller? Smaller?"

"About my height."

"What kind of build?"

"Similar to me."

Venusia was, like many slaves, a couple of inches less than the Roman average, perhaps because her distant origins lay in a province where the norm was shorter. Though not skinny, she was slim-built, with thin arms and her clavicles showing bonily above her tunic neckline. The plebeian rich led healthy lives, though they treated their slaves frugally. Laia Gratiana carried even less weight, which I had always seen as representing her lack of enjoyment in life, because there were no dietary restrictions on the mistress of a household. She was taller than Venusia, as was her friend Marcia Balbilla. That was normal.

"How old was Ino?"

"She would have been thirty next year. I know because she was always fretting on about it. She wanted to buy her freedom then, and take up with her fellow."

"What fellow was that?"

"One of the slaves in the house. Their house."

"Yes, I heard about him. Marcia Balbilla did not know, but it was a pretty open secret otherwise. Any other follower she was interested in? Someone from outside?"

"I don't reckon so. She would not have met anyone."

"It would be difficult," I suggested, "for anyone with mistresses like yours and Ino's, to take up with a man who was not in your own household?"

"Oh, impossible." That was nonsense. Plenty of slaves and freedwomen make outside connections. Some come and go every few minutes like bees from a hive. Venusia looked me straight in the eye, and made it almost pitying. Her own eyes were so dark brown they were almost black; they were fathomless, reminding me of gutter-water outside an industrial workshop. "Anyway, we are not all free-living creatures like prostitutes. Some of us behave morally."

She was aiming this at me. It was a cheap, nasty dig.

I felt my jaw set. "There's nothing wrong in seeking congenial company. And do you have a lover, Venusia?" She just shook her head disgustedly. "Have you ever had one?"

"I have not," she said in a bald tone, as if I had asked her if she ever dabbled in sorcery.

That was a crucial moment. Looking back, I could so easily have got this wrong. I might have assumed the brusque way she spoke meant Venusia shunned men because she was inexperienced and no men ever looked at her. Yet a sudden instinct told me it sounded more like the over-emphasis of someone blotting out a bad experience.

I cannot explain where that kind of impression comes from for an informer. Somehow a niggle starts. It is easy to overlook. Often it turns out to be right.

"Would you have liked to buy your freedom and set up independently?"

"No money."

"You must have had rewards. Don't you believe in savings?"

"Why bother? You only get swindled out of it."

"Who swindled you?"

"Nobody. I am not that stupid."

Why mention it then? I wondered.

I gave up shortly afterwards, exhausted by my long journey that day and the impossibility of breaking through the maid's stonewall resistance. You wouldn't think I was trying to identify a man who might be a threat to her. On principle, she had a dry-mouthed, derisive manner, like one who was deliberately being awkward and privately enjoying it. She despised me. It was not the first time I had been regarded as lightweight by a witness; still, it left me feeling unsatisfactory, my purpose unfulfilled.

I led Postumus away, via the deserted shrine. There we stood gazing up for a moment at the statue of Ceres, seated and representing the Loving Mother. This was not an untrustworthy figure who might abandon a baby girl in a rebellion or exploit a reluctant young boy as a high-wire acrobat. The Ceres of Aricia had the upward and outward gaze of a woman contented with her position and her busy role, nurturing her children whilst attending to many other tasks in the world. Her abundant hair was loosely swept back, caught at the neck in ringlets, tendrilled, fastened down with her light crown of wheat stems. She was handsome, wide-eyed, adorned with a twisted necklet and rosetted earrings. She smiled, she was calm and capable. She reminded my brother and me of the woman who had adopted us, our own Loving Mother. That made us smile. Yes, even Postumus.

It was too late to return to Rome that night. We had to stay at the inn. As the boy and I walked back there, I muttered wearily, "Well, that was a long way to come to hear nothing useful!"

Postumus turned and looked up at me. He assessed my statement. He might be eleven, but he was creepily observant. "She was telling you lies."

Well, I knew that. I just had to decide what the lies were about.

XLI

It took us all day to make it back to Rome. This was partly due to traffic tangles, but we had our own delays. By the time we reached and climbed the Aventine, and the cart rolled up outside the old laundry, the three chickens were down to two. Two very scared ones.

Felix, the driver, was in a filthy mood over that. He had been attached to all the chooks. He dropped off Postumus with me, pretending he had to take the cart off in the wrong direction for carrying my brother home. Postumus climbed out resignedly, with Ferret hanging around his neck. Ferret had stopped going crazy. Tragically for Diddle, Ferret had achieved his aim.

I felt worn out. I was ready to collapse at home, but now had to walk my brother to my parents' house. And my brain had been in turmoil, in between me being obliged to sort out crises with men and pets. I had travelled frequently with my parents so was well used to quarrels among my companions, though had never before had to catch hysterical poultry. Still, things always quieten down once everyone is exhausted. You just need to know when to fetch out the picnic hamper. Then the one grace of a long journey with an unfriendly driver and a boy who lives in his own world is that you have a chance to arrange your thoughts.

Mine had slithered into order almost of their own accord, and the results were disturbing for me. I no longer believed that the aedile had killed the maid—or any of the other people who died on the Aventine in mysterious circumstances. He was the wrong type.

That meant my friend Andronicus was stirring up trouble when he swore it was otherwise. I wondered if I really should meet the aedile to assess him first-hand, but Andronicus had also tried to implicate the runner Tiberius, and I was equally convinced that was wrong, so why bother? People like me were best advised to avoid all magistrates. It was definitely a bad idea to roll up to one who was in the throes of the main festival in his period of office and accuse him of committing a series of unspeakable murders. Everything I did know about Manlius Faustus said he would grow very hot under the tunic at that. Especially if he hadn't done it.

If he was innocent, I would be stuck for the rest of my career, working in a city where officials knew of my outrageous claim. Not sensible. I even had relatives who would annoyingly point out that the aedile had a right in law to compensation for me blackening his reputation. Some of the blighters were so keen to make names for themselves that in a promising cause célèbre, they might even rush to prosecute me on Manlius Faustus' behalf . . .

I had committed myself to plenty of stupid actions, though never before because somebody else incited me. I liked to make my errors for myself.

There was no reason to think anyone from the Faustus/Tullius household had been directly involved with the murders at all and, frankly, I was beginning to be annoyed with the archivist for suggesting it. Andronicus clearly felt resentment against the people he lived with, but it was irrelevant to my investigation and he should have kept it to himself.

I had met people like that before, people who thought my work was one big game. To them, trying to send me down the wrong track was a challenge, often a joke. Their theories were like ill-formed, pointless, wild ideas cooked up in a bar, which is indeed where they often floated to the surface. I ignored them—at least when I was sensible.

I recognised, too late, that I been lured into trusting Andronicus' judgement because of how I felt about him. I was furious with myself. I had behaved like a daft girl.

It was not that I blamed him for my wasted trip. Somebody did need to ask Venusia if she saw anything. I was half looking forward to telling Tiberius at some point that despite his sneers at my competence I had gone to those lengths—a twenty-mile, two-day trip—supposing we ever liaised on the subject again, which seemed unlikely.

Perhaps we should meet. I had questions he might answer and an idea to test. As I say, I had done a lot of thinking.

As soon as we arrived in Fountain Court, Rodan rushed up to tell me Andronicus had been there. I would have liked space to recover. I wanted to readjust, given some of the doubts that had struck me. I had certainly not spent that journey musing on the airy spheres of astronomical philosophy.

"That fellow of yours has been," grumbled Rodan, so churlishly I guessed they had had words about me being missing. I should have left a message. "He's an irritating bastard."

At that moment Andronicus himself turned up again. There I was, tired out, with a small collection of luggage at my feet, after Felix dumped us, with a fretful eleven-year-old, plus Ferret, plus Rodan staring curiously. Women have to handle such situations, postponing the demands of lovers. Andronicus could see my predicament, yet swarmed all over me. It struck me he was like a dog who could not bear to be left alone. He had the same kind of self-centred jealousy, and as it turned out, was equally prone to sulking, to spite me for going off secretly, without taking him on his lead.

"I had to attend a family occasion, then I needed to interview that maid, Venusia—it all came up rather suddenly, but I'm here now, so I hope you can forgive me."

"It was her birthday," announced Postumus. I expect he thought the detail might be helpful.

"And who is this?" Andronicus asked, with a glint in his eye, and pointing. Thank the gods, Postumus was far too young to be mistaken for a rival.

"My brother. He is not as evil as he looks, just never turn your back on him."

Andronicus assessed my brother, who was a chunky child as a result of his single-minded manner of eating. He loved food as his substitute for loving anybody else. Over his solid body, Postumus wore a good quality tunic, which he had managed to keep fairly clean because he was the kind of odd child who enjoys being careful. The unnatural creature had also been subjected to a very neat haircut, specifically for my birthday. He looked arrogant and superior. The ferret must have summed him up for Andronicus: such a pet may be a normal accoutrement of a working country dunderhead, but in the city it defined my brother as a pampered rich boy.

Postumus gazed back. Many people found his stare disconcerting. Even in my weary state, I found amusement in watching how Andronicus would react. Both were used to taking a specific position, observing everybody else disdainfully.

"She has to take me home now." Postumus claimed me casually, but effectively.

"Must you?" Andronicus was pleading in his most winning way. My heart fluttered. He knew how to make his attentions fervent. He knew, too, how to seduce and disorientate a woman who thought she had decided she wanted to be left alone. "Since when have you been a pedagogue, dragging little pupils through the streets?"

"Afraid I must."

"But what about me?"

"Andronicus, he is eleven. It's getting dark; he cannot be out on his own on the Aventine. He would frighten the muggers. Either he stays the night with me here—" I could see that would not fit whatever plans my friend had "—or I have to take him."

There was no reason why Andronicus should not have walked

down the hill with us, then come back with me. Nobody suggested that.

Instead he demanded abruptly, "What was so urgent, to send you chasing after Venusia?"

Oh Juno. Not here, not now. "I had to ask if she saw something."

"Any luck?" challenged Andronicus. I was conscious of Postumus assessing my friend like a scientific experiment put in front of him by his tutor (a cheap academic, but sincere and whom, you guessed, Postumus derided).

"No, none."

"So where is she?"

"Some place in the country. Do you need to know?"

"Of course not," Andronicus replied, so immediately and so reasonably I felt chastened. "We seem to be having an argument, Albia."

Though he spoke lightly, and wore his open-eyed innocent expression, Andronicus was tense. The people I knew called this kind of talk a discussion. Arguments were when you threw dinner bowls, first making sure they were full. Mostly we had those with bad-tempered toddlers. There had been many with Postumus.

"So your trip was pointless?" Andronicus asked, when I failed to respond to the argument comment. I wasn't ready for discord tonight.

"No, but it made me sure I need to see Faustus."

"I told you not to." While I was taking that in, Andronicus insisted, "You should do what I say!"

He should have known better. Anyone could see I was tired and tetchy, but in any case that was a bad move. "Because you are the man?"

"I am not your head of household," he conceded, as if making a belated attempt to cool the tension. I let the moment pass. Or so it seemed. When men start handing out orders to me, I can be a good actress.

Postumus slipped one hand into mine. That was unusual. I saw what he was up to. He loved a stand-off. He loved to stir one. My brother spoke up with his eerie self-assurance: "Flavia Albia's head of household is our father, Marcus Didius Falco."

With what seemed a single breath, Andronicus became all silkiness again. "Of course he is, little man, and we must certainly get you home to him! You go, Albia."

"If our father dies," Postumus announced, as if he had been working this out, "Albia's head of household will be me!"

That was too much. With a wince at me, Andronicus went off, swinging down the alley, after saying significantly, "Well, I may come along again later!"

I made no comment.

"You ought to stay with us tonight," my potential head of household instructed me. As a go-between in a love affair, Postumus made an efficient hatchet-man.

I left the luggage with Rodan and set off with the boy. I started at a fast march, but slowed down. We had to watch our step. In our absence, the Cerialia ceremonies must have continued on a daily basis; wherever a procession had snaked around the Aventine, remains of the nuts thrown at bystanders—Ceres' bounty—still lurked on the sidewalks, ready to make the unwary twist an ankle. I was wearing the wrong shoes. Even my brother was so tired, his feet were all over the place and I had to steady him when he stumbled. The last thing I wanted was for him to drop the ferret, and for us to have to persuade the slinky beggar to come out of a drain.

When we arrived home, my brother broke away from me, and scampered ahead into the house shouting cheerily, "Guess what! Ferret killed Diddle and he's eaten her!" He knew my sisters would start wailing.

He was eleven. Just a child. He seemed wise beyond his years, yet sometimes we overestimated him. Half the time he did not understand the significance of things he said and did. Never try to reason with a boy; it's pointless. We, who knew and tried to love him, accepted his eccentricities and even his rudeness. But other people could take him badly amiss.

I wished I did not at that moment remember the oyster-shucker, Lupus. It reminded me that what a boy says or does too casually to the wrong person may have terrible results.

I was grateful that my own little brother lived a sheltered life, kept in at home. He was never out on the streets where mysterious attackers prowled.

XLII

I could have stayed the night with my folks, as Postumus had slyly suggested, but I was not in the mood for company—theirs or anyone else's.

Andronicus did return to Fountain Court. It was almost as if he knew I preferred not to see him. I felt he was trying to impose his will, never a good trick for a man who wanted to impress me. I was in my apartment, the one on the second floor. I had not even undressed, but was lying on my bed as if I expected more to happen that night.

In Rome there would be other women lying in the centres of beds alone while men in separate rooms cursed them for it. One of the rites of the Cerialia required that as a gesture to chastity, women should preserve themselves from any male touch; to make sure, men had to sleep elsewhere. Of course this was a rite for the rich. The poor did not own enough beds.

I had heard that ladies who stayed celibate for Ceres drank a concoction of barley and pennyroyal to suppress their sexual appetite. Rumour had it, drugs were incorporated too, since grains and simple hedgerow herbs were not enough, supposedly, to overcome female lust. I needed neither herbs nor drugs. Nothing beats seeing a man in a new light to kill your passion.

Did you know, even in low doses, the oil of pennyroyal is poisonous? People happily cook with it, or make infusions, yet midwives are said to use it to bring about abortions. And it can kill. Was the mystery killer using some similar, readily available household poison? Or was he in a position to access something more specialised?

So, true to his promise, Andronicus returned. I wasn't surprised.

How many times do women lie awake, longing for a lover to appear, only to be disappointed? I had done it. This requires a degree of excitement about a relationship that I knew I had abruptly lost. Somewhere on the road out to Aricia, or returning home today, the Via Appia had claimed all my joy in the archivist. Tonight, I genuinely wanted to be chaste. It had nothing to do with religious observance, but reflected a cold drench of sense. I had lost the urge. Our rift was permanent. I would never again want Andronicus to touch me.

Did he know? Would he accept it? Was he a man who would let a disaffected lover go?

I heard him banging and shouting to be admitted, then Rodan growled in answer. I crept to the door, opening it quietly and not making my presence known. If the archivist gained entrance to the building, I was ready to press the door closed quickly and bolt it, then tremble on the inside, hiding from him.

It is odd how it happens: that subtle slither from being entirely wrapped up with a man, into not wanting him.

"Orders is orders," Rodan was maintaining, like some officious clerk. That was a change, and utter hypocrisy. With him, orders were for forgetting or ignoring. "The owners of this building are very particular. Once I lock up the grille, I can't let anybody in."

"What if I lived here?"

"But you don't, do you?" Sometimes I forgot how Rodan had spent many years as a landlord's enforcer. He knew how to remain unmoved, and indeed do it with a low-level threat of violence that would drain anyone's courage.

"I'm sick of this!" Even Andronicus sounded ready for a fight. I was against that happening. Rodan might be a failed gladiator, but he was still big enough to inflict damage; in pain, the archivist would probably turn vicious. Being selfish, I did not want to have to find a new porter, if Andronicus managed to hurt Rodan. He was cheap, too stupid to rob us, and had been known to the family for many years; who likes change?

Andronicus was still ranting. "First the woman is continually missing, then she thinks she can run rings around me—I'd like to kill that pestilential brat she had with her."

"Better not try it." That must have been the tone Rodan once used for putting frighteners on slow-paying tenants. With the grille safely between them, he was happy to play tough. It was a slow, easy offer to hook someone's organs out of them via an unusual orifice. Like an Egyptian embalmer—but with you still alive—at least you would be when Rodan started.

"I am not being made a fool of—somebody will pay for the inconvenience!"

"Send your bill!" jeered Rodan.

"You or her! It's all the same to me who suffers." Andronicus' Parthian shot was intended to chill. I could not help wondering if he guessed I might be listening.

When I was sure he had gone, I emerged from the shadows. In the entrance lobby, after I walked down, a couple of crude oil lamps at floor level shed a sickly glow in feeble patches. It was enough for me to make out Rodan as he stood, looking out through the grille, ox-like but flabby in his ragged one-armed tunic. He heard me and turned, showing no surprise.

We exchanged a long look.

"Thank you, Rodan. Do not let him in," I said quietly. "If ever he comes looking for me, say I am not here. Make any excuse."

Rodan said nothing; he just nodded.

I went back to my rooms. I made sure all the doors were barred. I was not frightened exactly, yet my heart was hammering.

It might be a difficult task to free myself from this situation safely. But I would have to do it.

XLIII

Next morning I wanted to be out of the house, somewhere people could not find me.

I went to the baths, partly to do yet more thinking. That never works. Physically and mentally I was so drained by yesterday, my mind just drifted.

Out of it did come two benefits. One, I was clean. An informer should start a hard day feeling neat. Two, I revived enough to decide on action. I dispensed with the interminable circles of speculation about the killing of Ino, Venusia's position, the crazy connections to the aedile and his long-ago adultery. Instead, I would use the informing trick that rarely fails: go back and re-check every event where questions still remained.

I went first to see Cassiana Clara. She could clear up immediately Andronicus' claim that the aedile had tried to assault her. But Fate was against me. She was not at home. I learned she had gone out of Rome (another fugitive?). Clara had not taken refuge in a shrine, but was staying at an estate belonging to her future second husband, at the seaside, way south in Campania.

I could only wonder whether this was to allow her to get to know her fiancé, or if it had some darker explanation. It was definitely too far for me to travel, and I felt the location could have been chosen for that reason. Nobody at the house would tell me more. I was refused admittance to ask questions of her parents. I could only curse the door porter, a bland functionary who hooked thumbs in his belt in a way that said he was used to being cursed and wouldn't give a fig for it, even if figs had been in season.

I had more success with my next attempt. I looped back over the Hill, using up more shoe leather as I made my way to the Fourth Cohort's station house; luckily I had made it a day for sensible shoes. I wanted to plead with the vigiles to let me interview Celendina's son, Kylo. That was assuming he had not been put before a magistrate and sent to an appalling death for matricide.

They still had him. In fact, it looked as if any case against him for killing his mother had been allowed to drop quietly. Hard men have to have a break from being bullies. Kylo was the latest fledgling sparrow who had tumbled into the exercise yard. He had been absorbed into the vigiles. They laughed at him, but they fed him, housed him, let him hang around on the fringes when groups were lolling in the yard. He even went out to bars with them.

If they could slim him down and make him mobile, he might even become a firefighter, though that was a long way off. Meanwhile, the men were using Kylo as a trusty, guarding the bare cells where they locked up temporary prisoners. The large young man looked more threatening than he probably was, and he devoted himself to the task solemnly. He was well able to subdue drunks and hush indignant arsonists. If the vigiles chose to foster him, it was his best chance. So long as no interfering official who needed something to do raised the issue, Kylo now had a job for life here. In a crude way, the vigiles were his replacement family.

They didn't care if I interviewed him. We sat on the ground together in the inner courtyard. One of the vigiles oversaw the interview, squatting on an upturned bucket, taking no notice, picking his nose. Morellus sauntered up, however; he propped himself against a pillar and pretended to be whittling a stick. Anything I learned, he was determined to know too.

Kylo's treatment here had transformed him from the terrified prisoner I saw first. The young man had settled and was more confident among people.

I spoke very gently. "Kylo, you do remember your mother, don't you?" He nodded. A slight frown of perturbation creased his forehead, nothing serious. "Do you think about her?" He dribbled a bit, but wiped it on his arm. "She would like to think you do. You must miss her badly. I met her, you know. We had a lovely chat at somebody's funeral. I thought she was a wonderful lady."

Kylo was looking uncomfortable but, so far, he understood he ought to talk to me, and not scarper. I carried on, keeping my voice low.

"You know who I am, don't you? I am called Flavia Albia." He stared at the ground. "You saw me once before, Kylo; I came and talked to you. And your new friends here in the vigiles all know me and are friends with me too. But we had never met at the time your mother died, had we? So when something happened to her, I am wondering why you said my name to people?"

Kylo suddenly looked straight in my direction. "Do you live here?" It seemed he could talk, and perfectly well, when he wanted to. I had no difficulty understanding him.

"No, Kylo, I have my own place. Why?"

"I was supposed to fetch you."

"When your mother was poorly?"

"She lay down. She said, 'I'm feeling funny, Kylo. Kylo, fetch Flavia Albia'—but I didn't know where I had to go."

"Kylo, this is important. Did your mother say why she wanted me?" He looked confused. "Kylo, had she mentioned meeting me that afternoon?"

He pondered. I waited quietly. "She always told me about where she had been out. She told it like a story."

"So what was this story, Kylo? Can you remember?"

"Oh I like stories. I always remember them."

"I like stories too. Will you tell me this one?"

He seemed wary to begin with, but my smiling stillness reassured him. Kylo sat up and in a rather formal manner related what happened, as if he was a street-corner entertainer reciting folk tales for money in the hat. He made little gestures to indicate new speakers and even altered his voice accordingly. "She said, 'I met that investigator. Nice little thing. Better than I expected.'" On the sidelines, I heard Morellus snort at that. Kylo glared at him as if he was a naughty child disturbing the class. "I answered, 'Oh, that is interesting, Mother.' Then she told me, 'When I was leaving, some man was waiting on the road by the tombs. He asked me, "Did you see Flavia Albia at the Salvidia funeral?," but I didn't like him so I told him to get lost. He really put my back up, Kylo, I really told him!' That," said Kylo, "is the whole story my mother told me that day."

I tried not to feel shocked by the connection to me. "I bet when your mother decided she didn't like someone, she could really let rip!"

Kylo and I laughed, thinking about it.

"And Kylo, one last thing. When your mother started feeling funny, did she tell you she thought someone had done something to her?"

"Oh yes."

"Who did she say, Kylo?"

"Am I supposed to tell you?"

"Yes, please."

"She said, 'It must have been him, the nasty little bugger. He jabbed me. The one who asked me if I had seen Albia.' Was it that man?" asked Kylo.

"Yes. I'm afraid it most likely was, Kylo. But don't worry. We are going to catch him and punish him."

"The nasty little bugger!" Kylo roared at the top of his voice, making us all jump.

"The nasty little bugger," I agreed, much more quietly.

Morellus bestirred himself and walked me to the gate. "Worried?"

"Not me."

"Don't be brave, this is serious, Albia. He wanted you. Celendina may have saved your life that day."

"At the price of her own."

"So yes, it's serious. You must know him. Why would some perverted bastard want to find you, Albia?"

"I don't know." I had an idea. "Well, look after the son carefully, Morellus."

"If we put him behind bars, I'd be afraid you would sneak along and set him free."

"Have your little dig!"

"You would do it."

"Oh, I would."

We stood for a moment, both thinking about other things.

This did not provide identification. Kylo himself had not seen the man. But this showed motivation. A psychopathic killer asked a simple question—"Did you see Albia there?" Celendina disliked his manner. Alone, on a road outside a necropolis at dusk, her first reaction might well have been alarm. Maybe he was too persistent, with a madman's arrogance and urgency. She snapped. So he was rebuffed with a tart answer by a tired old woman, anxious about the son she had left alone.

"Celendina took a shine to you, Albia. She tried to protect you."

"I thank her for that. But I would not have wanted her to suffer for it. Morellus, do you think he followed her home?"

"Could be. Judging by the other cases, if he stabbed her by the tombs, she would never have made it back before the poison overcame her."

"Then someone in the neighbourhood may have seen him."

"Jupiter! . . . I'll have a go," Morellus grumbled. "Seeing as it's you. I don't know how you persuade me into things. But I will send a couple of lads to the street, to knock on doors and ask."

I said thank you. I even said it nicely.

"Morellus, another thing. I tried to see that girl whose husband was one of the victims. She's out of town, for some reason, possibly significant. You may be able to clear up my query—you have met Manlius Faustus?" Morellus nodded. He made no comment, yet the look he gave me was distinctly odd. "Is he a satyr? Does he prey on women?"

"*Faustus?*"

"Are you deaf or just annoying? Does he?"

"No."

"Is that all?"

Morellus said heavily, "Manlius Faustus, plebeian aedile, does not grope, grab, fondle, squeeze, tickle up or insert his sanctified diddly-do into women."

"He likes boys then?" I punched back.

"I doubt it. I doubt it very much. He's normal. But he likes to keep to himself," said Morellus. "What a wise man!"

I was intending to leave then, but still lingered.

Morellus gave me the sceptical eye again. I sighed in response. We understood one another. He was so slow he made a snail look reckless, yet after half a day to consider a point, he possessed modest powers of reasoning. "What?"

"Morellus, I think I have made an appalling mistake."

"Looking at your face, I'm getting a horrible inkling . . . Jupiter," he said again, as I watched him working out what I meant. "I think I'm going to wet myself—you know who it is." A statement, not a question. He had realised too.

"I don't know what to do, Morellus. I have no proof, just that sick feeling when you see the answer. The answer that has been crying out to you all along."

"Oh that answer and I are old bloody friends! Come back in," ordered Morellus. He had roused himself as much as he ever bothered. I won't say he had livened up, but his gaze held a dim gleam of interest. "You know who you need to talk to. You can use my office. I'm going off-shift." Nothing interfered with that. The vigiles' main shift worked all through the night and were desperate to go home by morning. Apart from the fact Morellus had a wife, three children and that rusty-coloured puppy who would all want to climb all over him, the man was dead beat. "I pass his house. I'll tell him."

"He might not be there."

"He will. They've all been up until midnight, watching those plays. The black god of the underworld bursting onstage in his thundering chariot and snatching the pretty virgin while she gathers flowers. Who would miss that? All the audience is on the edge of their seats, hoping for a real rape of a real virgin. Real snorting horses. Real screams. Real blood. The finest Roman theatre."

"As far as I know, you animal, even in the name of culture, they don't show live deflowerings of maidens during solemn religious drama."

Morellus chucked me under the chin. "Hot stuff, this year's Cerialia. I heard that wide boy Faustus wants to popularise it, show something scandalous to bring in a new audience . . . Wait in my room. There's a nice map you can look at, so you don't need to read any confidential scrolls. If you play with my stylus, don't break the point or I'll stop your dress allowance."

I knew what the dozy article was doing there. Lightening the atmosphere, in his heavy-handed way. Telling me I would be safe here while I waited.

I watched him buzz off down the street, and by his standards, he was on the verge of running.

XLIV

When Tiberius strode into the enquiry office, he had dropped the pristine white flash of the other evening in favour of a street-style tunic that looked as if he'd filched it from a bathhouse manger while road-making slaves were cleaning themselves up. What made me really stare was that he had had all his facial hair scraped off. He looked almost unrecognisable.

The smartened vision took a seat, on the other side of Morellus' wooden table from me. I had been sitting alone for much less time than I expected. Although as he arrived he gave no sign of haste, once Morellus spoke to him about me Tiberius must have covered ground fast. I was unexpectedly grateful.

I gave him a survey. Barbering had revealed a good face, one that would stand daily familiarity. Neither too plain, nor too handsome to be trusted. With a few forgivable tweaks, a sculptor could make it noble. Straight nose, firm mouth, strong jaw, astute expression, those watchful grey eyes I already knew. The tanned skin of the Roman working class, who spend most of their day out-of-doors.

He endured my examination, though coloured modestly. That was good. Today I needed to like him, or at least not actively dislike him.

"You shave up well."

Typically, he ignored my compliment. "I have been looking for you." He leaned forwards on his elbows, resting his chin on his hands. "Things to discuss."

"Me too." I acknowledged that we would now work in partnership again after our recent tiff. "I went to Aricia."

"You need not have. I am having the woman fetched back to Rome."

"She won't come."

"No choice. Official custody."

"Well, I tried. She seems unlikely to give anything up."

"No, not to me either," Tiberius agreed ruefully. "Morellus can tackle her. I want him to keep her here at the station house." Seeing my expression, he was quick to add, "He can hold her for a couple of nights—for security—no brutal methods. That never brings out the truth. She has lived all her life in comfortable surroundings. The sights and sounds of a neighbourhood barracks should be enough to frighten her into a confession. To somebody." He meant me.

"Laia Gratiana," I said. "The maid will talk to Laia, if she talks at all."

Tiberius raised his eyebrows with a gleam that said I had had a smart idea. So; we were back on good terms.

I rode out an important pause. Tiberius began fiddling with the styluses and pens, the equipment Morellus had warned me not to break. We were both uneasy; we had to find a way to initiate a dark conversation.

Sticking with the maid, I approached the subject obliquely. "I doubt she herself has done anything wrong, but Venusia is shielding someone." The runner stopped fiddling. "I may be the only person in the Empire who believes this, but even if you fail to close the deal you wanted, a long journey is never wasted. You have a lot of time to think."

Tiberius leaned back again, arms folded. "Spill those thoughts?"

I braced myself to share all my sorry conclusions. I felt like Kylo—with the great difference that I understood the implications. "Start with Aricia. I went there the day after the Ides. I had a long and frankly tedious interview with the maid. She told me nothing, not directly. Venusia is . . ."

I was groping for words because I wanted to be fair to her; I had some sympathy with what I now saw as her personal predicament. Tiberius smiled wryly. "Yes. I have met her."

"Recently?"

"No, not for years."

"You are not her secret lover then?"

At that, he choked, full of masculine horror. "No! . . . Does she have one?"

"I came to think so, although not the man I was being encouraged to identify. According to Andronicus, it's your darling master, the aedile." Tiberius breathed visibly. "He alleges Faustus dallied with this maid, then dropped her for his patron's wife, causing Venusia to destroy his marriage out of jealousy. That is the Andronicus version. Mine is different." I was watching Tiberius closely; he was restraining a tetchy response. Our eyes locked; he still refrained from comment. He in turn was watching my emotions as I speculated. I liked the fact he waited to hear my verdict; I liked him giving me credit for reaching one independently. "I asked Venusia if she knows Andronicus; she denied it. I think that's untrue. I think she has known him very well. She mentioned that, as she put it, I 'went around with him,' and I had the impression it mattered to her."

"Which means?" asked Tiberius.

"Andronicus has engineered a connection with her." My companion pursed his lips enigmatically. "I can imagine his method, unfortunately. He wormed his way in close then tried to winkle out of her what she knows about Faustus."

"Was he successful?"

"Not sure. He knows about the old affair, but it's recent; he heard it from Laia. He is a manipulator," I admitted. "Venusia may have believed it was love, but I have heard Andronicus describe her harshly. He despises her—as he does many people." I tried not to think that perhaps he despised me, too.

"Contempt is the key to him." Tiberius almost spoke in parenthesis. "Albia, I tried to warn you not to engage with him. He bounces from woman to woman—has done so since his teens. He started early, I've been told. Why is he digging anyway? Blackmail?"

"I suppose so."

"It wouldn't work. Faustus has nothing to lose. Laia Gratiana already thinks he is dirt. His uncle doesn't care. His patron and the wife are both long dead."

I was not so confident. "It could make your aedile's life uncomfortable. Scandal always matters. A revelation of adultery, even now, would sully his term of office—and he could get into serious trouble with the emperor. Faustus may think it long dead, but you know how congealing flotsam bobs up again, with the same old stink. Andronicus believes he can control people through any knowledge they don't want him to have."

Tiberius frowned. "That was exactly why he was denied the post as secretary."

"He resents that so bitterly; he constantly harps on it . . . But let me finish. The mad fancies get worse. Andronicus wanted me to believe Faustus was so vengeful about Venusia informing, he actually stalked and attacked her. We are asked to believe he killed the other maid, Ino, by mistake."

"Oh for heavens' sake! Flavia Albia, you don't believe any of this filth?"

"No." I let a beat pass before I added, "Not now."

"Meaning?"

I paused again, then for once teased him. "You need to be careful. He blamed you first!"

"He's a fool then."

"Yes, luckily for you, that was what I thought."

"Thanks!"

Tiberius dropped his arms onto the table. I reached and took up his wrist. He had no bandages today, so without undue intimacy I could inspect that wound I had given him, flopping his hand over to see both sides. The punctures were drying out and scabbing over at last.

"I should have listened to you." His tone was easy. "It needed air. I was laid up briefly; one morning there was even excited talk of blood-poisoning, though I recovered and disappointed them."

"I heard you were feeling seedy." In fact, that was not exactly what I heard. Releasing his arm abruptly, I dropped my gaze from this new clean-shaven version of the runner. "It was strangely self-destructive for Andronicus to insist that the mystery killer comes from your house."

"That's him. Stupidly impulsive. You would never have thought of it, if he had left the subject alone." Tiberius clearly anticipated what I was going to say next.

"He knows how to create a story. His reasoning is that you, or Faustus, were well-placed to find victims in the street, directly familiar with all the relevant locations. But he, too, passes freely between your house and the temple. Nobody monitors his movements, well not much." I knew Tiberius did on occasions. "And once I started to wonder—" I took a deep breath. "Andronicus himself became my prime suspect."

There. It was said. I had made the accusation that had bothered me all the way along the Via Appia yesterday.

In his dour way, at first Tiberius barely blinked. This was not a man who sensationalised.

He must have heard how dry my mouth had become from tension. Without a word, he stood up, took a jug from a shelf and went outside, reappearing with water. He found beakers, selecting the least chipped from a misshapen collection that Morellus kept in a basket on the floor. After he poured, we drank slowly, our mood of bitter preoccupation ruling out enjoyment. That assumes anyone ever could savour the bouquet and undernotes of the sludge the vigiles had in their water fountain for fire buckets.

The situation changed at that point. The runner fumbled in a pouch on his belt, one of those over-elaborate leather devices men favour to carry their small change, notebooks and whittling knives. Their only benefit, it seems to me, is that they make good presents when you are stuck over relatives' birthdays. Men are so fussy about these things, they really want to choose their own, but you can fix that for them. Did Tiberius have someone with whom he would pre-arrange a "secret" anniversary or Saturnalia gift for himself? Somehow I doubted that, though he seemed like a man who would be amused to do it.

He withdrew a couple of objects, placing the first on the table in front of me, one-handed, while he kept back something else. This was a small, round glass flask, with a thong round its neck to carry it by. Green glass, brown thong, no distinguishing marks. A lock-up shop alongside Prisca's baths sold scores of them. That was repeated throughout Rome, and on all across the Empire. A standard ablutions flask.

"Mean anything?"

"Possibly. Andronicus had one like it the other morning. I assumed it was bath oil. Most people take their own oil if they can afford it."

"Can you identify this bottle certainly as his?"

"Not without perjury. Sorry; I am a classic bad witness." Informers hate being reduced to the level of general uselessness they themselves encounter in enquiries. Ashamed of myself, I reached for the flask, unplugging the wooden stopper to sniff.

Tiberius shouted, *"Careful!"* so I nearly dropped it. I don't know what the contents were; not oil. Some thinner liquid, with a strange odour that could be chemical or plant-derived. I had opened a palm to pour some out but then, abruptly wary, I made sure not to. Tiberius reclaimed the flask and closed it, still one-handed. "Silly girl, Albia! Tests will be carried out."

"How?"

"As a gesture to you, on some creature even you would see as vermin. How are you with pigeons?"

"Try a rat. You expect fatal results?"

"Don't you?"

"Where did you find this?"

"His room was searched this morning."

"So you knew the truth already?"

"Not 'knew.' I *suspected*. Because he and I are so constantly at loggerheads, I have been trying not to condemn him until I had to."

"Well, we don't want to be unfair to a multiple murderer, do we?—Gods, it is so much easier to form charges against a stranger."

Tiberius was looking concerned for me. "Has this become too personal? Do you want to stand aside?"

"I want to see it through."

"It's hard." Voice low, the runner seemed affected himself.

"It has to be done," I answered, though my jaw set and my tone was drab. "So what else was in your evidence haul?"

Displayed with a conjurer's gesture, his second item was my own bone needle-case.

"That belongs to me." I heard my voice croak. I felt hot, then sick, even though I was not surprised.

"Don't protect him, Albia."

"I don't even want to. He must have taken it."

I sat silent, remembering that afternoon when I had been stitching braid. I saw Andronicus examining my sewing box, hazel eyes bright with curiosity as he opened the box and explored the contents. He must have palmed the needle-case, right there in front of me.

I pulled out the plug, a tiny wad of old papyrus, and shook, aware once again that my companion flinched at the danger, though this time I was ejecting any contents safely onto the table. Nothing fell out; the case was empty. Tiberius asked how many needles I had owned. "One in this case, plus another still at home. Even two is a luxury. Do you know what needles cost?" In my head I heard

Andronicus say, *I don't do sewing . . .* Like so many of his utterances, it had had a double meaning.

Tiberius confirmed in a quiet voice, "Identical killings elsewhere have been carried out with poisoned needles. One was found stuck in a victim, over on the Esquiline. He felt something prick him, so spun around unexpectedly, causing his attacker to let go and leave the needle behind. That lunatic was caught, incidentally, so we can be sure the deaths on the Aventine have been caused by someone else. The method has been known for a while, but was deliberately kept from the public."

"Oh your damned secrecy! You got it wrong, Tiberius. Someone who did know could use the idea to make it look as if his killings were part of the general epidemic. That would divert attention."

"Yes."

"Andronicus must know."

"I never told him, Albia."

"Are you sure? Andronicus once said he has taken the notes at situation meetings with the four aediles. When they reviewed the needle killings, he must have heard the method discussed."

"That fits." Tiberius drained his beaker, refilled it, drank to the bottom again. He leaned on his elbows once more, in order to move a little closer to me. Mornings were quiet for the vigiles. There were no sounds of anyone outside in the colonnade, or beyond in the muster yard. Yet even though we were alone in the enquiry room, Tiberius instinctively dropped his voice: "So, Flavia Albia, let us say it: you and I are both convinced that the needle-killer on the Aventine is our archivist, Andronicus."

XLV

Andronicus was the killer. Now that someone else agreed with my suspicions, it all seemed horribly obvious.

To diffuse my panic, I fell back on nervous humour. "Oh he can't be a murderer; his eyes twinkle!"

The runner sat tight while I grappled with the truth. I was stalling. He knew it. For the first time, I faced up directly to the personal implications. It did not take long, because the dread had been lurking all last night. Not for the first time, I had given my heart impetuously to a man who then betrayed my trust—but this was by far the most sinister occasion.

"Story of my life," I admitted bitterly. "Being strung along by a bastard, taking far too long to notice it . . ."

Judging by his expression, Tiberius had met embittered women before and had little patience with my self-pity, but what he said was, "From my observations, Andronicus truly fell for you."

I flared up. "And I stonkingly, inexcusably, ridiculously fell for him!"

"Steady."

"But for a series of accidents—and my own unease, it's fair to say—it could have been worse. At least I never slept with him."

I wanted Tiberius to know. Why? It was none of his business.

He brushed the statement aside. Embarrassed perhaps.

"I am furious. He stole something of mine to use in his terrible attacks—worse, it was something I had been given by my dear young sister! That's a good needle-case, it had associations with Julia, but I will never feel able to use it again."

Tiberius took it back from me. He needed it as evidence anyway.

I buried my face in my hands, raging now at myself.

"What a mess. This is what everyone expects if you do a traditional man's job. Oh Juno; if you are an honest woman, it's what you dread yourself. Sheer bloody incompetence. You will tangle yourself up in some terrible case; make things far worse; sleep with a killer; compromise yourself, your future chance of work, even risk not convicting him—"

I need not say that while I ranted, Tiberius listened inscrutably. I doubt he realised there were few people to whom I would reveal such depths of feeling. I truly felt I trusted him.

He had pushed back from the table, arms full-stretch, while he settled himself to hear me out as if this was an unpleasant formality that had to be gone through.

I finished. I fell quiet. He applied what passed for a reasonable expression; he even cocked his head slightly to one side. The poser.

"You told me," he corrected me, "you did *not* sleep with him."

"You are being pedantic."

"Better," the mimsy swine intoned, "than being hysterical." After a moment he added in a serious voice, "You made a mistake. It lasted a few weeks. Some of us have to live with the fact that we harboured this creature for years. He seemed harmless. We would have ended his bad behaviour at home. He would never have been detected as a killer, without your enquiries. To my shame, I even tried to get the vigiles to stop you."

"Pax!"

"Thank you. So, Flavia Albia, shall we two sensibly together work out the sequence of events?"

———

I summed up first, while the runner indicated agreement to each point with silent nods. I had noticed he did this in meetings. It gave the impression he was waiting to catch people out, but I now realised he liked to hear from everybody else first, in case it affected his own contribution. If he saw any need to intervene earlier, he would do it.

"To begin where I first came on the scene," I said. "Andronicus killed Salvidia because she had visited the aediles' office and verbally attacked him; she was enraged about that wall poster calling for witnesses to the death of little Lucius Bassus."

"My fault!"

"Your fault," I agreed unrelentingly. He wrote the poster. "Andronicus was right that he was blameless, merely the man she had found in the office, but Salvidia's violent reaction shook him. It was unjust. He was overcome with outrage, as happens with him, so he took an extraordinary revenge by killing her. Then I turned up in the office, and perhaps he wanted to stop me investigating—I remember he kept saying, 'So you don't need to waste any more time?' I guess he went to the funeral and tried to find me, still hoping to make sure I discovered nothing against him. He met the old woman outside the necropolis. Celendina took umbrage in a way he found insulting, so he followed her home and killed her too."

"Morellus thinks you had a lucky escape that night."

"Andronicus could have killed me any time."

"Ah, but soon he was unable to resist you!"

"Skip the crass jokes."

"I was not joking," replied Tiberius mildly. "He spoke of you to us at home as a gorgeous creature. There was hope you might reform the irresponsible side of his character—though I'd like you to know, I never wished him on you." He paused. "I tried quite hard to keep you apart."

Feeling disconcerted, I carried on: "Prior to those attacks, he had killed Julius Viator—why? Can it be that when Cassiana Clara was sitting in the garden at your house during that dinner party, and

Andronicus found her, *he* was the man who assumed she was, as he told me very crudely, 'asking for it?' *He* made a grab for her? I wanted to persuade her to give me a witness statement—"

Tiberius shook his head and interrupted. "No need. The girl can be left to forget the incident, if she really can ever forget that it led to her husband's murder. I was in the colonnade on the other side of the garden, coming back from the facilities. Andronicus had not heard me. I saw it all. And yes, he tried to force himself on her. She was very inexperienced; the assault was a great shock to her."

"So he read the situation wrong? She screamed?" A nod. "Viator rushed out, saw his wife struggling, was furious, and like the other victims, he made his feelings known much too strongly for Andronicus?"

"Viator actually thumped him."

"Oh, now we see that was Viator's death sentence!"

"That seems to have been his first death," Tiberius said glumly. "One good punch from an athletic man caused his deterioration into a killer. And Andronicus was in severe disgrace at home for weeks after he assaulted Cassiana Clara," he told me. "Tullius gave him a warning. He came very close to being dismissed permanently that time."

"That time?"

"He has a long history of behaviour problems. Being reprimanded has no effect. He never admits he has done anything wrong. If forced, he blames other people; once you know him, you can watch his cunning brain devising excuses as he wriggles." Tiberius described it wearily; I had the impression he had been involved in trying to rehabilitate the culprit. "He wins over Tullius, who likes an easy life, with that charm of his."

"And Faustus?"

"Sees through him."

"One day Andronicus took me to the house," I admitted, knowing that Tiberius would raise a scathing eyebrow. On cue, he obliged. "I thought the other staff were friendly with him."

"That's how he gets away with it," Tiberius said, scowling. "You and I view him as a predator, but most people notice nothing unusual. He knows how to blend in. He has hidden his aggression and his lack of remorse in plain sight."

"When I said her husband had been murdered, Cassiana Clara was terrified he would go after her next. It seemed extreme then. Of course she is right. If he fears she might give evidence against him—say he assaulted her and her husband threatened him—Andronicus will attack her too. Someone threatens him, he just wipes them out of existence. Has Clara been sent away from Rome to protect her? Has the aedile warned her family?"

"Yes. To both questions."

That was a relief. "So," I concluded, "what do we think about Lupus?"

"Lupus?"

"The oyster boy."

Tiberius chipped in immediately: "We buy our shellfish from that stall. Lupus was a cheeky lad; I remember him. Liked to joke with customers, typical barrow boy, pain in the arse sometimes, basically too young to judge when his comments were inappropriate. The Porticus is over by the temple, so if no one else was on that side of the hill but Andronicus had to be at the archive, he would be ordered to pick up supplies. On one occasion, he came home complaining bitterly that a boy had been rude. Took it personally, as he always does. Refused to go again."

"Clearly he did go, once too often," I concluded grimly. "When I interviewed the family they reckoned they saw nobody the day Lupus was killed, but if we paraded Andronicus they might remember him."

"They might."

Tiberius stood up. The subject was affecting him. It was affecting me too, so I also lumbered to my feet. I felt stiff, weary and downhearted. He complained about us sitting in that enclosed stuffy room for too long to be good for thought; he urged that we left the station house and went somewhere with a new view and more air.

In the doorway Tiberius paused, looking at me from close quarters. He could see I was reluctant to go. "All right?"

"Fine."

"I don't think so."

"I will be."

He waited a beat, but when he saw my chin come up, he steered me into the colonnade and we set off walking.

XLVI

Slowly, as Tiberius and I walked through our city that morning, I recovered my courage. I had lived in Rome for fifteen years, most of them on the Aventine. These were my streets. I became determined not to be driven out of them by fear.

Our steps led away from the riverside, a direction in which I rarely went. We must have taken a turn around the Plane Tree Grove, a rather bare public park near the road that was named after it, though I was so distracted I had no memory of this afterwards. Then we worked across the southern side of the main Hill until we emerged out of the Thirteenth District into the Twelfth, beside the vigiles' Fourth Cohort headquarters, where I had been entertained by Scaurus and his henchmen. No mention was made of that.

For a long while, we did not talk at all, as we meandered down the wide Street of the Public Fishponds towards the Circus Maximus. Stopping short of a descent right down to the racetrack, we made our way above it instead, along the lower part of the Hill again, back past the two Temples of Venus and eventually that of the flower- and vegetable-covered garden god Vertumnus. I remember I commented to Tiberius on the Temple of Venus Verticordia that only in Rome could the goddess of love and lust be worshipped in a version that was propaganda for sexual purity.

"Venus the 'turner of hearts' towards virtue—meaning *women's* chastity, of course," I grumbled.

"Faithfulness in love," argued Tiberius, revealing a romantic side.

"If you believe in it!"

"You don't?"

"I do. My husband was faithful to me, and I to him."

"I have noticed you always speak well of your marriage."

"Well, it was short!"

"And a long time ago?—Yet you still wear your wedding ring."

Wrong. Lentullus and I had never bothered. I explained wryly that I acquired this ring only a few years ago from a house sale my family organised and wore it to imply respectability in my work. Sometimes it may have deterred men, though I had no wish to remind the runner that I ever looked available. It was bad enough that he knew I had attracted Andronicus.

"Have you ever been married, Tiberius?" He only wore a signet ring, its symbol a spirited fish-tailed horse. I had seen it when I inspected his scarred hand.

"Once."

"Oh—and never again?"

"I didn't say that." This man failed to say quite a few things, I was beginning to suspect.

Our meandering had brought us to the lower reaches of the steep Clivus Publicius. We had to pass the house where the child Lucius Bassus had lived, the very spot where he had been run over by the Metellus and Nepos wagon. On the wall where Tiberius had written up his fatal poster calling for witnesses, the family had now installed an oversize memorial plaque. They must have spent the compensation money Salvidia's stepson paid. A touching message commemorated Lucius:

> *Lived three years, four months, ten days: a little soul who*
> *loved only play, returned to the gods of the underworld:*
> *his parents' hopes are shattered.*

Tiberius muttered impatiently that the Bassus family would have done more good by using the cash for their other children. I felt obliged to murmur, maybe the plaque comforted them. He declared that kind of comfort was overrated.

He pointed out angrily that the door of the house stood open again. Nothing had been learned. Any other infant could have run out into danger.

"I wonder why anyone bothers!"

"Do you have children?" I asked.

"No, I never had the chance to neglect innocent offspring!"

Tiberius strode on, with me hurrying after. We looped up over the heights, through little streets with markets and fountains at crossroads, under the commanding bulk of the great Temple of Diana of the Aventine, through more local alleys and byways, until we returned to my home area. Much of the time we spent together, I was barely aware of my companion. I was lost in private meditation, sometimes of a neutral kind that serves to empty your brain of trouble, but frequently much darker. We walked; I was reclaiming my right to do so, after a long night and morning of apprehension. Exposing Andronicus had shaken me. What that callous killer had done left me bleak and lacking faith. Worse, before I calmed down on today's walk, I had been deeply frightened.

Even Tiberius wanted to warn me not to be complacent. "Until he is in chains, keep your wits about you, Albia. If you have said or done anything to upset him—"

"That's me! Unfortunately, I dropped him. He will not forgive me for that."

I saw no need to dwell on the end of my love affair. But I did mention that my brother had been dangerously obstreperous with Andronicus last night, probably in the same way that young Lupus once cheekily aroused his loathing, a lad doing what came naturally without realising it threatened his safety. Tiberius thought Postumus should be kept in at home, just to be on the safe side.

He offered no advice about me. Wise fellow.

Everywhere had a bright but relaxed holiday atmosphere. People were having lunch. There was no suggestion Tiberius and I should do that together. Instead, he left me at the Stargazer where I said Junillus would look after me. Looking tired, Tiberius said he had to go home. It had been a kind move to remain with me when we left the station house, although I could tell why he did it. He, too, had needed time to prepare himself for the next action.

"Andronicus has been kept busy at home with tasks for Tullius. It is time to confront him. Then make an arrest."

Despite myself, I thought about Andronicus, unwittingly working with the aedile's uncle while retribution approached. Tullius would know what was going on. He would be aware of the room search, and the evidence discovered; while Tiberius finalised the case, Tullius must have agreed to supervise Andronicus. What would it be? Lists? Rental dates and prices? Reviewing old contracts that could now be used for wrapping up fishbones, or simply dumped with the household rubbish? Presumably a hardbitten old businessman would be able to keep his archivist occupied, without showing signs that formal charges were in the last stages of preparation.

I had no wish to see Andronicus being made a prisoner, no desire to know what would happen to him in the judicial system. There could only be one end for a freedman who was found guilty of unlawful homicide, especially when two of the citizens he had killed—Viator and Salvidia—had been wealthy. Murder carried the death penalty. He was not important enough for his trial to be drawn out. The prosecution would be brutal, his defence sketchy. He could hardly rely on the traditional character witnesses to plead for him. Justice would be swift. There was only one outcome. He would be sent to the arena to be torn apart by the beasts.

I would make sure I was away from Rome then.

"Don't let it prey on your mind," said Tiberius heavily. "It is over. You can leave the rest to me."

Brave, manly words—a declaration which always sounds convincing and never goes wrong, does it?

The Stargazer provided its usual solace. Many a solitary customer had found oblivion there. A beaker of wine helped finish restoring me to full confidence. A second slipped down unheeded. Another made me positively defiant. I believe it is a known effect.

I went to my parents' house, needing to warn them that they should keep Postumus indoors. Easier said than done, I was informed rather spikily. My brother had become fascinated by the nightly rituals enacted as part of the Cerialia. He sneaked out when he wanted to. I said, stuff that, the horrid little beggar had upset the needle-killer and if they wanted to avoid a fatality, he must be made to obey orders. I may have added that looking after an eleven-year-old boy should surely not be difficult and I was surprised at the lack of discipline regularly applied to him in this airy-fairy house. My words veered to the wild and my logic to the incomprehensible.

It was suggested I might like to have a quiet lie-down, upstairs in the roof garden.

Oddly enough, I did what I was told. I slept for hours. Nobody disturbed me. Who would dare?

When I awoke on the daybed, feeling cold and sluggish, I could tell from the shift in the light that the whole afternoon had passed me by. Noises from the river—the daily racket of unloading, the crashes, stevedores' cries and squeaks from pulleys—were now fewer. Sounds from the streets below were different from daytime: hardly any donkey bells, more casual conversation. A blackbird sang his heart out on a nearby roof, designating territory.

The air was filling with drifts of hot oil and herbs as evening cookery began in homes and commercial kitchens. If I stayed here much longer I would be obliged to have dinner, with a lot of teasing. I slipped away, shamefaced, and skulked back alone to my own nest, going via Prisca's baths. The place had just opened formally; they were busy, which saved me having to talk.

At Fountain Court I saw no sign of Rodan. I made my way through the first-floor home of the Mythembal family. Children were wailing, in a room I could not see into. I heard the nightly protests as their weary mother attempted to wash them with cold water, and each one doggedly resisted her until they fell asleep in mid-sob. Locked in their desperate family ritual, none of them were aware of me. I went straight through my own room at the end of the corridor, passed outside to the walkway above the courtyard, climbed the narrow stairs, and fell into my hidden haven. Suddenly I realised how desperate I was to be home, solitary, in this deep silence where only motes of dust were moving. I kept my brain empty. There was nothing left to consider.

In the apartment was a tiny area where I could prepare food. I dipped a beaker into a bucket of cold water, drinking deep. I turned around to my main sitting room, barely aware I was doing it. I stood, looking.

This room was furnished with a wide couch that served as a daybed, its en suite bronze-legged footstool, a couple of elegant inlaid chests, a rug on the floor, a hanging lamp, souvenirs and paintings on the walls. Two high square windows, set in the thick outside wall, let in light.

There was still light that early evening. Enough for me to notice if things were not right. Nothing was missing. None of my possessions appeared to be displaced. But I had a sensation. You know how, when mice have recently taken up residence at the back of a cupboard, you feel their presence even before you glimpse them from the corner of an eye, long before the telltale droppings and the smell?

I had a glass platter that had contained three apples when I last saw it. Now there were two. My sewing box, untouched by me since my birthday, seemed to have moved sideways. Its lid was still down, but when I went over and lifted it, the short piece of ribbon into which I had stuck my sewing needle was now missing.

While I was out this morning, somebody had been in my apartment.

XLVII

I knew who it was, and why he had come. He was looking for me. I would be his next victim.

The doors to my bedroom were closed. Before real fright set in, I crossed with angry strides and threw them open. It could have been a foolish move, but nobody was in the room.

Panic hit me. I left the apartment by the main door, which I generally never used. Clambering over the flower troughs, I ran breathlessly downstairs. Rodan had reappeared from somewhere and was talking to two of the vigiles. It was no surprise when they said they had been sent to warn me: Andronicus must have sensed he was about to be arrested. He had escaped from the aedile's house.

When I reported that he had already been here, I was told to wait in the courtyard with the second paramilitary: Rufinianus. I knew him. He wrote the notes that time I had the other intruder, the one I stuck with a kitchen knife. Rufinianus was hopeless, yet his presence was comforting. The other man took Rodan. They hurried upstairs, first to search the office, then to work their way down, floor by floor, checking the landings and every other apartment. Rodan would open up the empty ones with the pass-keys my father had reluctantly left with him; if nobody answered at the rooms that were occupied, I knew he would push in the door by leaning on it. If tenants complained, he charged them for having the damage mended.

While I waited with Rufinianus, the lamp boy turned up for his evening duties, lugging a big round amphora of Spanish olive oil. I told him to use every light we had, filling them until they were brimming so they would last as long as possible. He looked amazed at the change of policy, but slowly set about it. The common areas eventually blazed more than stairs and open spaces ever do in tenements, to the shock of the inhabitants.

When the whole building had been searched, we knew Andronicus was nowhere there. I learned that Morellus had started on duty early and was leading the hunt. Rufinianus was despatched to bring him up to date about my unwelcome visitation.

"Tell him I lost another needle."

Rodan locked the grille. I was informed that on his return, Rufinianus was to remain in the courtyard. There would be guards all night. For added reassurance, the other man took me to my apartment and walked me through it, re-checking. He gave me the usual sombre vigiles advice to members of the public about keeping shutters closed, locking my doors and admitting nobody I did not know. I reckon he realised that for once somebody was actually listening. He tolerated my quip that what I really had to fear was somebody I *did* know, then he made a to-do of checking all the hooks and hinges on the window shutters. It made him feel better. Nothing would console me. Once I was left alone, I admit I sat on my couch, trembling.

I had overheard strict security instructions being given to all the other tenants on the first and second floors. Such special attention is never as reassuring as the authorities intend; it makes everybody more keyed up. Not that you ever believe them if, on the other hand, the vigiles assure you there is nothing to worry about. The words, "Everything is normal; please go back indoors" immediately make a neighbourhood jumpy.

I had asked if a message could be taken to my father's house, about protecting Postumus. "Oh yes, he killed a boy before, I believe." Clearly the vigiles on the ground had now been briefed in detail.

When Rufinianus did come back from seeing Morellus, he had two other troops with him. I took down hot drinks like a good householder. They were very respectful. I think their unusual good manners were what I found most alarming.

There was nothing else I could do. I lay on my bed all night, fully dressed and generally not sleeping.

XLVIII

I did drift off eventually. I awoke later than usual. A strip-wash and change of clothing helped make me feel more myself. I managed to drink posca, and ate anything I could find: a nub of loaf, a slice of preserved meat, a handful of wizened grapes.

I refused to touch the two apples; they would be sitting on that dish until they went mouldy.

Although I felt as if I was in mourning, I put on earrings I was fond of (my Etruscan filigree rosettes) and a coloured scarf. I had chosen sensible shoes and a sturdy tunic in heavy-weave linen, then speared up my hair very securely with more bone pins than usual. I was dressing for action today.

A member of the day-shift who was a stranger to me had relieved Rufinianus. He allowed me to leave the building, though with stupid reluctance considering I said I was going to consult Morellus at the station house. The man came with me; I deliberately lost him at the end of Fountain Court. I went to the station house by myself. I refused to be guarded by nincompoops. If that was the best the public budget could afford, I would rather not be guarded at all.

It was so early that on the streets I could see anybody coming towards me or hear anyone behind. Behind was what I had to fear with Andronicus. I walked in the middle of the road, wherever the road was wide enough to provide that extra security, not passing too close to any dark door- or stairways. Occasional stray dogs yawned at me. Sad public slaves swept pavements and I saw a long-faced burglar on his way home, disappointed and empty-handed. A couple of bars that stayed open all night during festivals were bestrewn with out-of-town visitors who were now devastated by their hangovers. One who looked as if he might not revive was being stretchered away on a builder's pallet.

Morellus was in his enquiry room, collecting in reports. Andronicus had not been spotted.

What I did learn was that Venusia had been brought in from Aricia last night. Late as it was, a covered litter had arrived subsequently, from which descended a rude woman who had a letter Morellus could not refuse, authorising her to see the prisoner.

"Laia Gratiana? What a pain!" I sympathised.

"Well, I tried to stop the lads from scratching their itchy bumcracks in front of her, but Hades, this is a working barracks, Albia! What did she expect?"

"What happened?"

"I was not party to the discussion. It was short and nasty, judging by the prisoner's state afterwards. I had to get the medico to dose her with a poppy cordial—which she, of course, eagerly took to. Madame herself emerged from the cell looking like a goddess of war, saying she had obtained everything we needed."

"Being Laia, she made it sound as though any idiot could have done the questioning and saved her the trouble?"

"Right! She obviously wasn't going to tell me, Albia, because I am just the man charged with tracking down the perpetrator, so that would be too bloody helpful, wouldn't it? She swanned away, ordering me to inform the aedile she will supply the details at his office, today mid-morning. Lucky him! Nobody was to go to her house to bother her."

"I could try," I volunteered, though not looking forward to it.

"Don't waste effort," Morellus counselled me. "What's another hour or two?"

"Long enough for Andronicus to kill again."

"Well that should be all right then. It's *you* our friend is after next, and you're here, aren't you, darling?"

I could not even raise the energy to order him not to be patronising.

"All safe and snug with me in my private office," mused Morellus. "We could have a bunk-up, if you have time to kill?" The flabby great lump was just raising my spirits by offering.

In lieu of bunking up, he took me out to an oily foodhall where the vigiles had meals when they went off duty, sat me on a bench in the corner behind a fortress-wall of large men, and gave me a second breakfast, this one of elephantine size. He called it the full Roman. It had all the refinement and quantity of a meal barbarians would devour before riding out on a three-day rampage.

I had to sit in the Armilustrium to let the stodgy feast go down. I did not see Robigo. I had glimpsed no foxes since the night of the burning-torch ritual. I knew my Robigo had probably been killed in the Circus.

At mid-morning I went to the aediles' office. A worried slave told me Laia Gratiana had already arrived, but she had ensconced herself with Tiberius and they were not to be disturbed. Had she been more bearable I would have barged in anyway, but in her case, I decided to forego the cheeky option. I would wait until the miserable cow departed, and get the facts direct from the runner. It was bad enough putting up with him.

I had nowhere else I wanted to be, so I waited in their courtyard. It felt wrong, being at the aediles' headquarters without Andronicus. I was glad to be alone while I dealt with that pang. Still, it would kill the demon. This was just a public office. Like them all, the furniture was dingy and the bastards made you hang about.

I had declined refreshments, which was a mistake because I soon felt violently thirsty after the vigiles breakfast. There had been slabs of cured gammon and even the doorstep slices of bread were salty; it was food for men who sweated themselves to wraiths in firestorms. Biffing away the mosquitoes that habituated the fountain, I took a drink of water there after which, since the flow was glugging feebly, I found a stick and began poking the outlet to make it run better. It is a tradition in my family that wherever we go we improve people's water features for them, whether they invite us to or not. You do have to make sure you don't block the thing entirely by mistake, or at least not when they are looking.

Laia and Tiberius must have taken refreshments, because while I was bent over working my water magic, a slave collected their empties. When he carried out the tray, he left the door open behind him. I could then overhear a low murmur of voices. Knowing this was confidential material, I tried not to listen, though not very hard.

Morellus was keeping Venusia in a small, bare, smelly cell, where she could hear horrible noises nearby of men being beaten, drunks screaming, and other unpleasant sounds she could not even identify. She became frantic. The mere appearance of Laia Gratiana, playing the concerned mistress who might use influence to have Venusia released, had been enough to break her. In tears, Venusia had admitted what she claimed was the whole story: Andronicus had made her acquaintance, seduced her, and subsequently made a fool of her. He had even conned the foolish woman out of her life savings. Laia gave Tiberius details which were horribly familiar to me, concerning the archivist's tactics. By the sound of it, he had even taken Venusia for lunch at the same place he once took me.

When she found her lover cooling off, Venusia had become demanding; she threatened to tell Laia he was making trouble for the aedile. His response was the attack that killed Ino. Terrified, Venusia told her fears to Laia, though without admitting the full relationship at that point; she was sent to Aricia. I heard Tiberius comment that it might have been better to ask first, in case official advice was different because of the investigation. At that point someone, probably Tiberius himself, must have noticed the open door and quietly closed it.

I got on with making an elegant job of fountain maintenance. I had no need to hear what followed. I could amuse myself imagining Laia's response to anyone who dared suggest she should have taken advice.

Eventually the door reopened. Laia bounced out first, exclaiming, "It's no use arguing. I will do it!" as if she meant to have the runner's balls toasted in a bread roll.

The elderly maid I recognised must have been chaperoning; she scuttled ahead, presumably to organise Laia's chair, which I had spotted out in the street when I arrived earlier. Tiberius, tight-lipped, escorted Laia as far as the atrium, whence she would leave the building. He took her down the colonnade, which had a certain amount of entwined foliage between the columns; as I remained beside the fountain in one corner, neither of them spotted me. I was therefore a secret witness to their parting: Tiberius leaned in and gave Laia Gratiana a deliberate kiss on the cheek. After a moment of hesitation, she even returned the favour, albeit with an angry peck. Then she swirled her skirts as she turned away; she left without another word on either side.

This was unexpected. I could easily believe that Tiberius would act as a trusted go-between, given that Laia could not abide Manlius Faustus. But the cheek-kiss is a formality for intimates; it is strictly reserved for close colleagues, friends and family. Such farewells should not occur in Rome between a woman of her status, an élite member of the cult of Ceres, and a man who acted as little more than someone else's errand boy.

Well, well!

XLIX

Tiberius stood with his thumbs in his belt, as if ensuring Laia was off the premises. When he turned and noticed me, I almost thought his expression lightened. I was innocently scratching moss off the shell-shaped fountain bowl. Dropping the stick, I brushed my hands clean. "Oh there you are!" I said off-handedly. If he feared I had seen his odd moment with Laia Gratiana, he did not blush.

I followed him into the room he occupied, which at least I had never been in with Andronicus. It must have been decorated for the aediles. Stirring wall frescos showed heroes shedding the blood of monsters, watched by vacuous maidens, in various rocky locations: the sort of lurid adventure people suppose takes place abroad. I had been abroad, and knew otherwise. None of the characters had all their clothes on. There were borders of pretty foliage and distant hints of the seaside. I could live with it. Not from choice, however.

I was offered a ladies' armchair, still warm from the thin backside of Laia. I hopped off that and found a cushioned X-stool. Tiberius took a hard man's stone seat. Not quite marble; Pa had several better ones in a corner of the antiques warehouse.

I sat meekly while my companion relayed all I had overheard Laia saying. He tipped back his head and looked down his nose at me, as if he guessed I had eavesdropped.

———

Tiberius sighed. "We have a problem."

"Really?"

"Andronicus escaped—"

"Yes, while you were sauntering round the Aventine to give yourself courage, he was calmly eating an apple at my place and helping himself to my last sewing needle."

"I'm afraid he just walked out of our house with a basket of old documents, saying he was taking them to the rubbish-heap. The porter had not been warned, because we did not want to alarm Andronicus with any whiff of trouble coming. But he must have sensed it; he never came back. At least we have found and arrested the apothecary who supplied his poison, and warned others. Apparently Andronicus was quite open about who he was. He claimed he needed the drug to paint on arrows to shoot rats in the archive store."

"Every poisoner says that," I grumbled. "You would think apothecaries would be trained to report mad-eyed people who have a rat problem."

"You know him," replied Tiberius wearily. "A few smooth jokes about the vermin being unfeasibly tenacious, that big-eyed confident look of his, and he would convince anyone."

Me, for instance.

"Sorry," apologised Tiberius, although I had not spoken. He became brisker. "Look, I haven't time to be delicate about your love life. Plans must be made. You are not the only person to be harried by Andronicus since he walked free. Laia Gratiana is in danger. She felt somebody was following her around yesterday, and when she arrived home from the station house last night, she definitely saw a man lurking outside her apartment. She is sure it was the same person she glimpsed when Ino was attacked. She described Andronicus' build and distinctive colouring."

I felt hard-hearted about Laia. At least her harasser had not invaded her apartment, and she did not live alone. People would always be around her, and in addition to her large household, Tiberius said she and her brother were to be provided with a day-and-night protection squad from those fine squaddies in the Urban Cohorts.

Well, jolly good for the cult of Ceres! Andronicus was probably unaware that Laia's brother even existed. I did point out that all I was assigned were a couple of near-useless vigiles. Tiberius annoyed me by saying that was because I was thought more capable.

Then I learned that the "problem" was more complex and risky than safeguarding a couple of target homes until the killer was caught. Tonight there was a serious risk that Andronicus could strike again. Despite having been stalked—presumably because Andronicus was enraged she had put Venusia out of his reach—Laia was insisting on joining in an after-dark ritual that was a high spot of the Cerialia: the cult women would be roaming the Aventine, dressed in white and carrying torches, as they re-enacted the goddess Ceres' search for her missing daughter. I groaned with disbelief, as I imagined the scene: women who had no street-sense at the best of times, running about in all directions as they called for Proserpina at all the crossroads. There were many of those on the Aventine, most of them in seedy areas, overlooked and underlit.

"Tiberius, we cannot allow this! Surely for just one year, Laia Gratiana can sit it out and weave at her loom at home?"

"She absolutely refuses." Well, who likes weaving?

"Get her brother to lock her in the house."

"No, he thinks she is wonderfully brave and spirited." The runner looked at the floor. "Of course, this has to do with Faustus."

"She sets herself up as a target, in revenge for his unfaithfulness? If anything happens to her, all the blame lands on him?"

"She won't think of it like that, not consciously. But you are right: as organisers, the aediles are responsible for the cult women's security. Normally all it entails is keeping drunks away from them." Tiberius dropped his face into his hands for a moment. When he looked up, he was unusually satirical. "And keeping them away from the drunks sometimes . . . Albia, this will be a nightmare. You must have seen it. You have a bunch of women who are not safe handling fiery torches, and who in my opinion have secretly tucked into wine fortified with very dubious substances. They run amuck like bacchantes, shouting their heads off and threatening to burn down the whole bloody region."

This was a deliciously intimate revelation about a ritual most people suppose to be sedate. I giggled, partly at his despair. "If it's that kind of wild party, I may join in myself."

Tiberius sat up. He said that was the best idea anyone had had so far. He would be one of the group patrolling the area, and I could go with him. Then he could personally look out for my safety while I could lend my eyes to assist him.

L

It would go wrong, almost certainly. Set up a woman as bait for a man who had already sent too many bodies prematurely to the pyre? An invitation to disaster.

I spent the rest of the day at home, supposedly resting. I had been taken back to Fountain Court by my vigiles escort, after the fool finally caught up with me. Later he delivered me to Prisca's baths. I enjoyed the amenities, but my real purpose was to proposition two people I thought could be helpful.

Zoe and Chloe, the women who wanted to be gladiators, were bemused by my story. I told them the truth about Andronicus and the danger he posed, because I wanted to be fair. I explained that he was out to get me, and also one of the cult members who would be cavorting on the Aventine that night. I knew from Tiberius that to give Laia courage, she would be with her friend, Marcia Balbilla; I wanted them to have bodyguards.

"The women will be in the chariot, because the chief priestess is too old. So we will always know where these two are, even if all the others are weaving about like escaped sheep. It's a women-only night, supposedly—well, participants—so we can't line the streets with soldiery; that would be out of place. But no one will object if the targets have two armed Amazons."

"This chariot—" Chloe was the facetious one. "I've seen it other years. It's towed by big serpents, isn't it? Can't we dress up as the snakes?"

"No. We shall have powerful men hidden inside the monster costumes. Strong enough to drag the chariot—or to help if the murderer is stupid enough to approach. If he does, we need you to be light on your feet. Keep him at arms' length, remember; don't let him strike you with a poisoned needle. Or the cult members while they are cuddling up together in the chariot," I felt obliged to add, having nothing against Marcia Balbilla.

Zoe looked deeply suspicious of the whole affair. "Are these women lesbians?"

"Of course not! One is married. The other had a husband once."

"Could be a cover."

"I really don't think so, Zoe. Marcia Balbilla has children, I believe." I could not believe I was having this conversation with two well-built girls who dressed up in breastplates and swords. "Look, the sisterhood is no big caboodlum anyway—what about you and Chloe?"

Zoe was shocked. "We are just close friends." *Very* close, I reckoned.

"So are Laia and Marcia. And if I'm wrong, they won't jump you, they are faithful to each other."

"We don't want to be seen with Sapphists. We have to think of our reputations."

"That never bothered you when you took up gladiating!"

I dragged these coy Amazons to Marcia's house, where the cult women were preparing. They were dressing up in their folded-over white Greek gowns and fake wheat crowns, twittering like a wedding party. As had been insinuated by the runner, the devotional dames were well supplied with great silver bowls of some warm liquid that exuded a powerful aromatic smell. Not, believe me, thyme and rosemary.

There, to my further amazement, I had a similar conversation with the two respectable matrons as I had had with Zoe and Chloe earlier.

"Just don't show each other too much affection," I warned wickedly. "You don't want the Amazons to get the wrong idea about you.

Myself, I really don't care what people get up to, but they are narrow-minded. No fondling!"

Balbilla and Gratiana looked put out, yet as I left I overheard them in fits of nervous giggles.

I went in a hired chair to the temple, my agreed rendezvous with Tiberius.

The Temple of Ceres was thick with people tonight, but as I arrived, he peeled off from a group of men and came up. He had been barbered again and was in white, though carrying a dark cloak. To comply with the law, he had to be unarmed. If I had been him, I would have broken the law, but as the aedile's man, I suppose he was stuck with compliance.

I was in white myself. I only owned one proper white gown, which happened to be in delicate opaque material. Luckily it was long enough to cover my sturdy ankle boots, inappropriate accessories with silk-weave gauzes, but excellent for kicking. Not possessing a wheat crown, I had threaded a gold necklace through my hair; that had been put up professionally at Prisca's bathhouse where, since I had had time to spare, a girl had also given me an eyebrow tidy and face-paint job.

This groomed effect made Tiberius gulp. "I see you are intending to stand out!"

"Give me a torch and I'll look like one of the others."

"None of them find it necessary to be in see-through."

I had a perfectly thick undertunic (though a little short because I had run out of long ones) making the filmy dress decent. "Oh shut up. I'm not fourteen and you are not my mother."

I let the prude stare. We had discussed the white dress plan; it meant I could blend in with the cult women.

His disapproval was spoiling the mood for me. Since so much of my life was spent looking dowdy for work reasons, I did occasionally like to lash on the cosmetics and jewellery. I admit Mother would have said *four* necklaces was one too many, but too late: my neat belt-purse was already full, with emergency cash and a small but deadly weapon which I could pass off, if challenged, as a fruit knife.

Every woman should own her own little decorative hunting dagger. You never know when you may need it.

LI

"Hail, goddess, preserve this city in harmony and prosperity. Bring us all the products of the earth, feed our kine and cattle and flocks, donate the corn-ear, give us the harvest. Nurture also peace, so he that ploughed may also reap! Be gracious, O thrice-prayed for, great Queen of goddesses!"

Laia Gratiana was having a tremendous time amidst the wreathing altar smoke. She *was* blonde Ceres for tonight. After solemn incantations at the temple, she had ascended an enormous chariot, pretending to shake the reins. Marcia Balbilla was in there behind her, relegated to the role of torch-bearer. As Laia leaned forwards, shrieking, in go-faster mode, two men inside large curly snake costumes heaved the vehicle along. It was a great, heavy, bucketing thing. The friendly-faced snakes towed the vehicle with hidden ropes attached to the wheels.

Their task was to drive around the Aventine, stopping at every crossroads as the celebrants gave loud shouts in all directions. Tomorrow Proserpina would be returned to her mother from Pluto's underworld with her half-eaten pomegranate, which would be a much quieter re-enactment. Tonight, Ceres was letting the crops die in winter while she hunted for her child. Each cult woman grasped a long flaming torch, with which they ran about, lamenting. They had produced classical costumes, with varying degrees of success; most managed a peplos with a folded top, pinned on the shoulders with brooches, while the daring left the sides open. Fortunately for modesty, Greek dress is voluminous so if it was properly done, many folds hid the peeking-breast look. (Men at streetbar counters were hoping otherwise.) Some women wanted such authenticity they wore their hair loose and went barefoot, as a sign of ritual mourning, though any who had done this before on the Aventine streets knew better and at least wore sandals. Most Roman women possess a pair of suitably Greek-looking toe-posts. You never know, do you, whether you may have to gallop about your neighbourhood in the name of ancient religion?

None of the women would have consulted a map beforehand; in the tangle of narrow, unnamed alleys they were liable to get separated and become fatally lost. Morellus had put vigiles out, ready to herd them back like sheepdogs.

I made one last attempt to stop the fiasco. "This is too risky! Can't you just for once forego the play-acting?"

"It is important," Tiberius argued. "Ceres brought us out of our barbarous condition, educated mankind, gave us civilisation. The point is to relearn our history. In this way, we may come to live happily and die with greater hope."

I laughed. "Someone has been reading up! You're defending your aedile."

"Don't be snide, Albia. He has to manage the Games with care and reverence, reverence to the gods through acts of worship. The intention is to intercede for favour, make Ceres well disposed to Rome, in order to guarantee a good harvest for the well-being of the city."

"Good luck!" I chortled.

Tiberius, scowling, marched behind the chariot; I, not scowling, strolled beside him. Zoe and Chloe skipped either side. The men in scaly snake costumes guarded the front. Laia and Marcia had a degree of protection simply because their driving platform was high up. Other members of the cult were flowing around wherever the mood took them. They had the reckless air of women who might be tipsy, though I was surprised how controlled they stayed. Tiberius deigned to grin, and said plebeian princesses could hold their drink.

On the uneven roads, the chariot was difficult to manoeuvre. It had an inbuilt axle flaw which made it lean to one side, another factor that slowed progress. The men hauling it had to skew themselves to force it in a straight line. If one of them miscalculated, sometimes their tall snake headdresses bashed together accidentally; the carnival beasts were beginning to look tattered and rakish. One had lost its forked red tongue.

We veered across the Aventine, stopping frequently. Each time, the women yelled lustily. Eventually the pageant ground to a halt at a particularly smelly junction, where a large crowd had gathered in anticipation. A man pretending to be a lame old woman accosted Ceres with a stream of filthy jokes and insults. This was part of the ritual; it represented an ancient servant, Baubo, daughter of Pan and Echo, the one person who had made Ceres smile as the depressed goddess searched.

Tiberius leant on a bar counter, signalling for drinks. "This will take some time . . . You will not believe, Albia, the stress in hiring an insult-giver. We even had a contract schedule, listing acceptable terms and how many times he is authorised to use the worst swear words. Faustus had to sit for hours, to audition actors telling him gutter jokes."

"Managing the rites with care and reverence," I reminded him gravely. "I suppose if he wants it to be a memorable year, he needs to make it sensationally crude? Are you auditing the ribald script? If only I'd brought my note tablet, I could tally up the 'fucks' for you."

"Flavia Albia, behave more demurely."

"As you once said, I am not a nice young lady."

"You are when you choose. Just be natural, can't you?"

"Spoilsport!" I muttered, though there was no heart in it. I felt like a chastised dog, though with no intention of rolling over. If I was a dog, it was a strong-willed, stubborn Britannia terrier. Tiberius might not know them, but they can never be mastered. They make up their own minds whom they respect; choice once made, they show bloody-minded, unflinching loyalty. Thankfully, Tiberius and I were never going to be on those terms.

He left his drink. What man does that?

He abandoned me too, and it took me a moment to see why. The crowd was even heavier at this junction, lasciviously keen on the Baubo scenario. Even the actor playing the rude crone was clinging to a chariot wheel to avoid being dragged out of the goddess's earshot by the press of merrymakers, while Laia could almost certainly hear very little of the bawdry with those shell-like ears—from which dangled *extremely* expensive earrings, I noticed. She and Marcia were beginning to look concerned about the sheer number surrounding their vehicle, though I spotted that one group of men was facing outwards and pushing back onlookers—clearly the vigiles.

They were preoccupied with crowd control, so had not noticed a worse danger: attempting to climb crablike up the opposite wheel from Baubo was someone with a familiar auburn head. Tiberius must have seen him and was working his way as best he could through the lively crush of bystanders. He was never going to make it. There was no point me trying to follow, so I climbed on the bar counter inelegantly, and stood up. I banged two metal jugs together above my head and shrieked at the top of my voice to alert the Amazon bodyguards.

Chloe was nearest. The more manly of the couple, she was short, wide and fearless. Chloe hurled herself onto Andronicus. He hung onto the chariot. She clung to him. The beautifully decorated chariot of Ceres began rocking so violently that the two women in it squealed and peered over the gilded coachwork. All credit to Marcia Balbilla: she then took a firm grip on her long ritual torch and banged down the lower end on Andronicus like a laundry worker with a washing-dolly. I think she aimed for his face, which would have been perfect, but she only hit his shoulder. She did dislodge him; he fell to the ground with Chloe on top, squashing him. Marcia lost her nerve and began screaming hysterically. Laia proved her quality and slapped her out of it, belting Marcia so hard I feared she must have lost teeth. She lost her balance, and fell off the back of the chariot.

Tiberius had reached the vehicle. He gestured furiously to the two snake-dressed hauliers. I heard him shouting, *"Go! Go!"* They took the strain. The chariot lurched forwards a few feet.

Zoe appeared, to find Chloe gripping Andronicus in a headlock with one arm, while with the other she pulled Marcia Balbilla to her feet, dewy-eyed with admiration for her exploit with the torch. Marcia stumbled tipsily and fell against Chloe. Zoe took that wrongly. Always pugnacious, she cursed and flew at Chloe, who had the sense to give Marcia a shove well out of the way. As they battled with their wooden swords, to the hysterical delight of the crowd, Andronicus squeezed free.

He made off and I tried to bawl for people to apprehend him. Useless. This was the Aventine. Any time you shout "Stop, thief!," strangers instinctively step in your way to prevent you catching the culprit, while he runs off laughing.

I was pulled down off the bar by eager men who liked a woman dancing on a counter in a half-transparent dress. They were too blissed out to cause me serious anxiety. I slipped through their grasp and wriggled my way through delighted people towards the action scene.

I saw Tiberius leap on the back of the chariot while the crowd surged forward and helped push it. This was so successful it shot ahead, rattling off at the fastest speed it had gone all night. Everyone tumbled along with it, except me. I was left, standing in a now dark and silent area, with Marcia Balbilla's dying torch. I picked it up and twirled it until the flame burned up. Holding it aloft, I set off steadily after the others, following the shadow I had spotted: someone who tailed the convoy, unobtrusively lurking at the back so nobody noticed him. I knew it was Andronicus.

LII

I lost him. He must have merged into the crowd.

By the time I caught up myself, I could see Tiberius looking back anxiously from the chariot, as if he had glimpsed our quarry or some other risk. The vehicle jerked to a sudden stop again; the Baubo actor was once more trying to earn his fee. Being re-enacted now was a traditional scene where the old crone groaned as if in the desperate pangs of childbirth (helped by the crowd chorusing along with *"Heave!"*), then lifted up her skirts to reveal her privates (was that what amused Ceres?—she must be easily tickled). Baubo then produced a child of Ceres' own—represented tonight for extra comic effect by a swaddled piglet. The dialogue was as refined as the events. Laia Gratiana looked pained, but was encouraged to smile by raucous spectators who did not know she was too snooty.

I had more to worry about. The mob had increased here, including a boy I recognised with horror. He had climbed halfway up a column on a fire porch for a better view and was hanging there by one arm. At least it meant I noticed him. Watching wide-eyed, with all his solemn, curious intelligence, was young Postumus. He was carefully absorbing every detail, taking in every obscenity. Dear gods, my terrible brother had a waxed tablet and stylus; despite his perilous position, he was writing down the jokes. Baubo had noticed and was looking furious at the breach of copyright.

Someone else saw this too. Postumus had not spotted Andronicus, but Andronicus had fixed on him. I suddenly made out the archivist, beginning to move purposely towards my brother.

I was too far away. I tried shouting but there was too much general noise. I began to push through the crowd, assailed by smells and grabbing hands, using my torch to clear a space. There was little room to swing it but I stabbed a few feet and ribs in passing.

I saw an arm grab Postumus from below. Sick with fear, I jumped up on a large pot outside a shop, only to see it was Tiberius, with Morellus close behind him. Postumus was pulled down, furiously wriggling as he lost his note tablet. Relief surged, as I watched my brother flung hand to hand like a victim being rescued from a blazing building, in the classic vigiles manoeuvre. Somewhere at the end of that line, Postumus would receive a dressing-down. If Morellus had told his men who Postumus was, he would be escorted home, in the hope of a moneybag from our grateful parents. If Papa had been happily organising his wine cellar, they might even get one.

Andronicus had vanished again. I began pushing this way and that, searching. I heard Morellus call to some of his men, "Keep looking for Ginger!" and I reached Tiberius and Morellus. Frantic gestures indicated where Andronicus must be, so we butted our way in that direction. He must have leapt among the pavement paraphernalia outside a shop, kicking over a large jar of tallow for lamps. It smelt awful and as it spilled across the road, the cobbles had become slippery. People were also throwing nuts now, purposely trying to sting others with the hard little missiles.

The chariot slumped then set off again, once more helped by the crowd. Now they took up the Baubo episode's cry of *"Heave!,"* as if the vehicle's painful momentum shadowed the birth process. It was a larger crowd, they pushed much harder, and as the lumbering vehicle swayed like a baby suddenly slithering out of its mother, one of the men in snake costumes at the front lost his footing on the spilt tallow. He fell, screaming in agony as a wheel ran over him. The chariot lurched spectacularly, then its axle collapsed.

Laia and Marcia were thrown out. The Amazons rushed to stand on guard over Laia, while Morellus strode across, grabbed Marcia and pulled her into the entrance to an apartment block. Closer to me, Tiberius had finally homed in on Andronicus. I scrambled after, treading on or elbowing anybody in my way. Just as Tiberius reached him, the runner's boot slid on a scatter of nuts. He was careering so fast he could not stop himself; he sprawled full length on the cobbles. Andronicus dropped onto him, punching him repeatedly with a fast, full arm stretch. The winded runner could barely protect himself. I still had the torch, so I ran straight in, swinging it as a weapon in wide arcs.

"Andronicus! Take on a woman, why don't you?"

Rearing backwards, away from the naked flame, he only just kept his feet. I was extremely angry and wanted him to know it. Prettied up at Prisca's and in my finery, I must have made a wild vision. He looked shaken.

Brandishing the torch, I really was trying to set fire to him. I would have killed him if I could. Tiberius stopped me. Still on the ground, he grabbed me by the ankle, shaking his head. I kicked free, but by then Andronicus had backed, cursed, twisted around and disappeared into a mass of people.

Tiberius struggled to his feet. "Leave it; we'll get him . . ." He was badly bruised and had a cut by his eye which needed to be mopped up. I checked; Andronicus had gone. I pulled Tiberius out of the crowd; we found refuge in the entrance where Morellus had shoved Marcia Balbilla, a sour stairwell to a typical multiple-occupancy block, stinking of damp, neglect, and uncollected urine in a great tank.

"*Cerberus!*"

"*—With bells on his tail!*"

We backed out fast. Morellus and Marcia were still there, closely engaged, and not locked in a discussion of public order control. I thought I might have to rescue her, then I realised that Marcia was doing most of the work. Morellus just leaned back against a bannister with his eyes closed, and thought it was his lucky day. Thank goodness he had had the presence of mind to put his fire-axe on one side or he would have disembowelled himself as they went at it. I left the torch, in case they needed extra light.

So much for festival abstinence.

Outside, Tiberius and I found space by a wall we could lean on. He managed to wipe some blood off himself with one arm. We settled our breathing. I found him a napkin that I kept folded small in my belt purse, which he pressed on his cut eye.

We watched the street slowly clear. The wrecked chariot was towed away by members of the vigiles. Laia Gratiana must have been rescued and taken home. Any other cult women had given up for the evening too.

Zoe and Chloe were looking after the two men in snake costumes; we saw them all go to a bar. The one who had been run over had to be supported by both women, but despite any cracked ribs he was clearly still up for whatever the night ahead might hold. Both men had the innocent seriousness of fellows who think they have picked up a couple of likely prospects. Zoe and Chloe were going to fleece them for drinks. Well, so I presumed. Who knows?

"Intriguing foursome!" Tiberius grinned.

"Gruesome scope for misunderstandings! . . . So," I mused, in a thoughtful tone. "What about that then—Morellus and Marcia?"

The runner and I looked at one another. We could not help ourselves; we doubled up together and laughed until we were breathless all over again.

Somebody was watching us.

It was me who felt the accusing gaze. It was me who first saw him. We were supposed to be tailing him, but how long had Andronicus been observing us? He could not know the cause of the hysterical mirth that had us clutching our stomachs and laughing until we wept;

he was staring at me like a man who had found his new bride in bed with her grandfather.

He had been motionless in front of a shuttered shop. Once he realised I had seen him, he tossed his head scornfully and set off away from us. I straight away ran after him, not waiting to explain to Tiberius, though he was so hard on my heels he could have stepped on my dress hem and tripped me.

We were close to the huge Temple of Juno the Queen—the exotic Aventine Juno, brought here from Veii when Rome conquered the Etruscans, not the grand Greek version who lived on the Capitol. Andronicus ran down the side of the building, then on across the frontage of the tiny Temple of Liberty, which is supposed to be Rome's oldest library, the place where slaves are freed. There were always a few people about there; he zigzagged through knots of them, perhaps unaware that wherever there was enough light from lanterns, that bright nut-brown head of his was a giveaway. Perhaps he knew and did not care. He enjoyed the chase, believing himself invincible. No one had caught him so far tonight. Why should he fear capture?

He was moving faster than it seemed from his relaxed lope; we were making no headway. He reached the long street that would take him to the Temples of Minerva and Diana. Now he began bounding along, springing up on goods piled outside shops and kicking them over, so our progress was hampered as the outraged owners came rushing out to resecure them. Rolling jugs and scattered buckets tumbled in our path. Unhappy shopkeepers dragged at our tunics, gesticulating in various foreign languages and pleading for justice as we broke away and rushed on.

He plunged into the backstreets. He fled down alleys clogged with years'-old rubbish, where dung paved the road. He dodged around fountains where ragged old drunks were lounging. He vanished into dark narrow entries that could be fatal dead-ends. The whores he pushed aside had collected their wits and were ready to abuse us as we ran up in his wake. Dogs he had disturbed stretched their legs and thought about biting chunks out of us. We were lucky, they were too busy peeing on cornerstones to bother. When I stumbled over litter, Tiberius grabbed my hand. When he slid a yard on slime, upright as a lake-skater in some frozen northern wilderness, I steadied him.

Andronicus crossed Greater Laurel Street. Delivery carts were out and about, now the festival proceedings were over. For a short stretch he confused us by dodging among the carts, then he nipped into a cross street, and was off again, veering past bars and workshops, pushing over a vegetable stall so we were handicapped by streams of rolling cabbages.

He burst out onto the Clivus Publicius, some way ahead of us. We lost sight of him. Suddenly we saw him again, now riding on the back of a startled mule he had unhitched from an unattended cart. He rode the beast full pelt down the hill away from us, looking back with his face alight with glee, one arm aloft as if wielding a triumphal banner, and whooping taunts. Ironically, we were only yards from where the ox-wagon had killed Lucius Bassus.

He knew he was safe. Just as we rallied ourselves to follow, a grim troop of Praetorian Guards marched past. The tall togate brutes were unmistakable, with soldiers' boots showing below their tunics and their swords under their clothes. They never wear full armour inside Rome, but they don't need to. They had probably been sent to execute some philosopher Domitian objected to for campaigning for a better world, but we would do for starters, just to get them in the mood before the bloody business in their orders.

Unable to pull up in a timely fashion and with no pillar to hide behind, we had run right in among this noble death squad. The big bored men were automatically unhappy about us. Breathless people running must be running away from a crime. People who give feeble explanations are people who ought to spend time in a cell, getting their story straight on a starvation diet in between visits from the torturer. As for women on the streets in opaque dresses, they need a good seeing to and these were the heroes to do it—one after the other, or several at once if there was no time for orderly queuing. If and when Tiberius argued about my treatment, he would be given similar attention. At the Praetorian Camp there was a scale of reparations, where people with complaints of harassment generally found they would not in fact receive compensation, but would be charged for those old military myths, "insult to a Roman officer" and "damaged uniforms."

We were in trouble. I assumed any quick thinking would be up to me, though my tired brain refused to cooperate. I was surprised, therefore, when Tiberius straightened up, hauled aside the centurion, a slow beast with ringworm, spoke a few words, showed his signet ring, and signalled to me to come and stand safely beside him. I was being taught new rude words and pawed heavily. One of the men had that clever knack of removing clothes from women without them noticing what he was up to.

Coins chinked. The centurion demurely uttered, "Have a good night then, sir!," glancing at me as if he assumed I was some blowsy piece Tiberius had paid for by the hour from a "manicure parlour." Neither of us had the energy to set him straight. I was too preoccupied, garment-wise. I had to retrieve one of my shoulder brooches from the gutter.

The Guards marched on to carry out their important work for the emperor. They left us like two misdelivered sacks, standing alone on the dark pavement.

LIII

Only much later, after I had been taken home and had flung myself on my bed in complete collapse, did it strike me how peculiar we must have looked there on the Clivus Publicius, so what a lucky escape we had had. Tiberius was not just coughing with exertion, but his face was bruised and cut as if he had been in a professional boxing bout. I had such a sore windpipe I could hardly breathe, while the sweat in my eyes from so much running must have made my cosmetics run. He had lost his cloak early in the proceedings; I never had one. We must have seemed incoherent and agitated even to Praetorians, who are used to meeting all kinds of bad characters, offering them all kinds of lame excuses.

Using his mysterious influence, Tiberius extricated us. We fell in with some vigiles. I was put in a chair and escorted to Fountain Court. A guard was posted. My brain was alive with wild images of the night. Despite that, I must have fallen into a deep sleep.

Next day I awoke knowing we had no plans. The situation seemed impossible. Yesterday the cult women had given us a physical focus for our hunt, but today's rites would all take place in the Circus Maximus. Even if our quarry bothered to go, among two hundred thousand people he would be invisible. He surely would not be so stupid as to attack the ceremonies. Otherwise, Andronicus had shown he had no fear of a vigiles' search—rightly. Even with no funds he was resourceful. If he lay low in the city, he could escape detection indefinitely. He might even flee from Rome. We had somehow to flush him out, and fast. As I struggled to rise, wash and change into normal day clothes, I had no ideas how to do that.

I went to the Stargazer. Seating myself stiffly at one of the inside tables, I signalled to Junillus for bread rolls and hot mulsum. Of his own accord he brought over the remains of the main cold meat platter; he shook out the ends of various olive bowls among the last slices of Lucanian sausage and shreds of smoked ham on the big dish from which he made takeouts and counter snacks for early workers. My vigiles minder stood upright, having something basic. Eating automatically, I fell into a vacant dream.

It was a warm day with a breeze, not chilly. Mid-morning, for I had slept in late. No other customers.

Life seemed bad. No hope, no solution, no point.

Without me being aware of it, Junillus had gone into the back kitchen, taking crockery to wash. In any caupona it was daily routine. He would be there for a while, starting preparations for the lunchtime rush. The vigilis must have gone out to use the lavatory, then being a man who could never stay quiet, he started talking to, or at least, at Junillus. He had been getting no joy out of me. I could hear him maundering on about the races or another tedious subject, with occasional grunts or short phrases from my cousin, among chopping and scooping sounds as he worked on food. I could not see them. I was alone. As a relative, I would be in charge of the bar if any customers came and I was accustomed to serving myself if I wanted anything, so Junillus would not bother to pop out to check. Junillus and the other man were out of sight and separated from me by several yards, when someone leaned over one of the counters from the street, a mere four feet from me.

It was Andronicus.

LIV

Oddly enough, even in this confined space, I felt little fear being alone with him. It was easier to be face-to-face than menaced by an unseen presence. Anyway, I knew him. Even with a killer, you feel that it matters. You have been friends, so he will not harm you. He will believe you can help him. You loved him once, so he cannot kill you. Alone among the people he threatens, you will be safe.

"Well there you are!" he exclaimed.

He had his weight on one elbow, leaning on the irregularly shaped, pastel-coloured pieces of marble that form the crazy patterns of most bar counters. He was giving me the old look, that flash of innocent, open eyes, the wrinkled forehead, the bright, shared, conspiratorial gaze. The past few days might never have happened. He was boyish and mercurial again, acting the man I fell for. This time the attraction failed.

I kept my voice level. "I am surprised you show your face, Andronicus!"

"Why? I have done nothing wrong." He would always believe that. It was at the heart of his madness, a disease of his soul. He had no remorse.

"You know what you did. You killed five people—five we know about. Viator, the boy, Salvidia, the old lady, the maid. Were there more?"

He shrugged. He seemed indifferent.

320

"Do you admit you killed those people?"

"Why not? None of them is a loss. Don't grieve. The stiffs deserved it."

"Were there others beforehand? Or when you heard about the needle killings at the aediles' meeting did you start then? Did that first give you the idea?" When he made no answer, I insisted, "Andronicus, were there others?"

He shrugged again. "That was all." I would never know whether I could believe him.

"So you confess to me, Andronicus? Five people offended you, so you murdered them? You knew poisoned needles were being used in an outbreak all across Rome. You reasoned you could do something similar, concealing your crimes?"

"It was not me, I'm just fooling you."

"It was you."

"Why do you care?"

"Because I hate injustice!" I railed at him. His lack of empathy exasperated me. There was no reasoning with him. "All of those people were taken from life before their time and for petty motivation. All because you are an emotionless, irresponsible, utterly cold-hearted bastard. Superficially charming—but in truth you are dishonest, arrogant and completely callous."

Finally, my agitation shook him. My failure of composure forced him to say, "If you are right, then I am sorry for it all."

I could see his thoughts already, finding excuses for himself, working up some new story to try out on me. "I had a hard life, Albia. You have no idea."

"Rubbish. I know about hard lives. You were never abandoned, starved, beaten, abused. What do you know of isolation and hopelessness? Bitter cold, curses, constant fear and misery? You never endured any of that. You have always had a roof and food, you never knew insecurity. Compared to me, Andronicus, as a freedman brought up in a comfortable home and given every opportunity, you were damned fortunate."

He would never accept my comparison. He was totally self-centred.

I was trying not to let him spot me watching for a chance of assistance. For the only time ever, it seemed, nobody at all came walking down either of the streets on whose corner the Stargazer sat. If I tried to attract attention from Junillus and the vigiles, Andronicus could easily reach me before they understood what I wanted. Nothing on my table would make a satisfactory weapon.

"I am trying to understand why, Andronicus. Why are you so resentful, why so unhappy? You are amiable and talented, well thought of as an archivist, with a good post in a prestigious temple." A thought struck me. "It sounds as if it all went sour for you when Manlius Faustus became aedile. You and he had already had a set-to over the position as secretary that he refused you—you see him as idle and worthless, favoured by his uncle and in high position simply because of who he is. Am I right?"

"Shrewd as ever," answered Andronicus, turning it into one of the compliments I now hated. "You see it as it is, dear Albia—why him? Most honoured in Rome? Aediles must be among the top hundred officials. What has he ever done for that?"

"Won votes and acted effectively—that's the system, you know! I think your main quarrel is that he is too strong for you," I told him. "He sees through you. He won't do as you want. Were all the terrible things you did to those other people caused by your naked jealousy of him?"

When I asked an uncomfortable question, Andronicus simply failed to answer me.

With no way yet to attract help, I was running out of ideas. I did not want to talk to him at all, and it was an effort concentrating on arguments with someone whose mind worked so differently from normal.

I dared not take my eyes off him. I knew I was tiring. "You found my apartment, I gather. And earlier, you took my needle-case?"

"Just a memento of you," Andronicus declared, as if it was a lover's trophy. "You can have it back, if you want?"

Determined to stop his games, I lost patience and snapped, "Don't lie. You cannot do that. Tiberius has it now."

I watched Andronicus adjusting his story, as Tiberius had described. "He and I are on good terms. I can ask him for it any time."

"You're not on good terms. He won't give it to you; he needs it as evidence."

"He would give it to *you!*" said Andronicus, smiling in a way I did not care for.

"Do you still have my sewing needles?"

"Probably not. Who knows?" He did have them. With luck, he had had no opportunity to coat them with anything dangerous.

I said to him, as if it was perfectly normal, "Well, I would offer you refreshments but you know I have to keep a good eye on you, in case you jump over that counter and stick me with a poisoned needle."

At that, he gave me a sweet, sweet smile. "I used the last one. Used it to kill the vixen." He was lying again, because I knew he had been in my apartment and taken the needle on the ribbon *after* he dispatched the vixen. "I had to help her, didn't I? I did that for you, Albia."

"I know." I remained quiet, despite my anger. What was the point in saying I would rather not have such consideration from a killer? I didn't need him. I could myself have found a way to do whatever was necessary. When the wounded fox was on the stairs, I could have been brave, held down her head with the broom, carried out the humane deed. "Yes, that was your only decent and honest action."

"And you know, it was horrible to do! Not a woman's job," Andronicus insisted.

That made me flare up. All my work is thought by some to be unsuitable for women. I hate that attitude. "According to you, a woman should only admire men respectfully and submit. Shut up and open up."

"I never treated you like that, Albia."

"What you did to me was worse. I was not someone you preyed on for particular ends like Venusia, trying to pick her brains about Faustus, and even stealing her money. You liked me. I do believe it. You wanted our friendship, as much as you ever truly value anything—yet even so, you lied, deceived, manipulated and played with me."

"You are so hard on me!" He grinned shamelessly.

"At least you never stole my life savings."

He feigned shock. Then he said, unbelievably, "Are you telling me it is all over?"

"Of course I am. Be realistic. Our so-called friendship died the moment I began to see through you."

Andronicus gave me his jealous frown. "So there is somebody else?"

He would never change. The fault could never be his. He would not accept that he had let himself down, that he had damned himself in a knowing woman's eyes. He would go through life—whatever he had left of it—continually blaming others. When he blamed someone too angrily, he would remove them. He would plan someone's destruction, secretly prepare his weapon, stalk them, attack them, then revel in their death as though he had somehow taken a responsibility upon himself—not to revenge his own imagined slights but to cleanse society.

For rejecting him, he would kill me too, if he could.

Suddenly, two things happened.

Junillus came in from the back, carrying a large pottery container of the Stargazer's horrible daily chickpeas.

Two men we knew came walking together towards the caupona: Morellus and Tiberius.

LV

All three must have seen my predicament at pretty well the same moment. All three started towards me. I heard a whistle, the summons that would make any nearby vigiles come running. Junillus put on a surprising burst of speed for a boy with his arms full of deadweight crockery, containing a hotpot he had just spent effort preparing. He would not want to spill and waste it. Being nearest, he staggered forwards and interposed himself with the pot so Andronicus, who had clearly considered leapfrogging over the counter to come at me, had second thoughts. He had experienced the lunchtime chickpeas; he would not want to argue with that powerful concoction.

Andronicus had the option of fleeing down the other street, but chose direct attack. He spun around and ran at the others. Instinctively they separated to give him two targets. He chose Morellus. Assuming the hefty Morellus could handle it, Tiberius veered around towards the Stargazer in case Andronicus had harmed anyone there. I was on my feet by now. Morellus briefly grappled with the fugitive, but he yelled when Andronicus stuck something into him. Knowing the outcome of a poisoned needle, Morellus froze in horror. Andronicus escaped. Tiberius checked me, shot a thank-you at Junillus, then bounded back to help.

Scrambling out to the street, I too reached Morellus. There was a needle still in his arm. He was now gasping for breath in a panic attack. I plucked out the needle, holding it carefully by the eye between my thumb and one finger. I dropped it down a gutter drain. Then all I could remember about poison was that folk remedy for snake and scorpion bites: I fetched out my little knife, then slashed across Morellus' reddened skin so I could squeeze and make him bleed as much as possible immediately. Tiberius put an arm under him and held him up, in case he fainted.

"Avenging Mars, he's done for me!"

Tiberius and Junillus were dragging him into the caupona where he could be given more attention. "There, Morellus, it was only a gnat bite. Albia has done you much worse damage."

"Be brave," I urged, though I did not blame him. "Fight it. Stay with us, Morellus. I'll ask my uncles the lawyers to sue me for compensation; you want to be here for your payout, don't you?"

I knew I was white-faced; the runner did not look much better. Our eyes met, facing up in despair to the fact that Morellus might be beyond help.

There were vigiles all over the place now; squads of them must have been stationed in nearby streets and alleys, combing the area for Andronicus. A crowd soon gathered, including the usual phony doctors, apothecaries, farriers, barbers and all those other charlatans claiming medical knowledge who hope to make fees from street accidents. Chair-men came at a run, jostling to be first in the queue to ferry any wounded home and charge them extra for alleged blood on their upholstery. All we needed was a seedy informer proffering legal advice, but I had that covered. Ever the professional.

Morellus was maundering about his wife and children, so he had definitely given up. Junillus brought him a cup of water, which he rejected, so I drank it. I remembered Andronicus had said to me that he had used his last poisoned needle on the vixen. I said this. Morellus calmed down slightly. Over his head, Tiberius was giving me the silent message that he would not trust anything Andronicus claimed, but what poor Morellus needed most was reassurance. Anything: in his line of work, he was comfortable with dishonesty. Either he was safe, or in a short while he would feel a strong need to lie down, then at least we knew he would pass away very peacefully.

I decided he would rather no one spelled that out.

The vigiles pushed back the crowd and ordered people to go home. During the pause while they arranged transport to take Morellus to the station house, I spoke to Tiberius. "This is beyond a joke!"

"Yes. I want to catch him today."

I reported my conversation at the bar with Andronicus. Tiberius and I were leaning against one counter. Around the tables people were clustering to bandage and fuss over Morellus. At the other counter, a couple of the Stargazer's regulars had turned up and demanded service as if they had not even noticed what was going on. They never let any emergency interfere with their rights as daily customers. The phlegmatic Junillus served them.

Despondently, Tiberius replayed Andronicus' history, as if seeking to find some clue to his character. "He had always been treated specially, maybe that was the problem. Tullius saw him as extremely bright—which in many ways he is. He was given education and training for a good clerical position."

"When Faustus came, after he was orphaned, did things change for Andronicus?"

"Andronicus may have thought so. Tullius continued to see him the same way, as a first-class slave—but for him, that was all Andronicus ever was or would be, whereas a nephew was a nephew."

"Family."

Tiberius suddenly opened up and confided, "Albia, the irony is that Andronicus could have a genuine grievance. Have you noticed his distinctive ears?"

Tragically, I had. I had nibbled them. Andronicus had ears where the tips took an unusual turn forwards, almost as if when he was a baby, the lobes had been folded by a silly nurse with pinching fingers.

"Uncle Tullius."

"What?"

"Tullius has the same," Tiberius told me in a sombre voice. "Quite a few slaves in the household have inherited the resemblance."

"Tullius fathered him?" It was hardly unusual. Legally, it would make no difference, because a child in Rome followed the status of its mother. Some slave-owners recognised their children, if they felt real affection for the parties involved, though there was no obligation. I guessed Tullius was a hard man.

"Imagine what Andronicus' deranged imagination could make of that!" mused Tiberius.

I thought failure to notice his probable paternity showed Andronicus was not as bright as he himself believed. The rich master's natural son? His jealousy of the nephew would have exploded.

Morellus was being carted off. I saw Tiberius exchange words discreetly with some of the vigiles, then he returned to me. "I am going to take you safely home." By then I was shaky, so disturbed by events that I did not argue.

We walked to Fountain Court, with a couple of vigiles following close. I could not help glancing around nervously; although I spotted no one lurking, I guessed Andronicus would not be far away. We walked in silence.

Outside the old laundry, the alley was the same as usual. The short row of run-down shops opposite had their shutters pushed open but were doing no trade. The ones farther down on the same side looked as sleepy. Disreputable blankets hung out over balconies. The Mythembal children were jumping in puddles, puddles that were probably animal urine, but they scampered away when we approached. There was slight sunshine, which in a park would have been pleasant but here just warmed up the midden, stewing its horrible contents and stirring maggots to life. Smells of industrial processes, fishbones and fresh dung shimmered above the irregular pavings.

A stranger would find this place ominous. To me, it was dirty, dank, yet depressingly normal.

Tiberius left me outside the potter's. He told me quietly that I should spend the day in my own apartment, locking the doors and admitting no visitors for my safety. He said this sternly and made a point of waiting until I agreed the instruction, nodding at him fretfully.

"Do what I tell you, Albia. Stay in!"

"Dear gods, you are tyrannical."

I picked my way alone across the roadway filth. There was no sign of anyone detailed to guard me. I could see Rodan out on a stool in the old courtyard for some reason; he would have been able to see any visitors, had his gummy eyes been open; he looked dead asleep.

As I reached the fire porch I glanced back. Tiberius held up an arm in farewell, then shouted unexpectedly, "Better get working, girl! It's about time you did something useful for your clients in your precious office!"

A moment before he had been telling me to rest up. He really knew how to annoy me. And the whole street must have heard him. It amounted to slander. Muttering, I strode indoors.

Tiberius was becoming as contradictory as the archivist. Imprinted with his first stern instructions, the idea of collapsing wearily in my apartment straight away held great attractions. Still, rebellious as ever, I chose to nip upstairs first. If there were any messages in the office, I could bring them down and work on them. *I* would decide how my work was done.

I went up, feeling the weariness in my legs as I climbed storey after storey. Amazingly, the rubbish boy must have cleared all the old amphorae off the top landing. I had been nagging him for years. To my annoyance, somebody—him?—had been in the office. The outer door stood open. Not only that, across the room, the balcony door was open too. I wondered if my father was at last having a contractor look at its stability; the ropes were no longer securing its old door. It was a feature that from inside the room you could only see part of the balcony, the part by the door. Strange material was blowing in a breeze that constantly raked it because of the height of the tenement. As this eye-catching stuff fluttered, I thought a woman was sitting out there until I recognised my own stole, one I always left in the office for when I felt chilly.

I walked over there. The stole had been tied onto a handle of one of the old amphorae. What in Hades was that about? The amphorae, about five of the dusty, heavy things, were all standing out there. So much for the boy tidying. He had just lugged them outside. I would have to drag them back in because the extra weight was dangerous. I bet he meant to heave them over and let them drop in the alley, but could not manage it. I knew better than to try.

We all loved that balcony. I cannot say how many warm evenings it had seen, with members of my family out there in ones, twos or threes for general pleasure or for solace in hard times. I had always adored it. Tempted, I stepped out.

It felt solid enough. True, where it was cantilevered off the side of the building, there were large cracks, enough to have perturbed Father and Uncle Lucius. Oh, but what a glorious amenity, if it was ever safely renovated. I had really missed having it.

This was, as it had always been, the best feature of the Eagle Building. The two dismal rooms tucked up under the roof were almost made desirable by its presence. You could see for miles. The view was fabulous. I gazed once again over the red pantiled rooftops. By some quirk of planning, you could look through a wide gap in the teeming buildings and see right across the River Tiber to the countryside beyond. You could hear the distant hum of life in Rome, catch its exotic miscellany of scents, feel that you were part of a great city and yet isolated in your private place. The sun on my face was marvellous.

I ventured across to the balustrade and looked down. The alley was full of men. One, seeing me appear high above him, began wildly gesticulating, throwing both his arms wide in an urgent movement. Others began looking up, pointing and shouting. Their words were inaudible.

Suddenly I understood. I was unwittingly embroiled in a stupid male plan.

I had to remove myself. Everything was unsafe. I was jeopardising the outcome. Those fools, Morellus and Tiberius, should have told me. Even if they had, though, I would probably have come up to look; I knew myself and my independence. It was too late now. We were all stuck.

As soon as I set foot back on the threshold of the folding door, a glance at the ropes told me. Each had been severed with a single blow, presumably from a fire-axe.

I ought not be here. When Tiberius brought me back to Fountain Court, his motive was deliberate and I should have followed his first instructions, ignoring that exaggerated afterthought about the office. I was supposed to have stayed well out of the way.

Andronicus had been set up. I had been used to do it.

LVI

I heard approaching footsteps. I was trapped. I had put myself in jeopardy; it had gone wrong.

Judging the sounds, the man was only one or two floors below now, heading up fast. The apartments on the intervening floors were unoccupied, all locked up. I had nowhere else to go.

I had no weapons. I am not a fighter.

I took the only evasive action. Quickly I slipped into the second room, my archive with the leaky roof, and hid behind its curtain. I was thinking fast. If he came in and didn't see me here, I had one chance. If I could get out past him, escape behind him, I might manage to be first downstairs. But he had nothing to lose and was light on his feet. The risk that he would catch me and stab me on the steps was too great.

I stood quite still. I heard him arrive outside. He stopped in the open doorway. He must be staring in from the landing.

He moved. His steps passed through the office, taking him to the folding door.

Now he would know I was not on the balcony. I had an instant to act. I slipped out through the curtain and straight across the room. I saw him; pushed him with both hands on the middle of his back; shoved him forwards hard. Surprise gave me time. Desperation gave me strength. I dragged the door closed, me indoors, him outside.

This could only end in disaster. He was trying to force the door leaf open, I was frantically holding on to keep it fastened. He was slim built, but it was a man against a woman and he was now openly violent. The door was a rackety bifold with battered panels, scene of much past mistreatment and even occasional violence. For years, people in drink had habitually crashed into it. Only the awkwardness of that dilapidated woodwork, which had always jammed and refused to operate properly, helped me.

I heard him say something to me. I saw him through the lattice, stepping back against the balustrade. He was about to hurl himself against the door, which would inevitably burst inwards. I jammed myself in the frame, full weight pushing on the door handle. It felt hopeless.

Shouts below. Someone was coming. He would not have time to reach us.

Andronicus was shouting too. He took his planned run at the door. I still managed somehow to keep it closed. He was so frustrated, he jumped right in the air and stamped down with both feet. At his next attempt, I could no longer hold the door, and he dragged it partway open. He was looking straight at me, when we heard a tremendous cracking noise. Vibrations ran through the soles of my sandals. A shudder rippled in the outer wall. He did not understand. I hope he never knew what was happening, though he must have done. I know he screamed. Any time I think about that moment, I can still hear him.

The old balcony split off from the building. The deadweight amphorae and our struggle were too much for the weakened supports. The ancient construction came away from the masonry and fell six storeys. Andronicus was taken with it.

LVII

A cloud of mortar dust bellied into the room and enveloped me. I swayed off-balance above empty space. As I toppled, strong arms crushed me. Tiberius hauled me to safety. One of us sobbed with shock; it may even have been him.

We heard terrible noises as the balcony landed with its tumbling cargo. Cries sounded in the alley far below. Then silence.

The runner turned me around for inspection. He apologised. I apologised. He meant for not telling me the plan and I meant for not understanding him. That was done. Neither of us would refer to it again.

He told me he had to go downstairs. I understood why. I was to follow as soon as I could. He left me. After his urgent steps faded, I could not bear it there alone and though still feeling fragile, I went down after him.

In Fountain Court there was a mound of rubble, but nothing terrible to see. The vigiles had covered the body. Somehow, no one else was hurt. Tiberius came up quickly and confirmed it was over; that was considerate.

I was taken to my father's house, where I spent the night and all the next day. Even after the office was made safe again, it would be some time before I wanted to go back, maybe never. Even my apartment held memories. I needed to adjust before I could be comfortable there.

It was the end of the Cerialia, so that night there was a big chariot race in the Circus. It would be the last event in the Games that the aedile had to supervise. He sent my family tickets, but none of us went. I stayed quietly at the town house until after lunch the following day. Everyone was going to our villa on the coast and taking me with them.

There were things I needed from my apartment. I walked back alone early that afternoon, slowly taking the Stairs of Cassius. First, I went to the vigiles station house, where I learned that Morellus had been stricken, but somehow survived. He was at home, and since they said he was slowly rallying, I left good wishes and did not bother his wife, Pullia. Seeking quietness, I made my way to the empty enclosure of the Armilustrium. I seated myself on my usual bench, where I stayed for a long while, reflecting.

I was still there, and beginning to dislike my solitude, when I heard someone approaching. I did not look up. A lone woman should avoid eye-contact with strangers. Not that this was a stranger. I knew the man. I recognised his tread. I knew exactly who he was, even though I had never seen him before resplendent in full Roman whites, complete with broad purple status bands on his luxuriant toga. He looked good. Very good. He could carry robes with confidence. As usual he had no bodyguards, but he needed none. By virtue of his high office, his person was sacrosanct.

Even before I looked, I knew he would have grey eyes and where he supported the toga's heavy folds on his casually bent left arm, that hand was now permanently scarred. This was, as I expected, Tiberius Manlius Faustus, the plebeian aedile.

LVIII

A corner of his mouth tightened. "You realised."

"You knew I did."

"Sorry about the secrecy. I like to see things for myself."

"All the fun of disguise—scruff, stubble, and best of all, low street manners; you can be rude to *everyone*." I played it cool. "Luckily I understand, aedile. Our family motto is: If you want something done, there are people you give orders to. If you want it done well, you must do it yourself." I could hear my mother saying it; my father worked that way. Helena herself too.

"You follow family tradition."

"I am my own woman."

Faustus, as I must learn to call him, sounded almost admiring, though being him, not quite: "Oh Albiola, you are that!"

Albiola?

My relatives never used diminutives. Even Farm Boy, who as my husband had the right to be sentimental, called me nothing more personal than "chick," which was the same as he called any donkey he was driving, and even a mouse he once had to entice out of our apartment. From the aedile I had no idea how to take it. He saw that and smiled faintly. For a heartbeat I was going to slap him down, but I left it. He had had enough of that from the ex-wife.

Now I understood why he kissed Laia so pointedly the other day. The formal salutation was his right as her ex-husband. He was asserting that she no longer cowed him. He had been penitent for ten years, but was finally finished with guilt.

I moved up, so the aedile sat down with me.

"What do you want, Faustus?"

"I was worried about you. I thought you might need comfort." I started to deny it, but he cut me off. "The truth is, I am tired and depressed myself. I hate what happened. Maybe I thought if I showed up, *you* might console *me*."

I laughed. He endured it. He was tough but tolerant. I liked this man.

So we sat together side by side, slumped and silent for a long while. He was famous for not speaking. I never chatter. I sensed that in his disguise as the runner he had learned to talk to me more than he ever talked to most people; for my part, I had felt able to be open with him. Yet he and I could communicate without words. Together we abandoned the struggle to remain unmoved in the face of appalling events. Silently, we faced our sad mood, our weariness, even our depression and regret for mistakes. Every time a major investigation ends, there is a period of melancholy. This time that poignancy was personal. At least we were sharing it.

I relayed the news about Morellus. Faustus told me he had been to a follow-up meeting after the festival, receiving congratulations for his contribution. He was modest, but I already knew this year's Cerialia was accounted a grand success. It would do well for him, though I did now accept he had sought no personal advancement, but acted as a devout man. Even so, he would, I thought, accept any benefits that ensued. I did not believe all his protestations that he lacked ambition. He wanted, he had told me, *to live happily and die with greater hope.*

For him, seeking the needle-killers would not end here. Many random deaths had occurred in Rome and the authorities would continue searching; Faustus was now seen as an expert, even though he did not relish the reputation. He offered me a commission to assist but, as he clearly expected, I declined. Too close to home.

Then Faustus fumbled under his toga and came out with something from his belt pouch. He dropped a packet in my lap. "The state wants to reward you, but who knows when or with how much . . . This is from me." While I investigated, he looked away.

He had bought me a set of sewing needles, well-made bronze that would not rust, with grooved eyes, in several sizes from tenting to fine embroidery. I thanked him, though I was mournful. Now I had to face it; my time with him as the runner had ended. An aedile was different. One of the top hundred. This was goodbye.

"Dutiful needlework, Albia. Keep you indoors out of trouble, busy in your household." I was surprised, both by the aptly chosen gift and the joke.

Suddenly his hand fell onto mine to grab my attention. Beyond the altar to Mars at the centre of the Armilustrium, above the enclosure wall, Manlius Faustus had spotted a pair of pointed ears. I breathed with delight and relief. It was my favourite dog-fox, Robigo.

I had left scraps, never hoping any fox would come. Now Robigo sat up there, watchful but relaxed. Almost as soon as I saw him, he decided to slip down the wall. We stayed quiet and observed: those busy paws brought him to what I had left to be eaten, his nose low. He was close enough for us to see his amber eyes, white muzzle, whiskers, black-tipped tail. He ate, then unusually sat there, looking casual. He yawned. He engaged in rapid scratching of the fur behind one of his black ears.

All the time, I felt Faustus' hand, heavily on mine as if he had forgotten it was there. Only when Robigo had silently streaked away did he release me.

The time had come to go. When I stood to leave, rather abruptly, Faustus screwed himself upright and steadied my elbow. That last afternoon, I was reluctant to break from his company. I wanted to take him to my apartment. Today, he was one man I would welcome there. Was it because he carried the aura of power? Or simply because his maturity and steadiness appealed to me?

My instinct said he wanted to come with me. It would be for inevitable reasons. I wanted to go to bed with him, to make spine-cracking, shout-aloud love so we obliterated recent pain and memory. He wanted consolation too; he had said so. It could be a once-only. We were strong people.

"Are you all right?" he asked, rather intensely.

"Not really."

I said he could see me back to Fountain Court, if he was desperate to be useful. "Nuts, olives—a little afternoon delight?"

We were standing close. I liked the faint smell of him. Close to, it was a lotion so light it could almost be the natural scent of clean skin.

He dropped his forehead lightly onto mine. "Don't tempt me!"

Why not?

I knew some reasons. His history said he could be passionate, but the past had made him wary. He was rich, occupying an élite position; he needed an unsullied image. I was on a vigiles' watch-list. No aedile with ambitions could afford the risk.

His excuse was not one I expected. "It would be more than enjoyable. But you know what would happen. Afterwards, we would be hiding down alleys to avoid each other. I liked working with you, Albia. I had hoped that in future we might help one another again. Let's stay friends."

That hideous cliché. Any woman understands what it really means.

I know to this day that if I had kissed him, he would not have resisted. But I smiled and stepped back, releasing us both from pressure.

I thought back to the day when I first went to see him, when I visited the Temple of Ceres and bumped into Faustus on the threshold of the aediles' office. I had dressed to impress a magistrate, amusing myself with how my sisters believed that when you go to that much trouble you will meet somebody special . . .

His interest in me as a colleague had a kind of innocence. I knew better. In Rome, you cannot overturn the rules. Still, the man possessed a good heart. He had, after all, taken it upon himself to write up that wall poster, calling for witnesses to the death of little Lucius Bassus. In our bleak world, where most people and few magistrates had consciences, such decency was indeed special.

I told him I was going to the coast; he looked disappointed. I said I would be back before long and his face cleared.

"Do you always have breakfast at the Stargazer?"

"Most days."

"Maybe I could come along and join you sometimes."

"Well, you know where it is."

He would be a no-show; he was fooling himself in the aftermath of a case we had both hated. I left it to him, whether he made good the promise. Working together again would be acceptable, if it ever happened.

So we parted in the Armilustrium, rueful and chaste. The aedile turned towards his uncle's house. I made my way alone to Fountain Court.

HISTORICAL NOTE

During this period some persons made a business of smearing needles with poison and then pricking with them whomsoever they would. Many persons who were thus attacked died without even knowing the cause, but many of the murderers were informed against and punished.

Dio Cassius, Roman History, *Epitome Book 67*